It Came From the Great Salt Lake
A Collection of Utah Horror

Griffin
Publishers

Horror Anthologies

Old Scratch and Owl Hoots: A Collection of Utah Horror

Copyright © 2016 Griffin Publishers, LLC
Cover Illustration Copyright © 2015 Carter Reid
All rights reserved. This book or any portion thereof
may not be reproduced or used in any manner whatsoever
without the express written permission of the publisher
except for the use of brief quotations in a book review.

Printed in the United States of America

ISBN-13: 978-0-9971970-9-9
Griffin Publishers, LLC

www.griffinpublishers.com

Contents

Foreword

Grandmother Who Breaks the Sky
by Michael Darling   11

The Great Salt Lich
by Nicholas Batura   29

Prissy, the Zombie, and Frederic Fekkai Hair Gel for Men
by Nikki Trionfo   50

Brine and Blood
by C.R. Langille   57

Voices
by Jace Hunter   73

The Hen Gathers Her Chicks
by Rachel Lewis   93

No U-Turn
by Christine Haggerty   106

Horsemen
by K. Scott Forman   118

In the Company of Salt
by E. Ellis Allen   129

Mine
by C.R. Asay   147

Slender
by Chadd VanZanten — 153

The Cellar
by Carol Nicolas — 160

Baby of the Lake
by Terra Luft — 178

Henry
by E.J. Harker — 199

The Dread
by Amanda Luzzader — 216

Dusky Spirits
by Jo Schneider — 229

Saltair Fire Waltz
by Angela Hartley — 237

Hydrogeist
by J. Anthony Gohier — 246

Exposure Therapy
by John M. Olsen — 262

Whoso Offendeth
by Jaren K. Rencher — 277

May 15th
by Johnny Worthen — 295

Foreword

As a child, my parents never wanted me to read horror. I distinctly recall the first scary stories I heard from friends in school. I remember the first horror anthology I borrowed from the library and the fear that my parents would see the rental slip. I read the stories late at night, under the covers, with a flashlight. I even moved to the foot of the bed so the light of the flashlight couldn't be seen. I hadn't realized there was a deep need within me to explore the depths of monsters and psychological terror before that time. For those of us with siblings and basements, we've experienced the fear of being chased up the stairs in the dark. Fear is powerful. Fear drives us to either fight or flight. When I was twelve, the kid next to me in school loved classic horror films and brought in a book cataloging their variety. I was repulsed and intrigued in their details and gruesome images.

From the tops of the Rocky Mountains, I'm pleased to bring the second anthology of Utah Horror, *It Came from the Great Salt Lake*. The first volume, *Old Scratch and Owl Hoots*, brought tales of darkness and evil from the Old West to the present. In this volume, the authors explore the fears from our unique landscape, the Great Salt Lake. What horrors wait in the murky depths? Local authors were asked to dive deep into their fears and draw out their poisons. I'm proud to say they exceeded the challenge and brought to life some of the most horrific and haunting visions of the Rockies. With this installment you will fight your fears and fly through each fear filled tale.

Don't stay up too late,
Daniel
Owner, Griffin Publishers, LLC

Grandmother Who Breaks the Sky
by Michael Darling

Before the poetry of autumn had a chance to start its verse, death came for Danny.

It started innocently, while Danny and the Mason twins walked home after school. With sidewalks wide enough that they could walk side-by-side, they trudged along, backpacks bouncing, whispering details about going to see the body of a girl.

"The museum kept her in storage for a hundred years. Mom showed us a picture. We didn't really want to go to the museum 'cuz it's just full of old junk, but my mom thought we'd wanna go see the dead girl, so we said yeah. She was the first person to drown in the lake, ever."

Aaron Mason was the older twin by six minutes and the most likely to make stuff up.

"When did she die?" Danny asked.

"Was like, a thousand years ago."

"No it wasn't." Zebadiah Mason was the younger twin and made everyone call him Zee because he hated his given name. "There wasn't anybody here then."

"No. They were Indians, Zee."

"Oh, yeah. She's an Indian. An Indian mummy."

"They said she was eaten by the monster in the lake."

"Now you're making stuff up," Danny said.

"Uh-uh. Am not."

"There's no monster in the lake. It's too salty. Except for brine shrimp. My sister did a science fair project."

"Yeah. Salty. That's why her body was preserved. She's like a big ole pickle." Aaron spread his arms to show how big the girl was. Not very big for a girl. Big, though, for a pickle.

Danny squinted. "If she was eaten by a monster, how come there was a body?"

Zee knew the answer. His eyes grew big. "The monster ate her *soul*."

Something traced a soft, cold finger up the back of Danny's neck like a piece of velvet that had been left in the freezer. He shrugged, adjusting his backpack to make the feeling go away.

"C'mon with us," Zee said.

Danny considered the prospect of seeing the pickle girl with his two best friends. Mr. and Mrs. Mason would probably make them look at tons of other stuff too, which would take forever. Grownups always did things like using a mummified girl as bait so they could get kids to look at *educational* stuff. But.

"Maybe," Danny said. "I can ask my mom."

"Tonight," Aaron said.

"'Kay. See ya."

Danny peeled off to walk up to the house of old lady Johanne. His mother had heard him say *old lady Johanne* once and had pointedly instructed him in old-fart etiquette. He only called her Mrs. now. At least out loud.

"Hello, Mrs. Johanne."

"In here, Danny boy."

Danny caught the aroma of tea coming from the kitchen. He was surprised when he saw Mrs. Johanne had put on a sun dress and fixed her hair. Something was up for sure. She hardly ever changed out of her bathrobe, and her hair was almost always under a net.

"Where's Thor?" Danny asked.

"In the back yard. Sit down, Danny. I was just having some tea."

Danny was afraid of what she might ask. Again.

"Don't give me that face, Danny. I'm not asking if you want some." She closed one eye halfway. "They'll let you look, won't they? Looking at tea isn't against your religion, is it?"

"No, ma'am."

Her half-shut eye popped open. "What if I told you my religion is older than yours?"

"Well," Danny paused to clear his throat. Old-fart etiquette reminded him to be respectful. "Our religion goes all the way back to Adam. So."

Mrs. Johanne nodded sagely. She crooked a crooked finger at Danny and waited for him to step closer. "There's things older than Adam in this world Danny. Eons older."

That frigid velvet crawled up Danny's neck again. He tried not to shiver. "If you say so, ma'am."

Mrs. Johanne sighed and leaned back in her chair. "Take my cup. Tell me what you see."

Danny looked. He saw a conglomeration of black blobs in the bottom of the cup. He had no idea what he was supposed to see. Put together, the blobs looked like a broken tree but he just shrugged.

Mrs. Johanne gave him a sour look like her tea had been all lemon juice. With a grunt, she got to her feet and reached for her cane, one of those industrial deals with four feet at the bottom for extra stability. She'd put bright yellow tennis balls on each foot so they wouldn't scratch her hardwood floors.

Thor waddled through the doggy-door from the backyard and panted in Danny's direction. Although named for the Norse God of Thunder, Thor was an aging pug whose nearest claim to thunder was a talent for flatulence. It was Danny's job to take him for a walk every day. Danny leaned over to scratch Thor on the head.

"Let's go," Mrs. Johanne said. "There isn't much time."

She moved quickly out of the house.

"Time for what?" Danny called.

He snagged Thor's leash on the way and clipped it to the dog's collar as they went down the front steps. The screen door banged shut behind them.

"Shall I lock it?" Danny asked.

Mrs. Johanne didn't hear. She was already crossing the street, her cane flashing in the late afternoon sun. Danny had never seen her move so fast.

Thor started wheezing before he made it to the curb. He hadn't moved so fast either. Not for a long time.

Mrs. Johanne lived across from Liberty Park, the oldest park in the city. It had an aviary and a lake with paddle-boats. Danny took Thor for walks there all the time, but they usually went alone.

Danny scooped up Thor, who groaned. Thor didn't really like to be carried. He was fat from Mrs. Johanne feeding him pancakes, and his belly was sensitive, but Danny didn't care. He dashed across the street, pug in arms, into the green shelter of the park.

He found Mrs. Johanne kneeling beside the ancient and towering oak that she jokingly called *Grandmother*. In the middle of summer, before the sun went down, the shadow of the tree fell right over Mrs. Johanne's house. She always said, "Thank you for the shade, Grandmother." Now, the little old woman was almost lost between the roots of the tree, deep in shadow.

The sun shining through the gaps between the leaves overhead gave the trunk a mottled appearance. Her hands rested on the bark, and her skin was so wrinkled it was hard to tell where she ended and the tree began. She chanted under her breath. Danny couldn't make out the words. He didn't want to interrupt her. Maybe she was praying. Old religions. He put Thor down on the grass to sniff around.

After a while, Mrs. Johanne stood and turned, a new light in her eyes. "Come, Danny."

Danny went to her.

"Put your hand on her." Mrs. Johanne took Danny's hand and gently, firmly, placed it on the rough trunk.

Danny heard music. Automatic reflex pulled his hand away.

"You hear it!" Mrs. Johanne said. Delighted.

Danny let the tips of his fingers caress the bark. A soft tinkling sound teased his ears, a piano made of glass, the music of stars. Danny looked up, expecting to see someone in the branches with an instrument. He saw no one. He pressed his palms into the bark and the sound deepened, a concerto of music with voices from other worlds. He stretched out his arms, moving his whole body to embrace Grandmother. He felt the bass notes in his chest as an entire symphony erupted inside his mind. The voices multiplied. The words were not discernible, but the tone was urgent, in a minor key. Insistent. Warning.

"She needs our help, Danny."

He didn't move away from Grandmother, but he heard Mrs. Johanne's voice in his ear. He felt wonderful inside. Like his feet could reach down into the earth and touch the strength of bedrock beneath them. Like his hands could stretch upward to draw life from the clouds and sun.

"Something is out there. Something terrible. Something evil. Grandmother's been warning me for a while. She's been watching you, too. She's chosen you to help."

"Me?" Danny asked. "What can I do?"

"Be a watchman," Mrs. Johanne replied. "Awaken yourself to danger, and if you find it, come back here. Like my family has done for thousands of years."

Danny didn't want to withdraw from Grandmother, but Mrs. Johanne wasn't making any sense. He pulled away, regretting it at once.

"What are you talking about?"

Danny had never seen a smile as wistful as Mrs. Johanne's.

"The Mother Trees have chosen caretakers since before there was ancient. Caretakers like me, and now you, have always helped them guard the world against danger. It's time to do it again."

"What danger?"

"Grandmother cannot see its form. Only sense that it is near.

Grandmother Who Breaks the Sky

Her leaves tremble when she feels it. Her branches reach up to break the sky and send us warnings on the winds of night."

Danny opened his mouth to protest, but Mrs. Johanne stopped him.

"Don't question, Danny. Just keep your wits about you."

A leaf from the tree fell at Danny's feet. Mrs. Johanne picked it up.

"Here. Take this. It's part of Grandmother, and it will help you."

Danny took the leaf. A sliver of song remained in it, a tiny piece of Grandmother's majesty. His mind felt dull now, as if the rest of the world had become less real without her touch. He nodded, wondering what all these new things might mean.

"You're a good boy, Danny. Go on home and remember what I said."

Danny walked home with the songs of trees.

* * *

"Son, quit whining. The museum's open for another hour."

Danny sat in the passenger seat of the van, fuming. He was late meeting Aaron and Zee. Mom had insisted on making dinner from scratch and having a conversation about Dad's day and Danny's day and her day, which was further complicated by the fact that Danny didn't know if he should talk about anything that had happened at the park. So he'd just said his day had been great while he pushed chicken parmigiana (delicious) and green peas (disgusting) around his plate for what seemed like hours. When he wasn't saying he wasn't hungry he was saying he wanted to go to the museum to meet his friends.

Finally, mercifully, mom had agreed to take him. He silently urged her to drive a little faster, even if it broke the speed limit, because he was afraid of missing out on seeing her. The big ole pickle. A thousand years old.

He paid the entry fee with money from his allowance and fumbled with his change. The twins had said she was on the top floor, and he scrambled up the stairs, growing breathless. He turned in a circle at the top, but didn't see anyone. He had to find his friends, not only to hang out, but also because he was supposed to get a ride home with them. They'd probably been dragged away somewhere else by their parents.

He'd take a quick peek at the dead girl first, then go find them. He had plenty of time.

Thinking about seeing a real corpse intrigued and repelled him. It was horrible to think that a person, who had once been running and laughing and singing, was now a still, silent package of bone and sinew.

But he had to see.

The area around her display was dark, unlit. Reverent. A single light illuminated her body, like heaven shining through a break in night clouds. Danny approached on quiet feet. Alone. His heart shifted into high gear in his chest. She'd been wrapped in a blanket, cocooned. He wanted to look. Didn't want to look. He read the sign in front of the display case.

Wa'ipi Baa' - Woman of the Water.

Finally, he raised his eyes. She looked nothing like a pickle. She had dark skin, pulled tightly over her cheekbones. Rows of perfect little teeth shone between her age-thinned lips. Her eyes were sunken, but her lashes were still long and dark. Even though she had passed away centuries ago, Danny could see she had been beautiful.

At the edge of his attention, he saw motion. Heard sound. Some part of him not captivated by the drowned princess registered the fact that the door to the display case had swung open. By itself. Danny smelled the lake. A briny, salty song with undertones of decaying brine shrimp.

Eyes that were not her eyes opened over the sockets. A voice that was not her voice spoke. The words were unimportant. The tone was inviting. A coolness, a current of quiet bliss, like the bottom of the lake.

A shriek cut Danny between the eyes. The sound, sharp and shrill, overrode everything. Danny recoiled. Pulled back his hand.

Grandmother Who Breaks the Sky

The hand that had almost touched her, The Woman of the Water. He covered his ears and backed away. Something inside him felt the presence of a leviathan passing between worlds. Something ancient and deep and hungry. It wanted to claim him. It wanted to come out of Wa'ipi Baa' and consume him.

The leaf, Grandmother's gift, called from his pocket. Making a sound his father had shown him once, down by the river when he'd trapped a blade of grass between his thumbs and pressed it to his lips and blown air through the narrow space. A whistle.

Danny, drenched in sudden sweat, jammed the leaf between his palms. Tried to make it quiet.

"Danny! There you are!"

He looked up.

Mom.

"You're shaking. What's gotten into you?"

She didn't hear the shrieking leaf.

"Nothing. Why're you here?"

Danny's mom put her arms around him, and he didn't mind. He had been shaking.

"Mrs. Mason said they had to go home. Aaron got sick."

Danny swallowed. It felt like drinking glue.

"Did she say why?"

"Uh-uh. She just asked if I could come back and get you. Let's go home."

A voice came over the loudspeakers, asking everyone to make their way to the exit. The museum would close in five minutes.

Danny blinked. Shocked. Had he been standing there, in front of Wa'ipi Baa' for almost an hour? He let himself be led outside. Over his shoulder, he watched the door to the display case close. By itself.

* * *

Danny walked, sweating from nerves. It was after midnight and a mist had invaded the late summer air. He'd never snuck out of the house before. He'd sat on the floor with his ear to his own bedroom door, waiting for his parents to stop talking and go to their bedroom. He'd waited while his butt got numb sitting in one place on the floor. Being a child seemed to consist of long periods spent waiting for adults. Being an adult must be a luxury, never waiting for anyone else.

Finally, when the house had gone quiet, he'd crept down the hall and out the back door. He'd left the leaf. It had gone quiet, fading as they left the museum, and silent by the time they'd reached the van. At home it had gone brown and dry. Dead.

Mrs. Johanne sat on the front porch, Thor snoozing at her side. Her house huddled isolated in the fog, like a drifting ship at sea. At first, she seemed to be wearing a dark bathrobe. As Danny got closer, he saw she was wearing a cloak of some kind. Forest green, with leaves woven in a pattern around the edges.

"It's here."

She knew.

Danny told her about the Woman of the Water and the eyes that were not her eyes and the leaf and Aaron getting sick.

"She wanted me to touch her," Danny said.

He needed to say things out loud. To make the unreal things more real.

"Or the monster inside her did. And I think Aaron did touch her. I think he touched the girl who died in the lake. And the monster made him sick."

Mrs. Johanne closed her eyes.

"If that's true, Danny, your friend may not be your friend anymore. He may not even be human."

A cold chain slipped around Danny's heart. The links almost stopped it beating.

"We can fix him though. Right?"

When she opened her eyes, Danny saw the answer.

"Grandmother knows about the monster in the lake. It's one of the Old Ones. Like her. Very ancient. Very powerful. Grandmother has lived many lives in many places. She keeps an eye on the Old

Grandmother Who Breaks the Sky

One in the lake. She watches and warns. She tells us the monster doesn't surrender what it eats. Ever."

Danny felt sick. If his mother hadn't shown up when she did, could he have resisted? Even with the leaf screaming its warning, he wasn't sure.

"The Masons are lake people, Danny." Mrs. Johanne looked solemn. "Always have been. It's not the first time the Old One has used their family. Their great-grandfather killed six people. Chopped them up and fed them to his hogs before Grandmother and I caught him. That was almost a hundred years ago."

Danny nodded. Wait. A hundred years?

A shuffling step made Danny turn. Aaron on the sidewalk. Mrs. Johanne inhaled with a sharp hiss. She saw him too.

Mrs. Johanne talked fast. Faster than she had walked.

"The Old One sent him to kill us. If we are eliminated, then Grandmother is vulnerable. The Old One could kill the tree. Send the Being that is Grandmother away. If that happens, there will be a lot more killing."

Danny had no reason to doubt her words.

Aaron wasn't Aaron anymore. His body shuddered, buried under a tangle of tentacles. He wore pajamas. His favorite superheroes. His gait was unsure, as if his legs had forgotten how to walk. Above the waist, Aaron's torso made a silhouette inside a mass of gelatinous scales and long, long teeth. And eyes. The same eyes that had opened over Wa'ipi Baa's empty sockets. Piercing eyes, deep blue, with the vastness of a universe hidden inside them.

Thor, who had once barked his head off at an empty french fry box, stayed silent. He was on his feet, though. Watching.

Aaron made almost no sound. Other than the dry shuffle of bare feet on concrete, there was just a funny gurgle like the first 100-degree day when Danny had chugged half a pitcher of lemonade on an empty stomach and jiggled his belly. Only instead of laughter, Danny felt nausea creeping up the back of his throat.

"Go to Grandmother, Danny." Mrs. Johanne insisted. "The Old One is here for me. If I can't stop it, you need to be there for Grandmother."

Danny hesitated. What could he do for Grandmother? As if she'd read his mind, she said, "Grandmother picked you. You'll know what to do."

He didn't share her opinion. Mrs. Johanne had pasted a determined look on her face but he could see her heartbeat beneath the thin skin of her neck and it was racing.

"Go!"

Danny ran. He crossed the street and took another look behind him from the sidewalk. Through the mist, he saw Mrs. Johanne chanting and Thor run down the steps and launch his little fur-covered body at the nearest tentacle. He turned away to watch where he was going. He wouldn't be any use to anyone if he broke his leg tripping over a rock. He hoped Thor and Mrs. Johanne would be all right.

Someone waited between him and Grandmother. Someone also wearing superhero pajamas.

Danny slowed. "Zee?"

"Hey, Danny."

"Are you okay?"

Zee had puffy red eyes and a web of wet lines on his face that shimmered in the hazy light of the streetlamps. Danny could tell that Zee was doing his best not to cry. All Zee could do was shake his head.

Danny felt his own face getting hot in sympathy. Aaron had been his friend—but he'd been Zee's brother.

"Did you touch her too, Zee? The Indian girl?"

Zee shook his head again. Harder. He's wasn't the one who made stuff up.

"No."

"That's good. We're just going to wait here for a while, okay?"

"Okay."

Zee stood where he was, but he swayed a little and his hands twitched. He looked like he wanted to give Danny a hug but didn't know how to do it manfully. Danny stepped closer.

He smelled salt water.

The sick feeling in his stomach came back, more nauseating than ever.

"Zee? You didn't touch her did you?"

"I said I didn't." Zee stuck his arms out in front of him. Took a step toward Danny. "When Aaron touched her, he fell down. He screamed. I didn't want to touch her after that. So I didn't." Zee took another step toward Danny. Danny took a step back. "I'm scared, Danny."

"Me too, Zee."

"It hurts, Danny."

Danny moved backward faster. Zee's steps growing more erratic. Tears poured out of Zee's eyes. They didn't stop. The tears turned into a stream and then water bubbled out of Zee's face. His eyes, his nose, his mouth. Even his ears streamed a flood.

Zee screamed through the deluge, "It hurts!"

"You said you didn't touch her!"

"I didn't. But Aaron touched *me*!" Zee sobbed, staggering. Trying to put his hands on Danny. "It HURTS!"

Danny ran. He made a wide circle around Zee and headed for Grandmother. Zee wheeled through a turn like a boat on choppy water.

"'Member when you told my dad you broke that window so he wouldn't beat me? 'Member, Danny?"

Danny couldn't stop his own tears. He didn't even try.

"I remember Zee."

"Help me again, 'kay? If you let me touch you, the monster won't hurt me anymore. Please Danny. It HURTS SO BAD."

"I'm sorry, Zee," Danny whispered. "The monster doesn't surrender what it eats."

Danny made it to Grandmother. He pressed his back against her trunk. He found unexpected warmth there. He looked at Zee. Tentacles sprouted out of Zee's face now. If Zee still hurt, he could no longer voice it. Clear blue jelly oozed up and over Zee's head. Stars sparkled inside it. And planets. And multi-colored nebulae.

Zee almost fell over. But didn't.

Danny had no clue what to do. He considered climbing Grandmother to safety. But her trunk was so big, he'd have to be a squirrel to get a grip. And what if Zee touched her?

He listened for Grandmother's voice, hoping for aid, but she remained quiet. He felt her looking through his eyes.

I am her eyes.

He picked up a leaf from between her roots. The siren shriek was there, but muted. Grandmother knew what danger was there. She knew Danny knew.

Zee shuffled closer. Danny moved around Grandmother's trunk and Zee struggled to readjust his direction.

I can move in a circle. He can't go faster than me. We can play follow-the-leader all night around the tree, and he'll never catch me. When the sun comes up, maybe he'll go away.

Another figure took shape in the mist. He recognized the cloak. Mrs. Johanne! She'd know what to do! The figure was just dark patches of fog at first. She drifted forward, like she was injured. The chains around Danny's heart grew heavier. Tentacles dangled from the sleeves of the cloak. The figure wore pajamas. Superhero pajamas. The thing wasn't Mrs. Johanne at all. It just wore her cloak.

Danny ran around the back of the tree to keep away from Zee. He didn't have time to wonder what happened to Mrs. Johanne. Aaron sensed his motion. Shuffled to change direction.

I can't play follow-the-leader. They can go different directions. Catch me in the middle. I can't leave the tree. I can't play games.

I can't kill my friends.

A window opened up in Danny's mind. Grandmother's pictures. Like a slide show from the worst family vacation ever, he saw the park with Grandmother's tree at the center. She'd turned gray and lifeless. Around her lay desolation. A wasteland. Small figures being ridden by tentacled things wandered past, eyes dancing. Moving toward the lake, long miles away. No. Not toward the lake. Toward the Old One in the lake. It rose into the sky like a helium balloon. Its bulbous head, tens of thousands yards wide, quivered.

Its hundreds of tentacles reached for thousands of yards, too, the power and dominion of a thousand universes orbiting in its eyes.

Danny blinked. The vision had come and gone in the space of a single breath.

Inhale. Indecision. Exhale. Desperation.

I have to find a way.

He had no weapons. As little kids, they'd played with guns and swords. He didn't have any of those. Not even pretend ones. He had brains. And a leaf.

A leaf. Serrated. A piece of Grandmother.

Aaron kept coming. Danny saw Thor caught in its jelly. The little dog was dead. A fierce snarl frozen on its face. He had been brave. Danny had to be brave.

Zee shuffled closer. Danny ran at Zee. He held the leaf by the stem and slashed when Zee's tentacle swiped at him. Danny dodged. His best ninja move. He'd almost been touched. The leaf bit into the tentacle and stuck. Zee barely paused. Danny backed away.

The leaf changed color, turning red. The tentacle still moved.

Danny checked Aaron's position. He was getting closer.

Backing against Grandmother's warmth, he stared at Zee. He created images in his mind. Images of what he wanted. Images like the ones Grandmother had shown him.

Her branches moved, sending him leaves. Stirring the air.

Leaves swirled down, falling haphazardly, without purpose. Grandmother curled the air on itself. Made a whirlwind. The leaves spun.

Faster.

The wind accelerated, the leaves in a blur. Danny focused back on Zee. The whirlwind went where he looked.

The leaves whipped around Zee, around the manifestation of the Old One that rode him. The edges of the leaves cut the jelly, so fast they didn't get stuck. The cuts tried to close. Tried to heal. Zee kept coming.

More leaves.

Another fall of green descended into the whirlwind.

Faster.

The leaves slashed, chewed. Turned crimson. Tentacles twitched, reaching out, almost close enough to touch.

More leaves.

More wind.

So many leaves now. He heard the gurgle still. Of the thing. Just under the sound of the whirlwind.

Zee stopped shuffling. Thousands of blades embraced him, all of them the color of blood. The leaves so wet now. Zee—what was left of him—toppled to the ground.

Danny sent more leaves. They sliced into meat. Cut into bone. Chewed until they were red and full. Bloated.

Trailing his hand around the trunk, keeping contact with the blessed Grandmother, Danny went around to find Aaron. And the Old One riding him.

Aaron was trying to leave. Awkwardly turning, trying to run away. His terrible shamble almost made Danny laugh.

He commanded the leaves to fall and the wind to blow. Grandmother listened. He sent the lethal whirlwind after Aaron. Caught him.

In her ancient wisdom, Grandmother wept.

Danny didn't need words to understand. This was not a victory.

The whirlwind swept through Aaron and the Old One. Edge after edge bit into the thing that possessed the boy. The boy with a boy's curiosity. Curious at the wrong time. In the wrong place.

When Aaron was buried under the leaves, Danny fell to the grass. Drained.

Sleep.

* * *

Someone called his name but it was just a sound. Was he at the bottom of the lake after all? He felt buried by a flowing coolness. It wanted to keep him under. But he couldn't stay under. The voice called again. He was sure now. From heavy depths he moved upward.

"Danny?"

He opened his eyes.

"He's awake!"

"Mom?"

"Sweetie! Are you all right?"

Danny blinked. The sunlight cut across his vision. He couldn't look up. He focused on the ground instead. Looked for signs of pajamas with superheroes. Signs of…

The ground was covered in leaves. Just leaves. Fat, red leaves. Leaves that shifted. Maybe the leaves were being teased by the morning breeze. Maybe not.

Danny would never be able to look at red leaves in the same way again.

He felt Grandmother at his back. She had cooled. She'd slumber until spring and new life.

His mother's hands slipped around his shoulders, comforting him. Someone had found Mrs. Johann's cloak. Put it around him. It fit.

"Mom. Have you seen Mrs. Johanne?"

His mom hugged him. "Did she get you out here?"

"Yeah." It was a good truth.

"This will be a shock, Danny. She's passed away."

"How?"

"It doesn't matter now, you just—"

"I need to know."

She paused. For a moment. "They found her in front of her house. But they're saying she drowned."

Danny nodded. "Oh."

"That's not all."

The cold piece of velvet put roots in the back of Danny's neck again.

"Mrs. Johanne left a note. Something about the Mason boys kidnapping her dog and running off. She said she went to our house and tapped on your window. Crazy old bat. You said they might have gone down to the pond, and you'd help her look for her dog. In the middle of the night!"

"Yes," Danny said.

Mrs. Johanne had made up a story for him. Grownups were good at that. He just needed to play along.

"That's not even the kookiest part." Mom was on a roll now. "She wrote that if anything should happen to her, she had you in her will. She's giving you her *house*! She said you loved the view of the park and—what was it?—Grandmother's shade? Isn't that the craziest thing?"

Michael Darling

Michael Darling has worked as a butcher, a librarian, and a magician. Not all at the same time. He most recently won the grand prize in the United Authors Association fiction writing contest. Michael has published numerous short stories. His first novel, *Got Luck*, is an urban fantasy set to debut in 2016 through Future House Publishing. Please visit Michael at www.michaelcdarling.com where you'll also find suspiciously easy instructions for stalking him on Facebook and Twitter.

The Great Salt Lich
by Nicholas Batura

1
The Drought and the Beginning of the End

The cracked lakebed stretched beneath Loco Moe and Griz like the scales of a sleeping sea creature.

Loco Moe passed the shovel onto his other shoulder and gnawed another splinter from his palm. Sweat dripped off his nose. Nothing, not even long lost Mormon treasure, was worth this much suck.

Griz lumbered ahead, shirt plastered across cascading fat rolls. His metal detector peek-a-booed around him with each sidelong swing.

Two hours earlier, Griz had lured Loco Moe into a plate-less Civic with the promise of fortune. A pink flamingo with High School Class of 2015 stitched across its belly dangled from the rearview mirror.

"You'll be rich, man," Griz had yelled.

Wind thick with brine and decay had buffeted them through open windows as they careened westward down Interstate 80.

"Shem said there's ten tons of Mormon booty buried out there. We find one hiding spot and you'll have enough to dump that meth shit and get some *real stuff*."

Safety glass littered the interior, glittering like discarded diamonds.

Loco Moe's enthusiasm for treasure had died the moment Griz cut the engine in Saltair's deserted gravel parking lot on the border of BFE and nowhere and handed him a shovel.

Sweat slid down Loco Moe's chest beneath his CHOOSE THE RIGHT . . . *to rock and roll*! t-shirt. Real stuff was why he'd followed Griz's fat ass out across the network of fissures that had so recently been home to brine shrimp and fuck all.

Loco Moe kicked a curled edge of sunbaked mud. "I been rambling down this old dirt road. Ba-ba-ba-ba-ba! Ain't no one coming around. Ba-ba-ba-ba-ba—"

"Shut the hell up!" Griz hunched over the Fisher-Price metal detector. It hissed and hiccupped.

"Get anything yet?"

"No, and I won't find dick with you singing that shit."

Loco Moe booted a chunk of dirt into the air. "I thought we were looking for gold rings and coins and stuff. Hell, if it's dick you want—"

"Shut up."

"Just saying, there's plenty of dick on North Temple and Redwood Road if you—"

"I said shut up!" Griz spun around. His girth, a millisecond behind the rest of him, caught up in a blubbery wave. His double chin quivered.

"Try me, you fat fuck." Moe adjusted his grip on the shovel.

"Fuck you." Griz turned and waddled onward.

Loco Moe let Griz get a shovel's length ahead of him before he followed. Next time the son of a bitch turned on him, he'd Babe Ruth the fucker's face to the moon. "Old Floyd says blues is the original soul music. Clearly you have no soul."

"Old Floyd would say anything for a hit. All that crippled hippy wants is your stash."

Griz rarely had anything meaningful to say, and although this was one of those instances, it didn't negate the fact that the blues was the greatest sound to hit human ears since cave men first thumped out beats on driftwood.

The metal detector wailed a high-pitched tone.

"I got something!" Griz pumped his meaty arm in the air. "This is it! We're rich!"

Loco Moe dashed forward.

"Right there!" Griz jabbed the metal detector at the ground.

Loco Moe began to dig.

Griz poked the metal detector over the deepening hole every few minutes and let out a piggish squeal at its metal-positive whine.

"That thing say how far down it is?" Loco Moe's arms burned.

"No, can't be that far, though."

"If you say so." The shovel thunked against something big.

Griz whooped.

Loco Moe scraped away dirt, digging around the edges of their find.

Griz eased himself onto his knees across the hole.

Loco Moe barked a laugh. Few memories from his childhood were worth retaining. One he held close to his heart was a visit to see the zoo camels. He'd lost it the first time he'd seen one kneel down.

"What's funny?" Griz clawed at the dirt.

"Nothing."

They hefted a rotting wooden box out of the hole. Rusted metal bands held its long planking together.

"It's fucking treasure! I knew it! What did I tell you?" Griz pounded on the box. Two crusty padlocks as big as his fist clanked on the side.

Loco Moe tapped the shovel against a lock. "Should we bust it open?"

"Oh yeah," Griz whispered. "Bust this box wide open." His words had a pornographic quality about them.

The Great Salt Lich

It occurred to Loco Moe that it would be an excellent time for Griz to try to take the treasure and run ... but he was the one with the shovel. And Griz was a fat ass.

"What you waiting for?"

"We split it fifty-fifty, right?"

"Yeah, man." Griz held three fingers up. "Scouts honor."

"You were a Boy Scout?"

"Just open the fucking box."

Loco Moe obliterated the locks with two satisfying blows. Iron flakes dusted the ground.

Griz scooted in front of the box. "I've been waiting for this my whole life." He craned his sunburned hotdog neck around and looked at Loco Moe. "It's all about to change, man; I can feel it."

The only thing Loco Moe felt was sweat drip off his balls and slither down the back of his knee. "Me too, man."

Griz lifted the lid. The hinges made a sound like a dropped egg, and the lid tumbled to the ground. "What the fuck is this?"

Loco Moe shivered. A reflection-less blackness filled the box, as if someone had collected deep space or a moonless desert night and trapped it inside.

"No fucking way it's empty." Griz pushed his arm into the darkness and gasped.

"What is it?"

"It's—" Griz looked back at Loco Moe, but his gaze was a million miles away. "You've gotta check this out." His face was the color of mashed potatoes.

An often unheeded voice in the back of Loco Moe's mind warned him not to put his arm in the box, but Griz's words from earlier crowded it out. *Have enough to dump that meth shit, get some real stuff, man.* It'd been too long since he'd had any good stuff. If the box was full of cash, then he could get enough heroin to last a long time. He knelt next to Griz and pushed his hand into the black. Electric ice jolted up his arm.

FEEBLE-MINDED CATTLE. The words blasted through Loco Moe's head like cannon fire. *Take me to your people. Freedom calls for a celebration, and I am oh, so hungry.*

2
Take Shelter

Big Slim twitched his head toward the homeless shelter's food serving line. "I'm telling you it's him." Liz had made it a point to put as little stock as possible in the homeless man's conspiracies, but sometimes curiosity got the best of her.

The evening's three volunteers stood behind the counter. Mr. Goberman and Mr. Schlittler, both high school teachers and regulars at the shelter, handed out donated pastries and water. It was the man next to them Big Slim was talking about. Dressed in black, he stood a head taller than the others. A wide-brimmed hat cast his face in constant shadow. He slopped stew onto trays with robotic grace.

"I'm telling you." Big Slim spoke through a mouth full of food. "Frasier said he'd found a new calling, said he'd gone to see that preacher-man." He jabbed a finger at the man in black. "Then bam! He up and disappeared!" Stew flecks dotted the table in front of him. "Old Crab Hands went a few weeks later. It can't be no coincidence, no, no."

Liz worked around a section of her tray that had been tainted by one of Big Slim's projectiles. "He's creepy enough, but how'd he do it? He's skin and bones. I bet it takes all he's got to lift that ladle." Big Slim had a wild imagination, but he was right; there was no way Frasier and Crab Hands Johnson would leave town without saying goodbye.

Big Slim stuffed a forkful of food in his mouth. "It's a shame." Spittle shot-gunned onto the table.

Liz set her spoon on her tray. There was no telling where the last blast had landed. Some things weren't worth the risk.

"Crab Hands was a good man," Big Slim said.

Crab Hands had always been nice to her. If that preacher was behind it all, they'd have to stop him. On the other hand, if he were behind Loco Moe and that shitbag Griz's disappearances, then maybe he wasn't so bad after all. But junkies disappeared all the time; one could only hope they were rotting in a mineshaft somewhere.

"Liz! Come on!" Liz's mom stood in the doorway to the shelter's back hallway, a cardboard box piled high with second-hand clothing in her arms.

"Shit, gotta run." Liz picked up her tray.

Big Slim swiped Liz's half-eaten hard roll. "See you soon?"

"Yeah. Mom has more winter clothes to bring in. And I still haven't found a life, so I'll be back in a few days."

"Fair enough," Big Slim said.

Liz mouthed *we're watching you* as she passed the Preacher. She dumped her tray in the wash bin and followed her mom into the hallway.

"Get your homework done?"

"First thing this morning."

"I didn't get a notification. Did you submit it?"

"Crap." The pros and cons of being a homeschooled teen were pretty balanced. On the one hand, she had a mom whose daily schoolwork checks were as consistent as sunrise, but on the other, it was that nagging that saved her butt when she'd forgot to hit the submit button online. "I'll send it when we get home."

Her mother snorted.

"You know, if I had a cellphone, I could put a reminder in—"

"I told you I don't want to hear it. Not another word until you're sixteen."

"But—"

"Case closed."

But May was so far away! It wasn't fair, especially not when half the damned homeless people at the shelter had smart phones. "Hey, have you and your social worker cronies seen Frasier or Crab Hands Johnson lately?"

"Why?" Her mother dropped the box next to piles of everything from flip-flops to squirt guns.

"Big Slim said he thinks they've been murdered."

"Big Slim also thinks it's only a matter of time before government robots take over the United States."

"Good point."

3
There's no Place like Home

A knock reverberated through the cargo van. Time passes, and yet so much remains the same, thought Voivode Batory. He slid the side door open. "Enter, my child." The cardboard scent of dried urine wafted into the van. Voivode Batory coughed. Though his gag reflex had disappeared centuries ago, his sense of smell had grown stronger with age.

"Preacher." The man stumbled inside.

"Close the door."

The man's filth was apparent even in the dimness of the overhead light. He shut the door and sat on the thick plastic drop cloth that lined the van's empty cargo area.

Voivode Batory sat on an upturned cook pot at the back of the van. "What is it you seek?" He always asked the question, though in truth the broken man's sorrow was uninspiring at best. So why the façade?

"Forgiveness." Gold glinted between the man's lips. Tears cut clean lines from eyes to beard. "Relief."

Was it the honor? No . . . it was for the ritual, yes. His show was no different than a priest's at mass. Ritual was personal, had meaning. "Would you give anything for relief?"

The man bawled into his palms. "Anything."

"Your life for forgiveness?" Voivode Batory was a being of honor, after all. But at the end of the day, he too had to survive.

The man dropped his hands. His face was a shade of cooked lobster, eyes bloodshot or infected. "Yes. Forgive me, please."

Voivode Batory stood, head grazing the exposed metal ceiling.

"Come to me." This was the worst part of it all.

"Thank you, Preacher." The man fell onto his hands and knees. He crawled across the plastic sheet, gulping in air like a scolded toddler. "Oh, thank you."

The man latched onto Voivode Batory's leg. His sobs mutated into choked gibberish.

A marriage of feces and alcohol invaded Voivode Batory's nose. He placed a hand on the man's head. "Be healed, and go with whichever god you've chosen."

"Thank you." The man's eyes popped.

Ocular fluid spattered Voivode Batory. Flesh crackled, smoke rose from his screaming palm; the man's life force coursed into him. It was molten pleasure, sex times a thousand, times a million. His knees buckled. The plastic sheet stuck to his face.

He lay for a moment next to the corpse. The smell finally pushed him to his knees, helped him strip the man, stuff the greasy clothing into a plastic bag, and tie it tight. He slid two twenty gallon cook pots next to the man. *Khanjara.* The word flashed in his mind; a translucent blade sprung from his fist. Although it used more energy than he preferred to expend, it was the right tool for the job. He got to work filling each pot, one with meat, the other with bones; the marrow would make a fine broth. Odds and ends went into black plastic bags.

Voivode Batory prided himself that he hadn't completely lost touch with the real world, unlike some of his kind. He still did a few things on his own, the intimate stuff, anyway. *COME!* The rest he left up to his minions.

The van shook. Sluggish thumps resounded from the sliding door.

ENTER.

The van door slid open. What had once been Griz teetered outside. Emaciated cheeks sagged below his jaw. Liquid seeped from sores that dotted his flesh. "Master?"

Dispose of the bags far from here. Be sure they CANNOT be traced back to me.

"Yes, master." Griz's spoiled sausage scent was hardly better than the homeless man's was.

Voivode Batory would have to have Griz dispose of himself soon.

4
The Tome of Truth

"Demon or wizard?" Liz pushed through the bookstore's double doors ahead of Big Slim. Although he'd had his weekly shower that afternoon, it would take years to scrub the homeless off him. Until then, she'd rather walk behind a garbage truck.

"Well, we only see him at night, and he's always got that weird hat covering him up." Big Slim tapped a book cover on the fantasy bestseller rack. "Wizard?"

"I think I know where we can look." Liz led them through the labyrinth of bookshelves to the tabletop gaming section. Some other kids from the homeschool co-op had introduced her to Dungeons and Dragons earlier that year. If there was anything that could help them identify the Preacher, it was the Monster Manual.

"Can I help you?" A twenty-something guy in a bookstore staff shirt materialized next to them. His nametag hung at the end of a lanyard covered with science fiction and fantasy pins, among them a Firefly class ship and a TARDIS. The geek was strong with him.

"Yeah, we're trying to ID a monster," Liz said.

A know-it-all smile crept onto the bookseller's face. He squared his shoulders and put his hands on his hips. "Description please."

"Well, he's really pale," Liz said.

"See-through skin?"

Liz glanced at Big Slim, who nodded. "Yup."

"Feeds on human flesh?"

"I don't think so." Liz looked to Big Slim again. "He's really skinny."

The bookseller gazed past them, his lips pursed, face scrunched. "Feeds on human souls?"

"Maybe," Liz said.
"Day walker?"
"Yes."
"Shape shifter?"
"Don't know."
"Magic user?"
"Possibly."
"Does he wear a ring of power?"
"No jewelry."
"Anything else? Anything at all?"
"Well, I don't think he bleeds."
"Really?" Big Slim said.
"Maybe? I saw him chopping onions for that weird stew of his, and I swear he nearly cut a finger off, but there wasn't any blood, so I thought maybe I'd made it up."
"Lich." The bookseller took the Monster Manual from Liz, flipped through it as if he'd memorized the thing and handed it back to her.
A skeletal face stared up from the page. "An undead being striving for immortality." She skimmed the text. "Powerful magic user, often controls slave army, not necessarily evil, keeps life force in a phylactery."
"A phylacta-what?" Big Slim stepped closer.
A musk of old sweat and perfumed soap crept over Liz. She handed Big Slim the book and stepped away. "So what is a—"
"It's basically a horcrux." The bookseller folded his arms.
"I, umm," Liz said.
"A whore what?" Big Slim looked up from the book, eyes like it was Christmas.
"You know, from the Harry Potter universe?" The bookseller's mouth hung open.
They'd clearly lost street cred, but the Harry Potter craze was one part of childhood Liz had missed out on. She'd have to watch the movies now.
"Destroy the phylactery, destroy the lich." The bookseller

snatched the book out of Big Slim's hands. "If there's anything else you need, please ask." He slid the book back onto the shelf and disappeared into the store.

"Jeeze," Big Slim said.

"Yeah, what a jerk. Let's go see if the Preacher's a lich."

"How?"

"I have no idea."

5
The Juice is Worth the Squeeze

Voivode Batory sat in the back of his cargo van. The hyper-floral scent of industrial detergent clung to the air. Water spotted the plastic drop cloth. Three dollars in change and a car wash power sprayer had been perfect to clean up the mess he'd made.

A milky crystal as big as his fist sat in front of him. Two months ago, it had been as big as his head. Hard work had paid off; the rest would be gone by the end of the week, and then he'd be free at last.

He picked it up. It was cool in his hands, and rough, like a cat's tongue. It glowed softly in the light of the tiny overhead bulb.

All of it used to be so much easier, he thought. Something had changed while he wasted away in that box. Appetite? Ambition? It had waned in the years leading up to his meeting with the Ute tribe. His struggle and loss to them had pushed it further inside, no, further away from him, for he no longer hungered for power. Prison had changed him.

He cupped the crystal and chanted the first of nine words of power. Silver twined about it, gaining speed with each syllable. Faster and faster it spun, thicker and thicker it became, until a newborn star blazed in his hands. Energy hung in the tiny cargo space, an electric mote that trembled, waiting for the final word. He spoke it, and the star imploded. A vacuum rush of energy stripped off his skin, tore away flesh, bleached his bones, yet nerves remained.

He woke next to a milk-white pile of sand. His skin was hot, but intact. He divided the crystal into nine equal piles, which went into

nine plastic sandwich baggies.
COME!
A thud shook the van a moment later.
ENTER.
A young man, handsome in an angular way, opened the door.
"Master?"
Go to your eight brethren in the eight kitchens. Give one of these to each. They are to speak the words RARE HUNGARIAN SEA SALT only to the head chef, then immediately hand it over.
"Yes, master." The young man took eight baggies and shut the door.
Voivode Batory placed the last in his jacket pocket.

6
The Taste of Victory

"Shem's gone."
"Shem?" Liz sat across from Big Slim. The newly donated cafeteria tables were an amazing upgrade from the second-hand patio furniture they'd been using when her mom had first transferred to the Salt Lake shelter.
"Yup, two days ago."
"Shem who?"
"You know, gold tooth."
"Oh, Shem! Really?" She'd met the guy a few times, but had never gotten a good vibe, something about his eyes; guilt lay within them. Plus, her mother and the other social workers had made it clear she wasn't to be alone with him. So not a total loss if he'd gone missing.
"What do you think?" Big Slim wrung his hands over the table; grime collected on its bleached surface.
"Well." Liz had started back into the scientific method this term, and it wasn't helping the situation. "I don't know."
"What do you mean?" Big Slim leaned across the table. "He's definitely a leech."

"Lich," Liz said. "You're probably right, but how do we test the hypothesis?"

"What?" Big Slim scratched his stubble.

"It's a science thing; we have to successfully test that he's a lich or else we're wrong and he's just a creepy old preacher with a thing for massive hats."

"Oh." Big Slim leaned back in his chair.

"See. How do we do it?" As much as her instincts screamed something wasn't right with the man, that lich was a likely possibility, the scientific method rang true. She needed proof.

Big Slim threw his hands up, eyes wide. "Holy water!"

"Won't work."

"Why not?"

"He's a lich, not a vampire."

"How do you know it won't work?"

"He's wearing a cross and posing as a preacher. I don't think holy water will do anything to him."

"Hmm."

The chow line dissipated to a handful of bodies.

"Let's get some food. Maybe we'll notice something. Act normal." Liz strolled to the line, selected a tray and silverware.

The Preacher was the last of the three servers. He stared into his vat of stew.

"Good evening, Liz, would you like a sourdough hard roll?" Ms. Loretta James, a local elementary teacher and frequent volunteer thrust a crusty grenade toward Liz. Clear plastic gloves revealed intricate copper spirals painted on her long fingernails.

"Yes, please." The roll thunked onto Liz's tray, crumbs exploding from it like shrapnel.

"Well, hello there, how about some broccoli?" Mr. Cockburn had an incurable case of optimism. "You've gotta get your vegetables!" His smile was a thing to frighten small children and foreigners.

"Okay."

He dashed a spoonful of emerald florets into a square of her tray. "You having a nice day?"

Liz moved on. She'd fallen into his trap before; engaging in any sort of conversation with the man meant fifteen minutes of rambling sunshine bullshit. She had more important things to do tonight.

Liz stopped in front of the Preacher. The brim of his hat stretched out for miles.

Now was her chance. "We know what you are."

Steam flitted up from the vat between them.

"You want stew." His words crept out from under the hat. Eyes like black holes held her.

"What? I said I—I do?" She'd had something important, but she sure was hungry.

"Yes." The word carried more than sound.

Liz held out her tray. "Yeah, I do."

The Preacher dumped stew next to her broccoli.

"Thank you." Her stomach clawed against her throat. What herbs had he used? What ingredients to make it smell so amazing?

"Would you like salt?" The Preacher opened a plastic baggie. "*Rare Hungarian Sea Salt?*"

Liz had always wanted to try Hungarian sea salt. She held her tray out.

The Preacher dusted her stew with fine crystals.

"Thank you!"

"Enjoy."

Liz left the line. Exotic spices wafted from the tray. When had she gotten so hungry? She walked back to their table and dug into the stew. Each spoonful was bliss.

Someone sat across from her.

"So." It was Big Slim.

Whatever he wanted couldn't matter. She was starving.

"Hey."

A handclap cracked through the air.

Liz jumped; her spoon clattered onto the table in a pile of wasted stew. "Hey! What is it?" Couldn't he see she was trying to eat?

"What do you think about—" he nodded toward the serving line.

"Huh?"

"The lich."

The Preacher popped into view. Synapses sparked back to life. A rotting earth funk wafted up from her plate. "What the hell?" Her tray lay before her like an opened diaper. A haze filled the gap of time between leaving and returning to the table.

"So he's a lich then?" Big Slim masked a smile with a bite of stew.

"Yeah, I think he is." She looked back at the Preacher. He winked.

"What's next with your scientific method stuff?" Big Slim crunched into his hard roll.

Fuzz lingered in Liz's head like the hand of a shady uncle. Spilled stew seeped toward her. "I need to remind Mom to level this one."

"What?"

"The table."

"Well, what about the—"

"I need a minute to think." Black hole eyes stared in Liz's mind. She mopped up the mess with some napkins, tossing them on her tray. The last one clinked. She moved the soggy pile aside and picked up something that gleamed in the sludge. "What the hell?" It was a gold tooth. "Holy shit!"

"Shem!"

A hand plucked the tooth from her grip. "Now what do we have here?" The Preacher loomed over the table, his hat blocking out the florescent overheads.

"A tooth!" Liz skidded her chair away from man.

All eyes were on them.

"Now, now," the Preacher said. "What tooth?" He opened his hand. A chunk of salt lay where the tooth should have been. "Why," he held the salt up to the room, "it's just *Rare Hungarian Sea Salt*."

The words burrowed into Liz.

The Great Salt Lich

Around the room heads snapped toward trays; clockwork hands shoveled food into mouths.

"No!" She jumped out of her seat. "Come on, Slim!" She ran for the exit and burst through the door.

Lamps cast the side street in yellow; shadows stretched across the homeless shelter.

A film coated Liz's mouth. Her stomach revolted. People. She'd eaten people. She lost it into a shrub that already smelled of stale acid. Now was a perfect example of a situation where her own cellphone would come in handy. If she died tonight, her mother would be damned sorry she'd left her only daughter without a way to call for help.

The shelter door slammed behind her.

"Why leave the party?" The Preacher tipped his hat at her. His eyes glowed in the lowlight.

Liz bolted down the street. She spat bile; her mouth watered.

"Help!" Her legs burned, lungs screamed for oxygen. The world shimmered ahead of her until a wall of black stretched across the street. "Shit!" The wall imploded in a swirling cloud that coalesced into a tall man wearing a huge round hat.

"Why the rush?" The Preacher's voice was warm butter.

There was nowhere to go but right. Liz turned, sprinting down the alley. A windowless cargo van was parked askew beneath a lone lamppost. The Preacher materialized in front of the van. Liz tried to stop on the loose gravel. Her feet skidded, caught, and she went down on her butt. The Preacher towered over her.

"You'd better stop it right there!" Liz's pulse hammered in her throat. Her hands stung.

"Stop what?"

"Killing people! You can't do it."

"Can't I?"

"No. And feeding them to us?"

"Waste not." He smiled.

"That's disgusting." She was dead. She'd be Big Slim's next topic of discussion if she didn't do something. Anything. Fight to the end, fake it 'till you make it, be all she could be. "Get out of here!"

"Or else?"

"Or else it's war."

"War?"

"That's right."

"What do you know of war?"

"I—" Her favorite twenty-sided die click-clacked in her mind.

The Preacher bent down, his face inches away. "Tell me of your wars."

"I—"

"Have you seen the Rhine run red with Gallic life? Felt flesh tear beneath the pressure of your war-weary gladius, hacking because it would no longer slice? Have you peeled the clotted blood of your enemies from your face?"

"I—"

"*THAT IS WAR!*"

The words blasted through her mind. A squeal erupted from her; involuntary tears dripped down her face. "You have to go."

"Why?"

"Because you eat people."

"Oh, they eat themselves." He stood up. "You may be too young to see it."

The Preacher took a step back and squatted at her level. "Tell me, the Utes who locked me in that coffin—what happened to them?"

"What?"

"The natives here, what happened to them?"

"We moved in, killed them all or pushed them onto reservations."

"See?"

He had a point.

"Well?"

"Well you can't stay." Her mother popped into her mind. Every moment he remained here was a threat to her. She couldn't let him stay, even if it killed her. "This isn't the place for you. I *will* witness war if you remain here. Would you wish that upon me?"

Liz's skull cracked against the ground. The Preacher was on her, pressing her into the asphalt, his knee an anvil on her chest. He grabbed her head with hands like deli meat.

"You wish for war, little one?"

Electricity scuttled across Liz's skin; lightning exploded between her ears and she saw... *A river, wide and bright with blood, a parade of bodies, naked and bloated, drifting to either side as far as the eye could see . . . A blow jarred her hands, her palms were raw, bloody flesh. Fear lanced through her ... and hate. She jammed her sword into the eye slit of her enemy's helmet; his scream gurgled into silence . . .*

Asphalt pressed against her cheek. An iron scent clung to her nostrils. The Preacher stood above her.

"Is that what you have in mind?"

Liz pushed herself up. She couldn't give in. "Leave."

His laugh reverberated off the buildings. "You." He shook a finger at her. "I admire your spirit."

The bookseller's words surfaced. It was worth a shot. "We found your phylactery."

"Oh?" He cocked his head.

"That's right, and we, uhh, don't make us destroy it!"

He pulled out an empty plastic baggy.

Liz had seen it before—it had been filled with—

"Quite impossible now, dear."

Sea salt! "What did you do?"

"Ensured my immortality."

"Does that mean you're a part of m—"

"It means my job here is done." A smiled cut across his face, the space around him shivered, and he was gone.

7
The Best of Both Worlds

Liz walked back to the shelter. Her head throbbed. She pictured herself as an overstuffed teddy bear, seams stretched to the limit, coal eyes bulging. The door shut behind her; the hall stretched ahead; fluorescent lighting flickered, died.

Nobody looked up when she entered the dining room. Big Slim had pulled her tray over and sat munching the last of her broccoli. His own tray had been licked clean.

"Hey." Liz sat across the table.

Big Slim stopped mid-chew.

"I said, hey." Liz waved her hands.

He blinked and recognition crept into his eyes. "Lizzy! How've you been?"

"I'm alive. Are you okay?"

"Fine as a foal, just finishing up . . . dinner." His gaze slid past her. "Weren't you just here?"

"Yeah. The Preacher is definitely a lich, but I'm pretty sure he's gone now."

"Preacher?" Big Slim crunched into Liz's hard roll.

"The creep-o with the hat?"

"Umm." Big Slim shrugged.

"The thing that killed Frasier? Crab Hands Johnson? Shem?"

"You're starting to scare me now." A hunk of dough rocketed from his mouth. "The names ring a bell, but they must've been gone a long time if I can't put a face to 'em."

Liz shook her head. "Forget about it." It shouldn't have surprised her. She'd been dealing with a frickin' undead wizard, after all. The Preacher's words returned. *Ensured my immortality*. He'd said his job here was done, and she believed him, which meant her mom was safe, and so was everyone else at the shelter, though her give-a-shit for them had reached a low point for the day.

"You sure you're okay?" Big Slim shoved a chunk of roll into his mouth.

The Great Salt Lich

"Yeah, it's just that—" Liz sat back. A wave of déjà vu crashed inside her. She took in the room, the bleached tables and high gloss floor. Something had changed. The long fluorescent tubes still cast the place in pale white. Tuesday's usual volunteers smiled at each other as they cleaned up the evening meal.

Big Slim stared into his tray, the last bit of roll smacking between his lips.

It wasn't the place, but the people who weren't the same. Liz's insides gurgled.

"Well, that was delicious," Big Slim said.

Black hole eyes ghosted through her mind. The shelter's patrons were less a gathering and more a herd spread out across the dining room, chewing their food like feeble-minded cattle.

"I'll go get your mom." Big Slim gathered both trays.

"No, I'm fine." Liz put a hand on Big Slim's arm. "It's just that I'm oh, so hungry."

Nicholas Batura

Nicholas Batura hails from Salt Lake City. He is just over half way through Seton Hill University's Writing Popular Fiction MFA program, and is hard at work on a fantasy novel. When he's not busy writing or working, he enjoys drinking wine and hanging out with his wife and their pit bull, the dog they call Jayne.

Prissy, the Zombie, and Frederic Fekkai Hair Gel for Men
by Nikki Trionfo

Prissy Jackson lived up to her name. Spiders? "Ooh! Save me!" Hand-crafted rose china? "Ooh! Lovely!" Backed-up sewer lines? "Ooh! Pee-you!" Stiletto heels stepped her through life—stiletto heels and satin red nail-polish and podcasts like the trendy Diversity Now with its accompanying twitter hashtag.

She stood protected from a rainstorm picking up speed over the Great Salt Lake. Her hometown of Magna didn't boast tap water that residents would actually drink, but it did have a covered bus stop at the high school. Not that Prissy cared about tap water or bus stops. She cared about first boyfriends.

Nothing in her life had been lacking when she'd been a freshman. But this year, she was eligible for prom. Her high school's current social-strata-pecking-order officially sanctioned it—sophomores going to prom. That meant she needed to acquire a living, breathing accessory. An accessory with bold, male features that would offset her turquoise Anthony Luciano handbag and advertised well on her twitter feed. #DiversityNow followers would appreciate her boasting something other than her boring blond hair and fair skin.

Thunder clapped and Prissy jumped right into the arms of a handsome stranger with a firm grip and a distinct smell. Prissy had a nose for these kinds of fragrances, despite the unfortunate perma-stench of salt water bacteria permeating the valley.

"Ooh! Dear me!" She inhaled deeply against the stranger's shoulder. "Calvin Klein Euphoria for Men Aftershave?"

"Why, yes. OM-gosh, you're beautiful," he replied. "Wait. I shouldn't say that. Why'd I say that? I've always wanted to fall in love in the classic way, the MKTO way. You know that song? I Wanna Do Ya Like Michael?" Tendrils of dark hair swayed as the older boy—probably a senior—set Prissy down.

Mm, dark hair. That was a start in the right direction.

"You haven't ruined everything," she said. "We could fall in love in the old-fashioned, love-at-first-sight way."

The gorgeous guy brightened immediately. "Great idea. I'm Braydon."

Thunder clapped and Prissy looked up.

A strange, dark figure limped toward them, and an overwhelming stench hit her—not Axe Kilo or English Leather, but something else. As the shape drew closer, it appeared to be injured. Lightning flashed, silhouetting decaying chunks of flesh hanging by a thread from the figure's face.

Prissy screamed. "It's a zombie!"

She'd never seen a zombie in real life before, and this one was darker and more striking than she'd imagined.

"I'll save you!" Braydon rummaged through his backpack while Prissy retrieved a nail file from the Anthony Luciano handbag at her side and pointed it at the zombie's peeling forehead.

She found her voice and projected from her diaphragm. One must always remember proper social etiquette. "No violence. #DivertsityNow says . . . says Less Fighting, More UnDying. You know, Live and Let Die. Peace for the Middle Beast and the rest."

The zombie reared back his head and moaned, causing the ground to rumble. Braydon and Prissy covered their ears.

It occurred to Prissy that it might be time to seek out a new

Prissy, the Zombie, and Frederic Fekkai Hair Gel for Men

Twitter crowd.

Braydon recovered first and threw something at the zombie. "Take that, you fiend."

A tube hit the creature in the shoulder and fell to his toes, visible through holes in his decaying sneakers. He picked it up and read the label.

"Frederic Fekkai Hair Gel for Men? That's all you could come up with?" the zombie asked.

Her nail file looked smaller than ever. She tucked it back into the handbag's third pocket, snap-side. For easy access later. Hang nails were worse than paper cuts.

She touched Braydon's arm. "Technically, you're taking the first swing, darling. I don't think political correctness allows—"

He shrugged her off and threw another item. "And that."

"A toothbrush?" the zombie fairly yelped.

"Personal hygiene directly affects quality of life. Something you could obviously learn," Braydon said, disgruntled. "And why aren't you attacking properly, so I can rescue her?"

"He's not attacking at all," Prissy pointed out.

Braydon shot her a look, hair-tendrils tumbling exceptionally well. "You can't be one of those Pro-Undeaders."

"Well..." She hesitated. Braydon would photograph perfectly against a prom backdrop. Plus, the zombie was terrifying.

Braydon turned back to the monster, stamping a foot. "You're supposed to put your arms out like this and moan."

"Well, you're supposed to hit me with things—large things—so my limbs fall off and I have to crawl back to the lake. You know the salt water bacteria are the only way to reassemble myself. All zombies come from the Great Salt Lake. Now, look here." The zombie grabbed a nearby streetlight and tore it from the sidewalk, dragging electric wires and chunks of concrete with it.

He slammed the streetlight against his opposite hand. The pole fell to the sidewalk with a crash, taking three zombie fingers with it.

"See," the zombie said, wiggling his thumb and remaining forefinger. "Only two left now. I can get my whole arm to fall off with a better angle." He bent for the streetlight, grunting.

"Stop! You're enacting your role as victim!" Prissy dropped her handbag. She darted into the rain. A self-tortured zombie, the exact topic addressed by last week's #DiversityNow podcast. Really, who would crush their own arm? Why weren't they teaching species-confidence to zombies in school these days anyway? Zombie Prep was running over at Saltair, even though those humans grossly violated property rights and rebuilt the building itself. The UnDead hadn't gotten around to burning it down again.

"Prissy, don't," Braydon cried.

The downpour pelted Prissy's loose curls as she ran to empower the zombie with slogans like Proud to Be Wound. Wait, that was for mummies. What was the catch-phrase for zombies? She lost what little balance stiletto heels had provided. She was falling until she felt someone catch her.

"Oh!" Prissy smelled fresh rain and dirt. She was in the arms of the zombie. Her heart pounded. He could throw her halfway to the Great Salt Lake, crushing every bone in her body. There was some great-uncle on her mother's grandmother's sister-wife's side that that had happened to.

"You saved me from falling," Prissy said, staring into the zombie's dark eyes. They were black as midnight. The perfect match to her Anthony Luciano handbag. She had trouble breathing. Swaying, she clutched his arm tighter.

"You fell into me." He set her back on her feet in slow-motion, gazing at her. "I can't move fast enough to catch damsels in distress."

"Show no compassion." Braydon was still under the roof of the bus stop, sounding flustered and fussing with an umbrella.

"Ooh, that brute," Prissy cried, watching him.

"That's quite a high-pitched 'Ooh' you have there," the zombie told Prissy, never taking his eyes off her face. "Try engaging the lower half of your voice box, right here." He put a wet, cool finger against the hollow of her throat.

"Why, I'd never thought of that," Prissy said. The zombie obviously knew the niceties of conversational speech. No one wanted to sound squeaky and high-pitched. And look at his shoulders bursting through his shirt rags. She'd never seen anyone as muscular.

Braydon threw the umbrella down. "Fine, then, I'm coming without it."

The zombie paid no attention to Braydon, still gripping Prissy tightly around the waist. "Gives you more volume. Listen to this." Grotesque moans erupted from his mouth.

"Aiiiiiii-ya!" Braydon smashed the Anthony Luciano handbag into the zombie's ear. The black appendage flew through the rain and landed in a puddle on the road.

"No!" Prissy screamed.

"Now he's got it." The zombie grunted terribly, louder than ever. He lost hold of Prissy. "Close range. My weakness."

"Stop!" Prissy lunged forward to throw her arms around the zombie, but lost her balance. She fell with her forearms on the pavement as Braydon smashed the purse into the zombie's collarbone.

The zombie collapsed onto the sidewalk, shielding his head with his arms. "You're much too quick for me."

"And, really, let's not get in the way, Prissy!" Braydon was leaning over Prissy, speaking through gritted teeth. He turned back to the zombie, bringing the purse over his head. "This'll be the last of you."

"Noooo!" Standing, Prissy slipped one of her stiletto high-heels off her foot with a satin-red fingernail. She brought the heel down on Braydon's head, knocking him out cold. "You take that!"

The zombie brushed Braydon's body aside like it weighed nothing and stood.

"Great angle," he said. "Where'd you learn that?"

"I've never even had lessons." Smiling and dazed, Prissy stared at the broken heel in her hand.

"No one's ever saved me before."

"Well, you shouldn't tell people how to beat you. Or go around taking your own limbs off."

"But I don't need them." Excited, the zombie grabbed the stiletto heel from Prissy. "Watch!"

"Please don't." She took hold of his wrist and he paused. She kept her hand on him. "I...I like men with their appendages attached."

He looked from her red fingernails to her face. "And the fingers and ear? You'll—"

"Wear your hair long until your ear grows back," she said, lost in the black of his eyes. "We'll hold hands on your right side only."

"Fair enough."

He glanced at her mouth and she closed her eyes. Kissing a zombie was cool and wet and wonderful. A zombie as her first boyfriend. She decided right then and there to pin a selfie of them together as her top Twitter post.

Nikki Trionfo

A California girl at heart, Nikki Trionfo writes, does those dance-step classes at the gym, swaps mom stories about her five kids, and considers her horror muscles—when fully flexed—to be as scary as pink sparkle frosting. Dinner is her nemesis. She recently signed with literary agent Josh Getzler for a hip, smart-sleuthing YA called Shatter. Find her at www.nikkitrionfo.com.

Brine and Blood
by C.R. Langille

Stories like these usually start with bad weather, which would account for the deluge attacking the Salt Lake Valley. We don't get a lot of rain in Utah in the summer months, and when we do, it's usually over before you could say, "It's raining." This storm, however, was different. It started two days ago and it hadn't stopped.

The raindrops hit my windshield loud enough to drown out the traffic update on the radio. The update wasn't necessary though; the sea of red lights in front of me mirrored by the Soviet bread-line of vehicles on the other side of the highway was update enough. I was a creature of habit though, and getting the daily traffic was more ritual than anything.

The ritual was shattered when the call came in on my cell phone. Holly, my secretary, had me install a nice Bluetooth system so I wouldn't have to mess with the phone. Something about hands-free being safer or some bullshit.

"This is Morgan," I said.

"Hey, Boss, I've got a woman here. Says she has a job for you."

Holly had a meek voice, almost a whisper. Yet, once you tuned your ear to it, it came in crystal clear. Caused problems sometimes on the phone with clients, but she had a way with organization that would impress any Wall Street tycoon.

"Stuck in traffic, Hon. Going to be another twenty minutes until I get back."

"The woman says she'll wait," Holly said. "Oh, and Boss?"

"Shoot."

"Don't call me Hon. We've talked about it before."

I chuckled. She had a quiet bark to her, and I liked the fire. Besides, it was a game we played, and I was sure she enjoyed it as much as I did.

Thirty minutes later, I pulled into the parking lot of my small office. The office of Bartholomew Morgan, Private Investigations was sandwiched between a Dollar Tree and a Great Clips in the middle of West Valley City. We had an advertisement in the phone book, but Holly was quick to tell me that we needed an online presence as well. I wasn't so sure, but when we only had just enough clients to pay the bills (during good months), I relented. Taking care of the site was one of her additional duties.

Even with the influx of clients from the website, times were getting tough. We had been late on rent last month, and if this job didn't go through, we'd be kicked out before the end of the next.

The door squealed as I walked in, and Holly shuddered. She stood up, grabbed a can of WD-40 from her desk, and marched over as I was hanging my hat on the coat rack.

"When are you going to get this fixed? I have to spray this thing at least twice a day," she said.

"Why do I need to fix it if you keep it working, Hon?"

She shot me a glare over the rims of her tortoise shell glasses. The look said the next time I said the word Hon she'd spray me in the face with the WD-40 instead of the squeaky hinges.

"Your potential new client is in your office. Ms. Whatley is her name."

"Why did you let her back there?"

Holly shot me a smile. It was payback. She knew I didn't like clients poking around in my office when I wasn't there.

"Touché."

I opened the door to my office, and it was surprisingly quiet. The subtle odor of lubricant told me Holly had already hit these hinges. However, it wasn't the audible state of the door that caught my attention; it was Ms. Whatley.

She had her back to me, but I could already tell that she was a looker. She wore a summer dress that was short enough to leave little to my imagination (and I have a big imagination). Long hair the color of coffee was pulled into a tight bun. The hint of a tattoo on the nape of her neck was visible, not enough to tell what it was, but enough that I knew I wanted to see more.

She turned to face me and caught me with the biggest blue eyes I'd ever seen. They were light blue like a pure glacier and contrasted with her dark hair in the most dramatic way.

She stood up and extended a hand. I shook it, careful to find that perfect grip, not too strong, but not too weak to be demeaning. The scent of sunflowers on a warm summer day greeted my nose.

"Ms. Whatley, a pleasure to meet you. I'm Bartholomew Morgan."

"Likewise," she said.

I sat down behind my desk, and my chair squeaked in protest. Apparently, Holly either didn't care about this squeak or purposefully left it to grate on my nerves. My vote was on the latter.

"How can I help you, Ms. Whatley?"

She returned to her seat and placed her hands on her knees. For a moment, she didn't say anything, only wrung her flower-print dress in her hands. Her lips, a shade softer than a bonfire, were pursed.

"I need you to track down my son."

A missing persons' case. Not typically my forte, but it wouldn't be the first time.

"I assume the police haven't helped?"

Her eye twitched and she glanced up at me. For a moment, those light blue eyes went dark. She let go of the dress and folded her arms.

"Technically, he isn't missing."

"Well, Ms. Whatley, if he isn't missing, why do you need me?"

Maybe he owed her money, or was in a bad way with some bad people. She glanced at her lap and her cheeks flushed. Before she spoke again, she started fidgeting with her dress.

"Rudy hasn't been himself for over a year now. He's been getting sloppy at his job, and I'm afraid his actions might get a lot of people killed. I want to know what he's up to before it's too late."

"What makes you think he's dangerous, Ms. Whatley?"

I pulled out a pad of paper and started taking notes.

"He's been acting out of character for a while, getting defiant. Things were okay for a short time, but I could tell he wasn't himself. I told myself it was just the run of bad luck he was in, but I don't think that was it."

The waterworks started, so I handed her a box of tissues, which was standard issue for my line of work. You wouldn't believe the amount of crying people who end up on the other side of my desk.

"You haven't said anything that indicates he's dangerous. What did you mean?"

She went on to explain some more about his situation. I wrote down a few notes, but still wasn't sure where this was going. She was keeping something hidden, that much I knew for sure. I've seen my share of liars, cheats, and people not telling the whole truth. However, I didn't want to be rude, so I proceeded carefully.

"Go on, please," I said.

She took a deep breath and looked me in the eye.

"He put a lock on the door to his room, heavy duty. One day, he forgot to lock it up before he left at night, so I did what any worried mother would do. The room was a mess, which was unusual. Rudy had always been very tidy, even as a young boy. In fact, he would clean the house for me without me having to ask. I was quite grateful, as any mother would be.

"His bed was untouched, but there were blankets on the floor. He had scrawled some drawing on the walls as well, but I didn't have a chance to look much further, because he came home."

Her hands started to shake a little and her eyes stared at nothing.

"He was furious, angry that I had entered the room. He started babbling on about his work and how important it was, and that he couldn't have me interfering. Rudy had a crazy look in his eyes. I'd seen that look before."

Ms. Whatley turned away to wipe away some fresh tears. Her shoulders convulsed as she cried. I wanted to go to her, put my arm around those soft shoulders and tell her it would be okay, but I was a professional. Well, I suppose that opinion differed depending on who you talked to.

"Ms. Whatley, I can conduct surveillance on your son no problem. However, if I do find that he's involved in illegal activities, I'll have to take the proper procedures, of course."

Generally the proper procedures meant calling the cops. I had been known to look the other way in certain circumstances, generally involving certain "fees;" however, never with dangerous individuals.

"Of course, I merely ask that you inform me first," she said.

I nodded. She gave me the rest of the lowdown. Apparently after the confrontation with her son, he left the house and hadn't returned. That was two days ago. I would need to see his room, and she agreed to that. Before we could move further, I'd have to discuss the logistics.

"Ms. Whatley, I'm sure Holly informed you of my rates, but I want to make sure you understand that my services don't come cheap. For surveillance, I charge fifty an hour plus mileage. No more than five-hundred a day. Is that going to be an issue?"

Something told me it wouldn't.

"No, Mr. Morgan, just please find my son and make sure he hasn't hurt anyone."

I still thought there was more to the story than she was letting on, but I could find out for myself.

"No worries, Ms. Whatley, I'll find him. I'm very good at what I do. Holly will take care of the details up front."

She rose, and I couldn't help but steal a glance at those lovely legs. We shook hands once again, and I asked her a question.

"Do you have a current picture of your son, Ms. Whatley?"

"Of course."

She dug into her purse and handed me a photo. Rudy had brown hair parted down the middle. It was already starting to recede. He wore thick-rimmed glasses that pulled on his face with their weight, giving the boy a kind of tired expression. His eyes, brown in color, seemed to look at nothing at all. He had a crooked smile as he held up a certificate which stated Employee of the Month in bold black letters.

"I've done a lot of research, Mr. Morgan, and I've chosen you specifically to undertake this task. Please don't disappoint me," she said.

"I'll do everything in my power to get the job done. You mentioned you had seen that look before in your son's eyes. What did you mean?"

She pulled her hand away. Not fast, but with some force.

"Actually, in my husband's eyes; burned out from duties and responsibilities, he put a bullet in his head. Rudy had the same look."

* * *

The rain was coming down even harder as I drove to Ms. Whatley's house. It was just past seven in the evening, but the skies were already dark. Pretty early for summer, but perhaps it was the overcast clouds.

I had all my equipment in the back seat. I had planned on finding Rudy as soon as I left the Whatley house; however, I needed to see his room first. More than likely there would be something in there that would put me on the trail.

The house was old, big, and located in the Avenues of Salt Lake City. It dug into the side of the hill like a parasite, unwilling to let go lest it roll down the street. Once the house was probably a glossy white, but now that color had faded and peeled with age. It looked more akin to an octogenarian marked with liver spots.

I parked the car and made my way to the front door. Several newspapers were sitting on the front porch in various states of decay along with several colorful feathers, which reminded me of tropical birds. Perhaps Ms. Whatley owned a parrot. I double-checked the address to make sure I had the right house. The numbers matched up.

The door was larger than normal, and made from a dark-stained oak. When I knocked, the heavy thud that resonated told me it was solid. Thunder boomed in the distance, as if answering my knocks. I raised my hand to try again when the deadbolt flipped, and the door opened.

The sultry form of Ms. Whatley greeted me. She had changed clothes since I last saw her at the office. Instead of a fun sun dress, she wore a pink bath robe. Her hair was damp and clung to her cheeks.

"Mr. Morgan," she said, almost a purr.

What was it about this woman? She screamed sex in a way both subtle and in my face. I had to focus on the task at hand.

"Ms. Whatley, thanks for seeing me tonight. I would like to get this matter resolved as soon as possible for you."

"I would be forever in your debt."

She opened the door wider to let me in. The house was dim, with bare light bulbs on the wall and ceiling providing a dull glow. The interior of the home was somewhat spartan, with only an old couch and an even older coffee table with a century of water stains. It wasn't what I expected. Ms. Whatley struck me as the kind of woman who would have a house full of niceties. This seemed barely lived in.

"Just moving into the place?"

Her lips screwed into a frown, but she didn't answer. My gut was screaming for me to leave, but I wanted to see the job through. We hadn't had a decent job in a few weeks, and the money was direly needed; the rent was coming due soon.

She led me down the hall, and even with the creepy house

surrounding us, I couldn't help but notice the sway of her hips. She shot me a glance from behind her shoulder and grinned. There was something predatory in her smile. Ms. Whatley was a dangerous woman; I'd have to remember that.

Rudy's room sat at the end of a long hallway which was just as empty as the greeting room. There were blank spaces on the wall where the paint was lighter, marking empty homes where pictures once hanged.

His door, like the front door, was solid. A latch in the upper corner with a padlock secured the door shut. It wouldn't be too hard to open.

I reached into my pocket and pulled out my lock picking tools. Unlike in the movies, it wasn't just a magical jiggle and then, bam, presto-chango, open lock. It took more time and a lot more precision. However, I was pretty good at it, and it didn't take long.

Rudy's room was musty, humid even, as if a swamp cooler had been blowing directly into it. Yet it was hot. With the rain outside dropping the temperature, it should have been nice and cool; however, the heat was oppressive.

I walked into the room. Like the rest of the house, it was dark with a single exposed light bulb to provide light. The walls were covered with writing in different languages, some I recognized and others I didn't. One phrase, in hastily scribbled English, caught my eye—*A sacrifice for the sun or we shall all drown in darkness, brine, and blood.*

There were printed papers depicting Mesoamerican sacrificial rituals, detailing methods, tools, and art. Dozens of depictions of people having their hearts and innards cut out, burned, and offered to old gods. There were pictures showing ancient Celtic peoples burning others alive in giant wooden structures shaped like people.

Other printouts detailed sunrise and sunset times, solar flare activity, and weather reports. I sifted through some of the papers near the bed and found something of interest. There were over a dozen photos of the miniature island called Black Rock at the edge of the Great Salt Lake. Each photo looked like it was taken in the morning as the sun was rising. They all had dates written on the back, ranging from the last few months to the most recent, a week ago. Upon further investigation, I found a pattern; the dates were weekly, exactly seven days apart. If this was the case, and Rudy kept to the pattern, he would be there tomorrow morning.

The rest of the room was filled with garbage and dirty clothes. There wasn't much else to go on.

"Do you think you can find my son, Mr. Morgan?"

"I think I have enough to go on; I'll get started right away. Please let me know if Rudy comes back."

"Of course."

I left Ms. Whatley's house with more questions than when I arrived. At least I had a direction to follow.

* * *

On the way back to the office, I put in a few calls and cashed in a few favors in an attempt to locate Rudy. If his car was spotted or he used his credit card, I'd be notified.

I called the office, but no one answered. Holly usually stayed late, so I was surprised she didn't pick up. I asked her once why she didn't go home after quitting time, which was officially six in the evening. She said it was because if no one was there to ensure everything was orderly, the business would go to hell. Guess she didn't have much confidence in my own abilities. Who was I kidding? Without her help, I would have gone bankrupt years ago.

The next day, wanting to get a jump-start on things, I pulled into the parking lot shortly after five in the morning and immediately knew something wasn't right. Rain still hammered the area, making it hard to see, but I could see enough to tell shit and a running fan had already been acquainted.

Holly's car was still parked just outside the building, the lights in the office were on, and the glass pane in the door was smashed.

Before I got out of the vehicle, I grabbed the revolver from my glove compartment. The weight told me it was still loaded. With the gun trained in front of me, I crept up to my place of business. Glass shards cracked underneath my shoes as I walked up, reminding me of the snapping of bones. A quick glance from the outside didn't reveal anyone in the waiting area, but I couldn't be sure. I opened the door and walked in.

The office was a mess—bookshelves were overturned, Holly's chair was on its side, and the contents of her desk were strewn about. My inner office door hung by one hinge with a small flicker of light emanating from within.

I maneuvered closer to the door, placing my shoulder on the wall. With a quick intake of breath, I rolled around, pointing the gun toward my office. Like the waiting area, it was empty and equally disheveled. However, sitting alone on my desk was a note.

It read: *A sacrifice for the sun or we shall all drown in darkness, brine, and blood.*

The note must have been from Rudy, although the handwriting was different. It wasn't scribbled or chicken scratch. This handwriting spoke of confidence, measure, and meticulous care.

I rushed out the door back to the car. I knew where he would be—Black Rock.

Attempts to dial 911 on the way to Black Rock proved fruitless. Perhaps the storm was affecting the phone lines; the rain was almost a wall of water at this point. Traffic was almost non-existent with people staying inside to avoid the weather. However, the lack of traffic didn't mean much because I had to drive at a snail's pace just to stay on the road.

I passed several big rigs pulled over on the shoulder as I made my way toward Black Rock. Their blinkers served as make-shift lighthouses, keeping me oriented and away from the figurative rocky shores. I tried 911 a couple more times, and met with the same results. However, on the final try, the phone connected, but before I could say anything, static blew through the receiver. A combination of stress, weather, and the situation must have gotten to me, because I swore I heard a woman's laughter through the static; even more disturbing, I thought it was Ms. Whatley's laughter.

The rain started to dissipate as I neared Black Rock. The eastern sky grew slightly brighter as the sun started to rise, chasing away the darkness. For being seven in the morning, the sun should have been higher in the sky, painting the heavens with reds, oranges, and yellows. It still looked as if it was just before dawn. Perhaps it was the clouds, perhaps something else.

A car fitting the description of Rudy's beat up vehicle was pulled over underneath an overpass. With the rain slowing down to a mere trickle, the stubby column of earth that was Black Rock jutted out of the shore of the Great Salt Lake. It stood alone, a miniature mesa next to a dead lake. A flash of movement near the base of the rock caught my attention. Two figures moved around the rock and out of sight: Rudy and Holly.

I parked the car, grabbed my pistol, and made my way toward the iconic rock island. The air was warm, warmer than it should have been. The rain made everything humid, creating a sticky sheen across my face. I hopped the railing along the road, and trudged through brush. It only took a few steps to soak my pants and shoes.

Everyone had differing opinions on what the Great Salt Lake smelled like. To me, it was a dead smell, almost sulfurous. Some days, when the winds were right, I could even smell it in my office. Today, standing in the heat and steam of the morning it was no less potent.

As I neared the rocky tower, everything went silent. The rain stopped completely, the wind died down to nothing, and only my ragged breath made any noise at all. Well, that and the squish-squish of my footsteps through the muddy shore.

I stopped to regulate my breathing, and the muffled sound of a woman's cry caught my ear. It was Holly, I knew it deep down. I rushed to the other side of the Black Rock with my gun at the ready. What awaited me almost broke my sanity.

Rudy was there, with Holly tied and gagged next to him. He looked different from the picture Ms. Whatley had given me. Rudy was gaunt, bone-thin, with a scraggly beard covering his face. His eyes and face were red, irritated, and angry. It seemed Holly hit him with an ample shot of WD-40. That was my Holly.

My presence didn't seem to faze him. He turned and began lighting candles. He had a large knife made from something that looked like obsidian. The way the blade seemed to radiate darkness made me think it was much more than mere obsidian. That, in itself, wasn't what made me stop and question my place on this earth; it was what was in the rocks above Rudy.

From what I could gather, it was Ms. Whatley. Her dark hair rained down on pale, naked shoulders, revealing the tattoo that was only hinted at during our previous meeting. The tattoo was a spiral of strange symbols and letters that didn't make any sense to me, but hurt my eyes if I looked at them too hard. She was entirely naked, covered only by her wild hair, but where her legs should have been a serpentine tail covered her in colorful feathers. She scrambled up the rocks, gliding across the vertical surface as if it were mere steps, climbing with long, clawed hands. She cast her gaze toward me and smiled.

Her eyes glowed a brilliant blue, and I almost lost myself in her hypnotic stare. She was beautiful, savage, and dangerous as ever.

If Rudy noticed her, he didn't give any indication. The boy lit the last candle, then grabbed Holly. She gave another cry, kicked out, and toppled Rudy. Holly tried to scramble away, but Rudy was quick to recover and grabbed her by the hair and pulled her to the ground. He straddled her prone form, bringing the obsidian blade to her neck.

"I'm sorry, I don't want to, but it needs to happen," he said.

His words broke my trance and grabbed my attention. I glanced back to Ms. Whatley, but she was gone.

"Let her go," I said, aiming the gun at him.

He looked up with ragged eyes sunk deep into his skull. It was still dark out, but I could tell he hadn't shaved in over a week. Tears streamed down his face.

"I... I can't," he said.

"Sure you can. Let her go and we can get you some help."

He started to sob, his shoulders shuddering with each cry. Rudy muttered something, but I couldn't quite make it out as he wiped his face with his free hand. Holly tried to roll away, but he pushed her head back into the sand.

"Don't hurt her, Rudy. Let's sort this out, get you back to your mother, and call it a day. How's that sound?"

"She's not my mother," he said.

"Come again?"

He looked up, boring through me with his dead eyes. I'd seen my share of crazy folk, but Rudy took the cake.

"Do you think I want to do this? Do you think I enjoy killing people? I detest it, but I was chosen. Chosen just like you," he said, pointing a finger at me.

He was talking crazy, but talking meant not killing. So I egged him on.

"What do you mean, chosen?"

Rudy still held on to Holly with one hand by the hair. With his other hand, he rubbed his forehead and muttered something unintelligible again. That was the hand with the knife, the dangerous hand. I took a few steps closer when he wasn't looking. If things went south, I wanted to be as close as possible.

The sunrise should have been above the Wasatch Mountains by now, painting the valley sky in brilliant hues. However, it was still dark, with only a slight hint of sun way behind the clock. I didn't have much time to think about it given the current circumstances.

"Only the Chosen can make the sacrifices. I don't know why. Brine and blood, brine and blood."

Rudy looked past me, and his eyes grew wide. He started to tremble and almost lost his grip on Holly. She fought with a renewed fervor as she glanced behind me.

The water behind me started to churn, and cold, salty spray hit my back. Not wanting to divert my attention from Rudy, I gave a cursory glance behind to see what was happening. The salty water was boiling and whipping up into a froth. Before I turned my gaze back to Rudy, something rolled above the surface of the water. I couldn't tell what it was exactly, but it was black, covered in a slick slime, and ropey.

"What's going on?" I asked, to no one in particular.

The scent of sunflowers crept to my nose, and I felt a presence behind me.

"A sacrifice for the sun or we shall all drown in darkness, brine, and blood."

It was Ms. Whatley's voice, or the thing that was Ms. Whatley. Still sexy and sultry, her voice made me think inappropriate things despite the events that were unfolding.

"The sacrifice must be made or the darkness shall drown everything," she said.

"No more! I can't, no more," Rudy said, slapping his forehead hard several times. Blood welled and rolled down his face.

"Rudy, just let her go. No one has to be sacrificed here," I said, taking a couple steps closer.

He looked up at me, then past me to the Great Salt Lake. Tears mixed with the blood and rolled down his cheeks. The sky grew dark, and only the dim glow of the candles gave off any light. Something large rose from the waters behind me. I wanted to look, but something deep down in my guts told me not to, that if I turned around, it would be the end.

Rudy looked to Holly, and wiped his face.

"I'm sorry," he said.

Rudy raised the knife high. Holly screamed, and I squeezed the trigger of my revolver. There was a blinding flash as the gun went off in my hand. The bullet struck Rudy square in the chest and arterial blood painted the rocks around him, dousing the candles.

The wind kicked up, roaring around us. I couldn't hear Holly's screams anymore, only the wind. With the candles out, I was cast in pitch dark. I fell to my knees and covered my face as bits of sand and rock whipped all about me.

I heard her voice. I no longer found it sexy.

"You are Chosen. I knew you wouldn't disappoint me. A sacrifice for the sun or we shall all drown in darkness, brine, and blood."

With those words the wind stopped and sunlight appeared

from behind the mountains. I turned toward the lake, happy to see nothing but calm waters along its surface. Wherever that thing, that leviathan, had come from, it had returned. I crawled over to Holly and held her in my arms. She wasn't crying anymore, but held her knees and rocked back and forth. She wouldn't look me in the eye, but kept a watchful gaze out to the water.

Rudy lay in the sand on his back, bent at the knees. He had a smile on his face. The obsidian dagger was gone.

* * *

I don't know what happened that morning, if it was real or not. I couldn't find Ms. Whatley after the incident. It was as if she never existed. Her house on the hill was just as I left it. After some digging, I found out that she never owned the house, nor did Rudy. I suppose they were squatting or something. Came to find out Rudy's parents died a long time ago in a car accident, and he wasn't even related to anyone closely resembling a Ms. Whatley.

Holly stayed on board with me, despite the incident. I think she found strength staying close to someone who had been there. We don't talk about it much, but I can only surmise what she saw in those waters. She doesn't go near the Great Salt Lake, and insists on being home before dark. Holly's still as strong as ever, giving me shit when I need it, hell, even sometimes when I don't, but a part of her died out there at Black Rock.

What I do know is it isn't over. It's been almost a year, and the days are getting shorter, darker earlier than normal. A few days ago a package arrived at the office. There were no post marks or a return address. It was a flat, rectangular box wrapped in plain brown paper. Inside were Rudy's obsidian dagger, a colorful feather that smelled of sunflowers, and a note.

A sacrifice for the sun or we shall all drown in darkness, brine, and blood.

C.R. Langille

C.R. Langille spent many a Saturday afternoon watching monster movies with his mother. It wasn't long before he started crafting nightmares to share with his readers. An avid hunter and amateur survivalist, C.R. Langille incorporates the Utah outdoors in many of his tales. He is the Organizer for the Utah Chapter of the Horror Writer's Association, and received his MFA: Writing Popular Fiction from Seton Hill University.

Voices
by Jace Hunter

"Kari, if you miss the damn school bus again you're walking."
"I won't, Mom," I call through the bathroom door.
"Like I haven't heard that before."
In the mirror, I hold a razor blade next to the new black hole the size of a freckle on my cheek. Its mosquito-pitched whine is the sound of a hurricane through a crack in a door. My hand shakes. If I don't get this right, missing the school bus is the least of my problems. I close my eyes.
Troops, I call to the people in my head. Report.
Just do it, Big Frank says. *Cut quick like we did on our thigh, a single long stroke to let the pressure out.*
But it's on our face, Bunny sighs from her burrow. *And the others didn't whistle.*
Exactly, Big Frank says. *We need to nip this crazy in the bud.*
I open my eyes and tilt my chin. As I move, the hole shimmers, twinkling like glitter or diamonds. It's the smallest of the four, smaller than the pea-sized hole on my thigh, the pinkie nail hole on my toe, or the hole hidden in ink on my arm. I put the razor down and touch it. Air flows out colder than star-breath. I gasp and stick

my finger in my mouth, sucking hard. Pulling it out, I see subzero blisters where my fingerprints should be. The holes in my body oozed cold before, but this ferocity is new.

I peer into the mental space where Granny Roz lives. Granny? What should I do?

Plug it, Granny Roz says.

With what? Big Frank sneers.

Bath tissue. Bum-fodder. The old TP, Granny Roz says, scratching her cornrows. She purses her lips and spits tobacco juice into an empty Dr. Pepper can. *Cover it up with face-spackle. Ain't no one gonna see.* She shifts her wad to the other side. *Nobody ever do.*

Plugging didn't work yesterday, Bunny says.

This hole ain't but a baby, Granny Roz replies.

Cut it. Get rid of the cancer, Big Frank says.

Spoken like a true military man, snorts Granny Roz. *Why fix what you can beat into submission?*

It's a hole in our face, Bunny says. *It's making noise. It needs to stop.*

The voices in my head advise, but the final decision is mine. I tug some tissue from the roll and lean so close to the mirror that my breath fogs it and I have to pull back a little to focus. I press a tiny piece of toilet paper against the shrillness. It doesn't stick.

Wet it, Granny Roz says.

I take a drop of water from the tap and roll a needle-sized plug. I twist and jam it into the hole. Like a teakettle lifted off the heat, the whistling stops. In the silence, time speeds up.

"Kari!" Mom calls. "I'm not driving you if you're too stupid to catch the bus."

I dab a bit of concealer over the lump and lean back from the mirror. The area looks red and swollen, a blemish about to erupt.

Good enough, Granny Roz says. *Don't forget our backpack. Put it next to you on the bus so none of Them can sit there.*

Big Frank growls, but doesn't say anything, just grabs his binoculars and heads to his lookout post. Bunny runs down her burrow to make sure all the dolls are tucked into bed. Bunny hates school.

Switch it on, Granny Roz says. *Let me see it.*

Mentally, I reach up to my master control panel and flip the switch that reveals a soldier's thousand yard stare. Big Frank taught me that last year when I went into battle with Them.

Now you're ready. Granny Roz settles into her rocking chair, picks up a bowl of peas, and starts shelling. *We're here if'n you need us.*

As I walk out the bathroom door, I tuck a tube of concealer into my pocket.

Might need a touch up later.

Not that anyone will notice.

I get to the end of the driveway in time to watch the bus pull away from the corner. Through a window, Becca Jameson points at me and laughs. Charlotte Hanamoto, that cow, joins in. Without thought, my arm raises and my finger flips them off. They laugh harder as the bus rolls out of sight. Big Frank, I say.

What? he says. *They deserve it.*

I look toward Mom's car.

Big Frank shudders. *Let's avoid that crapfest.*

How?

Granny Roz shakes her head. *You got two feet, Chile. It's not but a twenty minute walk.*

I'll be late.

Better late than getting into Mom's car, says Big Frank.

Bunny? I think.

Walk, she says, *you'll still make the second bell.* She curls her ears over her face and closes her eyes. In the background the shadow troops stand silent.

Walking gives me time to think.

The first black spot—holes I call them—appeared a week ago on my littlest toe. Covering my entire nail, it looked like a Goth pedicure gone wrong or the aftermath of a hammer's kiss. The rest of my toe was warm, but the arctic draft of air coming from the place where my nail had been froze my sock to my shoe. Walking across polished cement, I'd slipped and barely caught myself before tumbling into a spinning rack of paperbacks. Ignoring the glare from the librarian, I eased into a study carrel and pried icy laces loose. WTF?

There was something familiar about the hole and the thin thread of bitter air leaking from it.

The swan, Granny Roz said.

That's it! It reminded me of the swan inner tube I'd gotten for my sixth birthday. Something about its beak or eye. Maybe it was the way the swan was supposed to keep me safe that day at the Great Salt Lake, but slowly leaked until I was floundering, unable to keep my head above the wakes and splashes of the other kids.

That day the miracle of Granny Roz's voice saved me. I remember floating in the too thick water, salt sticking in my hair, not paying attention as the swan carried me away from shore and toward a diving platform. Bobbing in the lake, I watched bigger kids cannonballing and lying in the sun, white spots of salt pooling in the hollows of backs and knees. "Watch this!" a boy's voice called. I didn't see the giant tsunami of a splash that knocked me sideways, only heard the girl next to me snap, "Carl! Knock it off or I'm telling!" as she brushed water off her face.

Slip. Struggle. Slip. I remember the sound of wet plastic rubbing against skin. Slip. Splash. I felt a hand grab my ankle as I sank like a pocket full of rocks. Instead of buoying me up, water seven times saltier than the sea pulled me down, filling eyes and ears, gurgling in the back of my throat, burning like hellfire. My toes touched mud, feet burying themselves to the ankles in slickness. Raising my arms to the surface, I watched the deflated swan lift past arms, wrists, fingertips—buoyant only enough to save itself. Bubbles rose, trailing fish kisses against skin as the darkness closed in.

Jump, commanded a new and wonderful voice in my head.

I jumped. Only my fingertips broke the surface.

I said, jump, Chile! Jump like a frog in bucket of cream. Jump with all the might God give you!

When my feet touched mud again, I pushed harder and swung my arms, this time rising high enough to catch a quick mouthful of air before sinking back into the lake.

Good, said the voice. *Now not just up—you gotta jump toward something. Jump toward salvation, Chile. Jump like you're playing hopscotch.*

What's hopscotch? I thought.

Eyes screwed tight against the salt burn, I saw a young girl in cornrows and a hand-me-down dress, the blue faded by harsh lye soap rubbed across scrubbing boards and the heat of the sun. The girl tossed a pebble at a line of squares scratched in the dirt. Glancing over her shoulder, she giggled, then jumped one, two, three.

Like that, said the voice.

Is that you?

A deep rumbling like the sound of gravel in a wheel well rolled through my head. *No, Chile. That's not me. At least not how I am now.* Hopscotch girl smiled, then dissolved into a study middle-aged black woman in a white kitchen apron standing on a sharecropper's porch.

Who are you?

Call me Granny Roz. Now jump!

I jumped.

Bouncing from the mud to the surface and back again, my six-year-old legs finally walked up the shore, feet crunching through the thin salt crust over mud.

Mom looked up from her book. "Where's your swan?"

I sniffled, sucking snot and saltwater up my nose. "I—"

Mom shook her head and held up a hand. "Kari, I don't want to hear it. You lost it five minutes after you got it."

"That's—"

"Tough titty said the kitty. I didn't bring you all the way to the Great Salt Lake to listen to you cry. Go play with the other kids like a big girl."

"But—"

She flicked her hand in dismissal. "Go. You're dripping all over my towel."

I didn't want to play with the other kids. Instead I sat in the shallows and listened to Granny Roz's stories about a life spent on a dry farm in Kentucky. *Always save tater water for gravy,* she told me, *and be sure to set the water a boilin' before pickin' the corn.*

Later, as we walked past pavilions and balloons pointing the way to another girl's pretty pink princess pony party, Mom muttered about waste. I ignored her and watched Granny Roz crimp a scalloped edge on a piecrust.

"Don't expect another one," Mom snapped, grabbing my arm and twisting.

"What?"

I said you can lick the bowl. Granny Roz smiled.

Over the years when things got bad, I made my way back to the Great Salt Lake. I'd wade out until I could slip my head under the water. Holding my breath, I'd think about a trouble that couldn't be named and a new voice would appear in my head with answers. Big Frank taught me about the power of no when one of Mom's boyfriend's hands wandered where they didn't belong. Bunny held me after the scary voices shouted in the night and the fires started. There are others; shadow troops I call them; they lurk in the background, waiting for I don't know what. Only three keep me company: Granny Roz to guide, Big Frank to fight, and Bunny to comfort.

For the past week, my pinky toe hole has been easy to hide under a sock and tennis shoe. Out of sight, out of mind as long as I pay attention to the differences between grass and tile, carpet and cement. As I walk to school, I glide my foot like an ice skate or rollerblade.

My eye catches the ink running over my left hand, lines smeared by soap and scrub brushes. Bunny pulls blankets over her head. *That wasn't one of our brighter moments.*

It's fine, says Big Frank. *You're over-reacting.*

We got in trouble, Bunny mumbles. *I got us in trouble.*

Not trouble, I soothe. Dr. Susan gave us hope. Despite the holes, there's a chance we might get out of here in one piece.

Granny Roz clucks her tongue. *You better hurry, Chile. You gonna be late.*

Jace Hunter

I pick up the pace, but the ink still catches my eye. I push back my sleeve and remember how just yesterday morning the world changed again.

I was cutting a pattern on a square of linoleum when the second hole appeared on my left arm, the size of a silent dime.

Trouble at seven o'clock, Big Frank shouted. *Prepare for attack.*

Bunny's head popped out of her burrow, her nose wiggling furiously. Her eyes darted left, right; her head swiveled front, back, up, and down. *No,* she said. *We're good.*

Granny Roz rested her broom against the kitchen table and walked out her front door. *Show me,* she said.

I raised my arm to my eyes. The hole appeared shiny, like water on asphalt, black ice on a bridge. I could see the edges where skin ended and the hole began, but no blood or bone or sinew; there was no sense of looking through or into. The hole was a void, an abyss that led nowhere and was filled with nothing.

This is our arm, Granny Roz said, her words knocking the air right out of me.

Nothing. I am filled with nothing.

As my warm breath rushed out, it coalesced as mist and frosted the tiny hairs on my arm.

Just like reeds in truest winter, Bunny shivered.

Granny Roz shook her finger. *Don't you touch it, Kari. Hear me. This is the devil's work.*

I'll smash whomever is doing this to us. Big Frank put down his binoculars and picked up his sniper rifle. He chambered a round.

It's not Her, Granny Roz said. *She's not even here.*

It's somebody. I'm going to find 'em and make them pay.

No, Bunny said, throwing her paws wide, the pale pink of her ears standing tall. *We don't know why. It's better to watch and wait.*

The best defense is offense. We hunt. Big Frank slipped his buck knife into its sheath and pulled his canteen snug against his shoulder.

A sharpie is better than a bullet, Bunny said.

What are you up to, Rabbit? Granny Roz crossed her arms.

Voices

A picture formed in my mind. Tossing the X-Acto knife back into the pencil box, I picked out a thin sharpie marker. A flick and a twist, and the hole was now part of a butterfly's wing. I drew flowers and vines wrapping my wrist; leaves tickled my knuckles. I put the black ink down and picked up red, blue, silver, and green; highlights and shadows—
"What do you think you're doing?"
Lost in creation, I looked up, startled. Mr. Harcourt loomed. The design sprawled from elbow to fingertips. "I—"
"That's what I thought."
Near the pottery wheel someone tittered. "Crazy Kari."
"She's cuckoo for Cocoa Puffs."
"You think?"
Mr. Harcourt sighed. "That's enough. To the counselor's office, Kari. You want to tattoo yourself, do it on your own time."
The student chair in the counselor's office was wider than normal and squishy. It wrapped around my hips and sucked me deep into the padding like a hug. Big Frank squirmed. *Metal folding chairs are more honest,* he groused. *Give me a three legged stool any day.*
The light from the big picture window framed Dr. Susan in silhouette, highlighting bits of fly away hair rising from her scalp like a crown.
L'Oreal number 8g, Golden Summer Sunshine. Granny Roz rolled her eyes. *Just look at them eyebrows. Who does she think she's foolin'? No way that color's anywhere close to natural.*
I think it's pretty, said Bunny. *Like Goldilocks or Cinderella.*
More foolishness, Granny Roz said.
Dr. Susan tapped her keyboard. "How's this week been, Kari?"
I tugged on the edge of my sleeve, squinting.
Dr. Susan glanced up. "Sorry," she said, twisting the blinds closed. "It's that time."
I tugged some more on my sleeve and tried not to stare at the hole in my arm.
Relax, Granny Roz chided. *It's not getting bigger.*

The mouse double-clicked. My eyes darted to Dr. Susan's face.

"So tell me about this week. How're things, Kari?"

I shrugged.

Dr. Susan waited several beats. I fiddled some more with my sleeve. "Kari?" she prompted.

"What?"

"I asked how things were."

With a finger, I traced the edge of the butterfly. "Good," I managed.

Mouse click. Big Frank adjusted his binoculars. *She just checked a box labeled lack of eye contact.*

"When you say this week has been good, what do you mean?"

"Good," I said.

Mouse click. *She checked disengaged,* Big Frank said. *We're heading into the danger zone.*

"Are you getting your school assignments in?"

I nod.

"How are you sleeping?"

Another shrug.

Big Frank gasped. *Incoming! The cursor is hovering over parental consultation. We have a red alert situation, people. Mobilize.*

Sit up! Smile! barked Granny Roz from the porch. *You wanna get us locked up in the nuthouse?*

I sat up and forced my lips back. "I mean, I'm sleeping better. The pills seem to be working."

"No more nightmares?"

"No."

Yes, Big Frank said from the tree blind. *But you're right, stick to name, rank, and serial number. Everything else is strictly need to know.*

Dr. Susan peered over the rims of her glasses. "Kari, I'm concerned about the way you've drawn all over your arm."

"It's just ink."

"It's a lot of ink. What are you trying to cover up?"

Bunny's eyes widened. *Careful. There are wolves about.*

"Nothing."

"Bruises? Did Charlotte or her friends hit you?"

I have bruises, yellow, purple, and green, but not from Charlotte or her friends. Mean girls punch with their words.

Say nothing. Bunny pressed her lips tight.

Dr. Susan nudged a box of tissues closer. "Did someone shove you into a locker?" Bunny hid her head. "Kari? Talk to me. This is a safe place."

Big Frank placed the laser dot in the center of Dr. Susan's forehead. *Target acquired,* he rumbled. *Just say go.*

"Is it bruises, Kari, or something worse?"

Say something, Chile. Anything, Granny Roz said. *Silence is becoming her truth.*

"It's not bruises. It's nothing. I just felt like drawing."

Dr. Susan leaned forward. "Is it cuts? Are you cutting, Kari?"

Cutting? Bunny held her breath.

"It's okay. Lots of girls like you cut themselves. They think it relieves the pain. They think it gives them control."

I blinked. "What?"

"Kari, if you're cutting, I need to know. Cutting is dangerous behavior."

Slow, Chile. Relax. Think about flowers and vines. Butterflies. You're too tense. She thinks you're lying.

"Girls who cut need help, Kari. They can't do it on their own."

You're not alone, Big Frank said. *You got us.*

"I know you want to stop, but you can't. Let me help." Dr. Susan reached out to touch me. I jerked away.

"I'm not cutting. I don't even know what that means."

Dr. Susan leaned back, considering. "I get it. You don't trust me."

"I'm not cutting."

"Okay. You're not ready for this."

"I'm not cutting."

"All right. I believe you." She tossed a pamphlet at me. "This can help."

I slipped it into my backpack and stood. "We done?"
"Not quite. I've been talking with YWF."
"YWF?"
"Young Writers of the Future. I sent them your essay."
"I didn't say you could do that."
"Sit down for a minute. Mrs. Miranda thinks you're a gifted writer."
Wary, I dropped my backpack and flopped onto the chair.
"You've heard of the YWF's summer programs?"
I shrugged.
"They were impressed."
"I can't go."
"Yes, you can."
"There's no way—"
"They're offering you a full-ride scholarship. You just have to show up ready to work."
I bit my lip and studied my knees. There's no way Mom'd ever let me go.
"Things change, Kari. You won't be in high school or living with your mother forever. Remember that."
I flinched.
She's not a mind reader, Chile, Granny Roz said. *It's just a lucky guess.*
Play it cool, said Big Frank.
"Do you want me to talk with your mother about it?"
I shrugged.
Don't cry, don't cry, don't cry, Bunny chanted.
"Kari, you're a smart girl. High school isn't the end. You have a bright future ahead of you. Like that butterfly on your arm, you can be anything you want to be."
"We done now?" I stood up again.
"Yeah, we're done. Let me know about the summer writing program. You know I care, right, Kari? Come back anytime. I'm here for you."
And so are we.

VOICES

Later that same afternoon, the third hole the size of a pea appeared on my inner thigh. I was hiding in a bathroom stall with my regular clothes stuffed in my backpack. Everyone knew Coach Jensen did one shower check each gym class. Skipping the shower was easy if you changed in a stall.

As if gym wasn't awkward enough.

Unlike the hole on my toe or arm, this one wasn't streaming cold. I sat on the closed toilet seat and poked at it with a pencil. No pain; no pressure. I pushed harder and watched as the pencil slid inside my leg all the way to its nubby eraser. With a flick of my finger I let go. It disappeared.

WTF?

I pressed along the edges of the hole like it was an over-ripe pimple needing a little encouragement. No bulge of a yellow number 2. I kneaded my thigh like bread dough.

Nothing.

How many pencils and pens could I stuff in? Rummaging around in my pencil case, I found my X-Acto knife.

Linoleum carving was such a bore.

I popped the safety cover off the blade and considered. I felt the troops stir.

Power, Big Frank said. *Control.*

Pain, Bunny said.

Freedom, Big Frank said, *for girls like us.*

Foolishness. At her kitchen sink Granny Roz peeled carrots lickety-split. *There's only one good use for a knife.*

I listened to a locker slam followed by the sound of running feet. The tardy bell rang. White noise filled my ears, ebbing and flowing as I sat like a stone in a river. I rolled the X-Acto knife between my palms, then held it to my cheek, drinking in the coolness of metal against hot flesh.

Granny Roz shook her head. *Lord, grant me strength. Chile, you done wore me out.* Dropping her paring knife among the carrot shavings, Granny Roz left the sink and sat in her rocker on the porch. In no time she was napping, head back with a little bead of drool pooling against her lips. Bunny was curled like a kitten in her burrow.

Against my skin, the blade warmed.

From his hideout in the trees Big Frank nodded. *Power,* he said. *Control.*

I cut.

It was hard at first, rubbery like the surface of an egg or a squishy piece of steak. The blade teetered on edge, then bit, catching the lip of the hole. My skin split, popping like the seal on a jar of pickles. Red, sticky blood welled, filling the hole and flooding my thigh with warmth.

Relief.

Stupid Dr. Susan was right about one thing.

One cut was enough. I stopped the bleeding with a wad of toilet paper pressed flat against my thigh. It wasn't much, a teaspoon of blood at the most, but it cleared my head. Colors were brighter. The taste of lemons and grass filled my mouth. Exhaustion swept over me.

Sleep, Kari, we're here.

I curled around the toilet, resting my flushed cheeks on the tile, inhaling the faint scent of bleach and pee.

Writing camp. I'm getting out of here and going to camp. I'm going to college. I can break free and be my own person. Another little slice and I can feel like this again and again. The empty holes mean nothing. I closed my eyes and didn't wake until the janitor's bucket bumped against the door. I—

Kari, watch out! Big Frank yells.

Breaking from the memory, I leap back to the curb as a car swooshes around the corner and into the high school. "Stupid kid!" the driver yells. "Watch where you're walking. You got a death wish?"

Yeah, right back at ya, butt-head.

Keep it together, Granny Roz says. *That's the second bell.*

I'm late to biology. All eyes are on me as I slip into my seat.

"Let's get started," Mr. Cooper says. "Homework out, please."

Voices

"What's that on Kari's face?" Becca snickers under her breath.

"Looks like toilet tissue."

"Probably cut herself shaving," Charlotte says. "She's such a troll."

"Yeah, Troll, where's your bridge?" Becca taunts. "Go live under it."

"No, go die under it," Charlotte says.

Bitches. My eyes start to water.

"Oh, look. She's going to cry! Charlotte, you made her cry." Becca holds out her knuckles for a bump.

Sticks and stones, Chile, Granny Roz clucks. *Don't fret. I'll make you a cherry cobbler.*

They can't actually hurt you, Bunny says. *Not here in front of everyone. Mr. Cooper won't let them. All they can do is talk.*

Charlotte bumps Becca's fist with a laugh. "Now watch. Right after class the little loser is going to scamper back to Dr. Susan. That's what you do, right, Loser? Tattletale about the mean girls. You're such a troll."

I open my notebook and pick up a pen. *Ignore them,* Big Frank says, running a bore snake down his barrel. *I got your back.*

When Mr. Cooper walks by, I don't bother handing any papers in. He doesn't even break stride. Head down, I concentrate on drawing intricate spirals, circles, and loops between the ruled lines. As long as they're small it looks like I'm taking notes.

"Baby scribbles," Charlotte mocks. "You're so retarded."

I'm going to writing camp. I've got a scholarship. This is just a way stop on my way to a much better place.

With the homework stacked on his desk, Mr. Cooper clears his throat. "Jonah, you're up," he says. "Now I need all of you to pay attention to the presentations. I'm going to be marking participation grades, so don't think you can just check out when you're not up here with your PowerPoint. I want questions, class. Let's engage our brains. Tiko, dim some of the overheads, please."

It's warm and stuffy in the room. *Chicken coop. Incubator,* Granny Roz mutters. *Do we need eggs?*

Jonah drones on about energy and life coming from the sun. In the darkness, eyelids droop as graphics of leaves and cells blur across the screen. After ten minutes the class is comatose. It takes Mr. Cooper longer that it should to realize Jonah is finished.

"Very good. Any questions?"

No one can muster the energy to think, let alone raise a hand. My notebook is filling with ink.

"Thank you, Jonah. Eric?"

Eric bounces up like an over-caffeinated kangaroo. He rubs his hands and bubbles like a salesman making the pitch of his life. "My topic is how parasites rule the world. There is no free-will. It's awesome."

Granny Roz stands up. *Chile, we need to leave. Now.*

It's the middle of class.

Now, says Granny Roz.

I can't leave. I can't risk a zero for participation.

Mr. Cooper rolls his eyes. "Eric, we discussed this."

The class perks up. Eric is smarter than the teachers. Everyone but Mr. Copper knows that.

"But Mr. Cooper, I have proof! Check it—this ant lives in South America." Two large black ants, one with a cherry bulb for a butt fills the screen.

We have to go, Big Frank says. *You have to go.* Suddenly my stomach rumbles and cramps. *Or there'll be trouble.*

Mr. Cooper is annoyed. "Eric—"

Eric advances his slide. "And here's another ant that's controlled by a liver fluke. At night it makes the ant climb up a blade of grass so a cow can eat it."

"That makes no sense."

Kari, says Bunny, *if you love us, you have to leave now.*

We love you, Kari. From the shadows the troops surge; there are more than I can count.

At the front of the class Eric grins. "It's the cycle of life. Climbing trees and grass to get eaten is not natural behavior for these ants. They're being controlled. If it can happen to ants—"

Voices

"People are more complex than ants," says Mr. Cooper.

"It's not just ants. It's spiders—"

"Insects are not human."

Kari, Kari, Kari, the voices call. The cramps are unbearable. I'm going to barf.

"—fish, grasshoppers, worms, crabs—" Eric won't stop.

"All lower creatures, Eric."

"How about rats, Mr. Cooper? We use rats to test human drugs, right?"

"Eric."

The voices are a band saw in my brain, drowning out Eric and Mr. Cooper. I can't think, can't breathe.

"There's a single-celled parasite that changes the behavior of rats in ways that increase the likelihood that an infected rat will get eaten by a cat. You know why it does this?"

The situation's critical, Bunny says.

"Eric—"

"The parasites need to do it in a cat."

The class roars.

"Principal's office, Eric. Move it."

Now? Big Frank asks.

Not here, Granny Roz says. *Too many witnesses. Power down. Let's reassess the timeline.*

I fall out of my chair as the world fades to black. I can't see, only hear Skylar say, "Uh, Mr. Cooper? I think there's something wrong with Kari."

The whole ride home is torture.

"You made me miss work again, Kari." Mom whips the car into the driveway. "You're not a baby any more. If you've got a headache, take medicine like a normal person. Don't go whining to the school nurse."

"I'm sorry. I didn't—"

"Yeah, you never do. Get out. I'm late." I grab my bag from the floorboard and open the door. "I want the laundry and dishes done before I get home. If you're not going to school, you're going to work."

"Okay."

"Take chicken out of the freezer for dinner. And if you put my nylons in the dryer, I swear I'll—"

"I won't."

"You're not too big for the belt, Kari. Maybe you need a little reminder."

"I won't forget," I say.

Mom cocks her head at me. I don't like the look in her eyes. "Somebody's getting uppity. Thinks she's better than everybody else."

"I'm not," I say quickly. This is headed nowhere good.

"I got a call from that counselor of yours this morning. Something about a writing camp."

"She talked with them, not me," I say.

"So you don't want to go? Dr. Susan said it's free."

I take a deep breath. "I want to go."

"What?"

"I want to go to a summer writing camp."

Mom leans over and slaps me across the cheek. "Yeah, and I want to be a size six again. Forget it. Neither of us is getting what she wants."

The pain makes my teeth ache. For once the voices are silent. I don't care. This is my life, and I'm breaking free.

"I'm going to a summer writing camp."

Mom laughs. "Oh, look at you. Think you can take me? Go on, try little girl."

I can't meet her eyes.

"That's what I thought. You're not going to camp. I told Dr. Susan you're not well. You need to be here with me. End of discussion."

"When I graduate next year, I'm leaving and going to college."

"Not with those grades. You'll live here with me. You know you can't manage alone. You'll see when I die."

"I—"

Voices

"Why are you still sitting here with your mouth open like a retard? Get out and shut the door. It's your fault I'm late." I push the door closed and step back. Mom shakes her head. "I said, shut, not slam. College? Right. Only if they hire you to scrub toilets."

I stand in the driveway watching the car roll past the stop sign. The sun feels good on my face.

In the kitchen, I lift each glass out of the dishwasher and put them upside down in the cupboard. Dr. Phil is nattering on the TV, telling a woman with smeared mascara that she is on a journey to find her authentic self.

I'm going to writing camp. I'm going to college. I'm not going to be anyone's slave any longer. I'm going to tell Dr. Susan about Mom. There are places in the world for girls like me. I don't have to live like this anymore.

My stomach growls. First I'm going to eat. I get out the bread and make a peanut butter sandwich. There's no milk. I make do with water.

When I sit down in the living room I feel it—an itching, burning sensation under the delicate skin of my cheek. The slap.

Fire ants, Bunny says.

No such thing, silly, Granny Roz says. *Eczema. A little dry skin.*

Poison ivy, says Big Frank.

Hush, now. You'll frighten her. Go wash your face, Chile. Things will be better, you'll see.

I rise and head to the bathroom. When I flip on the light switch I see the terrible crackling lines spreading along my hand, arm, leg. In the mirror I see fine webbing on my face, neck, shoulders. "Crazing," I say aloud. "In pottery it's called crazing."

With a whoosh, the tissue cork in my cheek pops out. The hole tears and widens, but there's no pain, just the sound of a freight train's whistle.

It's time, Granny Roz says.

We're coming, says Big Frank.

Hello, says Bunny.

I lean closer to the mirror. The hole on my cheek is no longer empty. An eye peers out.

Jace Hunter

Jace Hunter is a pen name for Michelle Parker, an award-winning author, editor, and public speaker who also publishes as Lehua Parker and Lava Rivers. Jace's work walks the darker side of speculative fiction. His short stories and novellas are available in anthologies and as audiobooks, and his untitled debut novel will be published in 2016 by Makena Press. An avid scuba diver and volleyball player, Jace enjoys traveling and spending time with his family.

The Hen Gathers Her Chicks
by Rachel Lewis

Pewter clouds wisped down to touch the lake. She gazed out the window, beyond the gold star that hung there, while shuttle and thread passed through her fingers. It was precise work, but as she had done it since she was a girl, she could watch the storm develop while this bone-deep knowledge worked on.

5 – 6 – 7 – 8 – loop a picot, back again.

The delicate threads knotted together, emerging as lace, forming the familiar hen-and-chicks pattern.

She had forgotten her son for a spell. No. That was not quite right. She had forgotten her grown son. That boy with the flouncy blonde curls and knickers, trapping damsel flies by the lake—he was never too far. Sometimes she opened the door and called his name, flustering that he wasn't heeding. Then she'd sit and tat and remember. As her fingers flew, the boy's legs lengthened and the knickers changed to flannel pants. His hair darkened, and he wore a dark uniform, the white wings of a brevet on his breast. Then came the box delivered by two servicemen whose faces she couldn't remember. It read *Effects of deceased Officer 1st Lt. Robert Asel Reece.*

Her little boy wasn't coming in, and her mother-guilt brayed.

The Hen Gathers Her Chicks

How could she have forgotten? And how could she have failed to usher him into the great beyond? If a child is to die before his mother, oughtn't she to hold his trembling hand or sing a lullaby?

5 – 6 – 7 – 8 – loop a picot, back again.

5 – 6 – 7 – 8 – loop a picot—

A sudden blaze in the sky caused her to lose the loop. The ball of fire hurtled toward the lake, slicing through the clouds.

She stilled her hands.

It was a plane.

She stood, sending shuttle and skein clattering.

It was a warplane trailing black smoke.

She ran into the misting rain without night coat and shoes and without any sense of the tufa rocks and mountain sage cutting into her feet.

The plane skittered along the lake, kicking up water till the flames extinguished. Then it disappeared.

Her feet stung as they touched the salt of the receding shoreline, though she pushed the sensation aside and ran on, splashing into the lake. The brine flies lifted away. She did not bother to swat them. She stopped, uncertain what to do next. The rippling water settled.

Then, a few arm-lengths away, a gasping figure sprang up.

She lurched toward him and caught him as he fell. She knew him in the stoop of his shoulders, in the turned-up nose, in the timbre of his groan. Somehow, though he was a head taller and nearly double her weight, she scooped him up.

Her body was older now. It was rich with bone-deep knowledge, and there were some things a mother would never forget how to do.

"Oh, Bobby," she crooned as she carried him home.

* * *

There was little room for wonder, so overflowing with music and life was she. Laughter filled her mouth. A kind she hadn't tasted for years. It was that cooing laugh for when her baby stuck out his lip, readying a wail. Not cruel. Just delight in her boy, and the sure knowledge that his cry meant nothing more than hunger or boredom.

And here he was again, a figure swaddled in yellowed but clean bandages, propped askance on his old bed—a grown figure, though not a whole one. Still, much more than the shadow he'd been. She had known he would return. He was her miracle baby come so late in life, and now he was her miracle man.

She had known, and so there was no need to wonder. Her laugh tumbled out now, melodic, youthful, and clean. Like a young mother's.

"Never could wait for the biscuits to cool," she said. "Made it so you couldn't taste a thing for days. Not even a straight lick of pepper."

His mouth gaped and a bite of steaming biscuit fell to his lap.

"Though I suppose this one was my fault. Sorry, dearie." She took a handkerchief from her apron, and swept the bite into its folds, then lifted a tumbler toward him. Milk flooded over his lips and ran down his chin and neck.

He was trying to say something, but she couldn't help herself. His efforts were drowned by her laughter. It wasn't cruel. Spilled milk and bandages. Evidence of childhood.

His eyes glittered feral and foreign, and she pulled away, spilling even more milk down his front. He did not look like himself, but then his eyes closed and his breathing slowed. He was familiar again. She replaced the tumbler silently on the tray and carried it away, looking back only once, swallowing the joy forming in her throat.

* * *

The milk cow bawled from inside the barn, but it would have to remain uncomfortable a while longer. She was stuck on the porch pacing, occasionally covering her ears while the wind whipped around her skirts. A man inside was yelling invectives. They must be directed at her. Or Bobby. There was no one else, alone as she and her boy were on this little island circumscribed by reeking sulfuric water. All alone, except for the yelling man, her cow, and the incoming storm.

When the man wasn't shouting profanities, he was saying the same things. "Tell Derkins. DERKINS."

Then

"My leg. Oh please, my leg."

She softened when he said *please*, but not enough to go inside. Why should he shout at her?

Thank goodness Bobby was out roaming.

The man's yelling picked up again, and she considered walking to the barn where she wouldn't have to hear him so distinctly and where she could milk the cow. But she couldn't see Bobby return from there, and besides, the bucket was not where it should have been. Nothing seemed to be where it should.

The man shouted words she'd never heard before, and though their syllables meant nothing to her, she recognized the sound of violence, even as the man's voice grew hoarse and weak.

She crouched on the wooden steps, clasping hands to ears and moaning in concert with the wind and her bellowing cow. Clouds stumbled and pooled over the lake, and soon the wind brought mist.

She jumped up. Storms came fast here. She scanned the lake's edge, cupped her hands, and called. "Bobby!" She had meant it as a command, but her intonation lilted into a question. The wind carried it back to the lake.

It seemed to her that the black, black clouds answered her question by weeping.

* * *

5 – 6 – 7 – 8 – loop a picot, back again.

The stitches were coming out uneven. She would loosen her

hand and try again, but her mind kept fixing on *that* day, and her hands stiffened as the thread wound tighter round them.

She couldn't remember much of the two men, except how young they looked in their crisp uniforms, though one had an uneven tuck. That was before they handed her the box and offered their condolences. She had laughed and said, "My, what big words from such young men," and then the meaning of their words dawned, and she staggered into the doorjamb. They looked too much like boys to wear such somber faces.

5 – 6 – 7 – 8 – loop a picot, back again.

She took out her crochet hook to unpick the knots and try again, but they would not give. This hen-and-chicks sat twisted at the end of an otherwise perfect row of mothers and chicks.

Bobby lay before her, his hair wet and clinging to his forehead, but he was peaceful as he slept. Even with the reassurance that he would not be going back to war—he would NOT be going back— she could relive that grief as poignantly and raw as the day it came upon her.

5 – 6 – 7 – 8 – loop a picot, back again.

She went on, leaving the deformity as it was.

She looked at the gold star still hanging in the window. She should have taken it down, but she'd been too busy. Or maybe she'd forgotten. She had to acknowledge that *that* was a sad likelihood. The lake buzzed with an uncommonly thick swarm of flies for October. Her hands relaxed and took to their steady rhythms until she had formed six hens and their little chicks.

Bobby's croaking voice startled her.

"My leg," he said. Bobby gestured with his bandaged hands, but she cupped her hands, still holding thread and shuttle, over his.

"There, there," she said. "There's no shame. No shame. No matter what people say."

His face still held the signs of his youth, except for a sobriety that set his jaw. It was such a foreign expression, unlike the defiance of childhood that flared and extinguished in a matter of moments. It was a steady, burning flame, and she was afraid.

He opened that serious mouth. "Tell Derkins that the plane—"

She couldn't bear to hear the even words fueled by this grown-up displeasure. "I've done you one better," she said. "I wrote Mr. Roosevelt. He understands. You know he gets about in a wheelchair? Great man like him. He understands."

"My leg—"

"No shame, Bobby."

"I'm not Bob—"

"No shame," she said in that tone of irrefutable command only a mother perfects.

She sat back.

5 – 6 – 7 – 8 – loop a picot, back again.

He would not be going back.

5 – 6 – 7 – 8 – loop a picot, back again.

"Please look at my leg."

She could hear the exhaustion in his voice. She had just checked it, hadn't she? She would humor him, if it would erase that severe expression. She lay her tatting aside and rose.

"Leg giving you grief?" she said, pulling back the afghan. She unwound his wrappings, and he began to whimper, then weep. She wanted to embrace him and weep, too, but he wasn't a little boy anymore. She would not embarrass him, so she stared fixedly at his leg. The skin around his gash was taut and dark blue, and little tendrils of black crept up his thigh.

She wrapped his leg and kissed his forehead. "You'll be shipshape in no time at all."

She left him and went out to the porch where she could cover her ears to his crying. Had he come home only to die?

* * *

She had lied to him. It was the only thing that would soothe. He'd been yelling since breakfast, and she'd wondered, *who is this boy so taken to profanities?* Was he really her little Bobby?

So she'd left the room and didn't return until nightfall, letting him hunger. When she did return, he was sitting in darkness, and she did not light the lamp. She was no good at lying, and needed some cloak.

"I wrote that Derkins fellow," she said. Bobby's shoulders squared. "In fact, I wrote him a few days ago."

"Did you send it to Hill Field?"

"Yes."

"Thank you," he said.

The wind whistled outside the window, bearing witness against her lie. "He wrote back," she said, worrying she might misstep. Bobby was sitting much too still. "He said your services were no longer required. Those were his words. 'No longer required.' Isn't that wonderful, Bobby?"

The shadowed outline of Bobby hitched. She wished now that she had lit the lamp to see his face. He must be overcome by jubilation.

"Bobby, isn't that wonderful?" she said again. "You can stay home." She felt the impulse to run to him and embrace him, but something stopped her. A muddling of thoughts. Should this not make him happy?

Then he yelled, his voice filling the darkness. "I am not Bobby!"

When she was a young mother, such tones would have left her trembling or crying, but now she drew herself up, matronly and wise. War had changed her boy, and she could appease his need to be grown up. "All right," she said. "I understand. Robert. Isn't it wonderful?"

Bobby wailed, and she clasped her hands at her heart, delighting in that cry that she knew meant joy.

* * *

She had filled the bucket with milk, musing that Bobby always seemed to disappear when chores needed doing. As she hauled the bucket homeward, she scanned his usual haunt on the southern shoreline and did not notice the two men on the porch until she stepped upon it herself, and set the bucket down. She started at the low voice.

"Excuse me, ma'am."

The young faces were much too serious. She would have preferred patting them on their heads and reassuring them they could not fool her. She knew they were really boys. But she held back. Bobby was somewhere. She stumbled into the doorjamb. These boys were sure to take him.

The southern shore was empty.

The tall one wiped his boots on the boot-scraper, ridding them of salt crystals that sullied the otherwise pristine uniform. "We're looking for a plane that went down round here."

The short one said, "Plane and pilot, if we're lucky."

"You mean if *he's* lucky."

Both young men offered wan smiles and stood before her, blinking at her.

She gazed northward, at their boat resting half on the shore, half in the water.

There. A shimmer of white, thin arms, reaching out of the boat.

She could not return their smiles, and the men blinked at each other and set their jaws.

The short one cleared his throat and pulled a picture from a folder. "Have you seen anything? He likely would have come from the lake."

Both turned to look at the lake.

They would see Bobby. They would take him. It made no sense beyond mother's intuition, but she'd learned to trust that feeling etched on her bones—that feeling that came into her world the moment he did.

She called a little too loudly, "Yes," flapping her arms and leading them around the side of the house, then past the barn.

They followed. One asked, "What did you see, ma'am?"

She didn't reply beyond beckoning with a flap of her arms and a hurrying of feet through sagebrush. She halted and pointed east where the sage and rock was dense and rugged.

"There," she said.

The men stopped beside her, panting. One thrust the picture before her and pointed at one uniformed young man between two others. "This fellow? Did you see him?"

A groan escaped her. The image was grainy, but how the figure looked like Bobby, if he were a few years older. Same nose. Same sloping shoulders. Same sandy hair. They would take him, and for once, she was glad he was a scampering, wild fellow. Not one to cling to her apron.

She shook her head. "I don't know. I don't know. Just a man out there. Never came by the house."

"The plane disappeared four days ago. We would have come sooner had we known about this settlement. Quiet little place, isn't it? You here alone?"

She stepped back, toward home, her finger pointing all the while, wishing they would look where she bade them. "Just a man out there," she said, sidling backward. "Never came by the house."

"Thank you, ma'am" one called, and they turned their steps east.

As soon as they turned, she scurried home, searching for Bobby's whirling limbs by the boat or the shoreline, but there was nothing but a snowy egret lifting away.

She paced the porch until the men returned to their boat and motored off. Then she sat with her tatting, agitated with the twisted hen-and-chicks she had let go unfixed.

5 – 6 – 7 – 8 – loop a picot, back again.

5 – 6 – 7 – 8 – loop a picot, back again.

She stopped looking out the window for Bobby to return. She felt a little foolish.

She remembered. He was already home.

* * *

She had given up perfecting her hen-and-chicks doily, and now it was a scattering of bedraggled mother hens and their ill-kept chicks. She'd been tatting since supper, but her hands had long stilled, and she sat gazing at her boy, waiting for him to awaken. He hadn't woken much that day. She felt like a new mother, anxious that her infant was sleeping so long, and wondering if, when he opened his eyes, they would still be blue just like hers.

A storm broiled over the lake and subsided, but still he had not awoken. When dusk settled in, she set her handwork down and harrumphed herself out of her chair. She began to unwrap his leg. A horrible blackness extended from knee to mid-thigh. He turned his face toward her, his eyes fluttering open. The wrappings fell from her fingers as she fumbled for the afghan to cover his leg. He shouldn't have to see. He shouldn't have to know.

His voice croaked before it found sound. "I'm Glen Rivers."

She touched his forehead. "Shh. Shh. It's the fever, dear. Let's cool you down."

She'd never seen his eyes glitter so strangely. No. That was not quite right. He'd once spent an afternoon squatting just above a weasel den, a flour sack at the ready, and finally he'd caught one. Whooping in triumph, he'd leaned over the folds of the sack and peeped in. The weasel had sprung straight in the air with the strength of a jackrabbit. Bobby didn't holler then—not when the weasel flew out, and not when it took to his face. There was just a flurry of arms and legs, and then he'd run home wearing that strange glittering look. That look kindled by fear.

Here it was again. Perhaps he knew without seeing the state of his leg the journey he was now taking. If only she could give him some measure of courage.

The wind circled the house, picking up speed. Another storm was coming, and they came fast.

His fingers crawled over her wrist and took hold. Lightning alit them briefly. They didn't look like his long, elegant fingers anymore. These were blunt and masculine, but if war could change her jolly baby into this troubled soul, it could just as easily change his hands.

"I've a daughter," he said.

Thunder rattled the window panes, and she jumped.

She could not tell from the strange light in his eyes whether this was truth or delusion, though his voice held a soft urgency unique to mothers and fathers. It only took a moment to see. She recognized it as easily as she recognized her reflection in a mirror. She was a grandma. She tried to frown. After all, if Bobby had a daughter, then he'd been behaving contrary to his upbringing. Still, the prospect of being a grandma—

"What's her name?"

"Rose."

"Rose." When she said the word, it seemed magic on her tongue, as though she were releasing a thousand angels to protect her progeny. "Rose," she breathed again. She imagined fat little arms reaching for her, pulling at her hair. A little girl smelling of spoiled milk and urine and perfection.

"I'm a grandma," she said.

His fingernails dug into her wrist, but there was no strength behind them. "No," he said. "No."

His eyes flashed fierce beneath another lightning strike. Perhaps she had only imagined a fatherly tone. Perhaps *she* had wanted Rose to be real. Perhaps she wanted to extend Bobby's life through some living-and-breathing being who would carry his romping curiosity from generation to generation into eternity. It was *her* delusion. There was no Rose. Bobby was being swept away by fever and infection, and here she was swept away by fantasy. She had only one task. To do what she could to calm his fears. To usher him peacefully into the great beyond.

"Shh. Shh." Then she sang. "Hush my little one, my loved one, as I rock and sing. As the silent moon passes o'er us, o'er my little one. Lulla-lay, lulla-lay, lulla-lie."

He started to cry, but still his eyes were bright with fear and with madness. "I'm Glen Rivers."

She sang louder to cover this unbearable transformation.

He repeated himself again and again.

"I'm Glen Rivers. I've a daughter. Rose."

It was a cacophonous duet, with one partner failing. Soon his voice was mere hissing and she sang alone. She sang to cover the pit of disappointment. She was not a grandma. She never would be. Soon she would not even be a mother.

She sang and mourned till long after his eyes closed. She extinguished the flame of the lantern and went to the porch in the blackness that cloaked her grief. The wind moaned and so did she. Rushing round her, the wind carried the sound away, yanking it from her much too fast, as though it could sweep away the anguish that shadowed motherhood's joy. The sweeping was too thorough. Too harsh. As if it was trying to make her forget. She had held Bobby, an infant, in her arms, not comprehending how her body and soul would transform to accommodate his every need. He was etched on her very bones. How could she forget? She stood facing the storm, cradling her grief at her chest, pleading to the sky to let her keep something of Bobby, even if it was this pain. Pleading that she would never forget again. She could not bear forgetting.

Note from the author: Apparently, several planes have crashed into the Great Salt Lake under mysterious conditions. One of these was a World-War-II plane coming from Hill Field, where such planes were repaired and readied for war. The pilot and plane plunged into the Great Salt Lake. He was found some hours later, having no recollection of what happened.

Rachel Lewis

Rachel Lewis lives near Sacramento, California, with her husband, daughter, and infant son. Occasionally she feels nostalgic for Utah snow. She earned an MA in Literature from Brigham Young University and is currently earning an education in parenthood.

No U-Turn
by Christine Haggerty

Stupid day. Stupid argument. Stupid fucking everything.

Emma stared at the salt flats that blurred by the gray sedan's passenger window. On the other side of the car, her husband of three months gripped the steering wheel with white knuckles. Emma glanced at him, his lips tight and his jaw grinding. She huffed, folded her arms, and leaned her forehead against the window.

She was sure as hell not going to apologize. It had taken her two full weeks to talk JT into a weekend in Wendover to eat and gamble and screw. Now, on the drive where she was trapped inside by self-preservation and child safety locks, he decided he needed to lecture her on morality.

Morality. As if she didn't already walk the tightrope of religious judgment every day she walked out the door of their Utah County townhome. For all the living she had been able to do since she'd stripped out of that white dress, Emma may as well have married her mother.

She wanted life to be risky, exciting. She wanted more than just the rides at the county fair to ramp up her pulse and flush her cheeks. She wanted to redefine her boundaries.

And JT wanted to shrink the box.

While they were dating, he had indulged her with trinkets and daydreams. Now he talked about money and kids and being responsible.

She looked at the second hand GPS monitor mounted to the dash. Over an hour to the casino. Over an hour of getting lectured by JT like she was ten-years-old.

The lock dug into her arm and she shifted to get more comfortable. She would pay bills—that was the cost of freedom from her parents—but the thought of getting up in the middle of the night with a fussy baby and wearing sweatpants because her jeans no longer fit over the loose skin and stretch marks made her feel nauseated. A few of her friends from college had already spammed Facebook with ultrasound pictures of their blobs. Emma was not about to join them. Not now.

She frowned at JT's clenched jaw.

Maybe not ever.

Fuck responsible.

"I'm just saying," JT twisted his grip forward and back on the steering wheel, "that I think it would be okay if you stopped taking the pill now." He had a baby face beneath the scruff on his chin, smooth cheeks and rich brown eyes that squinted at the road. "The doctor said it could take months even if you weren't on the pill and we started trying."

"We're not trying." Emma fidgeted with the air conditioning vents and lowered the zipper on her hoodie. "We're not anything. This entire topic of conversation is ruining our weekend."

JT pulled off his ball cap, scratched his head, and slid it back on. Twists of dark hair stuck out from beneath the edges. He needed a haircut and a shave, and he still wore his dirty work shirt.

Emma had been so excited to leave when JT got home from turning brake rotors and changing tires that she hadn't cared then. But now the sweat stains along his collar and under his arms disgusted her. She smelled him, too. A mix of grease and body odor.

No U-Turn

Her phone vibrated on her lap. Mom. Probably calling to snoop, probably wanting to come over, probably going to show up at the townhouse uninvited anyway. Emma ignored the call and tossed her phone on the back seat with their duffle bags.

Staring out the window, she tried to find something to distract her from the frustration that pulled at the muscles along her neck and between her shoulder blades. The landscape zoomed by, a flat stretch of packed, salted dirt reflecting the red afternoon sun. Emma turned up the music on the pop music satellite station, the beat rolling and dipping and peaking in contrast to the view outside.

JT turned the music down.

"When, then? I have a good job. You'd be done with school by the time the baby was born, even if you got pregnant now. I thought you wanted to have kids with me."

Emma tightened her arms across her chest. "Are you trying to guilt me into having a baby? Seriously? If I wanted to feel guilty and have absolutely no fun, I would have just lived in my parents' basement for the rest of my fucking life. I married you because I thought you loved me and wanted to spend a little time having fun before I got fat and smelled like baby puke."

"Emma." He frowned. "Let's drop it." He reached over and slid his hand on her knee.

"No." She threw his hand off, knocking his fingers on the gear shift.

"Urgh, Emma!" He swallowed a swear word and shook his fingers out.

"No! Damn, you!" She shifted and re-crossed her legs so that he couldn't reach her and the steering wheel comfortably at the same time. "You don't get to just 'Emma' me and have it be all right. As soon as we said I do it's been nothing but baby, baby, baby. I want to have fun first."

"You keep saying *fun*. Define *fun*. Me working all day so you can go out for drinks with your friends up in Salt Lake, so there's no way a neighbor will see you and tattletale on you to your mom?

That kind of *fun*? Or do you mean giving me the list of things I'm not allowed to talk about? Because that's my favorite kind of *fun*."

JT leaned toward the windshield, peering at the road. "Not!"

Emma followed his gaze along the ribbon of pavement. A boxy shadow loomed up from the landscape, silhouettes of gas pumps queued beneath an odd roof of metal and vinyl.

A gas station. Soda and candy. Maybe even those stupid flavored condoms. JT might think those were fun.

He let off the gas and the car slowed.

"We're married. Period. We should be able to talk about anything. *Any*thing. Like nightmares and eye crusties and food we don't like. It should be as easy as breathing to share everything with each other. That's why I married you, Emma."

A warm, female voice interrupted JT's lecture. "When it is safe to do so, make a U turn and then make a right onto US Interstate 80 West towards Wendover, Nevada."

JT had named the voice *Danielle*. Emma thought Danielle sounded like an electronic slut.

He pulled off the road and coasted past the pumps, settling between two faded yellow lines that angled away from a span of greasy windows. He killed the engine and gave her a hard look. "I should be able to say 'baby' without you having a *fucking* tantrum."

He popped the lock and kicked the door open, then slammed it behind him and disappeared inside the convenience store.

Emma stared after him. He'd said fucking.

Shit.

JT never swore. Swearing was part of Emma's arsenal. He hated it, and she knew it. She only swore out loud when she wanted to challenge his smug self-control. She liked him edgy, a little rough. It made the sex better, although that wasn't always why she wanted to piss him off. Sometimes she had a bad day and wanted to share her misery.

Sometimes she was just a bitch.

Tonight she hoped for the sex.

Without the air conditioning running, the car smelled like

stale Cheetos and grease. Emma wiped dust from the dash. Maybe she'd go in and start to make up, buy JT some gummy bears and an energy drink so he'd be wired when they arrived at the casino. Yeah, that's what she'd do. She'd flirt and touch his arm, and they'd get past this stretch of flat, salt-stained misery. They'd get to the over-themed, glittering casino and forget about babies.

She popped open her door and stood. She coughed in a dusty gust. The wind tasted of desert and salt and scraped along the crumbling asphalt. Their gray sedan was the only car in the parking lot, and except for the glowing 'Open' sign above the door, the convenience store looked completely abandoned.

The sun touched the horizon, long rays of light streaking across the dirty glass that spanned the front of the store. Emma couldn't see anyone inside among the neat rows of Nutter Butters and fishing lures. JT must be in the bathroom. She should go, too, while they were stopped. Yeah, then the next place they stopped would be Wendover.

Lights. Food. Sex.

She closed the car door and walked around the hood. The trash outside overflowed with dirty towels and empty fast food cups. Brown smeared the edge of the outside mat and the sidewalk in front of the doors. A syringe huddled in a crevice near bundles of firewood.

The salty wind picked up the smell of rotting food and piss. Emma hesitated, her hand inches from the industrial metal handle. She could tolerate convenience store bathrooms, but it wasn't worth going inside a place like this and risking a venereal disease. She'd rather pee on the side of the road.

She still couldn't see JT, and there was no attendant at the counter. She bit her lip and hugged herself as bumps rippled along her arms. Turning back to the car, she stubbed her toe on an edge of the uneven sidewalk, cussed out the cement, and plopped back into the passenger seat.

The sun had sunk halfway below the horizon. Emma gazed at it through the tinted windows and sighed. No gummy bears for

JT, but she could still make this weekend great. She had a few new pieces of lingerie, bad girl-style with some leather and buckles and a pair of panties designed to be ripped away. She liked feeling powerful, naughty. She imagined JT tearing off the panties, his hands that had so tightly gripped the steering wheel gripping her hips...

Her body flushed and she looked down as if the bugs on the windshield could see the sex in her mind.

The driver door popped open and a plastic bag thunked onto her lap. She startled and blushed, digging out a bag of strawberry licorice and avoiding her husband's eyes. He sat stiffly and stabbed the key into the ignition.

Okay. Still pissed. Emma gripped the arm rest of the door as JT slid the gear shift into reverse.

The car squealed back, then jerked forward and rolled onto the highway. A strip of sun hugged the horizon, a final burst of light before it slipped from view and twilight turned the endless flats a shimmering gray. Almost pretty, and certainly better than the stretches of white salt-stain.

JT stared straight through the windshield, his hat jammed low over his eyes. The air conditioning kicked up and he jabbed the button to turn it off.

Okay. Still really pissed.

Emma tore open the licorice and peeled out a sliver. "Do you want one?" She held it out.

Nothing, not even a twitch.

Okay. Still really, really fucking pissed.

She tore at the licorice with her teeth and chewed, watching out the window again. He'd come around. He always did.

The dead air mixed a new scent with the sweat and grease and Cheetos. Briny, wet. Like raw shrimp.

Emma turned the air conditioning back on, chewed the strawberry candy, and stared out the window at the empty landscape. Maybe she could talk JT into taking a shower with her as soon as they checked into their hotel room.

No U-Turn

Warm water. His chest slick with soap...

JT jabbed the air conditioning off again.

What the hell? Emma straightened in her seat and scowled through the windshield at the stretch of road that blurred in the headlights. The last of the sunlight drew a strip along the horizon and gave way to an inky blackness dotted with stars.

The briny smell filled the cab, burning Emma's nostrils. She turned the air conditioning on again.

JT turned it off.

"What the fuck?" Emma swore and slapped the dash, then turned the air conditioning on again. "You smell like salt and shit. I need that on or I'm gonna puke. What the hell did you do in that bathroom?"

The car slowed and tipped off the highway, rocking over scree as the headlights bounced along a pitted dirt road. Emma's shoulder hit the passenger window. She braced herself to cuss out JT again and paused.

He twisted his face toward her, his scruffy baby cheeks slack, stretched pupils reflecting the dash lights in a flash of red.

"Are you high?" A chill ran along Emma's spine and spread, blanketing her shoulders and back and settling in the pit of her belly. Instead of JT, Danielle's electronic slut voice responded.

"When it is safe to do so, make a U turn and then turn right back onto US Interstate 80 West toward Wendover."

JT turned back to the windshield.

"No U turn. Home."

"You would like to return home?" Danielle asked.

"No."

Emma braced a hand on the dash and swallowed. JT's expression remained flat, his shoulders stiff, and his spine curved away from the seat.

"Home," JT repeated.

Something along his collar moved. At first, it twisted up beneath his hat like a lock of hair, and then it continued to stretch around JT's neck.

Danielle responded. "Calculating new route."
In the glow of the dash lights, Emma watched the thing coming up out of JT's collar. It thickened and thinned and stretched to his ear, forming a tip like a finger. The thing caressed the length of JT's neck and disappeared down the front of his work shirt.
What. The. Fuck.
Emma's stomach churned, and she gripped the armrest on her door. She knew she was moving, touching things, but the cold fear running through her body made her numb.
"Yes. Let's go home."
"Make a U turn and then turn left onto US Interstate 80 East toward Salt Lake City. Your route is clear and you should reach your destination in one hour twenty-three minutes," Danielle instructed.
"No U turn!" His voice had a hollow echo, as if he stood in an empty parking garage. His shirt bulged out between his shoulder blades, then flattened, and another tentacle slithered up the back of his neck and played along the back of his hat.
"Home."
The car continued to rattle slowly along the salt flats. Emma's heart thudded and flushed out the cold. Blood pulsed in her ears, and she bit her lip to keep from screaming. She didn't give a damn about what had happened to JT. She wanted out. She inched her fingers back along the door and up to the lock, one of the old styles that popped up like a stick, and pulled.
Click.
JT's head whipped around, his red eyes pinched in anger. "No." Emma tugged on the handle and the door swung open. "No."
JT's hollow voice mixed with the crunch of the tires and the sting of raw palms as Emma flung herself out of the car. She rolled to her hip and pushed herself to her feet. Her leg buckled on her first step, and she slipped on the fine scree that littered the flat, salty ground. This time she felt the impact, the jolt through her limbs as she landed on her hands and knees.
The car skidded to a stop. Dust. A door slammed.
Scrambling to her feet, Emma ran a few steps and turned

around. The headlights blazed into the dust, catching the edge of a stretch of water less than twenty feet from the sedan's fiberglass bumper.

JT's tall silhouette blotted out the light. Emma sucked in a breath and ran. One, two, three, four steps before a hard jerk on her pony tail wrenched her head back. Her foot slipped out from under her, and her back slammed to the ground.

"Home," JT repeated. "No U turn."

She clawed at the hand that held her hair. "Let me go, you piece of shit!"

JT turned and pulled her toward the water as if he felt nothing, steps steady. "Home."

"No!"

Her scream echoed off the car, the water. Wrapping both hands around his wrist, she pulled her shoulders off the ground, arched her back, and backed her feet under her. She twisted around and grabbed JT's sleeve and kicked his knee.

His leg buckled and he fell to his knees, bringing her with him. The tug on her hair ripped more from her scalp and she fell to her knees behind him. He shifted his grip from her hair to her neck and slammed her face down into the dry, packed earth. Her cheek crunched and her nose snapped. Warm, metallic blood filled her mouth.

JT leaned close. "No."

The single syllable ground into her ear. Pain came with it, beating through her head with its own pulse and blooming in her broken face. Shaking, Emma pushed herself to her hands and knees. In the foggy light at the edge of the headlight beams, she watched blood drip onto the salted dirt. The hollow, metallic sound that wove its way through JT's voice spread down her spine like a vine of ice.

Run. She needed to run.

She shifted her weight to stand. A hand clamped around her ankle. She sobbed, choking on a scream, kicking at JT as he yanked her into the headlight beam.

"No! JT!"

"Home."

He dragged her through the light toward the water.

Emma clawed at the ground. Her shirt and hooded sweatshirt hitched up beneath her breasts, her belly scraped raw.

She kicked again.

JT tightened his grip and chuckled.

"No U turn."

"Please," Emma begged. "Please, JT."

"Home."

His last few steps kicked up a splash.

Chill water soaked through the butt of her jeans. She sucked in a breath, gagging on blood. Water wrapped up along her shoulders and the back of her head.

Squinting at JT, she reached for his face.

"Please. Don't do this, JT. You love me, remember?"

Her fingers trailed over the stubble on his jaw. Then she jerked her hand back. A tentacle stretched out from behind his head, a long viscous finger silhouetted by the headlight.

She twisted to get up and JT slammed her shoulder back into the water.

"Home. No U turn."

The cold water lapped at her broken cheekbone. The tentacle twitched.

"Please, JT," she sobbed.

Something in the water pressed against her back, driving the cold into the muscles along her spine. A clammy slug finger probed behind her ear.

"No," another sob. "Please. I'll have a baby. I'll do whatever you want."

The slug finger pressed harder and the cold along her back buzzed into a million pinpricks.

"No, JT!" She squirmed.

He pushed down harder.

The pinpricks sharpened.

Emma arched her back and screamed.

The tentacle hovering by JT's face curved in and popped into his eye.

Blood running down his face, JT grinned.

"Home."

"No!"

Emma writhed, reaching up to scratch at his face. She managed to curl her fingers in his collar. The fabric tore.

"Nonononono!"

JT pressed a hand over her face. Water covered her ears, muffling her own screams. The pinpricks blazed into a solid sheet of pain.

JT chuckled , the vibration traveling through the tips of her fingers along with the beat of three words.

"No, no, no…"

Christine Haggerty

Christine Nielson Haggerty is an award-winning author of dystopian and dark fantasy fiction. Currently a creative writing instructor at a private boarding school, Christine is a black belt in traditional Japanese karate. She has gained a fan following from her presentations and ninja coaching for fight scenes. For fun, Christine practices karate, kickboxing, and spinning fire.

Horsemen
by K. Scott Forman

If it wasn't the sand fleas, it was the stink. That was why he left—that, and the peace treaty. The piers, the boats, the people—so many half-eaten fish on a refuse pile of carcasses swarming with feces-tainted flies whose appetites were never satiated: a memory. Now, he saw water and gray sand and foam formed of lapping waves. He licked his lips. At least salt was clean.

Salt and heat and sweat and ache: he had worked on many boats, and on many coasts, sometimes until he felt like a fish himself. Beachcombing followed, the smell of low tide, seaweed, seabirds, and kelp, all good reasons to move west, far from the sea, farther from her fragrance, the surf, the salt, and her voice.

She reminded him of others, men, women, even the beasts and the serpent, all in the past, a savor never lost, especially in the heart. The dead sea spread out before him, and he could see the Levant like it was yesterday. Another dead sea, another fisherman, a face he would see again, but not any time soon.

Inland he trekked from the sea, riding and walking on the dry land. Soon, the cool mountain air mingled with pine and even snow as he crossed the Sierra Nevada heading west. The smells and sounds were gone, but not the toil and soiled clothing, the loss and pain, and never having enough to eat. He did not miss the stench of the ebb and flow, of the flotsam and the jetsam.

When he and his horse had exited the mountains, a monolithic basin taunted him. Its endless sage brush and repressive heat reminded him of the salt-sown fields of war, the perspiration of whores, the salinity of tears, and the last sweat of regret that comes just before death. He blinked his eyes, but the images stayed.

His horse nudged him. He had ridden the old sorrel from the sea, walked and rode during the ascent and descent of the mountains, and then the basin and desert. Sometimes they rode with purpose, but mostly wandered on foot side-by-side. They had nowhere to go, other than away from the sea. He rubbed her muzzle and examined her red coat; she needed a good rub-down. The sweat on her sides mirrored the foam along the edge of the lake, fomenting the birth of shrimp and gnats, mocking the brackish shoreline: the lake could not kill everything.

"You don't want to drink this, old girl."

She had been with him a long time, so long he could not remember. She was his closest, maybe his only, friend.

He watched the shore of the cyclopean sea and all the nightmares of his whole life stared back at him from the life-sucking muck that was more firm than wet. The fisherman returned to his remembrance, the futility of his life, his mission, and the few followers that spent their lives in much the same way as he had done.

He shook his head and stretched. He felt aches, especially in his gut, and with it came a touch of hunger. The lake looked back at him, forcing him to think of the last time he satiated his appetite on fish and bread. He felt a spasm of nausea wash over him. Why was it always there with the fish and the salt? A past deluge or miracle might be the source, but knowing the source probably wouldn't help. It was part of who he was.

He had crossed this barren waste believing if there were any more fish they would have left their salty births behind, and he had been right. The trout had been fresh-water born, and the mountains were salt free. The briny shallows that stared back at him now had no fish, only white death. He felt it, and then the familiar tick.

It was an impulse, an unconscious twinge, not of pain, but of emotion, of fear. He looked over his shoulder automatically. He had forgotten the habit in the mountains, alone with the old red horse, that feeling, that sensation one thinks he has lost, like seeing a familiar face, the eyes, the nose, the mouth, all familiar like a dream, but forgotten. It was an unbridled worry, a false fear, nothing.

His mother had the same nervous malady, not with people, but with water. Water and stoves and cooking and bathing and locks, all endearing impulses buried deep in an unsettled unconscious mind. That had been a long time ago, before anything else mattered.

He looked again, seeing nothing but a vast wasteland edging up to a dead sea. He returned his gaze to his horse; she whinnied and stomped a hoof as if they had waited long enough in this godforsaken place and should move on. He waited, his eyes wandering back to the foam and water, his mind's eye to his mother. He couldn't shake the feeling.

His mother had only ignored the impulse once, and she had paid a terrible price. She had not heeded a premonition, not looked over her shoulder, and it had been a mistake. Lightning had struck, and it had changed both their live forever.

It was a long time ago, so long ago the earth felt young. Why think about it, or his mother; both she and the past were gone. Still, she could have warned him, should have warned him, locked the door and never let the visitors in. She had known what they were going to ask him to do, to be.

He lifted his gaze beyond the lake and cursed. It wasn't Luck, but Fate. He preferred the old ways of thinking; the Greeks, they had it right, or at least they had entertained adherents to their beliefs. The Three Sisters of Night had cursed him and his mother. Why did they prolong his suffering? He could see them, gathered around their spinning wheel, their sewing machine, their needlepoint, whatever, and they cackled, watching his life, mesmerized by the thread that held him to mortality, the shears poised, the scissors opening, so close to cutting what remained of the string of his life that a soft breath or a whisper could break it. End it. But they always refrained from the final snip.

"Today would be a good day to die," he said to the horse, "but if you drink that water you'll just wish you were dead."

He laughed. Were the three Fates really hags? They were probably beautiful women with a job to do, a task set before them, more like him than not. In another life, another world, he may have courted one of the Fates, proposed, even married her and, together, made a large family and died a happy man. He laughed again.

"Just a job, I guess. Maybe next time."

The horse shook its head, as if in understanding, and nudged him forward. It wanted to get to the next town and fresh water.

"And something to eat," he said absently.

Something moved; a glimpse of something where nothing had been before. It was a dot in the corner of his eye. He scanned the spot and everything in its vicinity; it had been in the lake, on the lake. He strained and barely made out signs of civilization in the distance beyond the lake's opposite shore. There was a city there; he had passed through it once before, but had forgotten its name. The movement had nothing to do with the city. He fixated on the spot. Nothing, he had imagined it, and then it was there again, just at the edge of his vision, something moving, coming across the lake. He squinted, tried to focus.

The endless salt flats had lulled him into complacency. Mirages were everywhere; the waves of heat or light displaying false shapes, ghosts, anything but reality. It had been troubling at first, but now he could tell an illusion when he saw it. This was no illusion. The sorrel stamped. She could see it too, sense it. She knew and he felt what she knew. The same thought had crossed his mind twice, but he had looked behind, not at what lie before them. The color would make it clear, confirm what he already knew.

It was dark, black, and it did not shimmer. It was no mirage. It moved slowly, but with purpose, coming across the deceased waters as if on an errand, as if some unknown power had willed it to move.

Horsemen

There was no unknown power, only a cast of unfamiliar powers. It was riding something, some animal, but not a horse. It had to be a horse. What else would a man ride, if it was a man, and what else could it be, but a man, or at least what had once been a man? How did he stay above the water? He had heard of water so salty that a body could not sink or even drown in it, but salty enough to ride on? This was no Jesus Christ or Peter, especially dressed in the color of night and riding a—

His hand went to his belt. The Colt was where it should be, the handle smooth and familiar from use. He had cleaned and checked it that morning. He went through the habitual procedure every morning when he woke up and every night before he went to sleep. He always had to be ready.

The figure continued to bear down on the spot where he and his horse stood, as if some magnetic power pulled it, an unseen hand pushed it, closer and closer. He could make out its definition now, shaped like a man, taller than most, and it was riding a horse, a pale horse that deepened to the black of midnight. The image had blended with the colors of sun and salt and water giving it a hue of silver, gloaming, and then full darkness.

He relaxed, but kept his eyes fixed on the pair, his fingers lightly on the butt of the gun. He moved next to his horse, a hand on her neck, and waited.

The rider and his mount hesitated. They still came forward, but there was a tension. He had not felt this kind of strain in a very long time—not fear or anticipation, but reluctance. He blinked once and refocused on the rider.

"I thought you might be coming this way. I see you've given up the sword for something a little more modern."

"Practical," he said.

He examined the familiar figure: dark boots, an oilskin coat, and a well-fitting ebony hat. It must have been burning on the inside of that getup, but did it matter? Blackie had always forsaken comfort, the *practical*, for style; it was all about the grand entrance, first impressions, and Blackie never disappointed.

"I thought only the destroyer rode upon the waters," he said.

His eyes moved down the figure; there was nothing but smooth lines, as if the horse and rider were one. He was sure there were two gun-metal gray .45s with handles matching a starless night sky beneath the water-resistant duster, both probably tied down to the rider's legs. Blackie spoke again.

"You might as well keep going. You're wasting your time in this town. It isn't the right time. I've already tried."

Blackie removed the bandana that had half-covered his face revealing a weathered countenance. He smiled, his teeth the color of his white skin. He dismounted. His horse moved toward the sorrel; they nuzzled, renewed acquaintances, and ignored the two riders.

"That was a nice piece of work you did in '49. Gold Rush, indeed. Kind of an enjoyable follow-up to the Treaty of Guadalupe Hidalgo," said Blackie. "Sorry to hear about that. It didn't quite work out, did it?"

"You get around."

"I keep my ears open. I hear there's some real trouble brewing, probably in the next year or so, '58 or '59, maybe later."

Blackie clapped a hand on his shoulder. It was friendly, but the touch reminded him that he was hungry. He felt his stomach twist and then complain, empty.

"My money's on Richmond," said Blackie, "but these people here seem to think one of the Carolinas is where it will start. Can't remember which one."

"I believe the *thus saith the Lord* goes something like *wars that will shortly come to pass, beginning at the rebellion of South Carolina, which will eventually terminate in the death and misery of many souls.*"

"Yeah, that's it," said Blackie. "I never was much for remembering scripture, Red. At least you were mentioned in this one."

"And Azzy," he said.

"Yeah, that old owl hoot. Never did like his nickname."

Blackie laughed, but his face was uncomfortable. He mapped its surface, navigated the lines and curves and movements, but there was nothing there other than fear of the pale rider they called Azzy. He spoke.

"I had nothing to do with the Gold Rush or Hidalgo or anything else."

"Sure, whatever you say," said Blackie.

They looked at each other. There was a certain empathy in the dark rider's eyes, an understanding. He opened his mouth, but then closed it. He looked at the two horses.

"Been a long time since these two had a roll in the hay. Maybe we should travel together for a few days, let them have a little fun, catch up, you know. What do you say?"

He said nothing. He was tired, thirsty, and hungry, more so with the appearance of his old friend. He liked being alone, away from people, and away from the few he could call friends. It was better, safer that way. He studied the path around the south side of the lake. As if reading his mind, Blackie spoke again.

"We could travel south. I hear there's a really nice place on the Old Spanish Trail, plenty of grazing and no shorelines or fish or salt."

His gaze snapped back, and he almost reacted, the words coming up his throat, stopping on his tongue, and then melting away with his saliva. His hand had already drawn his gun.

"Take it easy, I know how you feel about seas and fish, and especially salt. I just wanted you to like the place, that's all. Somewhere you don't have to think about the past."

"Or the future." He relaxed and replaced the .45 in its holster.

"The future?" asked Blackie. "It's the past that bothers you." Blackie frowned, a hand came to his chin, and then he smiled. "Most of that was Azzy's doing anyway, and you have to admit, it made the stories much more interesting. Turned it from straight up, wrath of god non-fiction horror to fantasy fiction, maybe even fan-fantasy fiction."

He nodded. He still felt tension, anger building up within him, but he pushed it aside. Azzy's doing, yes, and what could Azrael have done differently? Not much any of them could do differently, nothing they could change, the past, present or future; it was just one eternal round. They had all, each one of them individually, been called and set apart for a purpose. He looked at his old companion and almost smiled.

"Non-fiction horror and fan-fantasy fiction, huh? You're talking genre when they haven't even come up with the names yet. They still think it's the word of God."

"I don't know. Some of 'em are starting to think it might be fiction."

Blackie laughed again and continued.

"I mean really, a global deluge."

"Don't forget the plagues."

"Egypt, now that was a good time," said Blackie. "I was there for seven years."

"Yeah, I remember, and I remember what followed."

Blackie seemed lost in a pleasant recollection, a commemoration of better days. Neither spoke for several minutes. The wind started to pick up; he was thirsty and hungry. He had mounted his horse when Blackie spoke again. "Moses wrote some pretty good fan fiction, didn't he?"

"Imagine the day when they come to the realization that all scripture has been so messed up by man that there's hardly any truth left."

Blackie shivered and went back to his horse. He mounted in one fluid motion.

It was sad, really. The truth was still there, but people had to look, had to really look.

He nodded toward the south.

"Old Spanish Trail on the way to California? I just came from there, and I don't intend on going back any time soon."

"We're only going to stop for a night or two, and not even go west. We let the horses get to know each other again, and then we can move on, move farther south," said Blackie. "I hear there's a really nice cantina in this new place along the Mexican border. Tombstone they call it."

"Tombstone, you sure?"

"Well, if it's not Tombstone, it will be in a few years," said Blackie.

"When Whitey and Azzy show up," he said.

Blackie stared at him, as if considering. Two more friends, a possible rendezvous, and...

"Funny, I forgot about your jovial side."

"You mean sarcasm," he said.

Blackie paused. "You may be right about Whitey and Azzy." He watched his old companion and then pointed his horse forward around the south side of the lake. Blackie caught up and kept pace next to him.

"The weather will be better. You know how it gets here when summer ends. We can be to the trail by early September, and then down to Tucson before the snow really starts to fly," said Blackie.

"That reminds me, weren't you down there in '21 with these folks?"

"No," he answered. "That was the Mormon Battalion, and they captured Tucson without my help."

They continued in silence. The city was getting closer. Blackie turned to look behind them, and then in front. He finally spoke off-handedly.

"Who knows, maybe Whitey and Azzy will already be there."

"Like old times."

"Like old times." Blackie laughed. "Well, it's a heap better than this place. I really tried to do my thing, wind and rain, snow and ice, drought, I even brought in some black locusts in 1848, but somebody up there must like these people."

"Black locusts? Crickets?"

"Yeah, I thought it added a certain *je ne sais quoi*."

He shook his head and a smile started at the edge of his mouth. Despite everything that had happened over the years, he still liked Blackie the best. He had always envied the black clothing. He looked across the water; the city had grown, like the people that inhabited it.

"I heard you and the others have been riding with this group since 1820 and—"

"Now that's not true," interrupted Blackie. "I may have checked in on them a time or two over the years, but I haven't been riding with them. In fact, I ran into Whitey at Fort Bridger last year. He said he hasn't seen you or Azzy in years, except for that incident in 1844."

"Carthage, yeah, I remember."

He looked away. He felt the anger seethe again. "So, what are they calling this place now? It was Deseret, right?"

Blackie did not answer.

"What? Is there something about the name–"

"Salt Lake City."

Blackie interrupted and spoke so quickly that he barely caught it. Salt again: instead of anger, he smiled.

"Now that is irony, isn't it?"

Blackie laughed. "I knew you would get in the spirit of things."

Maybe a few days wouldn't be that bad, and there really wasn't that much between this great salt lake and the Mexican border. What could happen? It was a wasteland with a few scattered settlements and a displaced Indian tribe or two.

"I need to get something to eat."

"A few days on the trail, we can talk about old times, and—"

"Does our destination also have salt in its name?" he interrupted.

The man in black laughed. "You're going to love it. Not that many people, plenty of grass for the horses, and—"

"What is it called?"

There was a familiar twinkle in Blackie's eyes that only made his black clothing blacker.

"Mountain Meadows."

K. Scott Forman

K. Scott Forman is an eclectic writer with dark tastes: suspense, horror, fear. His most recent work has appeared in the literary journal, *O-Dark Thirty*, and the anthology, *Gothic Tales of Terror*. He makes his home in the Rocky Mountains.

In the Company of Salt
by E. Ellis Allen

Buildings stand as a eulogy of what was. Broken glass is spread out in webbed patterns on the concrete. No one is around.

"Lieutenant? Where are we?"

"Quiet."

"But the town?" It's his nerves making him talk.

"Shh."

"But what's it called?"

"Why?" I ask.

"I told my Mom I'd keep track."

"Didn't your mother die, Denninger?"

"Yeah. So? I still promised her. So, where are we?"

I shrug. "Well, it's not Syracuse."

I can tell he's looking at me. I don't turn my head. He's one of the younger soldiers, maybe fifteen or sixteen-years-old. I doubt he'll last very long. None of them will.

New recruits are afraid all the time. They're soft and quick to huddle in groups, shaking as bullets rain down upon them, too green to duck. But not Kale Denninger. He'd watch the bullets falling, his half-moon face unflinching.

In The Company of Salt

For the first week, the young ones shot at everything, at nothing. We lost five men because of it, though no one told them. It wouldn't do any good if they knew.

We march, pounding the cracked asphalt street with hard, succinct knocks. I curb the remaining fifteen soldiers in my Company around the corner. We funnel down a large street.

"What happened to everyone?" Denninger asks.

Corpses of women, children, and old men line the length of the road, arranged side-by-side as if sandbags in the gutter. I step over one.

"We did."

"They all dead?" Denninger asks.

I nod scanning the torn landscape from corner to corner. "Combat rubble."

"They look petrified," he says eagerly.

"Uh-huh."

Denninger bends low inspecting them. Bodies are covered with a cast of fine dirt and left undisturbed. Nothing remains that would disrupt them. No stray cats. No skinny dogs to rip them apart. When was the last time I'd seen any animal that wasn't a horse? Or rat? No birds or geese fly by anymore. Where are all the beasts and fowl of the field? Am I the only one left?

Denninger raises his foot and kicks the head of one of the corpses. The toe of his boot sticks inside the dead woman's caved in skull. A cloud of dust looms in mid-air.

"What are you doing?" I grab his arm and pull him. "Move out."

"You know what I miss?" Denninger is talking again. "I miss summertime."

"Quiet."

I slow the troop to a standstill. On the ground, small tracks indent the dirt.

"Moretti, come here, take a look."

Sergeant Aldo Moretti rushes to my side. He is one of the older boys, nearly twenty, an athletic build, with black hair and eyes, brown skin, and white teeth. He details the pattern in the dust.

"Elk?"

"Possibly, if there were any," I say.

"I heard bison used to roam these islands."

I shake my head. "That's not a bison track." I move carefully around the faded imprint in the sand. "Take a look, here. See how they sink unusually deep into the ground?"

Moretti nods. "So you're thinking fakes?"

I shrug again. "Just keep your eyes open."

With my hand, I motion the troop to move forward. The soldiers return to their uniformed march—left, right, left.

"I miss what it was like before the war," Denninger continues, "I remember riding down the river on inner tubes."

I pretend to listen to the young soldier's thoughts. The truth is I miss the world before the war, too. Lying in the grass. Chasing nothing but the wind. Dreaming.

I don't recognize the sun as reflecting across ripples in the river, but rather from it penetrating shrapnel bursts. Its rays illuminate the sharpened things, the ones that could pummel through my skin and wreck my body. Like this town, I'm waiting to fall.

"Back in line, Denninger," I say.

The sun is setting, bathing the gray world in rust-colored hues. Soon the night will be collapsing upon us.

"Fan out. Let's set up camp."

The soldiers step out of line and rotate with their rifles pointed upwards towards the city skyline.

"Moretti, take two men and post a lookout up there." I motion to the top of the street.

I lead the rest to a small grouping of overgrown shrubs in the corner of a parking lot surrounded by little one-story shops. I scan the courtyard. A wall with multi-colored bricks seems out of place from the building's facade. I walk to it.

I peer around the wall's edge and see down a narrow alleyway. The alley is dark and smells rank of moss and old urine. It cuts vertically west to a second street.

"Denninger, I want you and Michaels to take the first watch on the next street over. We'll camp here."

Two soldiers unravel a large blue tarp and hammer dense spikes with a rubber mallet into the asphalt. A second tarp, one with tan and cream camouflage, is unrolled and strung up by white nylon rope to four posts spiked to the ground around the outside. Four smaller tarps, sewn to all four sides of the camouflage one, fold down and are tied to eyehooks at the bottom of the posts and form an enclosure.

The soldiers file under the makeshift tent.

I give out assignments to the night watch before settling my pack in the middle of the tent. The soldiers pick spots surrounding me. I feel like a lightbulb gathering moths. We wait.

Soon the russet tinge of the sun fades. The dense cloud crusting over the earth's atmosphere stretches and expands to the ground. It scatters freezing mist in the form of tiny water droplets.

Inside the tent, the boys are restless.

"Settle down, settle down."

I roll onto my stomach. I can feel the cold ground seeping through the plastic tarp. The acid in my gut eats at the abscess in my stomach lining. I burp bile and sit back up.

"G'night, boys."

I lie on my pack and pull my knit cap over my eyes.

Most nights, I lie awake, distrusting sleep and the environment, even the soldiers around me. Silence unnerves and scares me, more than the whistle of a shell coming, closer, closer, splitting the air and then the earth. It can't be trusted; like this entire abandoned town, it lies in wait with its finger on the trigger.

* * *

At dawn, two creatures move side-by-side through the dirt. The older one leads; the small one stays in his shadow. They follow the soldiers around the ruined city. They do not disturb settled dust. They do not enter a building, not one. Instead, they lie in crevices that have formed on the structure's sides.

"Have they food?" the smaller of the two asks in a soft whisper, too light for the wind to carry.

"No."

"What do they want? When will they leave?"

"Us." The old man rubs the sides of his face. "They're looking for any people left. They'll leave when they don't find anybody."

She stares into the weathered face of her grandfather. It seems to have been simultaneously melted and toughened by the sun.

"What'll they do if they find us?" She asks though she has heard it all before.

"You'll be taken to mine the Flats. And they'll take me somewhere else."

His blue eyes dim and shift rapidly back and forth. A thin trace of white goop sticks in the corners of his mouth. She hears his stomach rumble.

"But where will you be taken?"

"Never mind, Alabama. Forget it." He squeezes her arm. "Let's go."

Alabama has gotten better using her walkers. At first, balancing on top of rounded moose hooves and boards was difficult and would often send her head first into the fields. Even with practice, she maneuvered in them clumsily, but her grandfather moved in his pair like an acrobat crossing a rope.

She looks at his skinny brown arms. His rib bones poke through the front and back of his t-shirt. *Where will they take you, Papa?*

From inside the soldier's tent, the two hear a cough and bound back to the safety of their crack in the wall.

* * *

"Lieutenant, wake up." Sergeant Moretti looms above me. A shadow covers his face. "More tracks."

"Where? Show me."

I pull on my boots and crawl over the soldiers strewn across the blue tarp. Moretti lifts a corner of the tarp knocking droplets of frozen dew onto the ground. Outside, Moretti reveals a pattern of broken heart shapes encircling our encampment.

"I found them this morning," he tells me. A breath cloud hangs over his mouth. "I was heading back from peeing in the alley. Elk?"

I squat. "Don't think so. Elk prints are round at the edges. They look like wisdom teeth." I place three fingers inside the sunken paw marks. "Also, elk travels in herds, well, at least the females and calves do… or they did before extinction."

"So what are these?" He crouches next to me.

"Moose tracks. Maybe a cow and her calf?"

Moretti's eyes shine. "Real, live moose?"

"Don't get ahead of yourself, Aldo. There's probably less moose alive than elk."

Moretti stands up. "So, fakes?"

"Yep." I move to another section of tracks. "Look how close the front hooves are to the rear ones."

"And?" he asks.

"I'm just thinking how two moose prints could make one footprint." A crease forms in between Moretti's furry eyebrows. "I've seen it once before. People take a piece of wood and nail old hooves to it."

"Why?" Moretti rubs his neck.

"Camouflage." I inspect the track marks from several angles. In the dusty dirt, I can make out two different strides, one long and one short. "Moretti, wake the boys. We've got some people to hunt."

* * *

I lead the Company through the city and to its edge, tracking. A treeless landscape of gnarled shrubs leaking out of the dirt rolls along the horizon. I can smell rotting brine shrimp on the breeze.

"Think we'll eat, today?"

It's Denninger again. I shouldn't have allowed him to talk when we first entered the town. It's all he has done since.

"Maybe. When we get to the lake."

A swarm of black gnats cloud around us. The troop begins to swoop their arms to rid themselves of the insects. Sergeant Moretti raises his arm above the boys' heads. Immediately, the gnats focus on the elevated limb. The boys seem amused, watching him moving side to side with the black haze.

"Let me try." Denninger lifts his arm above his head, but the gnats ignore him. He waves his arm. He snaps his fingers. Nothing. "Why isn't it working?"

"Your arm has to be the highest thing around," Moretti tells him.

"Let me try," Denninger says.

Moretti ignores him. Instead, he moves the gnats into a figure eight. The soldiers call out directions.

"Make 'em zig-zag!"

"Spell your initials!"

He does.

"I want to try it." Denninger's voice drops an octave. "Put your arm down."

Moretti doesn't.

Denninger blocks his way. "I said put your arm down."

"Jesus, Denninger. Do you know who I am? I'm the Sergeant of this whole company. If I want to hold my arm up, I'll hold my arm up."

Kale Denninger's face flushes. Moretti switches arms and pretends to conduct the gnats in a symphony.

"Back in line, Denninger," he orders.

Denninger thrusts his balled-up fists into the pockets of his pants. He spins on his heels and falls back among the faction.

Moretti drops his arm. Straightaway, the gnats infiltrate the group.

We trudge down the slope of a soft mound. The stench of the brine shrimp grows. I can see the green water of the lake and hear it lapping up the beach.

"Sorry, Lieutenant." Moretti catches up to me and leans in. "The boy's troubled."

"I know."

"Should I take care of him?" Moretti smiles.

I look over my shoulder. Denninger is coming around the dune trailing behind. His eyes are squinting, and his lips are in tight parallel lines. I blow out a breath.

"No. We can't afford to lose any more soldiers. He'll learn his place in time."

"And if he doesn't?"

"I'll let you teach him."

As soon as we reach the beach, uniforms are stripped off, and the boys rush the water. They laugh and dunk one another under the swirls of green spume and from their mouths, spew a stream of the saline solution.

"You're going to get sick," Moretti tells them.

Two older boys sprint out of the surf and drag Moretti back in with them.

I pull off my boots and stuff both socks into their nose. Then I roll up each pant leg and strip off my shirt.

"Why'd he do that to me?"

I turn around. Denninger is sitting on the sand, still dressed and still angry.

"He's the tallest, so the gnats followed."

"He didn't have to be. You could've let me be for a second."

"Yep. Probably could have."

Denninger's bottom lip sticks out.

"Come on, Denninger. Don't cry."

He springs to his feet. His face is red. I see a thick blue vein pulsating in his neck.

"I'm not crying!"

"Take it easy, kid." I stand up.

"I'm not crying, damn it!"

"Hey, what's going on?" Moretti is behind me. I can smell the salt water coming off his body.

"Nothing," I tell him.

"You better watch yourself." Moretti arches his height over the boy.

"Sergeant, let's go. It's a good day for a swim." I turn around and walk to the shoreline. The kid's troubled.

I watch the boys playing in the surf for over an hour. For a moment, I forget we're at war.

"Hey, Lieutenant?" An abstract shadow of Denninger falls across me landing on the beach. "How many people do you think live on this island?"

"None."

"You sure?" He looks smug.

"What's up, Denninger?"

"Just tell me how many people you think still live in this place?"

"Why?" I twist my neck to see him.

"Did your mom make you promise to keep a census, too?" Moretti laughs. He dives on his stomach, throwing golden sand upwards.

Denninger's eyes turn dark.

"I was wondering on account of that sand castle over there." He points to a boulder.

"Show me."

We pick through tumbleweeds with puncturing stickers and get to the face of the rock. I kneel in the sand. The gravity has begun to tear the structure down, but I can still make out its castle form. I turn to Denninger. "You didn't do this?"

"No."

"How'd you find it?" Moretti and the rest of the group crowd around us. "I had to take a dump." He points to a lumpy brown pile a few feet away. The wind picks up and assaults us with its scent.

"Damn it, Denninger!"

Moretti stalks toward the boy with his chest puffed out and his chin sticking forward. He grabs him by the shoulders and shakes him hard. "You bastard! You tricked us into sniffing your turd, didn't you?"

Denninger smiles.

Moretti throws him to the ground and straddles him. "You little asshole! I should shove your shit down your throat and make you eat it!"

"Go ahead! Touch my shit, I dare you!"

Moretti punches him in the mouth. I drag Moretti off. Denninger sits up. His lip is split open and blood gushes down his chin.

"You're the asshole, Moretti, you brown back!"

The boys groan and move back.

Moretti lunges again, but I have him restrained.

"Moretti, take a dip. I mean it, cool off." I push him to the group. "Here, make sure he cools off."

The boys surround him and escort him down the beach.

I unearth a rock and roll it in my palm. It's softball size and has a sharp nub on one side. I hand it to him. "Here, bury it."

Denninger goes to his feces and digs a moat around it.

"I should let Moretti beat the shit out of you, know that?" He looks up. "Why do you want trouble?"

Denninger lengthens his back. "Why does he want to give *me* so much trouble?"

I swallow the bolt of anger inside me and decide to take another approach. "Maybe you're right, Kale." I spit saliva into the sand.

Denninger drags his poop into the trench with the tip of his rock and covers it with sand and dirt. "I am."

I bite back my need to correct him. "What do you want from me, son?" It takes everything I have to sound sincere.

Denninger stands and tosses the rock into a pile of sticker bushes. He claps the sand from his hands. "I don't want Moretti to be in charge of me anymore."

I look at the boy. He looks so out of place. "What are you doing here Kale?"

"What do you mean?"

"How did you get here, in my army? You're not fifteen, are you?"

He drops his eyes and looks out at the water. "No, I'm not."

"How old are you?"

"Old enough."

"How old?"

"Twelve and a half."

"How'd you get in the military?"

"I lied." He doesn't blink. "I didn't want to mine the Flats."

"You an orphan, son?"

"No."

"Your mom's dead. Where's your dad?"

"Locked up."

"Prison?"

Denninger shakes his head, "No. He's in the B Institute."

"Oh. Crap! Sorry, kid."

"He's not crazy." His shoulders stiffen. "It doesn't matter what they say. I know he's not crazy."

"What do they say?"

"That he needs so much electricity he can't remember me anymore. But he's not crazy. He never was. He was sad when my mom died, that's all. He didn't mean to cut me so bad. He stopped after the first finger."

For the first time, I notice the tip of the kid's pinky finger on his right hand is missing. Denninger sees me looking and curls his hand into a fist.

"He told me he was sorry," Denninger says.

I feel a sharp pain in my stomach. "How long since you saw him last?"

"A couple of years. But I get word from his nurses about his progress...well I used to."

Icy sludge fills my body. "Kale, have they said your dad's been sick, lately? Like he has the flu or his heart isn't working, something along those lines?" I ask. The ice is replacing my blood.

"Yeah?" He scratches his ear. "He's not getting enough blood to his heart." I place my hand on his shoulder. "He's too sick to see me, right now."

"I bet you're right about your dad, kid."

"You going to turn me in?" He searches my eyes.

"No. I won't turn you in. But you've got to straighten up and listen to me."

"I don't want Moretti in charge of me anymore," he says.

"Okay, you report directly to me from now on."

Denninger smiles and agrees. The sun is in the middle of an anemic sky.

* * *

We backtrack through the city. Denninger marches in line with me. Moretti follows closely behind, seething. We round the curving street and stop.

A child is sitting next to a fountain. Her thin face is smeared dirty. Her dark hair hangs down in her mouth. She is watching something inching up her arm. A cricket. The child's eyes are shiny watching it climb. Once it reaches her shoulder, she raises her other hand and smashes it. She peeks at its yellow remnants underneath, then scoops it up with her fingers and eats it.

The girl's head snaps up, and she sees us. She slides into the fountain's basin and scales the opposite side.

"Better get her," I say.

The soldiers charge after her, some whooping as they run. I stay behind, replacing her sitting on the edge of the fountain. Within seconds, the army returns, dragging the child spitting and biting along with them.

Her face is deformed. One side is raised a half inch higher than the other and protruding outward. Her cheek is red with a deep purple line down the center of it. I reach out and touch it. She howls.

"Your cheek's inflamed. Do you have an abscessed tooth?" She tries wiggling out of her captor's grip. I lean forward. "Hey, kid, what's your name?"

Denninger level's his rifle at her. "Talk."

"Put it away, Denninger. She'll cooperate. Are you alone? Huh? Where's your guardian? Where are they hiding?"

The girl lifts her head and glares at me. My boys tighten their grip on her.

"I'll count to three. One…two…"

"Wait!"

From the shadows a rare creature appears. He is aged and ragged, but he's fast. He runs at us, his boney legs jettisoning him across the courtyard.

"Don't! She's mine! She's my granddaughter, Alabama. She's all right!"

Denninger switches his aim from the child to the old man.

The man stops in front of me. He's missing most of his teeth. He watches the barrel of the gun, and he slowly bows. A wisp of cotton white hair rims his baldhead and trails down his neck.

"Please, she doesn't mean any harm. She's starving, that's all. We'll go. We won't bother you anymore." He lifts his eyes toward the rifle.

"Put it away, Denninger." I tap the end of his gun. He slings it over his back.

I look down at the old man's feet. A rectangular board is visible between his toes and behind his heel. A piece of worn leather crosses the top of each foot. "Are you the moose following us?" I ask.

He raises a leg exposing a tattered hoof. Moretti gasps.

"You move fast on those," I say.

The old man nods.

"How long have you been out here?"

"My whole life, sir." He tilts his head. "So has Alabama. There's no one else, sir. No one else left alive."

"What happened?"

The old man twitches his nose. "Bombs. Starvation." He looks over his shoulder at the human sandbags. "Couldn't get any more in the ground, I'm too weak."

"You know I can't leave you two here," I say.

"I do not know that."

"Look at her! I think her tooth is abscessed. If we don't take care of it, she could lose her jaw."

The old man shakes his head. "No, sir. I've been taking good care of her. I irrigate it a couple times a day and make her swish with saltwater."

"The lake water? You might as well have her swishing piss!"

The old man glances sorrowfully at the child.

"Listen, if I don't bring you in, you'll starve to death," I tell him.

"Yes, sir."

"They'll take good care of your girl. She'll get food and medical attention and a place to sleep."

"Yeah, but they'll put her in the mines. She can't go to the Flats, sir. She's afraid of the dark."

I look at the child, still trying to wrestle her wrists free from her captors. "I think she'll do all right," I tell him.

The old man drops his eyes to the ground.

"You'd rather she stay out here, with you, starving, than to go to the Flats?"

He doesn't look up. "I don't suppose, so."

"We are going to take her." I stand up. The girl begins to scream.

The old man rushes to her and wraps his arms around her. He cradles her head. "He's right, Alabama. You'll be okay."

"No! No!" The girl bucks and head-butts one of the soldiers in the stomach.

"And what about me, sir?" Tears leave cleaned streaks down his face.

I shake my head. "Our mission is to find inhabitants. That's it." I look at the child. "And we found *one*."

"You're not taking me with you?" His voice cracks.

"No. You know what'll happen if I do."

He nods.

"Look, we're meeting a boat in ten minutes. I'll make sure your girl is put on the ship and given food."

"All right. All right." He pulls a piece of her hair out of her mouth. "You be good, Alabama. Don't give 'em any reason to bring you back here."

"What about you?" she asks. "Where are they taking you?"

The old man and I exchange looks.

"We need his help tracking other islands," I tell her.
"That true, Papa?"
"Yes. Besides, the island's not fit for anybody, anymore."
He presses his lips against her forehead and whispers something in her ear.
She nods.
"Okay. I'll go."
The old man kisses her again and lets her go.

* * *

We move quickly through the city, to the opposite side of the island. The girl hangs her head, crying. Far behind the troop, the old man's following.
"He's still there," Moretti tells me in a low tone.
"I know. He's making sure I keep my promise."
"You're not going to report him?" Moretti asks. "Or shoot him?"
"No. He won't last long out here on his own." I glance over at Denninger, who is staring straight ahead and keeping pace with me. I turn to Moretti. "As long as he keeps out of sight, nothing will happen to him."
We return to the beach and stand on the dock. On the horizon, an enormous white ship buoys along the waves. A yellow raft with a motor is skimming the water's surface towards us.
I crouch down in front of the girl.
"You okay, Alabama?"
The child puts her hand in mine, but her gaze is steady on the ground.
A patrol officer on the front of the skiff throws a rope to a soldier. The soldier loops it around a metal hook mounted on the pier.
I whisper in Alabama's ear, "Listen, don't you say a thing to him, understand?"
She nods.
"Ignore everything I tell him, all right?"
She nods again.

"Lieutenant." The patrolman and I exchange salutes. "You found one?" He inspects Alabama.

"Yep. She's a recent orphan. Parents' bodies just turned cold," I tell him.

"What's wrong with her face?"

"Bad teeth, I think."

I lift the girl placing her in the arms of the patrolman. He wraps a wool blanket around her and sits her down.

"How long you scheduled to stay on the island?" he asks. I see the child is watching me.

"Another week," I lie.

He nods. "We thought you might need some supplies." He points to a wooden crate in the back of the small boat. Moretti and two others jump inside and remove the box.

"Be careful with her. She's had it rough, here for a while."

"See you in a week." The man starts the motor. He turns the boat around and guns it toward the larger ship waiting on the horizon.

"Stop! Wait! Alabama!"

I turn as the old man streaks past and races down the dock.

"What does he think he's—"

A thunderous crack splits the air around us. The back of the old man's head rips open, spilling his brains. He is propelled forward onto his knees.

He tries to steady himself with one leg planted on the dock, the other dragging behind. He wobbles, standing for a moment. His left leg is dead. He takes one more step then falls sideways into the water. The soldiers and I hurtle around.

A thin taper of smoke rises from the barrel of Denninger's rifle. His static eye is peering through the scope while the other wrinkles into a squint. "Got 'em!"

"What the hell you do that for?" Moretti grabs the nose of the gun and yanks it out of Denninger's hand.

"What?" Denninger grins. "Lieutenant said he had to keep out of sight. But you saw him, he didn't stay out of sight." Denninger looks at the water. "Hey, look at that. I got 'em to do the dead man's float without even trying." He chuckles. "We warned him, right?" he says, facing me, but not taking his sight off the old man.

I shake my head. "Yep."

I take the gun from Moretti and cock it. I aim and fire. A crude hole in the middle of Kale Denninger's face opens. He is thrown backward to the ground. A veil of sand kicks up around him. He is staring upward, his half-moon face unflinching as white clumps of sand and salt rain down and are absorbed in the dark liquid bubbling out of him.

The soldiers stand with their mouths hanging wide. Moretti maneuvers around them and squats next to Denninger holding two fingers against the boy's neck.

"Dead."

I nod and look over my shoulder. I can see the old man's body sticking out from the underside of the dock. An arm and a leg stretch away from his body. They bounce on the current as if waving goodbye.

"You know, Moretti…" I look past the dead man. I can scarcely see the outline of the ship in the distance. "Of all my missions…the strangest by far, is this one…"

Across the water, at the point where the earth and the sky touch, the horizon is set ablaze in burnt oranges and blood reds of a falling sun.

"The one that came from the Great Salt Lake."

I hand Moretti back the gun.

E. Ellis Allen

E. Ellis Allen is new to the writing business. Since becoming a writer full-time, she has won the City of South Jordan's Literary of Arts Short Story competition in 2014 and again in 2015. Recently, she has started a new adventure in writing the biography of an ex-German soldier and POW.

Mine
by C.R. Asay

When Eli whistled, I came. It had always been that way. It was my luck to call him mine. My paws didn't make a sound in the slurry of silt and sludge at the edge of the Great Salt Lake as I loped to his side, tongue sagging across my canines. I didn't feel the wet or the cold. Hadn't for a long time. But none of that mattered now because Eli was here. Without Eli I was nothing. Only a void. I didn't exist.

"Thata boy, Kal."

His voice was hoarse, and though he stared at me, he didn't try to reach down to pat my head as he had in years past.

He slouched, hands deep in jean pockets, face lost in in the darkness of the night. I sniffed, perplexed at the lack of scent sending me signals. Surely, there was sauce from the Dragon Diner's Tai Pan Noodles staining his shirt. I loved those noodles. I sniffed the cuffs of his jeans. Nothing. It was worse than being blind.

Eli retreated a single step, a cool shiver traveling up his arms. I sat back with a whine.

Everything was different. He didn't share his noodles anymore, or even scratch my head. But when he whistled, I came. That would never change. Except that something had. What was different tonight?

"Come on, boy. I found 'em." Eli started walking down the beach, his feet squelching in the mud. Mine were silent beside his. "They're gonna get what's comin' to 'em."

He swung something long and heavy onto his shoulder. I recognized the old pump-action shotgun his old man had left him. I wagged my tail and then stopped. I had good memories of that gun. And bad.

We'd take it in the mountains every fall, trampling through the woods hunting pine hens and grouse. We'd even bagged a few; mostly there wasn't much left, just feathers and blood. We left the broken bodies to rot—not that I minded it too much because Eli was with me. I licked my chops remembering the taste of flesh and blood still warm, even the feathers.

My teeth tingled. A feeling I hadn't had in…

I rested my canines on my tongue and looked up at Eli. His face was hidden in blackness. The moon was lost behind clouds, but I could hear his breathing, short and anxious. The anxiety bled over to me, and I whined.

"It's fine, pal. Everything will be fine soon. Better than fine. Perfect."

He gestured ahead where an orange glow shown through the spikey branches of the lake's sparse vegetation.

I wanted to lick his hand to remind him that everything was already perfect. Well, almost. If only I could smell and have a tiny taste of his noodles. I pressed closed, begging for my nose to send me a signal. A whiff. Anything. Eli shied away. Very un-Eli-like. Where was the love? Where were the scratches? Where were the noodles?

"There they are, the bastards."

Eli pulled the gun from his shoulder and crouched with a rustle in the dead grass. My paws made no sound beside him.

The wind shifted, bending the grass around Eli's knees and whipping his hair. My lips and teeth tingled. I saw light through the grass, flickering light from a fire. And noise. Harsh laughter. Glass bottles clinking. The moon crawled from behind a cloud, illuminating the landscape in cool light.

I felt the sudden cold of the wind, as though reaching me from a frigid void. I shivered and *felt* cold. The encroaching light of the moon filtered a tickling awareness of scent toward me. I smelled! Wood smoke, beer, and hotdogs. And something else. Blood. Pumping heartily through healthy veins. I hadn't smelled anything in so long that I filled my nostrils with the scents. So many. I filtered through each one, remembering them all, especially...

I gulped and my haunches hit the ground, my tail curled between my legs. A scent memory quivered through my hackles, raising the hair on my back.

A concoction of spearmint, tobacco, the burning rubber of sneakers too close to the fire, sweat, beer, and the extra sharp scent of malevolence.

It was this last one that kept me frozen in place, paws tingling, nails digging into the cold ground, the hair along my spine rising. I remembered the last time I'd smelled it, everything had changed. Malevolence had sent me into the lake. The cold lake with clammy hands surrounded by shouts, gleeful, drunken slurs, the leering faces, and the harsh laughter. The pistol passed from hand to hand, the stomping of fire-softened sneakers as I tried to escape the box of bodies they'd pinned me within. Then the excruciating pop. The sizzle of fire through my chest. Eli's cries.

Eli? Eli! I leaned in for protection, terror surging through my tingling paws and up into my teeth. He stalked forward without a glance in my direction.

"We gonna do to them what they did to you, Kal."

Eli raised the shotgun, malevolence oozing from his pores in a sickening wave. I followed, tail tucked, ears down.

He stood, just outside of the flickering firelight; he pumped a shell into the chamber and pulled the gun tight into his shoulder.

"You sons of bitches are dead men."

The air grew still, the sounds of mirth silenced. I didn't like this.

Not at all. I smelled the blood and rot; I remembered the blood, feathers, and the rotting bodies; Eli was going to use his ol' man's shotgun to put these men in the lake; in the lake with me.

I didn't want them in the lake. I refused to let it happen.

With a snarl, I leapt out of the tall grass and into the circle of the fire. The cries of terror thrilled me, filling my mouth with a furious desire for blood. I saw a red glow reflecting in the first man's eyes as my paws smashed into his chest, his square teeth crashing together, his head hitting the ground with a thud. My teeth sank deep into his throat, and he gurgled, fingers clawing into my fur. I shook my head until he no longer resisted.

I tore into the next man who was frozen in place on a log, a beer bottle forgotten in his hand, his jeans stained, the rubber of his sneakers softening in the heat of the fire. A moment later, his bleeding body lay beside his friend. I whirled and ripped at the plaid sleeve of the last man as he scrambled drunkenly away, sobbing and cursing. I tore the high-pitched scream from his throat, blood sliding across my jowls. I released the warm flesh, the thrill burning through my heightened senses. I stepped back to stare up at Eli, tail wagging.

He stood just outside the circle of flame, shotgun loose at his shoulder, his mouth wide, showing yellowed teeth.

"Kal? Y-y-your eyes!" he breathed out.

My what? Why were we talking about my eyes? There were bodies. Just like he'd wanted. But not in the lake, blessedly. There was only one person I wanted in the lake with me.

I licked blood from my chops, teeth tingling, and launched myself at Eli's throat.

The blood was warm and delicious in my mouth as I dragged Eli down to the lake, his eyes wide, his mouth agape. His feet left a track through the sludge.

Once in the water, he floated, bloody ripples swirling from the mangled neck. The fire flickered in the distance. Quiet sobbing carried across the water, mingling with the rushing of the wind. The water didn't wet my paws and the taste of blood was no longer so strong in my mouth.

But none of that mattered, because Eli was here. With me. In the lake.

It was my luck to call him mine.

Forever.

C.R. Asay

I am the spectacular C.R. Asay, writer of science fiction/horror/steampunk, and author of *Heart of Annihilation*. I've been published in multiple anthologies and won an honorable mention in the illustrious Writer's of the Future contest. You are privileged to have just read one of my dog stories. I love these. They are always a pleasure to write, and this one was especially fun and bloody.

Slender
by Chadd VanZanten

The guy at the lumber store is around my age. Mid-twenties, maybe a young-looking thirty, but he's not like me. He's one of these rugged types. Big shoulders, good jawline. He jumps off his forklift and comes over. Without meaning to, I take a half step back.

I'm getting ready to tell him a lie. A lot of lies. I say, "Hi. How's it going?"

He says, "What can I help you with?"

His name badge says Chris, and he's here to help me. Because I can't help myself. I'm helpless, apparently. I watch him carefully.

Chris pulls off his leather work gloves, jams them in the back pocket of his Levis. They dangle out in a really rugged way, but I've been practicing my techniques, so I'm fine. I was out at the lake just this morning, rehearsing.

I learned about lying from a movie about this guy who has to lie to the FBI to save his daughter. See, he knows who kidnapped her, but if he tells the FBI, the kidnapper will kill her before they catch him. So the guy stands in front of a full-length mirror for hours and hours, rehearsing his lie.

I hand Chris the key and say it just like I practiced: "I just need a copy of this."

I don't have a big mirror, and my apartment's no good for practicing, anyway. My place is in an older building downtown, over by the warehouses. It's pretty crummy. Six floors, no elevator, tiny rooms, and the walls are like cardboard. If I rehearsed in there, the girl who lives next to me would hear every word I said, just like I hear everything she says. Everyone can hear everything everyone is saying. So I practice out at the lake. Great Salt Lake. I go out there a lot—to practice, to be alone. It's quiet. Nothing but the wind. Sometimes seagulls. Hardly ever any people.

Chris tells me to follow him to the key machine.

You see what I mean, right? He's in charge. I follow him.

As he escorts me through the lumber yard, he taps the key with the back of his rugged middle finger and says, "This has DO NOT DUPLICATE stamped on it."

In this other movie I saw, there was a woman who cheats on her husband, and her sister helps her cover it up. The sister says if you're going to tell one lie, might as well tell lots of lies. See, most people think it's dangerous to lie because you have to tell another lie to cover it up, and another to cover that one. The sister says the more lies there are, the harder it will be for them to find the lie you actually want to tell.

So I say to Chris, "Oh, I forgot about that." (Lie number one.) "I put that on all my keys." (Number two.) "I guess I could go find a spare that's not stamped, but you'd be closed by the time I got back, and I was hoping to have this for my girlfriend tonight. She's moving in. We just got engaged." (Three, four, five, six.)

Chris eyes me. I've never had a girlfriend, and if Chris would only look a little closer, he'd figure that out. I basically stopped putting on weight at age fourteen, but then kept on growing taller. I'm very, very slender, and not in the good way. I'm taller than Chris, but if I stood behind him, you wouldn't see any part of me except my head.

The girl who lives next to me knows I don't have a girlfriend, just like I know she used to have a boyfriend, but broke up with him. She accused him of not being over his ex, and he wouldn't say that he was, so she told him they were through. Then she called her sister and ranted about it. The next day, I asked her out.

She smiled, but scoffed hoarsely. "I don't think so. I'm seeing somebody."

"Who, Trent?" I asked. "No, you're not. You said he still has a thing for Janine. You told him you're through."

Her smile went away. "Stay away from me."

Then she stormed off, but before she got to the staircase, she turned her head and gave me this look. It's a look I get a lot. From girls. From guys, too. From Chris. He looks at me, then the key, then me.

"You stamped that on here yourself?" he asks.

I realize now that that was a hole in my cover story. How do you get DO NOT DUPLICATE stamped on a key? Do you have to be a locksmith? Can you do it yourself? Either way, it's a great policy. It was pretty easy for me to steal the key, but putting DO NOT DUPLICATE on all the spare keys is a massively decent back-up plan.

Sure, I could say, "Yeah, I stamped it on there—with my DO NOT DUPLICATE stamp." But I know that saying "yes" when the answer is "no" is the easiest lie to spot. Learned it in a movie about this military interrogator who's trying to get one critical piece of information from a terrorist, but the terrorist refuses to tell any real, direct lies. See, a really good liar doesn't just lie, he stays with the truth as long as he can.

So I say, "No, a locksmith put that on there. Obviously. You know, in case the keys get swiped. This town's full of criminals. For all I know, you're one."

Chris gives me a fake chuckle and says, "Right." Then he holds the key right up to his nose and squints at it. "It's just that this key looks like a master."

I straighten my collar and say, "That's what my lady tells me every night."

Chris laughs, for real this time. He grins his rugged grin. Usually, I can't get a real smile out of guys like him, but I swear he was this close to fist-bumping me. There are some things movies just can't teach you. Like how to think fast. But I also got lucky, and that is another thing movies have taught me—luck counts for a lot.

Like finding the little gray metal box bolted to the wall down in the boiler room of my building. Pure luck. I mean, what are the chances? I guess the manager hid it down there, and it had to be a long time before I showed up because it's got an inch of dust on top. I've seen the huge ring of keys he keeps with him, but he's got spares for all of them down there in the basement. A hundred keys on hooks with labels. UTITLY. STORAGE. ROOF. MASTER. The box has a lock on it, too, but it was unlocked. Really, what are the chances of that?

Funny thing is there's a spare key in the box labeled KEY BOX, which means if the manager ever lost the original, he'd either have an extra key for a box he never locks or an extra key inside a box he can't unlock, which if you think about it is its own kind of lie.

The lake is that way. If you walk up to the shore in the springtime, you'll realize that the lake is one big lie. Because you think it's dead. When you see it from far away, you figure that lake is completely dead. Like an endless puddle of battery acid with rocks and salt rime all around. It even smells dead, and it's saltier than goddam hell. No fish can live in there, no plants.

But walk up to the edge of it and you'll see the brine shrimp. Millions of little red shrimps smaller than your pinkie nail. If you ever had Sea Monkeys when you were a kid, that's what they were—brine shrimps from Great Salt Lake. I don't know what they eat. Detritus, I guess. Rotting bodies, maybe. The lake is full of them. It's like the lake itself wants you to think it's dead, but if you look closely, it's alive. Almost like it's hiding.

Chris takes one more close-up look at the master key. I shouldn't have given it to him right away. I should have asked him if he would copy it first, got a "yes" out of him, and then handed it over. This is the whole entire reason I came to the lumber yard instead of an actual locksmith—I was hoping they wouldn't know or care about the rules. I'm vague on the legalities here. Can he ask me for ID? Can he keep the key and report me?

Chris sighs and says, "You're sure this is your key, right?"

"Yeah, I'm pretty sure it's mine," I say, grinning. "But, if you can't copy it, it's really no problem. My girlfriend doesn't need it right this minute. I'll just tell her I have to go back to the locksmith to make a copy."

I know—improvising lies is not a good choice. When you improvise, you make mistakes. But Chris is already picking out the key blank. Probably needs to get back to his forklift. He screws the original into one vise and the blank goes in the other. The motor spins up. It's too loud to talk, so we stand there trying to find something to look at while the machine cuts the duplicate.

I'd just gotten back from the lake that morning, to practice one more time, and I walked up to the edge again and looked into that lake of acid. Maybe that's the real lie of the lake. Even though it's full of a billion-trillion sea monkeys, it's brine, not water, which means it's not a lake at all.

As the motor in the key machine winds down, Chris unscrews the master key and hands it to me. I close my fist tight around it and shove it into my pocket, way down to the bottom. Then Chris drops the copied key into my hand.

"Careful," he says. "It's still hot."

It burns me a little. I bounce it on my palm.

"Let's go up to the register," says Chris. "Get you checked out."

I follow him again, past the plywood and insulation, past the aisles of paint. He doesn't say anything or even act like he knows I'm behind him.

As we get to the cash registers I say, "Can I ask you a quick question?"

"Yeah."

"You put DO NOT DUPLICATE on a key so that if it gets stolen, someone can't make a copy and then return the original, right?"

Chris shrugs. "Right."

"Well, that's a good policy and all, but, how do you know that's not what I did?"

He laughs.

I laugh, too. Then I say, "Seriously, though."

"Well," says Chris, "I guess I don't." He gets behind the cash register.

I can tell he's nervous. Chris is nervous. Forklift Chris. He says, "But, I mean, what's the worst that could happen?"

Last night I saw this movie about a mafia guy who goes against his bosses and then has to lie about it. This was the best one. The guy knows if his bosses catch him, they'll kill him, and he knows the bosses are good at spotting liars because they do it a couple times earlier in the movie. So he tells the cops he'll give them information about the mafia if they help him lie to his bosses.

Here's what the cops teach him: when you say the lie, think the truth.

See, most people try to push the truth out of their head when they lie, but that's not right. Just like the lake: even though it's dead, it's full of life, and because it's full of life, it's a great place for the dead. If you're going to lie, you have to fill yourself with the truth.

"The worst that could happen?" I repeat. "The very worst?" I pause, but only for effect. "The worst is that I stole a master key and a bunch of people in my apartment building are going to end up raped, murdered, and tossed into the Great Salt Lake, starting with the girl who lives next to me. That's the worst."

Chris laughs again, but he's gone back to the fake one. He's looking up at me and my shadow is on his face and he's not very rugged at all anymore. I stare him right in the eye.

He looks away. "Okay, okay," he says, fiddling with the cash register, "but what are the chances of that?"

"Slender," I tell him. "Very, very slender."

Chadd VanZanten

The very first e-book Chadd VanZanten ever downloaded was the collected works of H.P. Lovecraft, and the second was *The Compleat Angler*. Chadd is a fiction writer and outdoor essayist whose work has appeared in *Backpacker*, *Big Sky Journal*, and the online journal *Eat Sleep Fish*. His first book, *On Fly-Fishing the Northern Rockies*, co-authored with Russ Beck, was published in 2015 by The History Press. His fiction can be found in *Between Places: an Anthology of Prose and Poetry*.

The Cellar
by Carol Nicolas

When the doorbell rang, I wasn't expecting a witch.

I was in my room, playing with my dolls while I waited for my friend to arrive. Bonnie was staying for dinner, and if the drizzle ever let up, we'd play outside. I galloped downstairs and arrived as Mom opened the front door.

The woman dripping on our porch was tall, beautiful, and seemed vaguely familiar. She looked at Mom.

"Hello, Margaret."

Mom looked puzzled.

"Can I help you?"

The woman's red lips curved up as she snapped her fingers.

"Remember."

All the color drained from Mom's face, and her eyes widened with terror.

"No. Not again."

She tried to shut the door, but the woman pointed, and the door flew open. Mom stumbled back. The woman laughed.

My older brother, Colin, came into the hallway.

"Mom, where did you put my—"

Mom turned and pushed Colin away. "Run!"

"Stop." The woman pointed. Mom jerked, as if she had been struck. She stood frozen, mouth open in a silent scream. Colin stood still, eyes wide.

The woman stepped into the house, set her wet suitcases on the mat, and closed the door. She stripped off her gloves.

"Hello, Colin. You've become such a handsome young man." She pointed at him and made a half circle gesture.

Colin gaped at her as if she was the most magnificent creature he'd ever seen.

"Who are you?"

"I am your Great-Aunt Tamora from Salt Lake."

Mom moaned. A steady rain began to fall.

Aunt Tamora looked at me and sneered.

"And then there's Francis. Such a disappointment."

I looked at my mom and brother, then back at her, and backed up against the wall.

"Leave us alone."

She hung her wet raincoat and hat on the coat rack by the door.

"Such a lovely home. I like old houses with all their secrets."

Aunt Tamora looked at me and smiled.

The hair on my arms stood up. What did she mean? Our house was old, built in the early 1900s, and Dad was always complaining about all the repairs. But secrets?

"Margaret, go in the kitchen and put the kettle on. It's time to make the tea." She patted her purse. "The special blend, of course."

Mom panted as if she strained against a great load. She turned and walked stiffly towards the kitchen.

"Mom," I shouted, but she didn't even look at me.

From the AM radio in the kitchen came Elvis Presley's latest song, "Now and Then There's a Fool Such as I." Rain began to drum even harder on the roof.

"Colin, would you like to join us for tea?"

"Sure." Colin smiled up at her.

Aunt Tamora ran a finger down his cheek. "So perfect. Go help your mother."

I stared at him, puzzled. What was wrong with my brother? He was only eleven. He didn't even like tea, yet he turned and followed Mom to the kitchen.

Aunt Tamora pointed at me.

"Francis, take my things to the guest room."

A curious feeling, like a heavy blanket, settled on me. I wanted to obey her. And then it dissolved, melting away from me, and I had my will back. Her spell hadn't worked on me. I didn't know what to do with this knowledge, so I picked up the smaller suitcase and hauled it into the guest bedroom, which was to the right of the front door.

The doorbell rang again. I gasped. Bonnie!

I tried to go out to the front door, but Aunt Tamora stood in my way. She ran her hands down the sides of her body. Before me now stood an exact copy of my mother.

"Stay in there and don't interfere."

She shut the bedroom door.

I ran to the window. My friend stood on the doorstep, pink umbrella over her head and pink rain boots on her feet. Her mother waited in the car in the driveway. Windshield wipers flipped back and forth.

Aunt Tamora spoke in Mom's voice.

"Hello, dear."

"Hi, Mrs. Simpson. Sorry I'm late."

"I'm very sorry, but Francis has the flu. She won't be able to play today."

I waved frantically from the guest window, but she didn't see me. I banged on the glass. She didn't hear me.

"In fact, you look ill, too. Better hurry home."

Bonnie took three steps away from the porch and threw up. She staggered to her car, and they drove away.

I turned to see Aunt Tamora in the doorway of the guest bedroom, once again looking like herself.

"Well? Don't just stand there. Get my other suitcase and put it at the foot of my bed."

"No. I don't like you. I don't want you here."

"I order you to obey me."

She pointed at me, but again the spell slid off me. Her eyes narrowed.

"Margaret's done something to you, hasn't she?"

I had no idea what she meant.

"Go away."

Her lip curled as she came forward and loomed over me.

"If you don't do exactly what I say, I'll put you in the cellar."

Cold shuddered through me. No. Not the cellar. Anything but that. I sank to the floor.

She laughed and started towards the kitchen.

I went back to the front door, grabbed the wet suitcase by the handle, and dragged it into the guest bedroom. Why was she here?

I tiptoed to the bedroom door and listened. They were in the kitchen now. Colin chattered away, keeping her entertained. I closed and locked the door, and went over and unlatched the larger suitcase.

I peeked inside: black clothing, folded neatly and slightly musty; a plastic bag stuffed with some kind of dried, crushed plant; a long, slim box; and an old, black leather-bound book caught my eye. I took out the box and opened it. Inside was a silver knife with strange symbols on the handle. A feeling of dread went through me. I replaced the knife in the box.

I pulled out the book and opened it. Inside, the title read, *Grimoire*. Curious, I opened to a random page and read:

Spell for fire: Give the right wrist a half twist and point as you clearly pronounce the word 'Burn.' Your intent is the power behind the spell. (Especially effective when used by elemental witches.)

Huh. I turned to another page, and began reading.

Between the autumn equinox and the winter solstice is Samhain, our most important celebration each year. The rites begin at sunset on the thirty-first of October. The traditional sacrifice to be made is of a male calf, lamb, or dog under the age of one year. However, when Samhain coincides with a new moon or a full moon, the sacrifice of a male human child not over twelve years old is required, one who has been prepared by administration of a tea made from Shafer's Sleep...

I turned the page. Before me was a diagram of how the body was to be positioned and cut. I dropped the book.

A letter fell out. With shaking hands, I opened it and read:

Tamora:

This year the new moon rises on Samhain, bringing with it an unparalleled opportunity for power for our illustrious sisterhood. The ley lines have shifted, once again running through the home of your great-niece, Margaret Simpson. Therefore, it is your great privilege to go before us, prepare the site, and provide the sacrifice. We shall arrive in the afternoon on October thirty-first. Be ready.

Your sister in power,

Hecate
The Coven of the Great Salt Lake

My heart pounded. I had to do something. But what? My hand reached for the necklace I had worn since I was very young. Whenever I was upset, I liked to slide the fine silver links through my fingers. After a moment I had calmed down enough to think.

I put everything back in the suitcase, carefully replacing each item exactly where it had been, then closed and re-latched the suitcase. I went over and unlocked the door. Their voices still came from the kitchen. I held my breath as I tiptoed to the front door, quietly opened it, grabbed my coat from the stand, and slid outside.

I dashed to the barn and found my dad in his woodshop, working on a project.

"Hey there, Franny, what's wrong? You look like you've seen a ghost."

I ran to Dad and threw my arms around him.

"Dad, you have to make her go away."

"Who?"

"Aunt Tamora. She's in the kitchen. Tell her to go away."

He peeled me off and set me on top of the workbench.

"What's all this nonsense? Who's Aunt Tamora?"

I stared at him. He didn't know her?

"Don't you remember? She was here before. And tomorrow is Halloween, and she's planning to—"

"Hello, Barry," said a sultry voice.

I whipped around and gasped. Aunt Tamora stood in the doorway, posed like a fashion model, her hair flowing in fiery rivulets around her shoulders.

"I'm so glad to see you again."

She pointed at him and made a circular motion with her finger.

I looked at Dad, but he was staring at her open mouthed. His face was flushed.

"You're so beautiful."

I jumped off the workbench, grabbed his arm, and shook it. "Dad. Dad!"

He didn't respond.

She sauntered over and ran a finger down his cheek.

"Barry, you're very tired. Why don't you go up to the hayloft and take a nice, long nap?"

Dad had a giddy smile on his face. He walked away and began to climb up the ladder to the hayloft.

"Dad, no!" I wailed.

Aunt Tamora whirled and grabbed my ear. Her eyes blazed into mine.

"Go back to the house. You have chores to do."

"I'm only ten," I whined.

I'd been helping Mom with housework for a long time, but I wasn't about to admit it.

Her fingers twisted, and I cried out. She pushed me outside into the rain and marched me back to the house.

Colin sat alone on the couch in the living room, an empty teacup before him on the coffee table and a stupid smile on his face.

"Mom!"

"She's making dinner," Aunt Tamora said. "She may not be much of a witch, but she can cook."

I gasped. "My mom is a witch?"

"Only a weather witch, and a weak one at that. You can blame her for the rain."

"What about Dad?"

"Your father and brother are mere mortals, easily manipulated. You, however, are a mystery. You have no magic, yet you are able to resist me. Why is that?"

Lightning flashed, and thunder rumbled. The lights flickered. She pointed at the orange candle on the coffee table. She twisted her wrist. "Burn." A small flame erupted. Her smile was cruel. "Perhaps I should test you again."

"Mom!" I turned, darted into the kitchen, and headed for the door.

"Lock," said Aunt Tamora.

The kitchen door locked. No matter what I did, I couldn't make the door open.

"Mom, help me."

She didn't even turn around.

I ran back through the house to the living room, but the deadbolt on the front door clicked into place. I rushed to the side window.

"Close."

I yanked on it, but it wouldn't budge.

"No."

I dashed to the black, rounded phone on the end table in the living room, but Aunt Tamora just pointed and said, "Heat."

The phone glowed red, and I snatched my burned fingers away.

I whirled around and faced her.

"What do you want?"

"I want obedience. It's that simple. Now go and set the table."

"And if I don't?"

"Then you go in the cellar."

Again cold fear rushed through me. An impression of a dark place crawling with bugs flashed through my mind. But I had never been in the cellar. Had I?

I hurried back to the kitchen. The roasted chicken sat on top of the stove, the beans were in a bowl, and Mom was mashing the potatoes. I set the table.

At dinner, the food I had been looking forward to all day now tasted like mud. I pushed it around on my plate. Mom sat silent and red faced, her teeth gritted. Her eyes held a desperate message for me that I didn't understand. Colin gazed in adoration at Aunt Tamora. Dad's chair was empty.

"What about Dad?" I said.

She made a sweeping gesture. "Forget him." Their faces went blank.

"Eat your dinner, Colin," Aunt Tamora said. My brother began to shovel in his food. "Very good. Now have some more tea." As he drained his cup, she smiled.

She poured tea for me. "Let's try some of this for you. Drink."

"I hate tea."

"Drink!"

"No." I knocked my cup over.

Mom whimpered.

Aunt Tamora's lips thinned, and her eyes narrowed.

"Go to your room. Now."

I fled.

As I lay on my bed, faint voices drifted up from below. I lay down on the worn carpet and put my ear on the heating vent.

"Honestly, Margaret, you're such a disappointment. We need strong witches and warlocks to carry our bloodlines forward, and instead you produce two mundane boys and a fractious girl who seems to be devoid of any magical ability. The most we can hope for is that she'll turn out to have some weak weather magic. And what good is that? You're a complete failure."

"Two boys?" I thought. My fingers crept up and rubbed my silver necklace.

"I'm sorry," Mom mumbled.

"I need to get ready for Samhain, and if it doesn't stop raining, it will make preparations difficult. You're the weather witch. Fix this."

My mom sobbed. "Why can't the Samhain be held somewhere else?"

"The Great Salt Lake Coven designated your home. It's a high honor to have it here. You should be grateful for this opportunity to show your loyalty."

"I am grateful, but…"

"It's a new moon, Margaret. You know what we require."

Mom's strangled cry was full of horror. "No. Please, no. Not Colin. Not him."

I bit my hand to keep from screaming.

Aunt Tamora's voice was sharp. "When you joined the coven, you agreed to the terms."

"You forced me to join. You took my memories so I couldn't object. Oh, please, please don't do this."

Mom began to wail. Outside, rain fell in torrents.

There was a sound of a sharp slap.

"Stop that noise at once. Don't bore me with your pathetic emotions. Your duty is to obey. Do you understand?"

"Yes. I will obey," Mom said in a toneless voice.

"Much better. Now, pay attention. You only have one child. Her name is Francis. One child, that's all."

"One child," Mom repeated. "Francis."

"Very good. Now go to bed. When you wake up in the morning, you will help me prepare for Samhain. You will not resist me any longer. And I want clear skies by morning."

"I will obey," Mom said in a dull voice.

I sat up, shaking. I had to do something. But what? I listened at the door until Mom had gone upstairs to her room, and then I crept into my brother's room.

"Colin, wake up."

He mumbled and rolled over.

"Colin, please. We have to get out of here. She's going to kill you."

His eyes finally opened. "What? Who?"

"Aunt Tamora. She's planning to kill you tomorrow night."

He blinked at me. Then he laughed and turned over. "You really had me going there for a moment, Fran. Nice try."

"But I'm telling the truth."

He sat up and scowled. "Why would she hurt me? She likes me. She's going to buy me a new bike tomorrow."

"She's lying."

"Go away."

He yawned, lay back down, and pulled up the covers.

How could this be happening? I went into the bathroom. The window looked out over the gently sloping roof. If I could get out, I could crawl over the shingles and drop down into the garden. I could run for help.

I pushed up on the window frame, but it refused to budge, so I climbed onto the toilet and put all my strength against it. It didn't move.

I'd have to break the glass. I looked around but couldn't see anything that would deliver a strong enough blow. Finally, I grabbed the plunger from under the sink, shouldered it as if it were a baseball bat, and swung.

The handle bounced off the glass, and I landed hard on the floor. I stared at the window. It should have broken. Why hadn't it? I bashed at it again, with the same result.

"Going somewhere?"

I whirled around, gasping. Aunt Tamora stood in the open doorway.

"Go to bed. Or perhaps you'd rather sleep in the cellar?"

Terror thudded through me. I crept past her, down the hall to my bedroom where I clicked on the small lamp by my bed. My attempts to open my window also failed.

The Cellar

She had won. She had taken over everyone I loved. I flung myself on my bed and cried.

I heard footsteps outside my door. I curled into a ball under my covers and squeezed my eyes shut. Thunder rumbled.

My bedroom door opened and closed. My heart raced.

The bed creaked. I almost screamed.

"Francis?"

I opened my eyes. Mom knelt beside me, her expression alert. A blood-stained towel was wrapped around her arm.

"Mom." I sighed in relief.

Hope filled me. She would pull a strand of white hair from her red curls, and she would wind it around my necklace and sing her song, just like she did every night. The hair would melt into the necklace, and I would feel happy and safe. And in the morning, everything would be back to normal.

But instead, she clutched my hand. Lightning flashed, and thunder shook the house. She put her lips next to my ear.

"I haven't got a lot of time," she whispered, "so listen carefully. Ever since you were born, I've poured all my magic into one thing—hiding you from them. I never taught you magic. I wanted a different life for you children, but she found me."

Mom sobbed.

"I can't get away. She's too strong. It's up to you to rescue us."

I stared at her. "But how?"

She glanced towards the door and turned to me again, speaking rapidly. "None of her spells work on you because you're stronger in magic than she is. You can defeat her. Please, rescue Colin. Get us out of here before it's too late."

"I have magic powers?"

"Look in the cellar. The answers are there." Her eyes were pools of sorrow. "Please forgive me for everything." Rain drummed on the roof.

She kissed me and fled.

Moments later, the floorboards creaked again just outside my bedroom door. I switched off the lamp and dived under the covers.

My doorknob turned, and the door swung open. A musty smell drifted in. My hair stood on end as Aunt Tamora stared at me. Though my heart raced, I kept my eyes closed and my breathing even. Finally, she closed the door, and her footsteps padded down the hallway and stairs.

I couldn't stop shaking. How could I have magic? What did Mom mean? I'd never done a remarkable thing in my life. And how was I supposed to go into the cellar? I could not go down there.

The next morning, sunlight poured into my room from a clear blue sky. I had overslept. Angry at myself, I jumped from my bed and ran into Colin's room.

He was gone.

"No."

I raced downstairs to the kitchen. There were only three place settings at the table.

"Breakfast will be ready in a few minutes. Sit down."

My mother's voice was expressionless. She spooned batter into the frying pan.

"Where is he?" I yelled.

Mom turned to me, a puzzled look on her face. "Where is who, dear?"

"Colin. My brother, your son."

Her face was blank.

"What are you talking about? You're an only child. We weren't able to have any other children."

She turned back to the stove and flipped the pancakes.

"Where's Dad?"

"Your father is gone."

I turned to Aunt Tamora, who sat at the table, smirking.

"No."

I ran through the house, searching and calling my brother's name, but I couldn't find him.

I returned to the kitchen. Mom had set three pancakes on my plate.

"Sit down and eat. Your pancakes are getting cold."

Her eyes were vacant.

I ate only because I needed the strength to escape.

"We have guests coming this afternoon," Aunt Tamora said. "Francis, you will help your mother prepare the house. I want bathrooms cleaned, carpets vacuumed, and all the laundry caught up."

I sucked in a breath. Unless I acted now, Colin would die tonight.

And I knew what I had to do.

I clenched my fists. "Why do I have to do all the work?"

"Don't you understand? You have no magic. Menial labor is all you'll ever be good for. Now get to work."

I scowled at her. "Why can't Colin help?"

"You don't have a brother."

"Liar," I shouted.

She pointed at me and made a circular motion. Her voice was low, dangerous.

"You will be silent. Now."

"I won't. I hate you." I stomped my foot and began to scream. "I hate you. I hate you."

"That's it!" She grabbed me by the hair and pulled me into the laundry room.

She pointed at the floor. "Clear." The dirty clothes and the mat flew to the edges of the room, revealing a trap door.

"Open." The door creaked opened. A damp, putrid smell hit me. I gagged.

"No! No!" I twisted, pummeling her with my fists, but she swung me up and dropped me into the gaping maw.

I tumbled down the four wooden stairs to the bottom. Bruised and sobbing, I crawled back up the stairs, but the trap door had closed again, leaving me in darkness. I screamed and banged and pushed on the door until my hands hurt, but it was no use.

I curled into a ball on the top step and rubbed my necklace. At first all I could hear was the pounding of my heart, and the air rushing in and out of my mouth. From above came the sounds of my mom's footsteps, the vacuum running, the washing machine chugging, and the dryer rumbling.

"Mom? Please, Mommy, let me out."

But she never came.

The sounds ceased.

Everything was quiet. I rubbed my necklace. My legs cramped, and I wondered how long I had been down here. The day passed slowly, and I dozed.

I woke with a start. What was that?

A moan came from somewhere in the dirt cellar, behind the shelving. I shrieked and pressed myself up against the trap door.

And then, a rustling noise, like a thousand insects rushing at me. Just like—

I gasped. *Just like they'd done before.* My memories flooded back. Four years ago, Aunt Tamora and her sisters had come here on Halloween. It had been a full moon, and women in black had invaded the house. Aunt Tamora had sent me into the cellar to get some wine off the shelf, and...

I had seen something down here. Something awful. Thousands of bugs had crawled all over me as I screamed and begged to let me out, but my aunts just laughed. The trap door had stayed closed. And when they finally let me out, Aunt Tamora had pointed at me and commanded. "Forget."

Something crawled on my leg, and I shrieked and flailed my hands. The bugs were coming for me, just like last time.

The light switch! Last time there had been a light switch! I felt along the frame of the trap door and the stairway and found it. But when I flicked it, the bulb was dead.

Then came the sounds of car engines, women's voices, and many footsteps walking back and forth on the wooden floor above my head. The witches were here.

I stared out across the cellar. My eyes were used to the darkness now, and I realized that the cellar wasn't completely dark: a chink of light came from the far dirt wall, where the ground sloped up to meet the underside of the house. I took a deep breath. If I could get over there, I could dig my way out. But first I had to get past what-

ever was down here.
My heart threatened to beat right out of my chest. I had to get out. I had to.
I crept down the stairs. When I got to the bottom, I crouched and reached out to the left. My fingers touched the solid wood of the shelves, some dusty canning jars, and a box. I felt the box all over. It was smooth wood, with a design engraved on the lid. 'The answer is in the cellar,' Mom had said. Could this be it?
I opened the box. Inside, my fingers touched a small pair of scissors and something flat, like paper. What did it mean? What did Mom want me to do?
And I knew.
I reached up and cut the necklace. The silver chain became strands of hair that fell away.
A strange rush of energy surged through my body, like pins and needles after sitting on a foot too long. I gasped. I was on fire.
I twisted my wrist sideways and pointed upwards at the useless lightbulb. "Light."
The bulb began to glow. I stared at it, astonished.
I really did have magic.
I took the second object from the box. It was a photograph of Mom, Dad, me as a baby, and two small boys in front of a decorated tree. I stared at it, then turned it over. "Barry, Margaret, Colin, Kenny, and baby Francis. Christmas."
For a moment all I could do was stare. My throat tightened. I had another brother?
A memory slid into place—me, Colin, and Kenny playing in the yard, happy and carefree. But what had happened to him?
I slid the picture into my jeans pocket. The muddy floor sucked at my feet as I made my way to the end of the storage shelves and looked into the bowl-shaped area beyond.
A large rectangular stone, stained with something dark, sat in the center of the floor. Beyond that, where the ground began to rise, was a half-exposed human skeleton.
And I knew.

"Kenny!"

The witches had murdered my other brother on that stone, and Colin was next.

"No."

My legs felt like overcooked macaroni. I hung onto the shelves and looked behind them. There was Colin, lying motionless. Cockroaches and ants crawled all over him.

I pointed. "Bugs, leave!"

For a few moments the muddy ground writhed, and they were gone.

I ran to him and fell to my knees. "Colin." He didn't move. I took his wrist. His skin was cold, but blood still pulsed within. "Wake up."

His eyelids fluttered, and he looked at me. Two tears rolled down his cheeks.

I put my finger to my lips. "Shhh."

He nodded. I helped him to his feet. He leaned on me as we sloshed through the mud, bending low as the ground sloped upward. We began to dig with our hands.

Above our heads, the wooden floor creaked as the witches walked in a circle. The chanting of a dozen voices and the cloying scent of burning incense drifted down to us, along with the sound of someone sobbing. It stopped.

Aunt Tamora's voice came clearly. "Margaret, I am tired of your sniveling. Get out."

"Please, don't do this. Please."

"You will obey me. You will not interfere. Go to the barn. Sleep."

"I will obey."

A door slammed. The chanting and heavy footsteps resumed.

Another woman spoke. Her words filled me with dread. "It's time to go down and prepare the sacrifice."

Colin and I gasped. Red light illuminated our dirty faces. We dug even faster.

"Let us out," I muttered. The dirt moved before us. The trap door opened. Colin squirmed through the hole, reached back in, and yanked me out.

"Close." The hole filled in.

I looked around. The front porch light shone over the dark yard. We were behind the bushes that grew on the side of the house, right beside a broken drain pipe. Mom was at the far edge of the yard, walking towards the barn.

From the cellar came exclamations of anger.

"They've gotten out somehow," said Aunt Tamora. "Quick, after them. We need the boy."

I faced Colin. "Follow Mom. Dad's in there. Use pain to wake them up. Bite them if you have to. Okay?"

He nodded again and stumbled after Mom. I ran to the edge of the front yard.

Shouts and cursing came from the house, and the door opened. Aunt Tamora stood in the doorway, her eyes fierce, her smile cruel.

I pointed at the door. "Close." It slammed shut.

I motioned to the entire house. "Close. Lock. Let no one in or out forever more."

She appeared in the window. Her face contorted with rage as she banged on the glass "Francis!"

I pointed, twisted my wrist, and let all my grief and hatred pour through me as I spoke one word.

"Burn."

The house burst into flames. Smoke billowed, and huge flames clawed the air. The witches screamed as they beat against the doors and windows, but they couldn't get out. I watched the inferno and listened until their howls were silenced.

Dad, Mom, and Colin met me at the barn door. We clung to each other and wept. Dad grabbed his car keys from the workbench, and we drove away. A siren wailed in the distance.

It was over. None of us would ever be the same, but it was over.

Carol Nicolas

Carol Nicolas is the author of *The Sixth Power*, a YA paranormal fantasy novel, and *Double Play: A Novel of Magic*, a YA urban fantasy novel. Her short story, "A Little Magic," won first place in the Short Genre Fiction category in the 2015 League of Utah Writers Creative Writing Contest. She is a member of LUW, SCBWI, and ACFW. "The Cellar" is her first horror story.

Baby of the Lake
by Terra Luft

Tegan awoke with a gasp as icy water hit her below the curve of her swollen belly. Clutching herself, she struggled through the sluggishness of retreating sleep. She hadn't sleepwalked in years, not since the night before her last college finals. The stress of pregnancy must have triggered it again. Or the nightmares.

Standing hip-deep in water, mud grabbing at her shoes from the bottom of the lake, she shivered, hands going numb where the water lapped over her belly. She couldn't feel her toes. How had she gotten this deep without registering the frigid water until now?

What have I done? she berated herself, sloshing toward the beach as the first light of dawn peeked over the Wasatch Mountains.

Her mind flashed a vividly detailed parade of seven months of recurring nightmares like a highlight reel—the baby swept up by a tsunami, swallowed by a river of alligators while she stood by, helpless to stop it. Her child pleading with wide eyes for her to help. Worse, someone grabbing her child and disappearing down a crowded street while she struggled, unable to give chase. Now she'd put herself in harm's way risking the life she had growing inside her. The life she and Chad had struggled for years to make.

She pushed the images away, willing the bile back down her throat. She needed to scream like she needed to breathe, but she resisted, focusing instead on splashing and struggled back toward shore. It was only water, but it felt like walking through quicksand. Why was it so hard to breathe? The air was thick and oppressive even though there was a chill to the early morning air. Water dripping, clothes clinging, she reached the shore.

Taking a slow, deep breath, she fought for calmness. Pausing, eyes closed, she imagined holding her bundled baby, fixating on the visualization like a mantra. She couldn't—no, wouldn't—lose another pregnancy. This one was different.

Sloshing and collecting mud on the sandals she didn't remember slipping on, she clomped toward her Jeep parked a short distance away.

She stopped short. She'd driven here. Asleep.

What if she'd plowed into an oncoming car on the Interstate? It wasn't a few blocks back to her house in Lake Point, it was a few miles. She could have killed them both, leaving Chad to—

No. She pushed the images from her mind. She was not the first sleepwalker to drive. She just needed more sleep, so it didn't happen again. She'd call her doctor and ask about sleeping medications.

The stench of rotten eggs and brine assaulted her sensitive nose. Damn it, she'd ruined her favorite yoga pants. She couldn't bring herself to abandon them on the shore. She hoped the wind from the convertible top would eliminate the odor enough to get home without vomiting. If she was wrong, the image of herself pulled over, leaning out the door, made her grateful she didn't sleep naked or scantily clad.

Chad would be home from his shift soon. She had to get there first and work out an explanation for her soggy clothes on the way. She could worry enough for the both of them, figure out the sleepwalking problem, then tell him once it was solved and behind her.

The expanse of the lake caught her eye as she opened the door. Nestled along the base of the rising mountains to the west, sunrise-painted clouds of pinks and oranges were reflected on its placid surface. It was as beautiful as she always thought when she'd come here to jog or walk along the shore.

It was the majestic scenery and her malfunctioning subconscious that had brought her here, not some unexplained force that had been pulling her to the lake the past few weeks. Sleepwalking was the only logical explanation.

With shaking hands she gripped the steering wheel for leverage and hauled herself up. She reached for her keys still dangling from the ignition, wet toes squishing in her sandals as she depressed the clutch.

She focused on the road, her knuckles white with the effort of keeping a grip over her emotions. She hated knowing she had lost control, even if she'd been unconscious at the time.

What if she had drowned instead of waking up or the cold water had harmed her precious baby?

What if it happened again?

Instead of spiraling into the abyss, she'd call Mom as soon as she got home and cleaned up. They could work it out together.

A freight-train of emotion hit her. Mom was dead. She couldn't come. She would never come again. How had Tegan forgotten, even for a second?

She pulled into the driveway, fighting to focus through the blur that had become the windshield. She lowered her head and allowed herself to be carried away like a leaf caught in a river.

Her car door whipped open. "Tegan! What's wrong? What happened?" Chad's voice was full of fear.

She lifted her head.

"I need my mom." It was all she could say, voice breaking.

"Why are you in the car?" he said, reaching for her. "Why are you wet?"

Shit. She had no explanation, her plans to spare him from worry forgotten in her grief.

"I woke up in the lake. I must have been sleepwalking." The truth gushed from her.

"How'd you get there?" She heard only accusation in his voice.

"You think I know?" she shouted, tears spraying from her lips, saltiness on her tongue.

"Shhh. Let's get you inside. You know stress isn't good for you or the baby."

She wrapped her arms around him, burying her face in his neck. His comforting strength lifted her and her belly past the steering wheel.

Damn hormones. Of course he didn't blame her; those were her own insecurities.

She wouldn't blame him if he did.

* * *

Face inches from the mirror, mouth open to apply mascara, Tegan's mind wandered ticking through her list of things to do today. The silence of the house soon had her dwelling on yesterday's sleepwalking.

The clatter of bottles and cans hitting the counter jerked her back to the present. Chad, home from the grocery store. How long had she been standing there, staring into the mirror?

Relief that he'd taken this small burden from her this week mixed with mild anxiety. He'd left without waiting for the meticulously crafted list she derived from her weekly meal plan, arguing he would just 'get it done' and they'd grab whatever he missed later.

Which meant she'd have to go back when the jerky and chips were gone.

"I'm home. Come help?" he called from the kitchen.

On her way past the window, she glimpsed their elderly neighbor, Gloria, lurking next door in her yard.

Was she looking at our house? she wondered as she joined Chad and his grocery chaos in the kitchen.

"Did you get my cereal?" she asked, rooting through the reusable bags.

"Damn. I knew I was forgetting something." He paused, soup can in hand, face scrunched in apology.

"The *one* thing I crave and you forgot it?" She sighed, continuing to empty bags onto the table, making mental adjustments to this week's menu.

"Sorry, babe, I missed that aisle when I was distracted by the small-town weirdness. I'll go back, I promise." He handed her a block of cheese to put in the refrigerator behind her.

"What'd you see? I'm still winning with stop-mid-checkout-to-smell-my-laundry-softener last week." Her irritation over the cereal vanished with their competition to find the quirkiest thing about Lake Point.

"There were a bunch of women talking, blocking the aisle with their carts. I had to stand there forever before they noticed and moved so I could get by."

"Not new, happens to me all the time. Still winning!" she said, slamming the refrigerator door harder than she meant to. Sometimes she was too competitive.

"That wasn't the weirdness. I swear they were talking about you," he said, stacking tins of smoked oysters on the table.

"Me?" There was a lump in her throat, which she pretended was because of the oysters.

"Yeah, I heard 'the lake' and one of them said 'warn them before she loses it like the rest.'"

Her face grew hot. She grabbed the crackers—an excuse to turn away from him. The sleepwalking scared her enough; she didn't want Chad worried about it, too.

"You just want to win. We're not significant enough to be the talk of the town," she said, reaching into the cupboard, hoping he bought her nonchalance.

"When they noticed me, one of them jumped like I'd goosed her. Another one followed me around the store like she was trying to approach me. Felt like I was in a meat market."

"Were you in the meat section?" she asked, turning back to wiggle her eyebrows at him. She couldn't resist a good joke, and it helped to lighten the mood.

He laughed, but didn't take the bait. "Why would a group of

strangers be talking about us losing our baby?"

"Good question. Logical answer: they wouldn't be. You're just paranoid," she said, putting the large bag of peppered jerky in the cupboard next to the corn chips. She rubbed her belly. *Your daddy is so predictable.*

"I know what I heard. Don't drink the water here; something in it causes small-town mentality," he said, looking up at her intently.

"I don't think small-town is something you catch." She lifted an eyebrow and took the spaghetti noodles from him.

"Let's hope not!" he scoffed.

"They say that about pregnancy, too, but I've still never seen another pregnant woman in town," she mused. Everywhere else she went, she saw pregnant women. But not here in Lake Point.

"Me neither. It's weird," he said, digging at the bottom of another bag.

"Shit! I'm late," she said, noticing the wall clock behind him.

"Late for what?" he said, looking up.

"The doctor, remember?"

"Right. Want me to drive you?"

"No, I'll be late for sure," she teased, slipping her moccasins over swollen feet and grabbing her purse by the door.

"Drive careful," he said, bending to her belly. "Keep Mommy safe, little bean."

"It sucks I couldn't find an OB closer than Salt Lake," she said, pausing to kiss his soft lips. "*That's* small-town mentality: not thinking it's weird to 'go to town' for everything. An hour drive, each way, is total bullshit," she said over her shoulder as she left.

Gloria was still outside, peeking over the hedge that separated their driveway from her yard. Great. She didn't have time to chat over the hedge.

Pretending she hadn't noticed her, Tegan made her way to the car, wishing for the anonymity of an attached garage. It wasn't the first time she'd wished it. Digging in her purse for keys she knew exactly where to find, she avoided making eye contact. She'd make a lousy actress.

Once there, she turned the corner and glanced up a second too soon. Eye contact established, Gloria raised a gnarled hand, silver hair flying in wisps around her face.

"Hi, Gloria! I'm late for the doctor, so I can't chat," Tegan called out in her friendliest voice, concentrating on pulling her girth up behind the wheel.

"I saw you come home yesterday all wet. It lured you there, didn't it?" Gloria called out.

At least she knew how they'd been talking about her lake escapade in the store today. How would Tegan ever get used to small-town living? The wind blew the leaves in the trees, sounding like a whisper.

"I was sleepwalking is all, nothing serious," she said, shutting the door between them. Gloria's mention of the lake mixing with her imagination raised gooseflesh on her arm.

She pulled out and headed for Salt Lake, her strange neighbor in the rearview mirror watching her from the sidewalk. Gloria's words echoed in her memory, an ominous weight behind them she couldn't explain.

* * *

Tegan crawled into bed and commenced her ritual of arranging the seven pillows into their strategic locations under her head, between her knees, under her giant belly, at her back, and cradled in her arms. It had taken her weeks to perfect this setup, which promised maximum relief from the aches and pains of pregnancy.

Until she had to relieve her tiny bladder or a nightmare woke her.

She was not avoiding going to sleep, she told herself for the tenth time tonight.

She shifted her weight and imagined her body back to normal, her baby in her arms instead of compressing her internal organs. How anyone decided to endure pregnancy multiple times was beyond her. Being pregnant dozens of times didn't count since she'd never made it this far before.

"Can I get you anything?" Chad asked, leaning on the doorjamb, beer in hand.

"Lie down and snuggle for a few minutes until I fall asleep?" she answered like always when he was home. The worst thing about his night shift was being on different sleep schedules. She hated sleeping alone.

"Don't I always?" he said. The mattress shifted as he laid back against his own pillows.

Tegan nestled her head into the hollow of his shoulder. Their bodies fit perfectly, even with the growing life and the pillows between them. She loved to fall asleep like this almost as much as she hated waking alone in the night to a cold empty bed.

"Love you," she murmured, the exertions of the day drifting her toward sleep.

"Love you, too," he said, kissing her forehead.

Seconds later, she jerked awake, lying on her back. Both arms were bent at the elbow, hands above her head, the pillows scattered. The nightmare retreated swiftly.

She rolled over; even sleepy she remembered the no-no of lying on her back during pregnancy.

She couldn't move.

She was awake, wide awake, but she couldn't open her eyes or move her limbs, struggling to do both. She was aware of her surroundings, the red glow of the numbers on her alarm clock behind her eyelids.

She tried to call out, but she couldn't open her mouth. The hair on the back of her neck rose, and her face tingled. Why did this pregnancy come with so many nightmares?

An invisible force weighed down her hands. She struggled, but every muscle refused to respond as if she were an insect stuck in amber.

Not this, please. This was worse than a nightmare.

She screamed. She heard it in her head, but her lips refused to part. It was like someone had forced her jaw open and shoved handfuls of cotton halfway down her throat then sealed her lips. She screamed again, harder this time. The scream echoed inside her head, but nothing escaped her lips.

Knowing it was futile didn't stop her from screaming over and over again, hoping some tiny sound would escape and draw attention to her struggles.

Where was Chad? Why couldn't he sense that she needed him?

Exhausted from her efforts, she surrendered to the force controlling her body and lay there, anticipating the violence she knew approached.

The baby kicked with enough force to bruise her ribs, possibly crack them. The pain knocked her free of the invisible bonds holding her. She cried out, sitting up in agony, hands protective on her belly.

"What's wrong?" Chad called as he rushed into the room and gathered her into his arms.

She couldn't make a sound besides huge gasping sobs. Her baby had saved her. She hadn't imagined it. Still cradling her womb, she vowed to figure out what was happening and put a stop to it. She would protect her baby at all costs.

* * *

The wind rattled the ragtop of the Jeep. By the looks of the dark sky, she wasn't sure she could beat the storm home. Tegan rounded the corner approaching the house. She didn't recognize anything amiss until she started breaking for the turn into her driveway.

That's when she saw them.

She slammed both feet down—brakes and clutch. The Jeep jumped the curb, her scream longer than the skid. The Jeep stopped halfway in the drive, still facing the tree that dominated the center of their yard, front wheel in the grass.

Naked babies hung from the maple.

So many dolls. Plastic, not flesh. Swinging by their necks with the gentle motion of the branches. Black Xs through their eyes.

She searched down both sides of the empty street, expecting to see kids watching for her reaction. What was it Gloria had said the other day about something luring her to the lake? The whispers behind her back were possible to ignore; women everywhere gossiped.

She had explained away the macabre parade of dismembered mice and birds on the back stoop: a cat whose owners had moved on and left it behind. The patterns she'd seen in the entrails were her imagination at work, nothing more.

This though, this was sinister and not easily dismissed with rational explanation. She wanted to run far away.

Keeping her eyes averted and her back to the tree, she made her way to the front door, shoulder blades tingling with the weight of eyes watching from all directions.

Once safely inside, she called out to Chad, voice cracking. He would have just gotten up at this time of the afternoon.

"In here," he answered from the office down the hall.

"Have you seen the front yard?" she said, voice still quivering.

He walked toward her, wearing only basketball shorts.

"Not since I got up, why?" His expression changed to concern the closer he got. "What's wrong?"

"Someone hung dead babies in the maple," she gasped, tears spilling down as the iron grip on her emotions crumbled.

"What the hell are you talking about?" He rushed past her toward the door, neck craning to see out the front windows on his way.

"Not real ones, dolls," she said, voice shaking to match her insides.

"Who the fuck would do that!" he said, slamming the door open against the wall.

The pile of plastic grew as he raged—leaves ripping, branches shaking as he pulled them all free.

"Who would've thought of that?" she said to herself, staring off into space. Was this what being in shock felt like?

Time stood still.

Where are the babies?

She was in his arms, his scent in her nose, not sure how or when she'd gotten there.

"Just a sick joke . . . gonna be okay," he murmured. His gentle rocking matched the rhythm of his hands rubbing her back. Their baby stirred inside her womb. She knew better. It was evil that haunted her.

* * *

"Hello," a voice called, startling Tegan. She'd been sitting there on the back patio, staring over the rim of her mug long enough her morning chai had gone cold.

Gloria's head peeked over the gate separating the house from the garage. She was the last person Tegan wanted to see after a sleepless night.

Gloria had said evil was stalking her before she'd known it herself. Maybe it was time to find out what Gloria knew.

"Hi, Gloria," she said, putting on her welcoming face instead of the default dismissal ready on the back of her tongue. She rubbed her burning eyes, wishing she had slept.

"I saw you out here alone, thought you'd want some company," Gloria said, waiting for an invitation.

"Sure, come on back," Tegan said, sounding as plastic as her smile felt.

Gloria lumbered toward her on a dragging hip, wearing her signature house robe, hair loose around her face, shoulders stooped. The years had not been kind to her. Tegan wondered how she'd come to live alone next door.

Did Gloria wonder how Tegan ended up here? Her thoughts were jumbled and random from the lack of sleep.

"I brought you a little something," Gloria said, lowering herself into the opposite bistro chair. She reached across and laid a small satchel next to Tegan's forearm.

The contents shifted, a pungent smell hitting her sensitive nose as she picked it up. She cringed, catching herself before outright disgust painted her face.

"What is it?" she asked, fingering the rough burlap full of questionable contents.

"I know it doesn't smell pretty, but hang it on your door. To keep evil spirits out. Made it myself."

"What if they're already inside?" she murmured before she could stop herself.

"I'm too late?"

The fear Tegan fought to keep at bay was reflected back across the table in Gloria's own eyes.

"I need to know what I'm dealing with. Do you have facts or just old wives' tales?" Even to her own ears her voice stung with curtness, but Gloria didn't flinch.

"Firsthand knowledge, dear." Gloria stared back, her voice hard.

"Tell me?" Tegan pleaded.

"Folks call it the Baby of the Lake because it drowns pregnant women. Usually *in* the lake."

The words were everyday ones, but strung together they sounded surreal. Like someone playing a joke on her.

"I don't want small-town superstition. I want facts. Why and how does it do this?"

She sat up, leaning closer to Gloria until her bulging belly nudged the table.

"It began in the nineteen-fifties when women had few options. A local woman in the family way with no husband searched out a discreet midwife willing to help her out of it."

"Abortion was still illegal?"

"Yes, although it still happened. It didn't always go smoothly. Iris was desperate, and when her aborted baby cried out in the night, she was horrified."

"How do you know this?"

"My mother was the midwife," Gloria said.

"Oh," Tegan said, words failing her.

"Mother was overcome, talking about how it was God's will that the baby live, while Iris screamed for her to kill it. Our house sat at the edge of the lake so no one could hear her, but I'll never forget trying to block my ears from the shrill cries. Iris snatched the still bloody baby while Mother's back was turned and fled. Mother tried to stop her, but Iris drowned it in the lake—a baby so determined to live that it had survived its own abortion."

"My God," Tegan whispered. How could someone take the life of her own child like that? Even an unwanted pregnancy? Her hand rested protectively on her belly.

A baby cried in the distance. Tegan turned toward the sound, the hair on the back of her neck raised.

"Did you hear that?" she asked Gloria.

"The baby's been haunting pregnant women, luring them to their deaths in the lake," Gloria continued as if she hadn't heard the question.

"There it is again," Tegan said. "A baby crying. It sounds like it's next door."

"I don't hear anything," Gloria said, leveling her eyes at Tegan. "And there haven't been any babies born around here in decades."

"Then why do I hear a baby crying?" She tried hard not to scream at Gloria who calmly sat there telling her of an evil she didn't know how to protect herself or her child from.

"Because it's coming for you and your baby now. Let me help you."

"How?"

She'd do anything to save her baby.

* * *

Candles flickered, their soft glow bathing Tegan as the warm water lapped at the base of her neck, soaking the tension from her shoulders. She would never regret the cost of the oversize tub. Her belly rose from the water like a flesh-colored island, the skin stretched taut enough she'd lost all evidence of a belly button. The baby was soothed by the bath, giving her a break from the usual kicking and somersaults.

Tegan closed her eyes, mind drifting away on the waves of cinnamon and mulled spice from the candles. Given enough time she could drift off to sleep, but she didn't want that. Too many nightmares. She wanted a nice soak and ten minutes of thinking about nothing.

Gloria's voice invaded her thoughts, details swirling and mixing with the soothing odors filling her senses.

What Gloria had proposed was both fascinating and frightening. It felt like the only answer but she wasn't sure she could go through with it.

She refused to lose this baby. She already endured a yearly parade of anniversaries etched into her heart marking the others they'd lost.

A pain started low in her groin. She dismissed it to the back of her mind where all the other aches and pains of late pregnancy went. Everything hurt now; what was a little more?

It might be a contraction though. What if it was preterm labor?

Every thought was banished as a sharp and twisting stab of pain hit her. Her womb clenched.

She splashed half the water onto the floor with the force of her hulk rising. Crying out, she bent at the waist, expecting to see blood in the water as her insides were ripped free. There was none but she couldn't focus enough to feel relief.

Chad was working.

She was alone.

Belly hard as a rock, knees bent, she clutched her shins, bracing herself against waves of pain worse than she'd ever experienced. Insides twisting and clenching, invisible hands wrung out her womb like a wet rag.

A scream tore free from her throat. Her back arched as a vise grip tightened down on her abdomen.

Unseen hands pushed against both shoulders, forcing her onto her back again. Clawing against the slick porcelain sides of the tub, she managed only to knock the candles over into the water, plunging the room into darkness. She was blind.

Her scream was choked off, her face forced under. The world changed. Sounds became surreal, echoing and quiet.

What do you want from me she screamed in her mind.

I want to live. Let me be your baby, answered a writhing darkness beyond her sight.

She sat up like a shot, spluttering and coughing, sucking in great gasps of air. Had the shock given her a boost of strength to fight back or had the consciousness she'd felt chosen to depart after answering her question?

The pain was gone, too.

What remained was an echo of a connection to that darkness, like the afterimage when looking at the sun.

Her mind raced ahead, making connections she fought against. The ghost wasn't trying to punish pregnant women for its mother's sins; it was trying to get a real chance at the life that had been stolen from it.

Tegan would lose her life or her baby. Perhaps both. The power she'd felt tonight proved that much. What if the ghost became her baby like it wanted? What kind of a child would it be, and could she live with that?

Gloria's proposal, the one she'd dismissed as lunacy but couldn't stop thinking about, took on a new perspective. Maybe there was a way to save both herself and her baby.

* * *

"Tonight is the last night of the full moon," Gloria said from across the kitchen table.

"I'm still not sure I can go through with it." Tegan elevated her swollen feet to the kitchen chair next to her. She busied herself with her mug of tea, unable to meet Gloria's eyes.

"We've been over this. You're being childish."

"I still have a few weeks to find another way." She sounded like a whiney child to her own ears.

"Sure you do. Plenty of time to drown in your tub or back at the lake."

Gloria did have a point. But witchcraft? If Chad knew what she was contemplating he would lock her inside at night when he went to work and take the key. Her logical mind knew her hesitation was a left-over objection rooted in the religious upbringing she'd rejected once old enough to make her own decisions.

"How do you know it will work?" She looked up, swallowing the lump in her throat.

"How do you know it won't? I'm not willing to sit here and watch you lose your baby when I know I can save it." The vehemence in Gloria's voice startled Tegan.

"You're the only friend I have in this town."

Gloria reached across the table and took Tegan's hand in her gnarled one. "I know, dear. The rest are just scared, that's all."

"I wish my mom were here; she'd know what to do," Tegan whispered.

"She'd tell you to listen to me; I know she would," Gloria said, patting her hand.

She decided it was better to have tried and failed than to sit and wait and hope she survived the next attack.

* * *

Tegan parked at the edge of the lake. The stench hit her nose, just like the morning she thought she'd gone sleepwalking.

A weight settled into her as she thought about what she was undertaking and what would happen if she failed.

Gloria, sitting next to her in the front seat, said nothing. Moonlight reflected off the water creating a beautiful scene, but looks deceived. Tegan ran through the plan once more, steeling herself to go through with it.

"Now or never," Gloria said finally, turning to Tegan.

She was right; time to save her baby. Tegan half climbed, half fell out of the Jeep. Everything was harder to do the closer she got to full-term. She walked around the car to help Gloria down. On her way past the backseat, she grabbed the bag of supplies they'd spent the afternoon gathering.

Together, they walked to the lapping shore in silence.

She stopped, dropping the bag onto the crusty sand. The sound echoed over the water in the stillness. Deep in her gut, she knew this was the spot.

She was starting to sound like Gloria.

"We should set up the circle here," Gloria said, handing two of the candles to her and pointing in two general directions.

Tegan walked looking for level spots in the hard sand. Unseen eyes watched them, burning holes in her back. She fought the urge to look behind her. Once she was sure both candles were not going to fall over, she returned to Gloria who was setting up the rest of their supplies.

"I've only ever seen a séance on TV," Tegan said softly, as if someone would overhear.

"Ready?" Gloria whispered back, holding out the long wooden stick from Chad's shed.

She nodded.

Gloria took Tegan's free hand. For balance or support, Tegan didn't know.

They walked in a circle, Tegan dragging the stick jammed deep into the hardened sand behind her, Gloria dragging her foot. They lit each candle they came to in silence, starting with the northernmost one, closest to the water's edge. The line formed by the stick was squiggly from her efforts and her shaking.

Once the circle was finished, they returned to the center.

"I'm glad there's no wind to blow out the candles," Gloria whispered.

Tegan said nothing. She didn't want Gloria to hear her voice crack. Instead, she reached for Gloria's other hand, forming a smaller circle inside the one they'd drawn in the sand. She hoped it would be enough to protect them.

Gloria squeezed both hands, and Tegan met her eyes. Gloria's determination and courage flowed into her. She joined it with her own, bracing herself for what was to come.

"We summon the one they call the Baby of the Lake," Gloria shouted, raising her face toward the sky. "Come to us here in this protected circle." The words floated away over the stillness of the water.

A gust of air hit them from above, filling the circle with a swirling tempest of wind. Tegan glanced at the candles through her whipping hair. They weren't even flickering. How was that possible?

Have you come offering a sacrifice? the wind howled, the voice echoing in Tegan's head. A voice she recognized.

"With conditions," she shouted back before Gloria could say anything.

Darkness shifted, enveloping her. Gloria, the lake, even the candles disappeared. She heard nothing but the voice on the wind.

No bargains! Give me what I want, and I'll let you live, the wind howled back.

"No possessing my baby." She didn't even know the gender of the precious life she was bargaining for. They'd been content knowing their baby was healthy.

I must live, the howling voice answered.

Not if I can help it, Tegan thought to herself, the weight of the knife in her sweater pocket like a talisman.

"Only by becoming my child completely—live as my child—and never harm another soul," she shouted. This was the only way she would do it.

Agreed. This time a whisper on the wind hungry with desire.

"Agreed," Tegan echoed softly, the sound lost in the wind.

Reality crashed back around her; she was back in the circle.

She opened herself willingly to the darkness, surrendering her defenses.

"No!" Gloria shouted, breaking the circle, eyes wild. "The circle will hold, I promise!"

Tegan hadn't told Gloria of her own plan conceived from the knowledge that the spell to banish an object or an entity couldn't be spoken by the person holding it. She had to be sure, had to have the evil inside her.

"It's done," Tegan said, tears spilling down her cheeks. "I'm sorry, baby," she whispered, cradling her womb. "Mommy loves you."

The wind hit her full force, knocking Gloria away. Tegan screamed as the tempest consumed her, breath replaced with wind. Her insides clenched, and she dropped to her knees, the pain too much to bear.

The nightmare she'd felt before whispered in her mind, overwhelming her senses as it consumed her.

Hello, Mommy. The voice inside her head now bypassing her ears.

Ethereal tentacles slithered down her spine, snaking around her womb. Her child kicked. Hard. Fighting.

Tegan's hand shook as she raised the knife to her throat, the pointed end of the blade digging into her neck above her artery. She was far enough along the baby could live without her. She clung to that fact for comfort in case Gloria's plan failed. She would not let her baby be taken.

"Now, Gloria!" she screamed. *Please let this work.*

Over the sound of the wind, Gloria's voice rang out.

"Ashes to Ashes,
Dust to Dust,
I banish this spirit
From its vessel.
Forever incapable
Of harming another.
Gone from this plane
Forevermore."

With the last word of the spell the wind ceased.

With shaking hands, Tegan lowered the knife from her throat and dropped it. She collapsed onto all fours in the sand, alone again with her unborn child.

"That was foolish and reckless," Gloria scolded.

"I had to be sure," she said. "It was the only way."

"You never invite such evil to enter your body willingly!"

With Gloria' support, Tegan rose slowly to her feet, reveling in the peace that surrounded her for the first time since moving to Lake Point.

"It doesn't matter now; we did it." She grinned, cradling Gloria's face in her hands.

"We shall see."

Gloria turned her back and walked away.

Terra Luft

Terra Luft is a speculative fiction author and prolific blogger. An overachiever by nature, she tackles every project with coffee and sarcasm and believes all rules exist to be broken. She works full-time by day and writes by night, always searching for that ever-elusive work-life balance people tell her exists. A member of the Horror Writers Association and a founding member of The United Authors Association, she lives in Utah with her husband, two daughters, their naughty dog, and a cat who stole her heart. www.terraluft.com

Henry
by E.J. Harker

Bear saw a foot come into the water and he reached for it. *That was odd*, Bear thought. He sat back down on the bottom of the lake and considered it. Over his many days, and he felt he had lived for many, many days, he had wanted things and reached for things before, but his paw had never responded. He looked at it. He felt his head tilt down to see it better. *Odd*.

Maybe it had something to do with the water. Maybe being submerged in this nasty, salty, bacteria-ridden water somehow made it possible for him to reach.

He reached toward the foot again, and his whole body drifted forward in the water. He was moving too fast, past the foot, and scrambled to catch it. Four sharp claws emerged from his paw and scraped across the foot leaving four perfect red lines across it. The foot immediately disappeared out of the water.

Bear floated in the water a little ways and sat back down on the sand beneath the surface. Claws. He certainly had never had claws before. He tilted his head again to see his paw more closely. No claws. He shook his paw, trying to set them free again, but no luck. Before he could think of a way to release his claws again, a hand wrapped itself around his middle and hoisted him up and out of the water.

"Tommy, what is it?" a voice shouted from a few feet away.

"It's a bear," the voice belonging to the hand replied.

"A real bear?"

"No, idiot, a stuffed bear. What would a real bear be doing in the Great Salt Lake?"

"What kind of stuffed bear scratches your foot like that?"

"I dunno."

Two hands felt him all over. Pushed at his paws, his tummy, his nose, his ears. Pushed and found nothing sharp.

"I guess he didn't do it. He's kind of cool. Maybe I'll keep him."

"Keep him? He's soaking wet and... and... he's green! And he smells funny. He's all covered in salt. Gross!"

"Maybe I can clean him up a little. Turn his fur back to yellow."

"There's writing on him. Did you see it?"

Bear was turned unceremoniously upside down. He was facing the water. He felt afraid.

"Brianne Alcott. 1408 Redford Drive, Park City, Utah, 84060. I know where that is. Maybe an hour's drive? Maybe my mom would take me."

"To return a slimy, green bear to some girl you don't even know? Don't you have anything better to do with your life?"

"Maybe she's pretty. Maybe she would be grateful. Maybe there's a reward."

"Depends."

"On what?"

"Did you ever stop to think that maybe she left it here on purpose?"

Bear was twisted right side up. He was eye to eye with a boy with green eyes and sandy colored hair. He had freckles all across the bridge of his nose. They stared at each other for another moment. Then the boy turned and walked out of the water to his towel on the sand. He placed Bear gently on the corner, sitting up, so he could watch the boys play in the water. Bear knew the boy meant well, but he didn't want to look at the water. He never wanted to see that water again. It made him afraid.

In the distance, Bear saw the wall of rock rising up out of the lake. It seemed to Bear that it had something to do with a train, but that didn't make any sense. The stuffing in his head was so wet, he couldn't think straight. At least he was away from there. Bear didn't know exactly what, but he knew bad things happened there.

Bear felt the water running out of him. He didn't know if his ability to reach would be gone when the water was gone, but he knew he would feel better when he was all dried out. The thought that he had been left behind on purpose started to spin through the stuffing in his head. He hadn't considered it before and didn't like it. Not one little bit.

Someone left me here to die! To be torn apart for fish food! Bear thought.

"There are no fish in the Great Salt Lake. Only little shrimp, and they can't hurt you."

What was that?

Bear looked all around himself, but didn't see anyone nearby that could be talking to him.

Was it a voice? A thought? Where did it come from?

"Who's there?" Bear whispered.

The sound of his own voice made him jump. He had never heard it before.

A giggle started that brought to mind the sound of rain hitting the lake. Bear didn't like it.

"I am here!" the voice said. "I am your friend."

"Who are you?" Bear asked.

"I am the Spirit of the Great Salt Lake. But you can call me Henry."

"Where are you, Henry?"

"Well, I am here with you, silly ol' Bear."

"But I can't see you. Are you hiding?"

"I'm not hiding." The giggle again. "I am a spirit. Spirits are invisible. Everyone knows that."

Henry

"Yes, of course," said Bear. He tugged at the bottom of his red shirt, "Of course, everyone knows that."

"I have lived here since the railroad tracks were laid through the lake in 1903. Sometimes I get lonely, so I make new friends. Today, I made you! I gave you your reach, your claws, your voice, and your teeth."

"Thank you, Spirit. I mean, Henry." Then Bear thought about it and added, "Teeth? I have teeth?"

Laughter again. "Of course you have teeth! Now that you're a you instead of an it, you're going to get hungry. You will need teeth to eat, unless you plan on eating porridge for the rest of your existence."

Bear felt around in his mouth for teeth, but didn't find any. Maybe like his claws they would appear when he needed them.

"I've never had porridge. Is it good?" Bear asked.

"You are a Bear. Bears eat meat. The fresher, the better."

The two boys came out of the water towards their towels on the sand. Bear went still. He wasn't ready for the boys to know he could reach yet.

"I'm gonna run down to the parking lot for a minute," Tommy said.

"What for?"

"I need to go."

"Go in the lake."

"No, I need to *go*."

"So what?"

"You're disgusting. We start eighth grade in a couple weeks. My mom said we should start acting like grown-ups. Set an example for the younger kids."

"You think grown-ups don't *go* in the lake?"

Tommy sighed. "Whatever. I'll be back in a minute."

The boy with the sandy brown hair and the freckles on his nose jogged down the path and disappeared behind the dunes.

The disgusting kid lay back on his towel and picked up Bear. He had black hair and his face was deeply tanned. He had bad breath, though, and Bear did not like being this close to him.

"You are one ugly bear," the boy said. "Maybe I should just throw you back in and tell Tommy you disappeared. He doesn't need to be worrying about getting you back to that girl."

Bear started to shake. He couldn't help it. He was very afraid of going back into the lake, of being left all alone in the water. There was something else in the lake. Something scary.

"What the…" the boy said, sitting up, "Do you have batteries or something?"

Bear felt deep jabs in his back and tummy as the boy searched for a hidden compartment of batteries. A deep rumble came from Bear's tummy. Somehow the jabs made him hungry.

The boy stared at Bear trying to comprehend what was happening. "Dude, what *are* you?"

"I am a frightened bear. And I am hungry," Bear said quietly.

The boy jumped to his feet holding Bear at arms' length. They stared at each other with curiosity and terror. The boy's head moved back and forth, as if he were arguing with himself. A look of resolve came over his face, and he cocked his arm back to throw Bear into the lake.

Bear instinctively reached for the boy's wrist. He wrapped both paws around it and dug in with his claws to hold on. The boy pulled his arm back in front of his face and stared slack-jawed. He was no longer holding onto Bear, but Bear was holding onto him. Blood ran between Bear's paws. The boy paled at the sight of it, but remained on his feet. He shook his hand hard in an attempt to dislodge Bear, but Bear held tight. The boy shook harder, and Bear began to slip. The boy looked around for something to pry the green bear from his arm. Bear flipped around on the boy's arm so he could wrap his back claws around the arm, too.

The smell of the boy's blood filled Bear's nose. His stomach gave another deep rumble. He felt teeth grow in his mouth, long and sharp. He knew he had to eat, and there really wasn't anything else around for miles. Bear's eyes rolled up to whites, his jaws opened, and he clamped onto the boy's hand.

Henry

The boy screamed twice and sat down hard on his towel. He watched the blood pour from his wrist where his hand had been just a moment ago. He fainted.

Bear savored the boy meat in his mouth. It was sweet and moist, and he chewed it slowly. The boy was not fighting anymore, so Bear relaxed. He released his claws from the wrist and arm, climbed up onto the boy's chest, and sat down to consider what part would be best to eat next.

* * *

Storm clouds gathered over the lake as Tommy jogged back toward his friend.

"Hey, Dylan. Do you want to go back to my house and play Call of…"

Tommy stopped when their towels came into view. He saw a lump lying in the middle of Dylan's towel. It had one arm, but the hand was missing. It had no legs and not much of a face. The middle of it was wet and torn, and it was covered in shreds of Dylan's prized Metallica t-shirt.

It was a trick. It had to be. Dylan was going to pop-up from somewhere, laughing his butt off and tease Tommy for being such a wuss.

Tommy looked up and down the beach, but there was nowhere Dylan could be hiding.

He looked closer. There were no footprints in the sand, nothing coming or going from the lake, nothing coming or going to the towels, nothing but their own tracks.

But there was blood. Strings of it in the sand all around the towels. And a small pool of it just beside Dylan's towel.

The thing on the towel took a final, shuddering breath.

The bile rose quickly up the back of his throat, and Tommy ejected everything he had eaten that day.

He ran as fast as he could toward his own towel. He skidded on his knees the last two feet, making sure he didn't look at the lump.

He pulled his backpack over and dug out his phone. He thought about dialing 9-1-1, but he was afraid they would dismiss him. He called his mom, talking fast.

"Dylan's dead. I don't know what happened…you have to come. Call an ambulance. They can't…there's nothing…I don't know where we are…you have to do it…just call them…make them come. CALL THEM NOW!"

He listened for a moment, and his eyes caught Bear sitting on the corner of his towel. But it wasn't the same corner he'd been on before.

I'm freakin' out, Tommy thought. *Maybe Dylan moved him. Maybe I'm not remembering right.*

But as he stared, he saw new stains on Bear. His paws and his mouth were dark with… dark with what?

No. It couldn't be.

Bear stood up on the towel. He turned his head slowly toward Tommy. He narrowed his eyes and growled.

Tommy's mind broke. He started to scream into the phone. He tried to run back to the parking lot, but he slipped and stumbled in the sand. Finally, he managed, "Bear! It was the bear!"

His foot turned in the sand and Tommy fell spread-eagle onto Dylan's remains. His screams rose two octaves as he stumbled and lurched away from the towels to the parking lot.

* * *

When Tommy was gone, Bear shouted at the lake, "Henry! What did you make me do?"

A wind came up blowing sand in Bear's eyes, forcing him to cover them with his paw. "I didn't make you do anything. I gave you tools. I gave you abilities. You did the rest."

"No! You told me I was going to get hungry. You told me I had to eat meat. Fresh meat. You put all those things in the stuffing in my head. You made me do this."

"I told you that you had to eat, yes, but it's the truth! You have to eat to survive. I didn't tell you what to eat, although, this did seem the logical choice."

Bear tried to cross his paws across his chest the way he had seen people do, but his arms were not long enough. He settled for putting them on his hips with a harrumph.

"Look at you! You're a mess," Henry said. "Go clean yourself up in the water."

Bear shook his head. "In the water..."

"I'm right here. I won't leave you alone."

Bear did as he was told while Henry talked. "He was going to throw you back into the lake. He didn't give you a choice. I know what it's like to be left all alone in that water."

Bear was suddenly aware of how very full he was. His eyes started to close. His head bobbed down to his chest. When he realized it, he yanked his head back up and forced his eyes wide open. He yawned and stretched, but he fought sleep to ask, "What happened to you, Henry?"

"Go to sleep. I'll explain everything."

Bear curled up on Tommy's towel and fell into a deep sleep. He dreamed he was a boy named Henry in the dormitory for the men working on the Lucin Cutoff.

* * *

Henry sat up on his cot. It was dark outside; he had no idea what time it was. Watches were expensive, and out here it didn't matter what time it was. If you were awake, you were working. Some sort of commotion downstairs had woken him. None of the other men around him seemed bothered by the sound, but Henry wanted to know what was happening. He crept down the stairs to the first floor, just in time to see Joe Danvers go into the boss's private room. Henry casually walked over to the door, paused and shook his boot. He made slow work of taking his boot off and shaking the gravel out of it while he listened.

"Boss, I'm sorry to bother you, but we got trouble," Danvers said.

"What?"

"All of the men from the first floor are gone. Up and left in the night."

"Why? What happened?"

"Well, sir, the last three loads of rock that we dumped there at the end? The rock you and I both stood on and jumped up and down on to make sure was solid? It's gone, sir. Just like before."

"Shit and shinola," Brian Alcott said. "Where in the blue hell is it going?"

"That's the problem, sir."

"I don't understand."

"A rumor sprung up last night in the first floor dormitory. One of the men said there was no scientific reason for all that rock and gravel to just keep disappearing. He figured we are standing right a'top the Mouth of Hell itself, and no matter how much rock and gravel we pour down there to hold up this railroad, it ain't ever gonna be enough. It will just keep gettin' swallowed up."

"The pilings are still there, aren't they?"

"Yes, sir. The pilings and the trestle are solid. It's just the rock and gravel that's poured to fill in the structure that disappears." Danvers sighed. "Anyway, around two this morning, the men decided the Devil himself was keeping us from moving forward, so they left."

"The nonsense people will believe," Alcott sighed. "As it happens, I've seen this kinda thing before. When we laid track down in… Louisiana, I think it was. My buddy and me put together a show of sorts that convinced the men it was okay to go back to work. We're gonna need a rat from back o' the café. And we're gonna need a *volunteer*."

Henry heard Alcott get out of bed and start getting dressed. He didn't want to be caught eavesdropping, so he finished tying his boot and tiptoed down the hall and out the front door.

Normally, Henry would have stuck around and volunteered, but something about the way Alcott had said it made Henry uncomfortable. Besides, if there were scared men around who wanted to leave quick, they would need money to get to town. Henry kept his hidden on the tracks, so no one would steal it. He decided he'd better double check his stash, just to be sure it was still safe.

Henry walked straight out from the boarding house and onto the railroad tracks and turned right. He counted the ties as he walked. Exactly twenty six. The half-moon gave enough light that he could see the faint heart he had carved in the twenty-sixth tie. He had met Joanna on the twenty-sixth of May and had fallen in love with her. He left her three days later to come to the railroad to earn enough money for them to get married. Now, if there were really men leaving the job, there would be more work for Henry. He thought he might be able to get back home sooner than he had planned.

Henry looked around to make sure no one was watching him. When he felt safe, he knelt down and began to dig into the gravel and dirt just behind the railroad tie. The cigar box wasn't far down. He opened it, and saw that his prized possessions were still there: a framed picture of his beloved Joanna and fifty dollars, a full month's wage less the charge for the boarding house.

Satisfied his belongings were safe, Henry reburied the box just where it had been, carefully covering the spot with gravel to make it difficult for anyone else to find.

"Hey there! You! What are you doing?"

Henry stood up and spun around in the darkness. Two men were running toward him, the man in front running in moonlight, while the man behind him had a lantern. It looked like Brian Alcott.

Danvers got to him first and threw something down on the tracks in front of him. Henry heard a sick-sounding splat, but never saw what it was. Men were coming out of the boarding house now and moving toward Henry to see what was going on.

Alcott got to Henry and shined the lantern on the tracks at his feet.

"Blood," Alcott said as he turned toward the men, "It's blood and something else. Some sort of sacrifice. I'm no expert, but this looks like Devil worship to me!"

Danvers grabbed Henry's arms by the elbows and held them behind his back.

"What are you talking about? I didn't—"

Henry started to defend himself, but Danvers pulled his elbows up, hurting his shoulders and making it hard for him to breathe. It was just as well; he didn't want them to know what he had been doing anyway.

"He started all of this! All of the trouble with the rock disappearing into the lake!"

"It's a lie! He's making it up," Henry gasped.

The group of men stared wide-eyed at Henry. A few of them were nodding. Some in the back started to shout.

Danvers yelled, "Maybe if we feed him to the lake, our troubles will end, and we can finish this thing and be gone from this cursed place!"

Henry started to fight, but he couldn't break loose. Danvers forced him to move down to the end of track where thirteen shipments of rock had disappeared. He turned Henry around to face Alcott one last time. There were close to two hundred men following them now, wanting to see what was going to happen.

"You have been found guilty of Devil worship, punishable by death. We will feed you to the Mouth of Hell to satisfy the hunger of the fallen angel. We pray to our Lord God that he will bless our work here and let us continue with no further delays."

All two hundred men replied with "Amen."

Henry could not believe what was happening. "I am no Devil worshipper!" he shouted.

Alcott took a carving knife out of the sheath on his belt, still covered with the blood of the creature he had butchered and given Danvers to entrap Henry. Slowly, Alcott pushed the tip of the blade into Henry's chest at the top of his rib cage. There was just enough flesh and muscle over Henry's ribs for Alcott to drag the blade through, carving in blood the only Devil worship symbol he knew:

Henry

the pentagram. He was trying to appease the Devil as much as God, after all. You could never be sure which one was paying attention. Henry screamed in agony.

Henry looked up at Alcott and said, "I thought you needed a volunteer."

Alcott smiled. "I did, and you're it, unwilling though you may be. I was worried there wouldn't be anyone out at this hour, but there you were. Must be fate. I'm sorry about this, kid, but I gotta get this crew back to work."

Henry's knees buckled. Danvers held him up and walked him to the edge of the rock embankment. Together, Alcott and Danvers threw Henry into the lake.

Henry swam and pulled himself up onto the rocks.

"I will get you, Brian Alcott! I will not rest until I take my revenge on you and all your kin." Henry shouted up from the water's edge.

The men could not let their sacrifice survive. They began to throw rocks and gravel at Henry, anything they could pick up. Two rocks hit him in the head and everything went black.

* * *

Bear opened his eyes. He heard sirens in the distance.

"Oh Henry, that's terrible! Is that how you died?"

"No, I didn't die until they dumped the next load of rock over my body." Henry sighed. "For some reason, it stuck that time, and they didn't have any more trouble building the railroad."

Bear shuddered. "Did you ever see the Mouth of Hell at the bottom of the lake?"

"No." Henry hesitated. "No of course not! This is Utah! If there ever were such a thing, it would be far from here." It felt to Bear like a drop of ice water ran down his back. He shifted uncomfortably on the towel. "I found myself in a peculiar situation, though," Henry said. "I was awake, and I could see and hear them, but I was a very weak spirit. They couldn't see me or hear me or feel me if I touched them. I had sworn revenge on Brian Alcott, but I was utterly powerless to take it.

"About six months after my death, the railroad across The Great Salt Lake was finished. All of the workers disbanded and went back to their lives. I tried to follow Brian Alcott back to his, but I quickly discovered that I could not go far from the lake. And so I sit here in this lake and wait to get my revenge on Brian Alcott." Henry paused. "Well, Brian Alcott is long dead. I have to take my revenge on his family now."

"Brian Alcott!" Bear yelled. "Henry, you don't think the girl, my girl, the one who left me here is related to Brian Alcott, do you?"

"She is. Brianne Alcott is Brian's great-great-granddaughter. She was named for him. I felt her the very first time she came to this lake. And now she is the last of his line. Her parents were killed in a car accident not long ago, and she has no siblings or cousins."

"Arg!" Bear said. "I know this all means something, but the stuffing in my head is still too wet. I don't understand."

"Bear, you can leave the lake. And when you do, you can take your reach, your voice, your claws, and your teeth with you. You can be my revenge."

"But Henry, she was my girl! MY GIRL! I couldn't."

"She abandoned you in an evil, haunted lake. Left you defenseless, alone and afraid. I know this isn't easy to hear, but she doesn't love you. She never did."

Bear felt cold all through his insides.

The sirens pulled to a stop just past the dunes. They heard car doors slam and feet running toward them.

Henry whispered, "Look at everything I have given you. I would not give these gifts lightly. I gave them to you because I love you, Bear. How could I not? You're going to save me."

* * *

"Miss Alcott? Brianne Alcott?"

The red haired teenager standing in the open doorway looked

frightened.

"Yes, I'm Brianne Alcott."

"Miss Alcott, I am Detective Dana Anderson."

Brianne's pale face blanched white, and her eyes seemed to bug out of her face. She clutched at the door for support.

"No, nothing's wrong. I'm here to see if this belongs to you."

Detective Anderson held up Bear for Brianne to see.

"Oh, um, he might. Let me see," Brianne said, taking Bear from her and turning him over. "Yes, that's where my mom wrote my name and address. He just, well, the last time I saw him he wasn't green."

Detective Anderson smiled. "He was found in The Great Salt Lake. Do you have any idea how he got there?"

Brianne looked down at Bear in her hands. "I… yes… I threw him in. My Mom gave him to me when I was six." A tear slipped down her cheek. "When my Mom died a couple months ago, he reminded me of her all the time. On one of my sad days, I threw him in. I thought he would be okay there. No fish to bite him, and I thought the salt would… I don't know… protect him somehow."

Detective Anderson nodded.

"But why are you bringing him back? Am I in trouble for leaving him there?"

"Oh no, nothing like that. He was evidence in one of our cases. We're done with him, so I'm returning him to you."

Brianne looked up into Detective Anderson's face and smiled.

"Thank you," she said.

The door was closed, and Bear was carried into the den and set on the coffee table. The girl, his girl, sat opposite him and stared into his eyes. He thought he would feel overwhelming love for her when he saw her again, but he didn't. Being here, with these things, in this place, brought everything back to him. He remembered the day she threw him into the lake.

"You lied," Bear said.

The girl's eyes grew large as she leaned back, away from him. She looked around to see if there was someone behind her who had spoken, but there was no one.

"You weren't sad that your Mother died," Bear continued, "you just wanted the Detective to feel sorry for you."

"How would you know if I was sad or not?" she asked.

"I was your Bear! I saw everything! I heard everything! You hated your mother!"

Brianne shook her head, "I didn't hate her. I loved her."

"Henry talked to you. He told you to kill your parents, and you did it! You are not a nice girl!"

Brianne's blue eyes were wide with guilt and fear. "No! I could never hurt them!" she shouted. "We were all at the lake; they were drinking wine. A lot of wine. We were just about to leave, when we ran into my friend Abby and her folks. They invited me for a sleep over. That's why I wasn't with them when they died. I went to a stupid party."

Brianne turned her eyes away and blinked at the tears welling there.

"Maybe if I had stayed with them, things would be different now," she whispered.

"Henry never spoke to you?"

"I don't know anyone named Henry."

Bear sat down to try to make sense of it all. The stuffing in his head was dry, and it didn't take him long to understand.

"He knows where you live now. It's written on my tag. That boy read it out loud. When he realizes I didn't kill you, he will send someone else. You have to leave. Right now."

Bear told Brianne the story of Henry. She found it difficult to argue with a stuffed bear. Brianne called her mother's sister in Denver. The arrangements were made. Brianne began to pack.

Thunder rolled over the house shaking the windows. That old familiar shiver went up Bear's spine as he placed folded shirts into her suitcase. The doorbell rang.

"Don't answer it," Bear said.

"It's just the cab," she said leaving him and going to the door.

Suddenly, Bear fell on his side. He could no longer reach. He could no longer speak.

Oh no, Bear thought, *Henry knows.*

The front door opened. A boy's voice said, "Hi, I'm Tommy. I found your bear in the lake? I called the police station, but they said they already brought him back to you. I really need to talk to you about that bear. He's not safe."

Bear heard Brianne say, "It's really not a good time. I'm on my way out. Could we talk about it later?"

"I came all the way from Salt Lake City. It's important."

"Ok, sure. Come in."

"Where is he?"

"Who?"

"The bear."

"Oh, he's put away where he goes. What did you want to tell me?"

"That bear—he's not what he seems to be. He killed my friend."

"Is it that green stuff on him? Is it poison?"

"No, he came to life, and he ate my friend."

"I really need to be going. My cab is going to be here any minute. I don't have time—"

"I told Henry you wouldn't believe me. But he was right about one thing. The story got me in the door."

* * *

Bear heard sirens and people as they came. Brianne, his girl, was dead. Tommy was in jail. Henry had won.

Without his girl or his reach or his voice, life was dull. Bear dozed. He dreamed he was Henry again. He dreamed he floated away from the lake, finally released after all these years. As he drifted over the railroad running through the middle of the Great Salt Lake, he saw a section of it crumble and disappear beneath the surface of the water.

Bear was afraid.

E. J. Harker

The appearance of *Henry* in this anthology marks E. J. Harcker's short fiction debut. She is a member of Rocky Mountain Fiction Writers and attends classes and workshops at Lighthouse Writer's Workshop in Denver. In her spare time, E. J. enjoys running, biking, and SCUBA diving, having earned her certification in Midway, Utah.

The Dread
by Amanda Luzzader

Something is coming from the lake. I can't see it, but I can feel it coming. I zip my coat higher and tuck my chin inside. January is colder in Utah than Las Vegas.

It was my idea to come see the lake. Something I read about salt's healing properties. This is the Great Salt Lake. It's full of salt.

The frigid wind stirs the sea air, carrying the sulfuric, rotting smell. I stare out at the rippling waves. I don't know what it is, but it's getting closer.

"They call it America's Dead Sea," says Brad. "I can see why."

He's right. It's rocky, desolate, and the putrid water stretches out forever. Nothing grows here. The salt is supposed to heal, but I realize now it can also kill.

From deep within the lake, the thing rises through the brine. It rises up and drifts toward me, and as it nears goosebumps form on my arms. I take a backward step, and then stagger back several.

Brad is instantly at my side. He grabs my arm.

"What is it?"

It was dread. Some kind of premonition. It'd come from the lake like a living creature and settled upon me. Something bad is going to happen. Something very bad.

"Let's leave," I say. My hands are shaking.

"Now? We just got here," Brad says. "You wanted to come. What's wrong?"

"No, it's just—I'm not feeling well. Let's go home. Please."

He looks at me a moment. "Okay, then. If that's what you want."

I'm not sure why he stays with me. Nine years. If our roles had been reversed, I'd probably have left.

At the hospital, I'd worn shoes with no laces and written in a journal using a floppy, rubber pencil. It'd taken several medicated months before I believed anything anyone said. It had all seemed so real, but eventually even I admitted that it had to have been just in my mind. No one was out to get me. No one was trying to kill me.

Brad told me the most logical thought I'd had in six months was the realization that I was crazy.

Nothing was the same after the hospital. I put on the same clothes and went to the same places, but my friends all wore forced smiles and watched me with close eyes. It was like I was a jagged shard of broken glass, and if they weren't careful they might get cut.

It's why we moved here—a fresh start. No one here knows me or what had happened.

When we get home, I can still smell the stink of the lake. It clings faintly to my hair and clothes. The dread is there, too, but it's even stronger now. It's a quaver that ripples through me with every heartbeat, and I can feel it in my bones.

But sometimes our mind tells us lies. I know this now. There is no killer hiding outside. There is no other woman. My mind tells me there is, but I ignore it. My mind tells me the gas will leak and the house will burn down, but I ignore it. I lie in bed with Brad's arms around me. He sleeps while I stare at the wall. I hear each one of my heartbeats, and they sound like this: bad, bad, bad. The feeling is dark and heavy. When morning comes, my body aches.

"What do you have planned for today?" Brad asks as he buttons his shirt.

I know why he's asking. The doctor had asked to speak to Brad alone at my last appointment, but I'd listened.

"It's important to keep her busy," the doctor had said. "Don't give her mind time to go to the dark places. It's when she's idle that the trouble will start."

"Well?" Brad asks.

"I don't know. Take a bath, maybe."

"Come on, babe. You can't just sit around all day. Think of something. How about the aquatic center? Swim some laps?"

"Yeah. Maybe."

He puts his hands on my shoulders. "Have some fun. Okay?"

"When will you be home?"

"Not until late."

"Again?"

"Yeah. I told you. Remember?"

I nod. And then Brad leaves. He goes to his new office, at his new job, in this new city. He left everything he knew because of me.

In the hot water of the bath, the dread feels like ice inside my veins. I submerge my whole body except for my face.

There's nothing bad here. There's nothing wrong. I am safe.

I say it out loud. Close my eyes and repeat it like a mantra. Nothing bad. Nothing wrong. I am safe.

The dread pulses, so I speak louder. There's nothing bad, nothing wrong. I am safe. There's nothing bad, nothing wrong. I am safe. I repeat it faster. But then the words mix up. There's nothing safe. I am wrong. The words echo off the bathroom tile and back into me like tiny arrows made of exclamation points. Nothing safe. Nothing safe.

I let the water out, watch it circle the drain. I sit naked and wet in the tub with my arms wrapped around my legs, too afraid to get out and face what's beyond the shower curtain.

The house is silent and still. I've got to snap out of this, or they'll send me back to the hospital. I'd been doing so well. I'd been doing so well until we went to the lake.

I take a deep breath and get out.

The mirror has fogged up. I rub a circle so that I can see myself.

My eyes look back. I don't trust myself. Who can you trust when you can't even trust yourself?

As I step into my bedroom, I smell something. It's faintly reminiscent of the lake—that eggy, sulfuric smell. Like gas. I follow the smell into the kitchen. Blue plumes blossom like flowers from all four burners of the stove. All four, turned up to high. The air above the stove wavers in the heat.

The hair on the back of my neck stands. I can feel the heat of the flames as I turn off each knob, but I force myself to stare at the markings—to be sure I'm turning the gas off and not on. And when I'm sure, I think of everything I did that day, trying to account for every minute, searching my memory for blank spaces. I wouldn't have done this. I don't want to die.

The dread tightens around my bones—squeezing them. I feel like screaming.

It takes three tries to dial Brad's work number, but before he answers, I hang up. Instead, I call my psychiatrist. I'm supposed to call her once a week. The last time I called was two days ago.

"What's up?" asks Mary.

"Nothing," I say. "I wanted to ask you about my meds. Maybe increasing the dosage."

"Why would you want to do that, Angela? What's this about?"

"Nothing. Just a feeling."

"A feeling? What kind of feeling? Talk to me. Tell me what's going on."

"Forget it. Really. It's nothing."

I hang up.

Only a few seconds pass before Mary calls back, but I don't answer. I just stare at the phone.

Before the hospital, I knew what real was. Real was something I could handle and touch. Real was absolute. Real was unquestionable. If I could see, hear, taste, or touch it was real. I knew when I turned on the stove and when I didn't. End of story.

Not anymore. I second-guess everything to see if it fits into the context of likelihood. Reality is something we take for granted—

The Dread

like the air we breathe—and when it's not there, it feels like drowning. I spend the rest of the day checking the stove.

A week passes, but the dread does not. The anticipation makes me jittery. I don't sleep. I can't eat.

Brad stares at me from across the dinner table. "You've barely touched a thing."

"I'm not hungry."

"Is everything okay? You seem—upset."

I'd like to tell him about the dread. How it keeps my muscles tense. How I'm always straining to hear. How it takes my breath away.

But the dread isn't real. I know it isn't real. And now that I know that, I should be able to handle it. Brad knows, too. If I tell him, he'll have to put me back in the hospital. And maybe that wouldn't be so bad. Maybe that's where I need to be.

"I'm just tired," I tell him. "It's the medication. Takes everything out of me."

He nods. "I was supposed to go back to work for a few hours." He puts his hand on mine. "But maybe I should stay home tonight."

His new job is more difficult than the one he left. He's having to work longer hours to keep up, and he's making less. He's never home, and it's my fault.

"No, I'll be fine," I say. "Really." The dread swells.

Brad turns on the TV for me and gives me a cup of tea. He kisses me on top my head. "I'll try to hurry," he says.

"No rush," I tell him.

I try to watch something on TV, but everything is murder, treacherous lovers, fire. I can't watch. The dread moves in, takes on a feeling of immediacy. There's risk and danger, and the worst part is not knowing when or how. I just want it to stop.

Even the TV room setup seems wrong. My back is to the entrance. I wouldn't be able to see if someone snuck up on me, and it feels like someone is sneaking up on me. But every time I turn around, there's nobody there.

Around midnight, our cat meows outside the front door. Brad

still isn't home. As I reach the front door, I have a memory. Or maybe it's my mind again, telling lies. In my mind I see another door, a different door. It's white, and it's shut. I know I'm going to open it, but I don't want to. I don't want to see what's on the other side. My hand is on the doorknob.

I open the front door and the cat darts between my ankles and into the house.

When I look up, there in the front yard is a man holding a flashlight.

I gasp loudly and recoil. The flashlight goes off. I stand there for a moment, clutching the neck of my nightgown.

At the hospital they kept asking me, "Why would anyone be trying to hurt you? What reason would anyone have to cause you harm?"

"I'm in the way. They need me out of the way."

"Who's 'they'?"

"I don't know."

The real answer was that there was no reason. No they. I am just an ordinary person. Yet, here in the doorway my breath hitches in my chest.

"Who's there?" I call into the blackness. I can see him, a blacker silhouette against the black night. He's not here for me, I tell myself. He is looking for something. Maybe he mistook my cat for his own.

But he doesn't answer.

"What are you doing?" I call.

The darkness of his presence moves forward, the grass swishes as he moves quickly toward the house.

"What do you want?" I cry. I get behind the door.

The swishing gets louder and faster. I slam the door and fumble to lock it. Then I crumple to the floor and scramble back, my heart nearly beating its way out of my chest.

I hold my breath, straining to hear. A long time passes, but I hear only myself. The cat approaches. He stares at me. He tips his head and meows, rubs against my leg. I'm frozen.

When Brad gets home, he finds me there by the door.

"I-I got scared," I tell him.

"It's okay. It's okay," Brad says softly, crouching beside me. He peels my fingers away from the knife I'm holding. "I shouldn't have left you alone."

In the morning, Brad is gone by the time I wake up. I call Mary first thing.

"I just can't shake this feeling that something bad is going to happen," I tell her. "Or that it's already happening."

"Like what? What bad things?"

"Like I'm going to die. Or Brad's not coming home. And I can't escape it."

"Do you see things? Like before?"

I hesitate. "I—don't think so." I think about the white door and the man with the flashlight. "I just have so much anxiety. Maybe it's this new house. Maybe it was a mistake to move."

Mary doesn't say anything, and I imagine that she's writing notes.

"What does Brad say?" Mary finally asks.

"He's worried."

"He said that?"

"I can tell."

"You two getting along?"

"He's gone a lot."

"Work?"

"Yeah. Every night, almost."

"I'd like to have you come in," Mary says. "Just for a little check-up. Can you make the drive?"

"Next week," I tell her.

Mary exhales. She's not pleased.

"When Brad's not so busy," I say.

After Brad gets home from work, I tell him that Mary wants to see me. He seems alarmed.

"When? What'd she say?"

"It's nothing serious," I say. "Just a check-up."

He rubs his forehead and then stands up. "You know what you

need? Not a check-up. You need a date. I've been so busy working. It's really not fair to you. No wonder you're so stressed."

"A date?"

"Friday night. They're doing a performance of *My Fair Lady* at the Pioneer Theater. I'm taking you."

I force myself to smile. "I think I'd like that."

It will probably be the last thing I get to do before I'm hospitalized again.

In the days leading up to Friday, the dread feels like acid under my surface. I jerk and twist. I want to peel off my own skin to escape it. But what's worse is what it's leading to. And death isn't the worst thing that can happen. I could be in pain, or be alone.

My mind fills with terrible thoughts. I see torture and loneliness. Faces flit inside my mind. Then, the white door again. It's shut. I put my hand on the doorknob, and I realize whatever is on the other side is what made me snap. All I have to do is open that door and look. I turn the doorknob, push the door open.

I see faces. I see screaming, twisted, horrible faces. My head spins like a cyclone. I run to the bathroom and vomit. My chest heaves as I wipe my mouth. I cry, and my crying turns to laughter.

Friday morning I feel better. The dread is with me, simmering in the background, but it's quiet. The eye of the storm, I think.

I spend extra time getting ready. Curl my hair. Put on makeup—eyeliner, mascara, lipstick. I pick out a nice dress—the black one that Brad likes.

I sit on the couch and wait for Brad. I look at the time on my phone and, a minute later, I look again. I try to read *Cosmo*, but I check the phone after every line. Finally, Brad calls.

"I'm running late, hon. Do you think you could meet me at the theater?"

"Umm—"

"Never mind. I'll just come get you. We'll just have to miss the beginning. It'll be okay."

"No, no. I can drive. I'll meet you there."

"You're sure?"

The Dread

"Yes. Of course." Even before I hang up, my heart is thundering beneath my ribs.

I open the front door slowly. It's already dark outside. I stare out into the yard—checking for the man, even while realizing he may not even exist.

The car door squeaks as I pull it shut. I take a deep breath and start the engine. I drive slowly. Tentatively. Like I just got my learner's permit.

For a while, everything's okay, but then I squint as the light of the car behind me glares in my rearview mirror. The car is too close, much closer than I'd prefer. Instinctively, I slow down, and the car gets closer.

I lick my lips, try not to think about it. I make a right turn. So does the other car.

I turn on the radio. It's sports. I change the station. Jazz. The car behind me is following so close, I'm worried it might hit me.

When I turn right again, so does the other car.

My hands grow sweaty, and I tighten my grip on the wheel. I try to keep from looking in the mirror, but I can't help it. In the darkness, I can't tell what kind of car it is, but I can see that one headlight is dimmer than the other.

I take two more rights in a row, and so does the other car.

It's following me, the same car—the dim headlight gives it away. I know it's real. In my gut, I can feel that it is real. And the dread screams, "YES."

I slow down even more. Ridiculously slow. So slow I'm barely moving. The other car backs off a bit.

Could it be a coincidence? I chuckle nervously. A cop, maybe? Could they just be lost?

I get an idea. I wait until I see some cars coming the other direction and then I make a sudden U-turn. Someone honks at me. I look back over my shoulder to see what the car with the dim headlight will do.

It makes a U-turn. It is. It's following me.

There are a couple cars between us now, but I can see that the other driver is edging around the other cars, looking for a space to pass. I drive faster.

I reach for my purse and knock it over. My cell phone falls to the floor. The car pulls to the right as I reach forward and grab it.

Struggling to the see in the darkness and to keep the car on the road, I phone Brad.

Please pick up. Please pick up.

One more ring and it will go to voicemail.

"Hello?"

"Brad!"

"Honey, what's wrong?"

"Someone's following me, Brad. They're chasing me."

There's silence on the other end. One second. Two.

"Where are you, babe?"

"I—I don't know. On the road somewhere."

"What do you see around you?"

"It's dark. I can't see. There's some houses. I can see the lake. Kind of."

"Just go home, Angela."

"Home? I can't go home. He'll find out where we live."

Brad sighs. "Go to the lake, then. I'll meet you there. Go to where we stopped before."

"Maybe call the police?"

"Okay, babe. I'll call them."

The car is behind me again. I can see the dim headlight.

"I'm scared," I say.

"It's all right," Brad says. "I'm going to call the police now."

"No, no! Don't go. Keep talking to me. Please, Brad. I'm so scared."

"Okay, okay. I won't hang up. I'm in the car right now, and I'm on my way. Just get to the lake. The turn-off where we went. You'll see it. I'm almost there."

The city melts away as I get closer to the lake. I get a whiff of the lake's rotten odor, the smell of dread. The houses and businesses fade away, and the traffic dwindles. Still the car follows, it's dim headlight leering.

Brad stays on the phone. "Hang in there. I'm coming."

I have almost reached the lake when abruptly the other car stops.

"He just stopped," I tell Brad. "He's turning around."

"You still moving?"

"Yeah." I breathe a sigh of relief. "He's gone, Brad. I can't even see him anymore. There's no cars anywhere."

"Okay, well, where are you?"

"I don't even know. It's so dark. I think I'm almost to the place we stopped that day."

"Okay," says Brad. "Meet me there so I can make sure you're all right."

I reach the spot and drive down the short road to the lake's edge. It feels safer here, away from the road. The water is still, and the moon reflects off it like a mirror.

"Go back," I say. "Go back to where you came from."

"What's that, babe?"

"Nothing."

"I'm almost there. Stay put."

I watch the lake until Brad pulls up behind me. I run to meet him, and we embrace between our two cars.

"Oh, babe," says Brad, "you're so cold. Here, give me your keys. I'll get a blanket." I press the keys into his palm. He pries my phone from my hands, and then he draws me closer.

"I'm not crazy," I mutter, pressing my head against his chest. "It was real. Someone was after me."

Brad puts his hands on my shoulders and looks me straight in the face. "Listen to me," he says. "I believe you."

And the dread leaves.

"You do?"

He nods as he walks to his car and opens the trunk. He pulls out a blanket and a toolbox and sets them on the ground.

"I've always believed you," he says.

Brad slams the trunk, and in my mind, the white door looms

again. It's shut. My hand is on the knob, and I turn it, push it open. On the other side I see Brad. And I see her. I see Brad with her in our bed. I see their faces, shocked and shouting.

Brad spreads the blanket on the ground, as if we're having a picnic. Then he puts on a pair of leather work gloves.

"It was you, Brad," I say. "It was you behind the door. With her."

He buries his face in his gloved hands and cries. He moans, and his shoulders heave. He cries and cries.

"Brad?"

He wails as he retrieves a roll of silver tape from the toolbox, and then a bundle of rope.

"Brad, what are you doing?"

He sniffs, wipes his face. "This is how I'm going to cry when I tell Mary about how you fell apart and drove off. And when I call your mom. I've been practicing."

As Brad sobs, I realize that one of his headlights is dimmer than the other.

"This is how I'm going to cry at your funeral," he says. "They didn't believe you. I did. I've always believed you. Do you think they'll believe me?"

Amanda Luzzader

Amanda Luzzader is an award winning author of short stories and a professional editor. She is also the mother of two energetic boys. Look for Amanda on Facebook and Amazon.

Dusky Spirits
by Jo Schneider

Waking up in a strange place never bothered me—sometimes those were the best mornings—what I hated was that first moment of prying my eyelids apart, which in this case seemed a vain attempt at best.

My addled brain tried to recall my last location. No luck. No hint of why when I flexed my fingers nothing happened, or why I didn't smell the expected blend of cigarette smoke and cheap perfume. Shadows draped around me like curtains.

No doubt, I'd been drinking. So why couldn't I taste the dry tang of cheap whiskey?

I focused. Reached out for anything but the dark.

I parted the curtains far enough to allow a gray murmur of conversation to slip through. It hovered over the soft clink of silverware on dishes. I strained to listen, and made out two voices. One man and one woman.

"This place is a dump." The woman said.

I imagined a skanky girl with stringy black hair and more eye make-up than should be worn.

"No, that last place we met was a dump."

The guy sounded reasonable. I pictured a white shirt, a plain tie, and hair so neat it made me cringe.

"What, Nanny's? They have the best blood pudding in the western hemisphere."

"That's disgusting," said the man.

The woman laughed. A low, grinding sound.

"Just because it's not all sunshine and lollipops there doesn't make it disgusting."

"No, you're disgusting for eating a triple portion of it."

"And you're a sissy," the woman said. "Where's your robe today, anyway? Did you have to sneak out again?"

"The ends of your hair are singed. I'd say you had to crawl out the hard way."

The man's dull voice had an edge. The same edge my family used to give me whenever they didn't approve of my lifestyle.

A brief silence. The woman spoke again, her voice dark. "What do you have?"

I heard the faint slosh of liquid being poured into a glass.

"Yellow? Really?"

The guy snorted. "Not the sunshine kind, trust me."

"I'm not drinking that," she said. "It looks like pee."

"You've sucked down two glasses of Mountain Dew in the last ten minutes."

"Don't knock the Dew."

"Just try it," he said. "Why would I bring you something bad?"

"Trying to ensnare me? Banish me?"

The frustrated dad tone, another one I could relate to, emerged. I could practically see the guy rubbing the bridge of his nose. "Then I would have to break in another representative. Why would I want to do that? I may not like you, but at least I get you." A pause. "Sort of."

"You drink some."

"You know I can't do that. They'll detect it when I go back. Just drink it."

"Fine."

I imagined a teenager's eye roll. The kind that practically takes their heads off of their shoulders. My daughter could be the queen of eye rolls. Could have been.

Slosh, sniff. Another sniff.

"Good bouquet, right?" the man asked.

"Don't rush me."

"Fine."

A pause. A sip. Then a smacking of lips.

"Pungent," the woman said.

"Pungent?"

"Not bright, which I chalk up to the source. Good, but not exceptional."

"Give it a minute," said the man.

"What exactly am I wait—" A sharp intake of breath interrupted her retort. It morphed into soft moan. The kind that spider web pleasure from your core out into the tips of your toes.

"Well, well." The moan turned into a relaxed, sensual purr. "Where did you find this one?"

"Texas."

"Nothing good comes out of Texas."

"I think you mean nothing bad enough to be this good comes out of Texas."

"What is this?" the woman asked.

"A homegrown local vintage—full of wasted potential. I pulled it just before the gates."

"How much did you get out of it?"

"Six bottles."

Whatever was in the bottles, it sounded like I needed some.

"I might be able to work with that. What else did you bring?"

The world tilted, and I felt myself falling. Like those moments when you're dreaming of flying, but then gravity ensnares you, and you plummet toward the ground. I expected to wake up, and find myself lying in a cheap motel room with mirrors on the ceiling, but my mind stayed shrouded in the dark curtains.

"The color is dark."

"So was the source," said the man.

"How close to pure is this?" Another sniff.

"Pure? I find it entertaining that you, of all creatures, would ask about purity."

"Pure sources keeps it happy." The woman's voice lowered. "It's in all of our best interests."

"Open your mind. Black and white don't exist anymore. We work in layers of gray now. Which, as you just experienced, can be infinitely more satisfying."

"What if it doesn't like it?"

"You just did," said the man.

"But it's not like me. It's not like either of us. We don't know what it will like."

"Look," the man said. I pictured him leaning forward on the table. "I have a couple of bottles of pure stuff with me. Give this new one a try. If it doesn't like it, you can toss in the old stuff."

"You're crazy. You know the job. Why are you here if you don't want to keep this thing asleep?"

"So you won't even try?" the man asked.

"No."

"Fine then, we're finished. You can explain to your superiors why it woke up and why the Great Salt Lake will drain and become a gateway into a place worse than hell."

The woman growled. It set my teeth on edge. Or would have, if I could feel them.

"Why are you doing this?" the woman asked. "We had a deal."

"I'm just trying to expand our possible marks. There are only so many perfectly terrible people out there, and the archangels are going to get suspicious if none of them come in for sorting."

"So you're looking out for yourself?"

"I'm looking out for all of the realms" said the man. "I'm trying to think out of the box. I realize you're trapped most of the time, so I can see the difficulty for you to try something new. Trust me. This one will keep it happy for years."

"How do you know?"

"Try it."

A fist slammed down on the table.

"Tell me why."

The guy spoke through gritted teeth.

"Fine. I happen to know that this one was bad. Through and through. Then he saw the light. Cleaned up his act for a couple of years. Then he slipped. One little thing and he crashed back to his former depths, where he continued to dig deeper and deeper."

Sounded a whole lot like my life. Without warning, my stomach flipped and churned.

"If this is a trick, I'll rip your throat out."

"As if that's going to help."

The world tilted again. I made a mental note to lay off the whiskey, and whatever else I'd ingested.

A blast of cold shot through me, the most potent sensation I'd felt since waking up, turning my bones into brittle icicles. The memory of the fight I'd had with my wife before I strangled her flashed through my mind. The words she had screamed at me. The blood-red anger that had swelled until I'd snapped. The moment the light had slipped out of her eyes and she'd gone limp in my grasp. It swirled once, then slid down into a black gullet. Part of me went with it, feeling the tunnel pressing in around me.

A piece of my soul ripped away. I felt the tear and the gaping wound left behind.

"Well?"

"It's...unique," the woman finally admitted. "Where did he come from?"

"The Salt Lake Valley."

"You're kidding."

"I never kid."

The woman chuckled, then said, "You knew him."

"Does it matter?"

"I suppose not. How much do you have?"

"Eight bottles."

"Your price?"

"Triple the usual."

The woman paused. "You're serious?"

"Quite."

More silence. More swirling. More cold. Another memory, this just one of many times I'd taken money from my brother. I'd stolen his wallet and maxed out his debit and credit card. All for drugs. The wound on my soul ripped again. The memory slipped down the gullet. Part of me, lost forever.

"You want three people on the border let out?" asked the woman.

"Three a month for three months."

"Damn it, you know how hard it is for me to get those guys through."

"It's worth it," said the man.

"I hate you."

"I know."

The woman paused. "But not as much as you must hate this guy. How long did you wait for him?"

My survival instincts kicked in, and I tried to think. Who hated me this much? The list was extensive. Could I bargain with them? What could I offer them? I still didn't know where I was.

The man's words lowered to a whisper. "Long enough."

"Is this why you took the job?"

"One of many reasons."

The woman laughed again. "Well, whoever he is, he's delicious."

"Can we call that a deal?"

Those words. They echoed through my head, and my mind froze. That's what my brother, Howard, used to say to me when he was trying to keep me in line. I could still see the expression of hope mingled with resignation on his face.

I'd let Howard slip down that embankment five years ago. No one had ever questioned it as an accident.

"We can."

My soul ached from the tears, but I knew Howard wouldn't help me now, even if he could. I'd always known that the day of reckoning would come, but I never thought my own brother would bottle my soul and sell it to the highest bidder.

I had been ready for Hell, but not this.

Jo Schneider

Jo Schneider is both a novel writer and a kung-fu fighter. It took almost as long to get her black belt as it did to go from typing her first fiction on the screen to getting published. Hey, no one said it was a race. Schneider writes mystery satire and YA science fiction and fantasy. If nothing else, she cracks herself up and imagines that her action scenes will be used as examples of how to write badass action scenes in writing conferences for years to come.

Saltair Fire Waltz
by Angela Hartley

Once upon a time, a man stared down from Promontory Point at the Great Salt Lake and declared, "This is the place." Believers said he was a prophet, capable of recognizing the world beyond the veil. I often wonder if this seer simply sensed evil hovering close to the water and mistook it for good. Humanity assumes the best in what it doesn't understand. Where divinity abides in slumber, we arouse with curiosity. The compulsion is in our nature.

After my death, I understood.

The dreams started shortly after my fifteenth birthday, the kind that make a young woman blush. They were always the same and began with me walking through a set of ornate doors to find him standing there, waiting for me, the handsome suitor who swept me off my feet.

A lovely, lovely dream, I thought.

But one day, as I poured over the latest fashions on the society page, I happened upon a photograph of the entrance to Saltair's dance hall.

Near the turn of the 20th century, busy bees built Saltair, a luxury resort complete with an amusement park on a pier suspended over the lake. Rivaling Coney Island, it was grand. The stained glass and brass handles of the entrance in the photo sparked recognition, throwing me into a frenzy. For weeks, I'd begged relentlessly to celebrate my 16th birthday there. As always, my parents indulged their only child and gave in to my greatest desire.

I can still remember the first moment I viewed the spires from the train, rising to heaven like quilting needles. It was 1924 and life was berries. The floating palace from my dreams was before me, real and tangible. I tingled with excitement. If the castle was real, my dream suitor must be real, too.

"We're here," Mama beamed, pulling me out of my reverie. She'd recently bobbed her auburn hair and fussed with small curls pinned close to her cheek. The starlets in Hollywood couldn't compare to the beauty of my mother with her long, elegant neck and fine ivory skin.

Papa jumped down to the platform and reached up with his strong, working-man arms. My new low-waisted yellow dress swirled against my knees as he lifted me from the train. There should've been a chill to the late April air, but there wasn't. The wind rested calm; the earth held its breath.

The Saltair dance hall floated on top of the lake like a Russian castle surrounded by a moat. In twilight, the water blazed orange instead of blue. Side-by-side in matching dresses, Mama and I walked up the planked boardwalk together. She'd modified our outfits from the latest patterns, perhaps too modest for New York tastes, but fashionable by Salt Lake City standards. I marveled as the setting sun bathed the silky fabric, turning the chiffon lace overlay blood red in the fading light. Papa came up from behind and stepped in between us. "I'm a sorry dew-dropper between two fine tomatoes," he teased.

"Applesauce," I said. "I think you look rather dashing in your boiler cap." And he did, in his tailored dove grey suit, standing next to Mama. Placing his arm around my shoulders, he squeezed affectionately.

Grabbing Papa's hand, Mama leaned into his side. His handlebar mustache twitched at the corners in an easy smile. "Well, I'm ready to step the night away with my two beautiful bits of calico," he said.

Mama laughed. "Sorry, love, but you're my beau. Baby girl has to find her own partner."

"My little princess dancing with some cake-eater? Nah," Papa teased.

"But I'm sixteen," I protested.

"She's right. Our Lydia isn't so little anymore," Mama said. "Someday soon a young Johnny will sweep her off her feet, and it will just be the two of us rattling alone in the house."

Papa kissed Mama's cheek, and I burned with envy. Oh, how I wanted what they had.

"Together we'll never be alone, Mama." He took me by the hand and twirled me down the boardwalk. "We'll have to count that as our dance," he said. "I'm sure once those Oliver Twists get a load of you, your dance card won't have a spot for your old man."

"Oh, Papa!" I said, but secretly I was glad. I didn't want to dance with Papa. Another partner filled my thoughts.

We were almost to the doors when movement caught my eye. As I stared out across the lake, I spotted a dark figure striding a few feet above sunset's rippling flames. The sight of him walking on water should've prompted me to run.

It didn't.

I caught my breath. *Bee's knees.* My temperature rose by five degrees just looking at him. His impeccable suit was coal black, the same as his hair worn longer than society deemed appropriate. As I marveled, he raised his head to meet my gaze. What struck me most were his eyes, radiating like a fire burning too hot. Blacksmith blue, I thought. When he reached the pier, he stepped onto the boardwalk in front of the dance hall. Smiling at me, he exposed perfectly white teeth behind plump lips. "My Lydia," he mouthed and disappeared through Saltair's doors.

His words, that smile, stirred feelings awakened by my dream suitor. Thoughts of us alone and intimate, like my dreams, but real, caused butterflies to flutter. My nighttime visitor and the gorgeous creature waiting inside the hall were one in the same. He was real... or was he?

A quick glance at the crowd entering the doors as if nothing extraordinary happened left me wondering if I'd only imagined him. I started to doubt my eyes, but my heart knew better, pattering fast and out of control. Anticipation drew me forward through the familiar ornate front doors and into the music. A sense of urgency whispered that I needed him to touch me in the flesh more than I'd ever required anything. Destiny had spoken, and *he* had chosen *me*. I could hardly contain myself, bouncing on the balls of my feet, impatient with Mama and Papa's pace. They couldn't hear the insistent low voice, persuading me onward under the melody. *Lydia, come to me.*

The ballroom rested under a large dome with grand crystal chandeliers hanging from the tall ceiling and a wooden dancefloor shining with orange oil. A bandstand stood at the far wall, the red boxes inlaid with gold. The conductor led an easy waltz, and with little trouble, I coaxed my mother and father to join the parade of couples twirling in front of us. As they merged with the other dancers, I admired their beauty and grace before they disappeared in a sea of faces. Here was my chance to slip away.

I turned. He was there. He stood against a post, as debonair as I had imagined, yet something feral twisted his grin, like a cat about to swallow a canary. The thought gave me pause. Staring down at my yellow dress, the first seed of doubt sprouted in my stomach, blossoming to terror as he chuckled.

Backing away, I spun on silk slippers to flee in the opposite direction, but found myself facing my dream suitor once again. Time shifted, slowing and then speeding up as the sound of my blood rushed through my ears. Dizzy, I struggled to remain on my feet. I stepped forward to catch my balance, taking a breath to cry out for help, but one look at the fiery demon beneath the façade of a man and my voice stuck in my throat.

"Did you think I would let you escape so easily, my sweet, sweet little bird?"

His voice was smooth and sugary, like hot chocolate drizzled over strawberries. It played along my skin, silken as memory. In my dreams, he'd only been lovely. No monster could possibly be that lovely. As instinct stood my hair straight on end, I tried to dismiss what my eyes had just seen, wanting to believe in the dream. But being the monster he was, he showed me his entire hideous demonic form, delighting in my knowledge of the torturous truth. The heat I'd felt in dream burned in reality.

A scream passed my lips as a whimper, but my feet marched on until I was standing right before him. Wherever his leering eyes lingered, my skin jolted as fire shot from his sockets, burning me in the most private places. I cringed, but couldn't move, pinned in place by his stare.

He reveled in my reaction.

"Now, now. Don't pretend you don't like a little heat. I know better. I branded everything inside you long ago. This is all you've longed for, isn't it?"

He'd returned to his beautiful form, but I could still make out the cracks where the demon leaked through.

In a sense, he was right. A night of dancing with a handsome bloke, a few stolen kisses, and perhaps something more was all I'd dreamed about. But that night each wish he brought to life twisted desire into fear.

He moved faster than lightning, pinning me against the post he'd been leaning on only moments before.

"I know your darkest desires. Here I am, willing and ready to give you precisely what you want. You shall have it, my love, and you will burn for me," he promised as he possessed my mouth. Brutally he razed, but oh, how I wanted the searing heat his full lips offered. Pulling away, he laughed. "Oh, the fun we'll have tonight!"

Taking me around the waist, he pulled me close and spun us onto the dance floor. We waltzed as he led us away from the crowd into a dark corner. His flaming hand grazed my cheek, scorching a trail of fire along my skin. Even as I cried out in pain, my body betrayed, arching to press closer, molding to the contour of his heat, begging for the fire of his fingertips. A familiar dreamy bliss coursed through my flesh as it succumbed to the pain of his touch. In his arms I became saltwater taffy, pliable and compliant. The beast had returned in all of his brimstone glory, but the true horror rested in my knowledge that his form no longer frightened me. I belonged to him. I'd pledged myself the moment I let him enter my bedroom through my dreams.

Gleeful in his absolute control, he scorched me again and allowed me to puddle to the ground. Unable to stand, I averted my eyes, ashamed and disgusted by how much I longed for his fire's kiss. When I looked back up, he was beautiful again, a smug smile twisting the ends of his mouth.

"Mmmm, that was good. Please forgive my lack of propriety. But you, little darling, make me sooo hot. Allow me to introduce myself." He bowed low, a perfect gentleman. "I am Nero."

He kissed my hand, searing his lip print to the back of my glove. "And you, of course, are Lydia. My dear, sweet, succulent Lydia." He cast his eyes toward the water. "This lake was my prison. The salt makes the water so pure, I cannot bear to touch it. Think of it, Lydia, even if I wasn't born of fire, to be suspended for eternity over water, trapped over a circle of salt that I could not cross. Imagine how I rejoiced when busy little bees constructed this magnificent wooden palace, breaking the sacred salt circle as it sat on top. Imagine how great my joy in finding the world had turned. Repression makes desire particularly sweet. And you, my dear, shone like a beacon in the night. Rarely have I found a partner so naïve, yet so eager, so willing to dance." With a flourish, he held his arms out and leapt in wild circles. Seated on the floor I watched as couples glided past, not even sparing a glance at his fiery spectacle. He flicked sparks in faces, but no one even blinked.

"I confess. You make me want to show off, Lydia." My name rested intimate on his lips. His hand reached out to me. Our fingers joined and I stood. "Tonight must be special. Our joining has to be more than memorable; it must be seared into hearts of those who rejoice with us. Do you feel it? Destiny drums through your veins, my love, pulsing with every manic beat of your heart. Tell me, as the catalyst for our moment of greatness, have you ever felt more alive?"

I didn't have voice to answer; my breath hitched out of control.

"What do you say, doll? Should we show these folks a *smoking* hot time?"

With a snap of his fingers Saltair's doors slammed shut. Startled, the musicians stopped playing. Couples stopped dancing. Fancy men in tailcoats assured everyone in the hall that there was nothing to be alarmed about, just an odd breeze from the Great Salt Lake. Their reassurances didn't comfort me, but my dream suitor was right, I'd never felt more alive than the moments right before my death.

His eyes blazed blue fire as he beckoned me closer with a fiery finger. He was a beautiful monster, and I was his. He opened his arms to me, and in his eyes I recognized my fate. In the middle of the dancefloor, he played out my fantasy in his truest form, and oh, how I burned. My yellow birthday dress lit up like a Roman candle bathed in orange flame. Where my satin slippers touched the floor, streams of fire licked out like the claws of the monster scorching my flesh as he ravished me. Everyone screamed as the fire spread, running toward the exits, but the doors remained closed.

No escape.

The screams were maddening. I wanted to shout for them to stop, but then realized the shrieks of agony were the lyrics to my song, the melody to the horror I experienced, naked and burning for my lover.

As I looked up, the ceiling collapsed, and for the briefest moment, the spires reached toward heaven, pointing the way to ascension. A strange peace came over me when I realized Mama and Papa would remain together. As the last soul escaped, the voice to my song ended, and the spires collapsed.

"Thank you for being the key, love," he whispered in my ear. The final tie to the dock broke free, and my master leapt to shore. He

Saltair Fire Waltz

left me alone, burning and locked inside his prison.

I've never stopped wanting him.

For nearly a century, I've burned in this place, neither willing nor capable of departure. As a demon born of fire, the water's too pure for me to touch. I keep close to the edges of the shore, patiently waiting for my master's return. When enough time passes, people forget, and busy bees build again. Where divinity dwells, humans trample like moths to a flame. It's in their nature. The Great Salt Lake calls.

After all, this is the place.

Angela Hartley

Angela Hartley has created worlds, published novels, built and managed several writing organizations, and has also entertained and educated at universities, symposiums, and conventions. In her spare time, she's studied religious theory, psychology, psychic abilities, and psychosis to gain a better understanding of the human condition. She currently resides in Midway, Utah.

Hydrogeist
by J. Anthony Gohier

Bodies float in salt water. That's what they tell me. It came up because the movie I was working on that summer was based on the true story of a grave robber who was exiled to Antelope Island and drowned trying to escape. There were several debates over whether anyone could actually drown in a saltwater lake, but it's hard to argue with history, and they say you can drown in your bathtub anyway, so the show went on.

Filmmaking is rarely as glamorous as people think, and a day on the lake was no exception. Of course, the talent, the equipment, and everyone above the line had to stay dry, even when filming on the water, which meant the rest of us spent the day in the lake pushing various boats and rafts around the rickety old fishing boat the actors were rowing and trying to ignore the scent of generations of decaying brine shrimp.

That still might not have been so bad if it weren't for the salt. I don't know if it made me any more buoyant, but I do know that it got everywhere. I was glad I wasn't wearing much, because after the first couple of hours, every inch I was wearing itched as it rubbed against my skin. By noon, it was hard think of much else. Luckily, it didn't take much brainpower to tread water or swim in the direction someone was pointing, hands pressed against the side of a boat.

As the sun's reflection crawled westward over the surface of the lake, I tried not to focus on how miserable the whole thing was. I had a love-hate relationship with water anyway, and I was determined not to let the scales tip any further toward hate. The truth is, I want to love water. That's probably the reason I'm so afraid of it now.

The first time I remember going swimming, I couldn't have been more than three. The pool was at the local high school where my dad taught French. I remember going with my family, and I remember how excited I was. The next thing I remember is sitting in the kiddie-pool while everyone else headed for the deep end. And when I say kiddie-pool, I am using the term generously. It was really just a wide square cut out in the edge of the pool, just deep enough to let in about an inch of water.

I know I was only three, but I still remember that day vividly. I watched as everyone around me wrestled and played with churning water. They laughed as they soared by, all but flying in the fantastic liquid that seemed to have a life of its own. And I stood there getting my ankles wet.

That didn't last. When you are three, you don't stop to ask yourself questions like *do I know how to swim?* And the bright red rope holding a few buoys over the inch of water wasn't much of an obstacle either. It only took one step to reach the water that drew me in ravenously.

For a moment it was miraculous, like being wrapped in smooth, soft light. Then I noticed all the legs thrashing about. I looked up. All the faces hid behind the shimmering wall that now cutting me off from everything above. And in that second moment, I realized there was nothing I could do to reach that wall, let alone break through into the world of air.

Obviously I survived; someone saw me, fished me out, and handed me off to my dad. But since that day, dark undercurrents of helplessness and inevitability have always tinged my love for water and swimming.

I tried to learn to snorkel once, but the idea of breathing while all of my senses told me I was underwater didn't go over too well. I kept cutting my breath off, gulping down pockets of air that would push against the contents of my stomach rather than ever reaching my lungs.

I wasn't thinking about any of those things while I pushed up against the raft loaded down with camera equipment and personnel and kicked my legs frantically. Or rather, I wasn't thinking about any of them until my legs caught on something. As I slipped under the surface and watched that terrible wall of water close over me, I found myself thinking about all of those things.

I kicked my legs harder, but felt myself pulled inch-by-inch further from the rippling barrier. I panicked. Reflexes gulped down the air held in my throat. My lungs burned in desperation. I thrashed my limbs against the darkness swirling around me.

My mouth jerked open, useless air escaping from my lungs. Salt stung my lips and tongue. My throat burned as I gulped in the murky water that threatened to fill my chest.

Kicking out once more, I closed my eyes against the oncoming blackness. Vainly, I tried to think of anything other than the inevitable. Then the cool breeze rushed over my face, brushing off the last of the receding water.

I blinked a couple times against the sudden brightness of the sunlight. Then I spluttered out all the lake water that I hadn't swallowed to suck down the salty air. I didn't worry about what my vocal chords were doing, and apparently they reacted with a throaty, possessed-goat kind of noise, because suddenly the entire cast and crew were looking at me.

With my lungs drinking in oxygen once more, the irrational panic dissipated, quickly replaced by embarrassment that burned along my cheekbones. Trish, the lifeguard, immediately jumped in beside me, hooking her arms under mine.

"I'm all right," I gasped against the flood of questions, "I just swallowed some water." With my face free of the water, the panic subsided as my brain started running through the mantras it had learned that day at the pool. *Water is only water. Water is only dangerous if you lose control. People only drown because they don't know how to swim.*

"You sure?" Trish asked. "You looked pretty freaked out for a second there."

"Yeah, it's fine really. I'm just a little hydrophobic."

"Really?" the director asked, leaning over the edge of his raft.

"Only a little," I replied. "Just when I think I'm drowning."

Apparently, that was the wrong thing to say, because I was immediately hauled bodily into a raft and chauffeured back to shore.

Trish radioed Scott, the crew medic, who was waiting for us in the production trailer. He checked my pulse while rattling of a bunch of questions.

"Really, it's no big deal," I insisted. "It was like two seconds. I'm fine."

That was when my head started spinning. I caught a glimpse of Scott lifting my eyelids and shining a penlight at me. Everything went black.

* * *

I awoke in the dark and rolled over to discover I had been laid on a sleeping bag spread out in the craft service tent. The budget was too low to afford more than one trailer, so craft, grip, and even editing had tents pitched along the edge of the base camp. The floor of the tent was covered in salt and sand as usual, and I grimaced as I crawled out of the flap. Someone had thought to put my jacket on me, but I was still wearing my salt-riddled shorts. I snagged a few bottles of water on the way out and poured them over everything from my waist down to relieve the worst of the chaffing.

The moon crept up over the lake, framing a dark silhouette unloading coolers from the last of the rafts onto the beach. That had to be Mike, the location manager. It was a pretty thankless position—

always the first to arrive and the last to leave.

The full moon played its light across Mike's profile as I approached.

"Everyone gone?" I asked, grabbing one end of the raft Mike was tugging across the sand.

"Pretty much. You all right?"

"Guess so. I was out for a while. Dizzy spell or something."

Mike nodded his thanks as we dragged the raft in line with the others.

"What about the boat?" I asked, jerking my head toward the dinghy.

"Leave it," Mike said. "It's tied to the prop dock, and it won't hurt to see if it actually stays afloat tonight."

I nodded my agreement. The old boat had been painstakingly stripped down and refinished to look old and worn out, which had taken priority over making sure it was seaworthy. Only that morning, prop hands had been furiously plugging all the holes that appeared once the boat was actually placed in water.

"Brandon? Is that you?" Trish's voice called. "Why weren't you answering?"

I turned to see the slender lifeguard half-jogging across the sand. She had pulled on some jean shorts and a hoodie over her swimsuit.

"Oh, Jon. You're up," she said, stopping next to us. "Where did Brandon run off to?"

"Couldn't tell ya. Mike's the only one I've seen."

"Oh." Her narrow eyebrows pinched down across her nose. "He was supposed to be checking on you. Steve's coming to pick me up, and I don't want to be here a minute longer than I have to."

"I must have missed him. Do you want me help you look?"

"Would you? I hate the dark."

"Sure, as soon as we get the coolers up here."

"I got'em," Mike said over his shoulder as he headed back down the beach. "I can't leave 'til you all do anyway."

Trish held her phone out lighting a few feet ahead of us as we returned to base camp.

"You know, I'm pretty sure we have actual flashlights in one of the tents," I said.

"I don't care," Trish responded. "Those tents creep me out once the sun goes down. That's why I made Brandon go after you."

The craft tent was just as empty as when I crawled out of it, but I snagged another bottle of water and dumped it down my shorts.

Trish turned away, pretending not to notice. "I'm going to try calling Brandon again before my battery dies."

I smirked as I reached for the nearest open box rummaging through it until I found a flashlight. A soft buzz came from inside the tent.

"Still not answering," Trish said, glaring at her phone.

"Listen," I said.

The buzz sounded again. I crawled deeper into the tent, tugging more boxes open as I went until the buzz grew louder.

"Is that Brandon's phone?" Trish asked. "What's it doing in there? He always keeps it in his pocket."

"Looks that way," I said, pulling Brandon's vibrating pants out of the box, scattering more salt through the tent.

That was when the shouting started.

I backed out of the tent and turned the flashlight toward the beach. Moving as fast as I could in the gritty sand, I scrambled down the beach to find Mike splashing in the shallows. Trish and I each grabbed an arm and pulled. Something jerked him back. Dark shapes swam around him. I splashed forward into the shallows and grabbed his legs. The water was bubbling now. I ignored the tightness in my stomach as Mike's shouts turned to screams.

I lunged backward, and Mike's legs broke free of the lake's surface. He wriggled up the sand, clutching his knees close to his chest. I snatched up the flashlight from where I'd dropped it on the sand and turned it on Mike's legs. Long, red, burn-like marks stretched across the skin.

"Something grabbed me," Mike said, "something in the water."

I flashed the light across my own legs, but they were as pale and white as always. I peered into the lake, still rippling under the moonlight and jumped at the sight of the face peering back at me. You know it's been a long day when you don't recognize your own reflection.

"Trish? What's going on?" another voice called.

I turned and Steve held a hand in front of his face as he came into flashlight range.

"Something in the water," Mike blurted out. "Something big!"

"I don't see anything out there now," I said. Handing the flashlight to Trish, I grabbed the last cooler and tossed it up the beach.

"Either way," Steve said, "let's get out of here and get Mike looked at. We can make a report tomorrow."

"What about Brandon?" Trish asked, looking out into the mist starting to form over the lake. "Do you think he went swimming? Do you think…?"

"I don't know," I said as Trish trailed off, "but let's get Mike back to the cars, and I can look some more."

We helped Mike to his feet and started the hike back to the parking lot. Trish led the way, flashlight in one hand and Steve holding the other. I tried to help Mike, but he shrugged me off, hobbling along ahead of me. I stared at them as we walked, trying to ignore the darkness lurking in my peripheral vision and thoughts of who or what it might be hiding. It wasn't a long hike, but long enough to make me glad I'd gotten most of the salt off my skin.

"What do you think it was?" Trish whispered as we crested the hill that hid the cars from the set.

"A lot of strange things live in saltwater," Steve replied. "They say life started with saltwater if you look back far enough."

I stopped short, almost running into Mike who was craning his neck to look over Trish. I stepped off the trail to get a better look myself, and my mouth actually fell open.

The water had risen. A lot.

The bridge to the mainland, which was really just a road shored up enough to be above the water level, was lost in the deathly stillness of the lake. The parking lot was covered, too; water caressed the tires of the three vehicles still there.

"What's going on?" Trish asked, grabbing at Steve's jacket.

"Let me check it out," Steve answered. "It doesn't look too deep, and we've got good clearance. We might be able to make it out if we go slow."

He waded in, the deep shadows lapping after him with each step, and climbed into the white truck. Mike tentatively stepped into the shallows and moved to his own car. Opening up the trunk, he pulled out a tire iron. Steve's engine chugged a couple times and turned over. Shifting into gear, he let the vehicle creep forward. Almost immediately the back wheels began sliding toward the lake.

Locking up the brakes, Steve brought the truck to a halt and shifted to a lower gear.

"Come back," Trish called. "I don't like this."

"Hold on," Steve called back. "I think I got it."

As Steve applied the gas, the whole vehicle slid backward. He threw it into park and cut the engine.

"Nope. No good." He slid over and opened the passenger side door.

Then the wave broke.

Unseen currents surged through the still surface of the lake, gushing into the air and slapping over the truck. Steve grabbed the doorframe as the tide pulled the vehicle out with it. The shocks groaned as the truck pitched heavily and rolled onto its side.

I dashed into the water as Steve climbed out, one hand to his head. The current had vanished as quickly as it had come, and the lake returned to its eerie tranquility.

"You all right?" I asked.

"Banged up a bit, but nothing too bad, I think."

He started wading forward, but his legs jerked backward, and he fell face first into the waves. The lake surged forward and slurped him back around the overturned truck.

I splashed forward, wrapping my arms around Steve's chest. Digging my heels against the gravel I pulled, but something else pulled back.

"Steve!" Trish cried.

Mike jumped in, slamming the tire iron over and over into the water around us. My feet slipped, and Steve gasped deeply before his head was jerked under. The water began to bubble. My stomach quivered. The lake frothed around me for a long minute as Steve lurched in my arms. I felt Steve's skin bubbling under his shirt. I twisted against the waves and kicked out. Steve's shirt came free as I leapt backward.

Trish was sobbing now. Mike was still thrashing the dark waves. I picked myself and yelled at him. "Mike!"

"Come on!" he yelled, swinging again.

"Mike, get out of there!"

"Come get some!" he continued. "Come on fish freak! I know you're in there!"

"Mike! There's nothing in the water!"

He slammed the bar again.

"Mike, it *is* the water!"

Mike stopped, then lunged backward, tripping and scuttling out of the waves on all fours, the tire iron forgotten under the throbbing tide. I helped him up and then put an arm around Trish's shuddering shoulders. On the other side of the parking lot we waited for her to catch her breath.

As she choked down a couple deep breaths, she reached for Steve's shirt. The soaked material flopped against her as she took it, dumping several handfuls of gray-white grit down her front.

She let out a half-screaming sob and dropped the shirt in the brush. Slapping at the salt covering her clothes, she sunk to her knees gave in to silent tears. Mike stood by staring.

I took a couple of deep breaths and knelt and touched Trish's fingers. Her hand shook, but she let me take it and lift her to her feet.

"Come on," I said to Mike, but he didn't move. "Mike, come on," I repeated.

He glared at me.

"What? We need to move," I said.

"Where?" he snapped. "Where exactly do you think you're going?"

"We're getting off this island! There are rafts back at the set, remember? Are you coming or not?"

I led Trish up the trail out of the parking lot. Mike didn't answer, but his sandals scuffed along against the trail behind us. We made the hike back in silence. The full moon hung overhead, casting its reflection across the drifting rafts. The lake had risen here, too.

Trish's breath quickened, and I nudged her toward Mike before she could start crying again. "Go find some paddles or something."

Not waiting for a response, I licked my lips and headed down the beach. Both of the supply rafts had already drifted out to swimming distance. The camera raft was tauntingly close. The water lapping around it probably wouldn't reach my knees, but that was still deeper than I wanted to get. But it was only a yard or so, I could probably jump that.

It was that or risk the boat.

I gauged the distance from the edge of the climbing waves to the raft for a moment, and then gave up with the realization that there was no way I was going to jump over the raft.

Backing up a few paces, I bounced in place a couple times to warm my legs up. One deep breath in and out, and then I ran. The first few steps were sluggish, the sand offering little traction. But as the sand grew wetter and firmer, I picked up speed.

The creeping tide reached out for my feet as I leapt. I flew for a moment, darkness around me and the silent waves beneath me. My feet touched the rubber edge of the raft, and slid backward off the wet surface. I fell forward, my chest striking the raft, and wrapped my arms around the large tubular edge. My legs hit the water, and I kicked, tucking my elbows to pull. The raft tipped threateningly toward me, but without the buoyancy of the water, the far side quickly dropped back.

The water licked at my thighs, and panic bubbled up from my subconscious. I forced a deep breath, and the three-year-old mantra started in my head again. *Water is only water*—except when it's not. *Water is only dangerous*—when the water is in control. *People only drown*—when the lake wants to eat them.

Shaking the unbidden thoughts from my head, I kicked again and writhed, pulling with every muscle I had, and as the raft slapped back against the lake, I rolled panting to its floor.

I pushed myself to a sitting position. The paddles tucked into the straps reached the bottom of the lake, and with a few punting strokes, the raft came up against the sand. Trish grabbed the straps and pulled as I clambered out.

"Mike's getting buckets," she explained.

Soft squishes in the sand announced his approach. I let myself catch a breath or two as I turned to him. Then the water swelled behind me.

I dove sideways, plowing into Trish and rolling across the sand as the wave crashed over the raft. Trish gasped and scrambled away, her knee striking my nose as she fought to get clear of the spreading wave. I blinked back tears and climbed to my feet. Mike just stood staring toward us. I held my breath and turned around. All three rafts were drifting for the middle of the lake.

"The boat it is," I said.

One by one we inched down the rickety dock. The boat seemed to hold our weight as we cast off and drifted around the end of the dock. A leak appeared, seeping out from under the seat at the back of the boat. Mike immediately put one of his buckets to use. Smart guy that Mike.

The night wore on as we rounded the tip of the island, and the lake was so still there were moments where it was hard to tell if we were moving at all. Eventually the roofs of the submerged cars came into view, and a while after that, the far shore began to creep out of the horizon toward us.

That was when the lake started bubbling. All the water churned and frothed. Small waves broke the surface rocking the boat. Mike handed Trish the second bucket while I paddled for all I was worth. I tried to shift my weight as I paddled to counter the boat's lurching from side to side. The shore ahead was growing, but so were the waves. I grabbed the boat as a large wave threatened to capsize us and glanced down. I bit my lip, pulling back from the face that stared up at me. It was my face, but those weren't my eyes. Something was wearing my reflection and glaring at me.

Trish's scream was swallowed up in the splash. I turned and lunged for the ripples where she had disappeared, but Mike was faster. He knocked me aside, leaning over the side of the boat and reaching into the lake up to his shoulder. A long moment later, he pulled the sputtering, coughing Trish above the surface.

I tried to help lift her into the boat, but Mike shoved me away. "Keep paddling," he said, "and lean that way."

The waves thrashed around us awhile more before giving up. I glanced down. It was slow going, but in time, we hit the far edge of the bridge and clambered out onto the road. Somehow the tide hadn't risen on this side.

"Steve's house isn't far," Trish said with a quiver. "I've got a key."

We plodded to the house in silence. I tried to ignore the salt that saturated my clothes. Inside, Trish offered a bathroom to clean up. I started the shower, then shuddered. The thought of water on my face threatened to bring back shadows of panic and helplessness. I set the tub filling instead.

Pulling my jacket off, I returned to the living room while the water ran. Trish huddled on the couch, a cordless phone in her hand. Mike stared at me.

"I don't even know who to call," she droned, rocking back and forth.

Mike laid a hand on her shoulder, not taking his eyes off me. "Go lay down for a bit, and we'll figure it out together."

Trish nodded and moved upstairs. Mike stepped toward me. "What do you want?" he asked.

I tried to raise an eyebrow at him, but as tired as I was, I'm not sure it responded. "What are you talking about?"

"You got us off the island, now what?"

"I don't know. We clean up, call the police, and go home? What do you mean?"

"I mean it was you!" Mike hissed at me. "It was all you. So what do you want?"

"Mike, I told you it was the water!"

Mike shoved me and I stumbled back against the wall. "The water only boiled when you were in it. There was no way you could have seen that wave coming before you pushed Trish out of the way." He stepped forward and grabbed my collar. "And you're wearing Brandon's shirt!"

I sucked in a deep breath, sweat collecting in my eyebrows as I looked down at the orange shirt I was wearing. I hate orange. The sound of the steadily filling tub poured through my head, and dizziness crept over me. I grabbed Mike's wrists, and my stomach lurched. I could feel Mike's skin bubbling in my grasp.

Mike's scream was choked off as he pulled back. I tried to let go, but my hands squeezed tighter, salt chaffing my fingers. Sweat streamed down Mikes face, streaking his shirt with salt. He dropped to his knees. His voice grew silent, but the scream was still twisted into his face. His hands came off in mine, salt spilling out around my grasp.

My fingers weakened, and I dropped graying hands onto Mike's limp form. He continued to shrivel and crumble until all that that was left was a heap of salt covering his empty clothing. I staggered into the bathroom, breath coming fast and shallow, frantically brushing the salt from my hands, and stopped as I stared into the tub.

My reflection stared back with someone else's eyes. I tried to run, but my feet refused to move. My mind kicked and wrenched against the confusion churning in my head, but my body remained still. My stomach clenched and pushed my legs forward one step at a time until I was looking directly downward into those empty eyes.

"It's been too long to let you go," my reflection said. "We haven't had a compatible host since we were a much bigger lake. We should have moved more slowly, but we're not as patient as we used to be. We've been asleep so long we'd forgotten how hungry we were. And now, to find not one but two hosts. The excitement is almost too much."

I pulled back, but my body pulled against me. My brain reeled, silently screaming its childhood mantra. *Water is only water. Water is only water.*

The face that used to be mine smiled up at me and flexed a hand. Tendrils of pain slithered from my abs up to my arm, and my hand mirrored the gesture. *Water is only dangerous if you lose control.*

More tendrils crept outward toward my limbs, wriggling through the muscles that still pulled me close to the rippling water. One more time thoughts of a much younger me flashed through my head. Thoughts of water all around me, closing me in, stealing the life out of me. *People only drown...*

Trish's voice called down the stairs. I couldn't make the words out over the faucet still pouring into the tub, but footsteps followed close behind. Footsteps heading downstairs, where she would find Mike. Where she would find me, or whatever was left of me. And the thing inside of me would find her.

Water is only dangerous when people lose control. I stopped resisting, lurching forward instead and plunging my head into the tub. My body screamed at me. Darkness lashed against every side of my mind. Resisting them both, I breathed deep and let the darkness have me.

* * *

The first sensation was dizziness. Air forced its way into my chest, and suddenly I was coughing, sharp hacks that burned as they expelled liquid from my lungs. My head was turned and the water splashed against my cheek. Soft fingers turned my cheek upward and lips pressed against mine.

My stomach knotted. I gagged and vomited. My throat burned as the saltwater burned its way free. A familiar voice choked off a smothered squeal. Forcing my eyes open, I blinked upward; the halogen light increased my dizziness.

Trish knelt over me, wiping salt from her lips. I stared up at her, and she stared back with eyes that were not her own. I tried to reach up, but jerked my head to the side as more racking coughs splattered water across the tile floor. I lay still for a moment, feeling my lungs suck air.

When I looked up again, Trish was gone. Eventually I dragged my way to the couch, where the cordless phone still lay. I remember bits and pieces of the ambulance ride. And long stretches in a hospital bed, trying to offer coherent explanations to a police officer that kept scratching his head at me.

When the hospital released me, I caught a bus home. There was something on the news, four missing-persons cases were opened. As far as I know they are still ongoing. No one seemed to believe my version of what happened to Steve and Mike. They gave me a psychological evaluation and assigned me a case worker

The crew resumed production once the cops were finished going over the set. I didn't go back, and no one seemed to expect me to. Without me there, production wrapped up without any word of further incidents.

As for Trish, I don't know what happened to her. I hear rumors sometimes that make me wonder, but I try not to think about them. The cops never found any trace of her. Still haven't decided if that's a good thing.

The film turned out all right, I guess. It's on Netflix now. I hear they are talking about a sequel. I won't be going back. I'm done swimming in salt water.

J. Anthony Gohier

J. Anthony Gohier has been writing for many years. He is a member of the League of Utah Writers and has won awards at the League's last two annual competitions, including Best in Show in Poetry.

Exposure Therapy
by John M. Olsen

"It's just a cave, Valerie. People have used caves for thousands of years. There's nothing to be afraid of."

I shivered, but not from cold. It was a dark, damp, oppressive enclosure, and it smelled of mud and decomposition. It ran back into the mountain below the Bonneville Shoreline Trail, just east of the Great Salt Lake. I didn't move.

"What's so special about this cave of yours?"

Brad grinned and waived his meaty hand toward the cave entrance at his feet.

"Nobody else knows about this one. I finally found one nobody's discovered, less than a mile from city limits. My cave hunting paid off."

He had told me about his caving hobby when we'd met a few months back. He had spent hundreds of hours in the canyons and along the benches looking for signs, hoping for that big new discovery. His only disadvantage was that he was six foot three and over two hundred pounds, built more for football than for spelunking.

His large crowbar lay beside the hole, unneeded now that he'd levered the rocks out of the way. He had told me in the car that he'd used block and tackle to move some of the heavier rocks the day before.

The thought of entering the cave gave me shivers. "Maybe you could just take lots of pictures to show me. I don't need to go in."

"I'll be with you the whole time. You have my best flashlight and a helmet. What else could you ask for? Here, I'll go first and you can follow right behind me."

He flipped his backpack around so it rested on his chest and sat next to the hole with his feet dangling.

Very little could scare me. I'd earned a black belt in Taekwondo with more armed and unarmed sparring than I would like to admit. But caves? No.

I put some of my mental training into play and calmed myself with a deep breath. "Okay. We can do this. You know I have claustrophobia, right? I mentioned it before." Sweat ran down my back.

"Yes. Dozens of times. I figured a little exposure therapy might help."

He grinned as he eased his legs down between two boulders and into the opening. He looked up and beckoned for me to join him. "There's a room almost big enough to stand in just a little ways down. You can help me laser map where it opens up farther in. It wasn't safe for me to go by myself."

Of course it wasn't safe. It was a cave. A dark, smelly, wet place that made me feel like my arms were tied to my sides, like I was in a coffin or about to drown. I restarted my breathing exercises as I waited.

"So how long has it been here?" I figured history might be a good distraction.

He looked up as his head descended into the entrance. "Near as I can figure, it formed while Lake Bonneville was here thousands of years ago, before it dried up into the Great Salt Lake. It was probably an underwater geyser before the lake receded. The flow of water dissolved some of the stone, then the shrinking lake left it open to the air. The walls are mostly made of calcium deposits in the first cave."

His voice had been growing fainter and more muffled as he descended.

I sat and poked my feet into the hole with my helmet's lamp pointed down to where I could see Brad's helmet below. I checked my back pocket for my small spare flashlight. My hair was tucked up under the helmet because Brad had warned me to expect mud. Lots of mud. I wasn't sure how to reconcile his description of underground beauty with the expected soggy glop. I shivered in the dark.

"It opens up about ten feet below me. It's an easy climb."

Footholds were easy to find, as promised. If I could concentrate on the climbing instead of the narrowness of the passage, I knew I could make it. I hoped I could, anyway. I was a lot skinnier than Brad, so I knew from a technical viewpoint I couldn't get stuck.

A damp, cool breeze rose slowly from below. I stared downward into the dark.

Brad tried to distract me again with information. "The cave has been sealed at least since the area was colonized in the eighteen hundreds. Before that, who knows? That means we don't need to worry about any big animals."

The room below was large enough for me to stand, but Brad had to stoop. To one side, the ceiling sloped down to where it met the floor. The other side ended in a wall of delicate rock formations. Brad said they were called soda straws.

"So what caused you to dislike caves?" It was the wrong question to ask if he meant to distract me, but I figured I should level with him. We'd been together long enough that he deserved to know.

"I tried to climb through an irrigation pipe under a road once when I was little. I got stuck halfway. They got me out a few minutes before the water got diverted to that ditch from upstream."

He closed his gaping mouth and shook his head. "I'm sorry. It was wrong of me to pry."

He glanced around the cave as if he were reacquainting himself with an old friend. The surfaces varied from jagged to smooth across the ceiling, walls and floor.

"See over here? I've mapped this area and as far as the laser can see into these two tunnels." He pointed at two openings, the larger of which looked barely big enough to crawl through, the smaller was no more than two feet across at the most. A breeze, similar to the one at the entrance, came from the larger opening. "This must open up again farther in. We can map it as we go."

Brad got out his tablet computer and a miniature laser scanner. "I just need to push this in front of me with my backpack and scan at each bend. The software assembles it all into a single map."

His longer legs forced him to shimmy through the opening like a snake while I was able to stay on my hands and knees behind him, lighting up his feet with my headlamp. He was right about the mud.

Brad had scooted forward several times to scan when his feet suddenly vanished around a sharp corner. I jumped and banged my helmet on the low ceiling of the tube.

"Brad? What happened? Where did you go?"

Panic crept into my heart as I looked at a sharp turn ahead of me.

"Woah. I don't believe this. Val, come on out while I set up the scanner."

I gritted my teeth and convinced myself it was a tube just like the slides at the kiddie park. Nothing was ready to grab me, crush me, or leave me alone in complete darkness to be lost in a contest between madness and starvation. Unfortunately, I have a good imagination.

"Here, Val. Let me help you."

He reached out and took my hand as my head cleared the tiny tunnel, my face down to the floor. I shrieked at his sudden reappearance, and then choked down a reply he didn't deserve. This area was much bigger. We could both stand and walk around.

The room was filled with crystal formations which reflected and refracted our helmet lights, leaving flickers of rainbow to play along the walls and ceiling.

"This isn't normal. You shouldn't get quartz and amethyst

crystals like this from a geyser blow hole. I've got to record this or nobody will believe it. Once I start the scanner, be sure to stay out of the laser beam. It will circle all the way around, and I don't want to scan you. Not right now, anyway."

Good. Concentrate on the flirting instead of the tons of unsupported rock above us. I unclenched my teeth. "I'm sure I look like I'll catch my death of mud. This isn't exactly a fashion runway."

Brad activated the camera on his tablet and aimed it at me. "Give me a good supermodel pout."

He took a picture and left my eyes with an afterimage of the flash before I could do anything but gawk in his direction.

"Great. If I see that on the Internet, you die."

We walked around the scanner as it rotated through a full circle, scanning the entire cave with its green laser light. Brad watched on the tablet as the data was assembled into a 3D view of the cave.

While he was occupied, I stepped around a large crystal pillar and leaned against a raised section of the floor near the wall. As my eyes traced the sharp edges of the rock, my hand rested on a hard, rounded surface. My fingers found their way into holes as I shifted my weight. I looked down to see my fingers resting in the eye sockets of a skull.

I screamed and backed away to the far wall, falling backwards to sit in the mud. I found myself staring at the leg and foot bones of another skeleton sitting in an indentation that looked like a crystal throne. Sharp quartz spikes covered the floor all around me. I had barely escaped impaling myself on one of the crystals.

A series of creative and loud words escaped my mouth as I scrambled on hands, knees and feet to get back to Brad. He met me halfway and wrapped his arms around me.

"It's okay. I'm right here. Breathe, Valerie. That's it. There. Now come sit down over here and have a drink of water." He pulled a plastic bottle from his backpack and continued in his most soothing tone. "Now, what happened?"

"There are bones. Some on the raised platform over there and more in a chair at the back of the cave."

John M. Olsen

"I'll go take a look. We may have stumbled on an old Indian tomb. The archeologists at the University of Utah will have a field day." He walked over to the raised area. "Yup, it's a skeleton all laid out like a burial platform. With all the moisture, there's almost nothing left but the bones." He leaned in close to examine the remains. "Huh. There's an obsidian dagger here in the middle of the ribs. This looks like more than just a burial spot. I think this one was killed here. It's amazing what belief will do to primitive people. People can die of their own choice, believing their leader is a god."

He wound his way back to the other skeleton. "You're right. This one hasn't fallen apart. I wonder why."

He lit up the skull with his headlamp and ran a finger along the nose ridge between the eyes. "Were you a god to your people? Perhaps you were a curse, instead. King or killer?" Brad gave it a Three Stooges poke in both eye sockets.

"Please stop messing with it, Brad. I'm barely able to sit here right now, thinking of human sacrifices. I need to get out. Old bones or not, I'm done."

I felt the hair on the back of my neck stand up, and gooseflesh covered my arms as he walked back over to me. The air felt wrong as he approached, as if we were not alone, even though I knew that couldn't possibly be true.

"One second and we can go. I just want to make sure the scan caught both sets of bones." Brad sat at the entry with his tablet and zoomed in on the map.

"Oh, yeah. Not perfect but they're there. Let's pack up and get you out of here."

He was reaching for the scanner when there was a loud crack. I glanced up as Brad shoved me forward into the middle of the room. A long crystal fell from the ceiling and crashed to the ground next to him at the entrance, spraying glass-like splinters in all directions.

Brad cried out and fell to the ground clutching his left leg.

"We have to get out now," I said. "We can get your stuff later."

I reached to help him up, and my hand came back wet. "Brad, you're bleeding!"

"Tear my sleeve off. I need you to bandage this leg and my right shoulder. Watch out for the sharp rocks."

"I need to get you out of here, not sit around while the cave collapses!"

"Gotta stop the bleeding first, Val." He winced as he held his left hand out so I could grab the cuff.

I nodded. "Okay. I can do this. Tear the sleeve. Bandage the cuts."

The shadows felt like they were closing in on me, but I split the sleeve from cuff to shoulder and pulled it free. I tore it in two and tied the makeshift bandages around his wounds, leaving the razor edged shards in place. Removing them in the dark might cut an artery.

"Now, out." I grabbed his good arm and helped him scoot over toward the exit. At the edge of the room, we leaned for a moment against the wall. I looked for the exit, but couldn't see it. "The way out should be right here."

Brad played his headlamp around the wall. He winced at every move. I could tell he was trying to look like he was okay. I knew better. The large crystal pillar which had broken free from the ceiling blocked the exit, embedding itself in the ground right at the entrance.

My heart raced as I strained against the rock and realized it was too big for me to move. Brad sucked in a breath. "He doesn't want me to leave."

"You can't be serious, Brad. The skeleton? It's just bones. It doesn't *want* anything."

He shook his head as if clearing cobwebs, then blinked at me. I wasn't sure if it was blood loss or shock, but he was drifting.

"Um, you're right. We need to get my crowbar out."

I looked through his pack, but didn't see it. Then it dawned on me. "You left it on the ground at the entrance after moving the rocks out of the way."

He flipped the computer tablet around one-handed to look at the map, then rotated the image around to get a top-down view.

"Look here." He grunted in pain and continued, "It scanned part way into this other small exit. I think it connects to the smaller tunnel from the other side."

I gawked at him. "You're in no shape to climb through that. You would barely make it through the big tunnel!"

"Not me. You. Bring the crowbar back." He rested his head against the wall. "You can pry the rock out with it."

"No. I can't go. Not through there."

I shook my head and clasped my hands together to keep them from shaking.

"You already tried to move the rock. I'm just going to get weaker. Think. Is there anything else?"

I pulled out my cell phone. Of course there would be no reception underground. I nearly threw it against the cave wall, but managed to put it back in my pocket instead.

Calm. I needed to be calm. Deep breaths.

"Crowbar. Okay, I can get the crowbar. There's only a third of the tunnel not on the map. How bad can it be?"

I tried to focus on the task as I checked to see if I would fit into the smaller tunnel. My shoulders cleared as my helmet scraped along the top. I would need to slither through as Brad had done in the larger tunnel, but with just scant inches of clearance on all sides. There was no way he would fit, so this was the only option to get him out alive.

I scooted forward around a bend, and my hands hit water as the tunnel dipped.

"Brad? Can you hear me?"

My voice was muffled as much by my own body as it was by the narrow stone passage. I was on my own, and I needed to hurry.

The puddle grew deeper as I inched forward to where the water reached the top of the tunnel in front of me. It felt just like the irrigation pipe of my childhood all over again. I tried to feel through the cold water to the far side, but couldn't tell how far it ran before it rose again. I sat for a moment considering how little difference there was between starving and drowning. Finally, I decided the water was the only chance to avoid death.

I sucked in one large breath and slid forward into the frigid water. I felt my way with my eyes closed. The waist of my pants caught, and I had to stop. I eased my hips to the side and twisted free.

My lungs burned as my hand broke the surface, but the air gap was too narrow to raise my face to the air.

I pushed forward still holding my breath, fighting the urge to fill my lungs. The red glow went to a sudden and complete black as the headlamp died in the water. I had to get to air.

I twisted and got my face into the narrow air-filled gap. I gasped air, gagging and coughing. The pool still reached up above my ears, but I could breathe.

I shivered as I inched forward in the dark. The cold water drained heat from my body. At long last I felt dry earth as the tunnel angled upwards again.

The tunnel was wider than it was tall, so I couldn't flip back over onto my stomach. Dust and grime dropped onto my face as I squeezed through.

Finally, the passage widened beyond my reach. I pulled myself out and saw dim light filtering down through the entrance shaft. Tears of relief rolled down my face as I scrambled up the entrance and grabbed the crow bar.

I was out. I had saved myself. Did I really need to go back in? It was too much to ask of me. I could just call for help. I got my phone out, but it had been soaked and refused to work.

I sat there for a moment.

"You are not a coward. Brad needs help right now. Nobody else can do it."

Having only one option reminded me of the discipline I had learned in my Taekwondo training. This was no different. I sighed and descended as fast as I could, forcing my needs to the foreground of my fears.

I wanted to take the larger tunnel, but I would have too little leverage with the crowbar in the tight confines. It would only work if I was in the far room. Through some miracle, the small flashlight from my pocket still worked, so I steeled my emotions and squeezed back into the narrow passage, pushing the small light and crowbar before me as the tunnel walls tugged at my clothing.

I started face up so I could breathe as long as possible, then flipped to face down as the water level reached the ceiling of the passage. As I broke back to the surface, the little flashlight gave its last flicker and died.

I stood dripping water onto the muddy floor. "Brad? I need some light."

No answer.

I felt my way over to the larger entrance, but neither he nor his backpack were where I left them. I felt around and came across his miniaturized laser scanner. It wouldn't be much, but it would be enough. I heaved a great sigh of relief between shivers.

A green light began to play around the cave, lighting up Brad's form stretched out among the bones atop the platform.

I climbed over and flipped the switch on his headlamp. Blessed light filled the room, but to my horror, the bandages on his leg and shoulder were loose and soaked through with blood. A crimson trail led from the entrance to the little platform. The obsidian knife I'd seen on the platform earlier was covered in blood and rested nearby.

"Brad, that's not funny. Don't mess with me."

I was shaking, but couldn't tell if it was from the fear, the cold, or the anger.

"You could die from blood loss if you keep moving around like that."

I patted the side of his face, but didn't get much more than a grunt out of him. I rewrapped and tightened the bandages in an effort to staunch the blood flow. That brought him back awake and cussing. He sat up.

"That hurts. Why is it so tight?"

"So you don't bleed out on the way out of here. Any more questions or can we go now? I got the crowbar. I hate this cave."

It might not have been fair to give him a verbal smack-down, but I figured after the prank with the platform and the knife, he deserved it. I helped him to sit up, then to stand with his good arm around my shoulder.

As we made our way between the formations, Brad spoke. "You're soaking wet and freezing. What happened?"

"Exposure therapy," I snapped back. If I stayed angry, the fear of the cold, wet, engulfing darkness might not overcome me and turn me into a blubbering pile of flesh unable to move. "Now sit down while I knock this rock loose."

I eased Brad to the ground to the side of the blocked opening next to his laser scanner where he slowly packed things one-handed into his backpack.

The stone blocking the exit was wedged in, so I worked the stone back and forth to pry it loose. Once I relocated the crowbar to the base and got it hooked under the edge, I was able to lever the stone up and tip it out of the way with a crash.

"Let's go."

I looked over to where he had been sitting and he was gone.

"Brad?"

The light from his helmet made it easy to spot him back at the platform. He picked up the knife again.

"Put it down, Brad. We're going now. The exit's clear. Do you hear me?"

I watched as he ran the sharp, jagged edge of the knife up his damaged arm, leaving a thin streak of red.

Rage and muscle memory from my Taekwondo class flooded through me as the pressure of being underground demoted the rational side of my mind to simple observer. The crowbar lashed out as I leapt across the cave. It hit the knife just above his fingers and shattered the blade.

"Stop it! I can't keep this up." My scream turned into a sob as I grabbed his blood-slicked hand to pull him back toward the exit. The smell of mud mixed with Brad's blood made my stomach churn as the darkness pressed in wherever his light wasn't shining.

My grip on his hand slipped as he pulled it free. He turned and took a step toward the other skeleton and the sharp rocks in front of it.

"Brad, talk to me. What are you doing? We have to leave."

He breathed out a long sigh. "He says it's time." He knelt next to the sharp rocks.

"You're hallucinating! I am so done with this."

Rage pushed my fears back to a far corner of my brain where they whimpered like a beaten dog. I hurled the crowbar overhand like a spear at the only other target I could see, hitting the skeleton's right eye socket and shattering the skull into pieces which rained down onto the floor as the skeleton collapsed.

A quick leap forward put me to where I could grab Brad's collar to keep him from collapsing forward onto the sharp rocks.

He raised both of his hands as I grabbed him.

"The curse of the ancient one is released!"

I yanked him to his feet, much harder than necessary.

The room shook like before when the stone had blocked the exit. This, and Brad's rambling hallucinations, brought my shrieking terrors to the foreground, but things looked different this time. The large crystal pillars were shedding small flakes which shattered as they fell, leaving behind crushed crystal which dulled as it settled to the ground as ordinary dirty sand.

Brad looked up at me. "Valerie? Why are we over here?"

I grabbed his hand and slung his arm over my shoulder again. The dull sand from the collapsing crystals had covered the floor and would soon block off the exit tunnel as it continued to gather.

I hauled him through the sand to the exit. The breakup had to be a natural event of some kind. Things were just settling somehow.

"Brad, go. I'll be right behind you."

He gasped as he bent down to crawl, and had to flip over onto his back to shimmy through so his wounds wouldn't scrape across the ground. As he snaked through, I grabbed his backpack, ready to push it in front of me as I'd seen him do.

Once he was completely into the narrow tunnel, I brushed away some of the dirt and squeezed in. Dirt fell at an increasing pace and threatened to trap my feet, but I pulled into the passage as the exit into the cavern closed off with a whoosh. After the watery secondary tunnel, this one was luxuriously large. I could crawl on hands and knees as I had when we entered. Contrary to the laws of nature, more dirt pushed into the tunnel from below, but I kept just ahead of it. Low rumbles continued to shake the passage.

Brad stopped, so I braced myself and pushed against his feet to help him scoot farther up until he finally called out that he was clear.

"I can't make it the rest of the way out, Val. I can't climb the entrance tube. You go out and call for help."

I shook my head. "The ground's still rumbling, you idiot. This whole thing could collapse. I need to get you out now!"

He winced as he leaned against the base of the exit shaft. "You can't lift me out. Not without help. I've got rope, but I don't think you can do it alone."

I racked my brains for the fastest way to get help. Then I remembered the pulleys Brad described for moving rocks at the entrance. "I think I've got it."

I emptied his backpack on the cave floor and grabbed his climbing rope. I looped one end through the belt at the front of his pants.

"Quick, mister caving guy. How much weight do I have to lift if I tie this end to a tree, and pull on the other like you were wearing a pulley? Is it good enough?"

He sucked on his lip for a moment.

"Two to one. I can help, but you'll be pulling close to a hundred pounds."

The crumbled, dry sand started to flow out of both paths from the lower chamber as the walls shed their formations.

"I'll manage."

I looped most of the rope around an arm and played it out as I climbed out into the glorious sunshine.

I used a square knot to tie one end to a tree, then removed all the slack. I pulled the other end around the tree as well, so I could send the rope down to him into the hole as he climbed.

"You okay? I'm pulling now."

There was a muffled reply, which was good enough for me. I alternated hoisting and taking up slack as he was able to push off the footholds until enough rope allowed Brad to help. A few more tugs, and he pulled himself out of the hole with a gasp. I grabbed his good hand to help.

"Slack please. You have no idea what it's like to be hoisted by the pants without a climbing harness. I may never have children."

Brad was covered in drying, mud-caked blood. At least his bleeding had stopped. Despite it all, it was wonderful to be with him, especially since we were out of the accursed darkness.

The ground settled, and part of the hillside dropped two feet with a grinding rumble. Brad said, "Sinkhole! Back away from it. Those laser maps might be about all that's left of this cave."

As we backed away, the cave continued its slow collapse.

"I need your phone to call for help. You still need an ambulance and shouldn't even think of walking."

"It's in the backpack with the scanner and tablet."

He looked around. I joined him in searching until I came to a horrible realization.

"I emptied it out to get the rope."

I ran over to the hole, ignoring Brad's protests that it was unsafe and that the ground could collapse. The hole only went down three feet before hitting dirt.

I stood in the hole and gave a pitiful shrug.

"I'm so sorry, Brad."

He laughed.

John M. Olsen

John M. Olsen has been creating things his whole life through a mixture of technical and creative processes, whether building family, stories, art, software, woodworking or anything else. He has dreams of becoming a Renaissance man and loves to learn new things to add to his store of randomly accessible information (otherwise known as irrelevant trivia). Writing is one of his loves, inspired by having read most of his father's extensive fantasy and science fiction collection in his teen years.

Whoso Offendeth
by Jaren K. Rencher

"It came from the Great Salt Lake." Sam Becker plopped a sealed evidence bag on the table in front of his partner. "It's a bad one, Doug. That's why it's all hands on deck."

Detective Doug Reed looked up at his partner. Seven years Sam's senior, Doug was six feet tall and retained an athletic build into his early fifties. Sam Becker towered over Doug; he stood over seven feet tall and far outweighed Doug with what was mostly solid muscle. Sam was a big man, physically, mentally, and emotionally. They had been friends for years, partners for even longer; it wasn't like him to lose his composure. Puzzled, Doug squinted at Sam, then turned his attention to the evidence bag.

The harsh fluorescent lights reflected in the plastic, glinting off folds and wrinkles enveloping a headless teddy bear. Sam laid a glossy photograph atop the bag. Doug tilted the photo slightly, enough to see the backside of a teddy bear; the ruler framing the bear proclaimed nine inches. Without the head, there was no telling the bear's exact size. Doug cocked an eyebrow at Sam, who nodded, cleared his throat, and continued.

"Fish and Game pulled it out of the water at the marina this morning. Forensics already worked their magic, pushed this one through processing, then dried it out."

Sam pulled a small notebook from his shirt pocket. His place was marked with a golf pencil wedged inside. Sam opened it and scanned his writing.

Doug shook his head in disgust. "So a kid drops his broken woobie into the lake and we all lose a day off?"

"It's not that simple, Doug."

Sam placed another photograph on top of the first. Doug turned the glossy photo around, right side up. This one showed the front of the headless bear. One arm and part of the midsection of the bear were stained a deep carmine color.

Sam clicked his tongue twice and said in an affected accent, "And I think, technically, a 'woobie' is a blanket, not a teddy bear." He waggled his pencil at Doug, chuckled, and thumbed over the notebook page. "Anyway, dispatch got the call from the Game cops. Fish and Game were investigating a Drunk and Disorderly at the marina last night, early this morning, I guess. By the time they got there, everything was quiet."

Sam turned another notebook page. "They started canvassing at sunup. It took them an hour of checking slips, but they finally found…something."

Sam drew the manila file folder from under his arm and slapped it on the table, stirring up a breeze of stale coffee. He flipped it open so that the front cover tented against the decapitated toy and put a finger down atop a photograph. A school portrait; from all appearances, it had that cheesy photographer's *trying hard to be dramatic, but not quite pulling it off* quality to it. Similar photos stood on Doug's desk. The red-haired girl looked six-years-old, maybe, seven at the oldest.

"Rachael Bradford," Sam said.

"Pretty girl."

Freckles flocked around her nose while deep dimples accompanied her toothy grin, a gap where her bottom front tooth should have been. She looked a little like his own daughter, Annie, especially the dimples and the missing front tooth. "Please don't tell me…"

"She's beautiful," Sam nodded, "and still alive. She's not the vic. Well, not exactly. She was *almost* our vic."

He drew Rachael's photograph aside and revealed a booking photo of a slightly overweight older man. Unlike the usual mugshot, this photo showed neither resignation nor defiance, but an obvious arrogance. Doug could tell that the man oozed confidence; he clearly believed that he was not just innocent, not just wrongly accused, but *above* the law. The set of his jaw said that someone would pay for this humiliation.

"He's our vic," Sam continued. "Eloy Gentry: 57 years old, white, male, lawyer at one of the big firms downtown, dead at the scene. He was found on the deck of his sailboat. A gorgeous thirty-footer, by the way. Forty-six foot mast."

Sam lifted the mugshot to show Doug a picture of a white sailboat. Doug grunted; all he knew of sailboats was that they floated and had a sail sticking up from the middle. Sam read his partner's mind.

"The 'Knot Guilty' if you can believe it."

Doug made the obligatory groan. "You say he was a lawyer? Which firm?"

Sam flipped to the booking sheet stapled to the folder and pointed. Doug nodded; he knew of the firm. Those in the know called it *The Tower of Power*. This evinced another groan, this time one of frustration.

"You don't work there, Sam, if you're a slouch. This could be trouble."

"Don't I know it. My second ex-wife, Mary? She used one of their lawyers. He crucified my guy and then ate us both for dinner with fava beans. Never even broke a sweat. You're lucky Maggie didn't do that to you."

"Great. A high-priced legal eagle dead on his boat—"

Doug's cell phone buzzed out a tune about the sun coming up. The caller ID displayed the name "Annie." He barely hesitated before he rejected the call and slipped the phone back into his pocket.

"Annie? You sure you don't need to take that, bro? You left her home alone again, didn't you?"

Doug waved away Sam's questions. "It's barely lunchtime. Maggie will pick her up in an hour." He gestured toward the school picture. "You say she was *almost* the victim. Where does she come in? What's Rachael's connection with this ambulance chaser? Gentry... Bradford... No relation there, right?"

"Nope. No relation. No, our barrister had a dirty little secret. You didn't look at his rap sheet too closely, did you, Doug? He's got a prior. Our vic was a pedophile, an S.O., and Rachael was his next intended target."

Doug looked up sharply, his piercing blue eyes blazing. "That son-of-a... Rachael? Did he... How is she?"

Sam shook his head. "She hasn't had a full physical yet—just the EMTs—but all indications are that, well, whatever happened to Gentry happened before he had a chance to do anything to her. We think he just nabbed her and took her to the boat for some privacy. Then..."

Sam shuddered and scrubbed his bald head with both hands as if trying to erase a memory.

"You didn't eat yet, did you?"

Doug ran his hand over his face; down, up, then squeezed his forehead at the onset of a sudden headache. Doug knew his friend; if it had affected Sam this strongly, it had to be bad. He sighed.

"All right, Sam. Give me the rest. Details, man. What happened to Gentry?"

* * *

Detective Doug Reed shook his head in disgust when the video ended. It had not revealed much. Shot with a security camera no doubt purchased from Hammacher Schlemmer. It provided a view of the boat from an odd angle, secreted on an outside corner of the cabin. The scene pictured was in the harsh green reverse exposure of a night vision camera.

The sequence began with an image of a man matching the file photo. Doug mentally labeled him "Gentry." The still-living vic dragged a struggling young girl by one arm into the scene. She clutched a teddy bear in her other arm. There was no sound with the video, so Doug could only assume she was screaming. He labeled the girl "Rachael" and nodded when she turned her face toward the camera. Rachael managed to get her feet underneath her long enough to stand upright and sink her teeth into Gentry's arm. Doug winced at the sight, anticipating what came next. Gentry shook her off and pushed her roughly to the deck, looming over her and ranting.

Doug glanced over at Sam; they locked eyes and shared a slight smirk. The lawyer looked ridiculous waving his arms wildly and stomping his feet. It would have been comedic if it hadn't been real and a little girl hadn't been involved.

Back on the screen the silent tantrum continued. Gentry became more and more animated, swinging his fists, but never quite striking Rachael. Finally, Gentry brought one foot back, clearly aiming at the terrified girl. The expected kick never landed.

The video flickered. A flash of white briefly overloaded the camera. The image pixelated and slowly resolved back to the green-on-black. When the image cleared, Gentry stood still, one hand clutching his belly, blood pouring from between his fingers, his other hand now holding Rachael's teddy bear. As they watched, the lawyer's mouth opened in a silent scream, one hand pawing at the wound and the other frantically waving the bear. After a few seconds, the bear slipped from his grasp and flew out of the camera frame. Gentry sagged, then dropped to his knees, his face frozen in a terrified rictus. With one last shudder, Gentry's arms fell to hang limply at his sides. Ropes of intestines snaked their way out of the six-inch hole in his shirt. He knelt that way, motionless, for nearly a full minute, then toppled slowly forward.

Gentry laid there completely still, his face on the deck of the boat. The time counter on the video rolled. No more than a foot away, the terrified girl huddled on the deck, trying to simultaneously cover her head and pull her limbs into her torso. Scared, she was doing all she could to get away from the remains.

The two veteran officers sat stunned watching the screen. For all their experience, neither of the men were sufficiently hardened not to be horrified at the sight of Gentry lying on the deck and Rachael quivering, afraid to even look at the body. Several minutes passed until the camera's sensor realized there was no further movement and the video shut off. The monitor sat black and empty.

Doug reached over and pressed a button on the monitor. "Once more, Sam."

Another few silent minutes passed. The second viewing did nothing to lessen the impact; Doug mustered all the willpower he could. "That was…" he started and then trailed off.

"I know, Doug. I watched it through a couple times before you got in."

"Something happened during that flash of light? Any theories? A bug in the camera or a digital glitch?"

"Nope. The time stamp tracks. There are no gaps and no glitches. Just that damned strange white streak."

Hoping to see something from a new perspective, Doug worked the monitor buttons again, this time watching the events play out in reverse. He reached the beginning of the video. Nothing. "What about Gentry? Do we have a cause of death, yet?" Doug pressed [PLAY] once again.

"We have the prelims. At first glance, it's pretty obvious. Massive blood loss following severe trauma to his abdomen. They found—"

"There, Sam!" Doug pointed at the screen. "What's that?"

They watched while something moved and rolled under Gentry's skin. For a moment, Doug thought of the scene in *Alien* just before the chest-burster emerged. "What in the world?"

"I was just getting to that, Doug. The coroner found this inside him." Sam reached into the file box and dropped another plastic-bagged item onto the table: a crimson-stained teddy bear head.

"You've got to be kidding. How on earth?" Doug's mind jumped from *Alien* to Annie's old Winnie-the-Pooh VHS. He saw the silly old bear stuck in Rabbit's hole. This was a breaking point; he wanted to laugh, it was all so insane. He put a hand to his neck and tried to clear his throat. Instead, he coughed once, twice, three times with the effort. "Do we have any suspects, Sam?"

"Not yet. But Psych just finished up with Rachael. She's in Interview One if you'd like to talk to her; her dad's in Interview Two. I have to warn you, though. She's still pretty upset. I mean, she'd have to be, right?"

Minutes later, the two detectives walked into the sterile interview room. Seeing Rachael, Doug was again reminded of Annie; the thought of her sitting alone in an interrogation room, scared, traumatized, and shoulders bowed inward upset him.

"Hi, Rachel." Sam gave the little girl a broad smile. The stark surroundings made the girl appear even smaller. He pointed at himself and said, "My name's Sam and this is Doug. We just want to ask you a couple questions about yesterday, all right?"

The girl looked from one to the other and nodded.

Sam opened his notebook and readied his golf pencil. "What can you remember, Rachel?"

"I already told 'em. The other men and the nurse? I already told 'em everything. First I said 'no.' I told 'em all about it before. I told him before. This time he got mad, really mad. He was my friend. He was nice 'til I told him, then he got mad. Like Oscar when he gets mad, but worser. He blew up. He hurt Uncle Eloy 'cuz I was hurt. He hurt Uncle Eloy 'cuz he was mad, 'cuz I was hurt. 'Cuz he hurt me, and I was scared. He was my friend, before—"

Suddenly, Doug's phone sang into the quiet room about the sun coming up: Annie again. Rachael stopped talking and Sam watched while Doug pressed buttons to mute the phone.

"Go on, Rachel. Doug's sorry about his phone." Sam shook his head slightly while Doug put his phone in his hip pocket and smiled at Rachel.

"Go ahead, tell us what else you remember."

"I told him everything. He was mad. He was the one that hurt Uncle Eloy. It was him. He's kinda scary when he gets real mad. He's the one. He came from Cantaloupe and protects me and keeps me safe."

"Who is 'he,' Rachael?" Doug pressed. "And what do you mean, 'Cantaloupe'?"

It was no use. Rachael just kept repeating her previous statements, but each time in a different order and with degrading coherency. Finally, after five minutes, she buried her face in her hands and started sobbing.

"This is all I have left of him," she wailed. A simple faux leather collar with a pet tag on it fell from her hands. Doug picked it up and started as he looked down at the symbol on the pet tag: a stylized bear track. Rachael took it from his offering hand.

Two hours and a fishing expedition later, Doug and Sam shut the door to Interview Room Two behind them.

Sam let out a frustrated sigh and ran a hand over his scalp. "Rachael is a broken record and her dad's a joke. Did you see him? Do you think he's in on it, somehow? I could see him having scared her silent."

Doug shook his head, putting himself in the same circumstance. "He doesn't know anything. I'm convinced. You saw him. He didn't even know she was being abused. You saw the shock in his face, the tears, the crying? He's not that good of an actor. He didn't know what his golfing buddy, Gentry, had been doing. He looked betrayed. He's really crying in there. He was stunned. Those are tears of anger and fear. Besides—" Doug's mind returned to the bear-track medallion.

"Yeah, but Doug, he's also our only suspect. He—" Sam stopped as Doug's telephone sang about his bottom dollar.

This time, Doug looked at the screen, exhaled, then answered the phone. "Hi, Annie-bug. Look, Daddy's really busy right now, sweetheart."

He listened for a moment.

"Yes, I remember we were going to the zoo, but Daddy has to

finish up some things at work."

Another pause.

"No, we'll just have to plan on another day. Daddy's not going to be home for a while. I'll pick you up at Mommy's later tonight. Why don't you watch *Winnie—*"

The image of the bloody teddy bear popped into his mind and Doug wanted to kick himself: NOT *Winnie-the-Pooh*.

"I mean, *Magic School Bus* until Daddy comes. Have some cold mac-and-cheese. It's your favorite, and Mommy's sure to have some in the fridge."

Doug smiled.

"I know I promised, honey. But this is important. I need to go now, but I love you. Kisses and hugs."

Doug swiped a finger across his phone.

"Sorry," he said to Sam. "Y'know how it is. Kids."

"Annie's a good girl. Don't apologize to me, old man. Go home. You're beat. Take my goddaughter to the zoo. Go to a movie. She's only seven once, y'know. And the thing with Maggie was hard on her, too."

"I know. But right now Rachael needs my help more. Lemme have the file."

Doug took the folder, slapped his notepad on top, and made his way back to his desk. He stopped to pour a tall cup of coffee. It was going to be a long night.

* * *

Ten days since Gentry's death and little progress had been made in the case. The funeral, held at the university, had been very public and quite well attended: politicians, sports figures, national entertainment figures. The news stations had their cameras rolling 24/7, and both of the Salt Lake papers were crucifying the SLPD for the lack of results. Of course, everyone was focusing on Gentry's gruesome murder while sweeping the dirty little secrets under the rug. Doug ran both hands through his short black hair, scratching hard, trying to wake up.

"Hey, old man, we've got another one."

Through bleary, bloodshot eyes, Doug looked at his partner. Sam's color was terrible, and he sported a two-day growth of whiskers. Sweat rings stained Sam's shirt, his shirt buttons strained, flecks of pastry stuck to the cotton, and Doug caught a whiff of perspiration and day-old aftershave. If the younger man looked that bad, what on earth did *he* look like?

"Another one?" asked Doug. "Seriously?"

"Yup. Similar M.O. An abusive father though, rather than an S.O. A little boy, rather than a little girl. Kid had a bunch of bruises ranging back a few weeks, they think. Dad's torso and gut shredded. Literally. Another teddy bear nearby, all four paws torn open and bloody. The bear's head was intact. The call came in yesterday. I didn't want to bother you because I knew it was your day off with Annie."

Sam dropped a stack of pictures on Doug's desk.

"There's no connection to Gentry that we can find."

"You should've said something. I was out at the marina again. I had to skip 'Annie's day' anyway. I've been here since—" he looked at his watch "—two this morning. Eight hours already. The press is killing us on this case. Rachel's dad is becoming a local television celebrity. I hear that Fox has even offered him his own 'True Crime' show."

Doug picked up the pictures and shuffled through them. "Anyway, Friday... you'll come over. We'll have pizza. Annie hasn't seen you in weeks. It'll be a special 'Annie's Day.' And bring your guitar. She misses your songs. She misses you more, you know that? And—"

Halfway through the stack his fingers numbed and his mind jumped. The pictures fell from his nerveless hands.

Sam watched, then looked down. The picture on the top of the stack was a close-up of a faux leather collar with a pet I.D. tag hanging from it. On the tag was a stylized bear track. Sam jabbed his finger down on the picture.

"Okay, brother. Spill it. You know something about this symbol. That's the second time you've jumped when you've seen it."

Sam fixed his partner with an icy glare—his 'bad cop' face—for a full minute.

Doug sagged backwards into his chair and groaned. He took several deep breaths before he spoke again.

"You know I was raised by my grandfather. I was named Sky, after him. He taught me. He forced me to learn what he called 'lore' even when I didn't want to. 'This, little man, is the sign for bear,' is how he would always begin. Grandfather would then sketch a few lines in the dirt and repeat three times the word for 'bear.' Then he would do the same for 'wolf,' 'moose,' and 'lion.'"

Doug still remembered the words, and as he thought each one in succession—just as his grandfather had taught them—the symbols rose unbidden to his mind's eye.

"He would say, 'These are powerful, sacred signs, Sky. Not to be shared or taken lightly.' Grandfather ended every lesson the same way, saying this while smoothing out the dirt, erasing the symbols.

"And then one day, he went a step further. 'This one, perhaps, is more sacred than most.' He made the normal sign for 'bear' and then added an additional stroke. It was this symbol here." Doug pointed at the picture. "This is the symbol for one of the guardian spirits, one who favors the aspect of the bear. That was his last lesson. He died three days later. "

Doug felt Sam's skeptical gaze.

"We need to find out where the kids are getting these bears."

"Doug, c'mon, they're teddy bears. You can get them almost anywhere. Are you seriously telling me you think that these toys are our murder weapons?"

"No, Sam, they might be our murderer."

Doug ignored the look Sam gave him. He had never bought in to his grandfather's spiritual beliefs; in fact, he barely identified as Native American himself. That heritage meant little to him as a child and meant next to nothing as an adult.

"I know it sounds insane, Sam. I do. I barely believe it myself.

Whoso Offendeth

I don't *want* to believe it. But Grandfather had some stories. Weird stories. Weirder than this, so—"

"Where did the bears come from?"

Doug opened his mouth to answer, ready to admit that he was as lost as Sam was, when his eyes fell on the scattered photographs. Doug shuffled through them until he found the one his subconscious told him was there: an extreme close-up of the bear's head showing the remains of a tag attached to the toy's ear with a bit of plastic thread. There, on that scrap of paper, was part of a sticker.

"Here, Sam. This is where they came from."

Sam took the picture from Doug's hands and looked closely. It was fuzzy, slightly out of focus, but it clearly said "Antelope." Sam cursed.

"Geez," Sam swore again. "This thing sounds like a campy monster movie on Saturday morning TV."

Doug smiled for what felt like the first time in days, and nodded. "You're right. Heaven knows it's nuts, but it's a break. This thing that's killing child molesters—"

He shook his head, changing his mind.

"Child *abusers*? I don't know what it means—I can't *fathom* what it means—but we have a break. It's something at least. I'm headed out there."

Sam rolled his eyes.

"Thanks, partner, make me out to be the crazy. Junior gets to go in and say, 'Yeah, Captain, we think a possessed Pooh Bear killed one of the most powerful lawyers in the state and his other psycho bear friends are on a rampage through the city.'"

Sam whistled a few bars of *Teddy's Bear Picnic* in a minor key and laughed. "I hope you know, Doug, that I'm gonna be throwing you under the bus."

"I wouldn't have it any other way, Sam."

* * *

With rush hour, the drive took nearly two hours just to reach the state park pay station. Doug flashed his badge and the ranger waved him through. It didn't always work, but sometimes he got lucky.

It had been a long time since he'd been out here. He'd forgotten how desolate it was, yet how beautiful it was in its desolation. The water was markedly different in color on either side of the raised roadway that split the Great Salt Lake into two sections. Dark on one side and light on the other; the drastic differences in salinity had its own beauty.

Doug thought how much Annie would like this. She loved the water and loved nature. Most of all, she loved him and loved sharing nature with him. He frowned. He needed to find the time to bring her out here. Hell, he needed to spend more time with her, period. *She spends too much time alone.*

Sam kept telling him what he already knew: the year since Maggie divorced him had been tough, tougher still on Annie. He mentally counted back the days since he'd seen her awake, then mumbled.

"If only the work would slow down, let me go home before she's in bed." Something from the gift shop would make her smile: a magnet or a toy.

A few minutes later, he parked and pulled himself out of his car outside the Antelope Island visitor center. He walked down the sidewalk, noticing as he reached the building that it was covered in spiders. Every six inches of the building was another spider. Webs stretched from the ground to the window sills and across the windows and from the floodlights to the eaves. He stopped and turned, only now seeing the webs and strands he'd passed in complete oblivion. He saw the rippling wind passing through the webs and the different angles of light. Orb weaver spiders. Everywhere. Grandfather had tried to calm his childhood arachnophobia. He'd had a saying; he'd had a saying for everything, really. Try as he might, Doug could not remember this one.

A young couple holding hands stopped next to him to look at the sight. He smiled as he looked at them.

"My worst nightmare come true."

They nodded and together the three of them ran for the door, unconsciously ducking their heads to avoid the spiders. Annie would most definitely not like this part.

Inside, the couple split off to view the mini-museum displays. A rack of Utah postcards and magnets welcomed him to the gift shop, what he liked to call the "Land of Supplemental Government Income and Unconscious Taxation." Doug worked his way around the various tables laden with t-shirts, tote bags, sea monkey-related objects, and there, on the wall, was his quarry, run to ground.

Alcoves of zoological playthings lined the wall. Doug quickly pawed through the haphazard mounds of stuffed toy coyotes, owls, and other local fauna, recalling folklore and beliefs about each of the native animals. He hadn't thought about his grandfather in years. After talking to Sam about him, he was reminded of the old man at every turn.

He finally picked out a teddy bear he knew Annie would like, grateful that there were several styles on display. Annie loved bears, but there was no way he was taking one home that reminded him of Gentry's fate. He could already see that Annie would take it from him and stare deeply into its eyes, marking every feature in her mind before proclaiming, "He was lonely, Daddy. That's why you picked him, wasn't it?"

Doug smiled at the thought; he could hear her sweet voice saying the words. He hugged the bear to his chest, just as he would hug Annie. Something metal dug into his chest. He looked down and ran his fingers around the teddy bear's neck until he found it. A medallion, on a faux leather collar, stamped with a stylized bear track. Doug's smile vanished, turning into a slight frown.

For a moment, he considered a different animal, but bears were Annie's favorite. Sam was probably right; it was a crazy idea, and Doug was on a fool's mission. He wouldn't find anything here. Anyway, there was no one violent in Annie's life that would be a problem.

Telling himself the I.D. tag was nothing more than some

government lackey's kitschy marketing ploy, he tucked the bear back under his arm and turned toward the front of the store. There, standing behind the counter, was his grandfather wearing a Park Ranger's uniform, alive and breathing. He fumbled the bear, and it fell to the floor. His eyes never left the ranger. It couldn't be his grandfather. He glanced at the floor and retrieved the toy. When he stood and looked again, it was clearly not his grandfather, just an old Native American man—ancient, and weathered by time—dressed in a Park Ranger's uniform.

Doug had been thinking of his grandfather and this man shared the same cheekbones, the long peppered hair pulled back into a long ponytail, even the same wrinkles around the eyes, eyes filled with centuries-old wisdom and mysticism.

Doug walked to the counter, smiled, and spoke a remembered traditional greeting; he watched and grinned as the old man's eyes grew large. He waited several seconds until the old man composed himself and nodded a greeting in return. Doug handed over the teddy bear, followed by several bills and a handful of coins; he declined a bag. He tried unsuccessfully to engage the old man in conversation. The old man only inclined his head, holding the teddy bear to his ear, then he simply stared at Doug with an implacable, knowing look. The entire process took only a minute, but felt interminable.

Finally the old man broke his silence.

"He knows you, Sky," he said. "And he knows all about Annie."

The old man's stare unnerved him; his inexplicable, simple words scared Doug even more: it sounded like his grandfather's voice.

"How do you know my name?"

The old man smiled and walked away.

Doug walked out of the visitor's center barely noticing the spiders. The day was somehow dimmer, but the change was completely lost on him. He shuffled his way back to his car, seeking its comfortable metal womb. The shrill squawking of a gull somewhere overhead broke into his thoughts. Only then did he feel the unnatural cold in the fall air and the unusually bitter lake stink. He cursed softly, shaking the teddy bear.

"What was I thinking? I don't believe any of this. I don't know what to believe anymore."

He shook his head again and tossed the toy bear into the backseat. This was not happening.

A turn of the key and the engine began to purr. A flicker of movement in the corner of his vision caused him to look into the rear view mirror. His heart leapt, nearly bursting from his chest. There was a man in the back seat. A Native American, a shirtless warrior of indeterminate age, whose visible flesh was painted a harsh white. Doug recognized the medallion hanging around the warrior's neck, the stylized bear track stamped on its surface.

"Who are you?"

Doug's hand reached into his suit coat towards his service weapon.

The warrior held up the brand new teddy bear.

"*Not all harm or danger that comes to a child is of the body.*"

The warrior smiled a predatory smile.

For one endless second, Doug saw in his mind little Annie, all brown curls and dimpled cheeks. He saw her as a newborn, cradled in the crook of his arm, smelling clean baby smell. He saw her first steps, heard her first words. He knew he'd missed a lot of firsts lately. He hung his head down in shame and then realization dawned.

"Wait! Don't—"

The warrior disappeared in a white blur.

***

Sam Becker held his goddaughter on his knees and wept silently. Annie jumped at the three-volley salute, the crack of the rifles echoing across the cemetery. He hugged her tightly to him, as if he could somehow shield her from the pain; he loosened his grip only to allow her to accept the folded flag.

A long way away, on a large island in the middle of a dead sea,

Jaren K. Rencher

a little girl pulled her daddy towards the shelves at the back of a gift store.

"*That* one, daddy. I like *that* teddy—the one with the necklace!"

An old Native American man swiped a credit card and said nothing. He simply smiled.

Jaren K. Rencher

Jaren K. Rencher is a consumer bankruptcy attorney by day and spends his nights reading, writing, gaming, painting tin soldiers, or in work for his church, all while surrounded by his five wonderful children and his beautiful wife of 20+ years. He wishes on a daily basis that he could flee from the rat race to a mountain hideaway with his family and live there for the remainder of his days. He already has the meadow picked out.

May 15th
by Johnny Worthen

6:19 a.m.

Jeremiah took a deep morning breath, tasted the air, and did not like it.

He waited, listening to the cars below and above him move slowly by on their ways to another day, wondering what his would be. He stayed beneath his trash and rags as long as he could before finally being driven out of his hole under the overpass by the heat and the stink.

The sun was up and bright, though he could not see it. It turned the smog to light, the brown air a refracting cloud of particles, translucent and luminescent like dirty frosted glass. In the shade, looking out, he had to squint to see anything. The smog was thick. For all the light, visibility was maybe twenty feet, which explained why the cars were moving so slowly on the freeway. Some would call the smog "pea-soup," but the color was wrong. It was umber, chestnut, sickly yellow at the fringes, shit brown in the depths.

It was still hot from the day before, would get hotter still. The heat made the thick air angry, reactive, sticky like grease, acrid like mosquito spray.

May 15th

"Gonna' be a bad one," he said to no one. "Worse it's ever been. Bad. Bad. Gonna' be a bad one. The worst."

Sitting up he put a finger to his nose and blew it out with a trumpet snort. Then the other. Two black ochre spots oozed over the dry concrete abutment. He rumbled his throat and spat a like blob beside them. "Ain't healthy," he said. "No. No. Bad. Oh, God, the worst. Saw it coming. Saw it. Bad."

He gathered his things, rags and trash, a half empty bottle of water, a coat he'd not need for another six months, a dog-eared paperback, and extra socks and stuffed them into a plastic bag. Lastly, he looked at his sign and read it out loud, "Hard times. Anything helps."

He read it again, sounding the words out, his lips cracking and his tongue tasting the putrid air. He turned the cardboard over and found a pen in his pocket. He wrote something new and then read it and squinted against the glare. He coughed and spat and then retraced the new letters thicker and blacker until his pen gave out. Folding it once, he tucked it under his arm and slid down the embankment to the off-ramp.

Once his belongings were stashed behind a utility box, he stepped out into the warm Salt Lake City summer smog, coughed, and faced the traffic. He found his bucket and turned it upside down to sit, facing the cars. With both hands he held up his new sign.

Most drivers drove by pretending not to notice him, but sneaking glances as they could. Some slowed down to see, reading and re-reading what he'd written. Some stopped and stared. He stared back.

The peculiarities of the state of Utah were known well before May 15. Utah, an original American theocracy, had a history and a reputation unique among its brother states. Founded in 1847 by Mormon settlers, a radical religious sect at the time, it took nearly fifty years for it to be admitted as a state. A full decade before the South's succession, Utah fought a war against the Union which many say it won—The Utah

War. Some called it a Holy War. The bulk of the casualties, however, were from a single innocent Arkansas wagon train en route to California which was cornered and massacred at Mountain Meadow near Cedar City by Mormon militia. There are some in Arkansas that say the events of May 15th were a direct result of that, a preternatural feat of vengeance, a singular divine act of retribution upon a sinful people.

Though human activity was doubtlessly at play, history does not speak to such things. The events, connections and coincidences were as they were, caused by human choices years in the making set against and alongside a history of a place, centuries in the waiting. Bad luck, poor planning. Retribution. It's all the same to the dead.

8:40 a.m.

Ms. Alsop called the roll for her eighth grade homeroom class and felt the cloying in the back of her throat like she'd been gargling glass. Halfway through her list of forty students, she stopped and popped a lozenge in her mouth to finish.

Eight kids were absent. Five of them she knew were home with medical leave due to the air. Asthmatics. The others she couldn't guess, possibly just late due to the slow traffic or maybe getting an early start on summer vacation which was only two weeks away. Short-time syndrome had hit the middle school like a contagion with students and teachers ready to be done. Lessons were busywork, classrooms day-cares, the school year surrendered; everyone giving up.

"Students are restricted inside today again," she said. "Quiet study time in the library or cafeteria after lunch."

Moans and complaints.

"Open up your textbooks," Ms. Alsop said.

She looked at her notes and took a deep breath. She'd sprayed air freshener before class, but already it was overwhelmed by the acrid smells carried through the doors from outside or sliding under the windows. She waited for the shuffling to settle down,

May 15th

for the fidgets to lessen, and dreamed of clear skies and beaches. Summer so close. She needed to get out of the valley for a while. Her headaches were only getting worse.

"We were discussing Ulysses and the Cyclops," she said when she thought she'd be heard. "Who can tell me about the cave?" No hands went up. She shushed the class and asked again. Several hands now. She pointed to Tami.

"Ulysses and his men followed sheep into the cave and ate a bunch of them. Then the Cyclops found them and trapped them in the cave with him."

"Why didn't he just kill them? Why'd he only trap them?" It was Alex. He had behavioral problems. He was bright, but didn't follow rules well. It was a good question, so Ms. Alsop ignored the outburst.

"He wanted to eat them later," Tami said.

"But it was so dangerous to leave them alive. I mean, look at what they did."

Becky raised her hand.

"Yes, Becky?"

"My father said that back in those olden days there weren't so many people. Like only a few thousand maybe, so killing them was a bigger deal."

"What about the war then? Hundreds of thousands of people died before the walls of Troy."

"My Dad says that is an exaggeration."

"But the Cyclops was an idiot. He should have killed them when he had the chance." Alex was speaking quickly, getting excited. Not a good sign. "They blinded him."

"There could be lots of other reasons why the monster let them stay as long as he did. But in the end, as Alex says, it was a mistake."

"He was cocky," said Bill. His hand was raised but he spoke before being recognized. It wasn't worth the fight.

"Exactly, Bill, that's where we are today."

She was pleased with the children's excitement with the story—well, some of them. The dozen or so who'd read it. The dozen or so who were good students. She was just grateful that the dozen who made her life hell were still too tired to do that.

"Brent?"

"Can I be excused? My throat hurts."

"No. Class just started."

"But–"

"No."

Reading her notes she said, "Does anyone know what hubris means?" The same hands went up.

"Claire?"

"It's when you piss off the gods," she said. The class laughed.

"Not exactly," Ms. Alsop said. "It's pride."

"And stupidity." Alex again.

"Yes, that's good. Who can give me an example of hubris?"

"The Cyclops thinking he could keep the men in his cave and not get blinded."

"That's a good one. Can anyone think of a bigger one, one that Ulysses did?"

Several hands went down.

"Tami?"

"When Ulysses is on his ship?" she said.

"Go on."

"So, he just blinded the guy, stole all his food, and got away. Then he rubs it in by bragging about it."

Alex: "He didn't think anything would happen."

"Exactly," said Ms. Alsop. "Alex, remember to raise your hand and let me call on you."

"Sorry."

"But he did get caught. Something happened. Something unexpected. The Cyclops was the son of the god Poseidon who got revenge on Ulysses and his men for what they did."

"Spoilers!"

Brent raised a wet dripping red hand above his head. "Ms. Alsop, my nose is bleeding really bad."

She saw his desk was a puddle of gore. "Go to the nurse," she

May 15th

said. "Alex, go get the janitor."

The two boys got up and dashed out the door. The class went into an uproar over the blood. She'd lost them. She didn't even try to quiet them right away. Instead she looked out the window at the sickening tangerine light. They were in the middle of another infamous Salt Lake inversion. The air was impenetrable, refracted bright and orange-tan as if the world itself were mustard. It's what grated her throat and kept the kids at home and had bloodied Brent's nose.

Two weeks for the school year to be over. Another ten days later and she was out of the valley and out of the muck. She'd spend the summer on a beach somewhere, smelling nothing but salt spray and flowers. She popped another lozenge and rolled it over her oily mouth.

Some of the scale of the catastrophe, whatever the cause, natural or manmade, can at least be laid at the feet of specific geography.

The Wasatch Front constitutes a narrow band of desirable land on the western slopes of the Wasatch Mountains. Extending roughly eighty miles between Ogden and Provo, including the Capitol of Utah, Salt Lake City itself, the vast majority of the state's inhabitants made their homes there. Though a fraction of the state's immense area, eighty percent of Utah's population lived along the narrow isolated Wasatch Front. Roughly 3.5 million souls on May 15th, according to FEMA and the CDC.

More peculiar still was the Salt Lake valley. Bordered on the east by the Wasatch Mountains and the west by the low Oquirrh range, it was hemmed in at the south by a rising slope and jutting bluff much like the similar one to the north that ran alongside The Great Salt Lake. The valley was in essence, a gigantic natural cauldron.

10:35 a.m.

The smell was different but no better. Corey James stood in the shallow waters of the Great Salt Lake and peered into his test tubes trying to make out the color shift of his reaction. Was it crimson or burgundy? The light betrayed his senses.

The inversion, the thick smog layer lying over the valley behind him, had bled out onto the Great Salt Lake and mixed with the brine stink the lake was best known for. It was not uncommon for the Department of State Ecology to receive complaints both about the stink of the smog trapped in the valley and the stink rising from the ancient lake when the wind shifted. But something was different this time, and Corey had left his sealed and filtered air-conditioned office to visit the salty brine to see if he could figure it out.

There was something going on in the chemistry of the lake. Something new.

He waved the brine flies away from his face to get a better look at his test. He was dressed in full mosquito gear, beekeeper hat and gloves, but still they bothered him in their sheer numbers. They didn't bite, but they'd find crevasses like nostrils, ear holes, and tear ducts and make a beeline to die there as if they were created to do it. The swarms were the thickest he'd ever seen them. They moved in undulating clouds, like living smoke, and cast macabre twisting shadows under the sick yellow light filtering down on his tests. Some had crawled into his tubes, their dead bodies floating on the surface while their cousins, the brine shrimp, danced beneath them in writhing contortionist wiggles.

And the smell. It was the worst he'd ever known it.

It was thick and organic, but different—tinted, spiced he'd say if it were a meal. Heavy and thick. A sulfur base with a petroleum hint, but also a strong fleshly decay like rotting road kill in Yellowstone. He knew the chemistry of hyper-saline environments, the bacterial sulfate reductions into hydrogen sulfide, the anaerobic bacteria working without oxygen to consume the dead and dying organics of the lake. Recombination of waste. The turning over of death into new life. Honorable, but disgusting.

May 15th

He tried to break out the competing odors: the smells of the sewage treatment plants that bordered the lake to the south, the human waste and chemical clean up going on there that added their stench to the lake; the refinery way across on the other side, pinched between mountain and shore, an ever-present array of lights like a city to itself, the perpetual orange burn-off flame atop a tower, a beacon on all but the most smoggy days, like this one. These smells he detected under the new stench and wondered if what he was sensing was not new at all, just a rare combination of all the bad smells the place collected.

The summer inversion had never been this bad before. In the winter with cloud cover, you could look down into the valley from the ski-resorts and see the brown layer of muck and pity the people beneath it until you had to return to it in a few hours. The snow came down in brown oily flakes and windshield wipers smeared it like snail trails, clearing the air. Now in the summer, the inversion was back, but there was no precipitation to clean it. Instead, it cooked in the hot air and settled like grease on all things and all surfaces, top and bottom, side and front, crevice and orifice like the brine flies looking for weaknesses to pollute.

The winds had not come. May was notorious to the city dwellers as the stink month, even before the wood stoves, industry, and cars smoked the air with pollution and refolded it all into an inversion. As far back as the first settlers, the May northwest winds were known for bringing in the rotten egg stink of the lake, the highpoint of the brine fly and shrimp season visited upon the population by seasonal pressure systems.

Corey had grown up with the winds and the smell, but to him it was not a bad thing. It stank to be sure, was unpleasant, but it wasn't bad. Hadn't been bad. It'd been his compass and clock. A companion he'd grown up with it like a fickle brother. It had led him to his career, to his wife, Beth, and their upcoming child, yet to be named. The squirming brine shrimp in his test tubes made him think of the little thing in Beth's belly, growing, becoming, about to be. He would teach his child what the smell was and explain how it was necessary.

Corey looked toward the city, seeing not the buildings, but only the brown haze on the horizon. The people there would probably be more than happy to trade their oily air for the rotten-eggs of the lake, at least for a short time. It would be a change. Something different from the months of soot they'd put up with.

He brushed the flies from the netting of his mask and shook the sample tubes again. It was no use. He couldn't see the subtle color differences. The haze and the flies were too much. He'd have to use the daylight flashlight and comparison card he had in the truck.

He sealed the tubes with rubber corks and put them in his case and locked it. He waved his hands to raise the flies and headed back to his truck a quarter mile away on the road. The water was barely ankle deep, but it was a muddy sucking quarter mile wade before he was on solid ground again.

The walking was hard. His breath came in gasps, and he stopped several times to rest on the way.

The chemistry was different. Something had happened. He thought back to the recent earthquake. A small 2.6 that nobody noticed, but had nevertheless sent everyone to the survival stores in droves after the news media sensationalized it with talk of an overdue Wasatch Fault catastrophe. The epicenter hadn't been the fault. It'd been the lake. Somewhere beneath the lake.

The aquifer.

There was not enough water for the valley. Not at the current rate of development. Not by half. The aquifer had been tapped and drained and the levels were not being replaced. His office had postulated a cave-in of the aquifer for the cause of the quake and no one had suggested otherwise. They'd written reports, started studies, alerted the people who needed to know so they could plan the future, and then everyone went about their usual work as if nothing were different.

But Corey knew something was different. At least in the lake chemistry. The stink. It cloyed and burned his eyes and made it hard to breathe. Methane? Butyric acid? An open casket? How could he describe it?

Choking.

He brushed the flies from his mask, thinking that they were somehow cutting off his air, suffocating him. It helped.

He was in shade, the flies surrounding him like he had his own fly-specific gravity. He waved his hands and sped up, sloshing and splashing as best he could the last yards to the shore. The flies in slow pursuit, his case slapping against his hip. His lungs burning from exertion—among other reasons.

On shore, he climbed the low embankment to the road, leaving most of the flies nearer the water. He opened the cab, tossed in his case, climbed in and closed the door. His face dripped with sweat. His gloved hands felt like water balloons. His eyes stung. Starting the car, he turned on the air conditioner before peeling off his equipment. He leaned back and looked over the still, hot lake and caught his breath.

He'd just begun breathing easy again when he saw the flies all rise up together. They blocked his view of the water like a dark curtain. At first they hovered, thick and undulating, a waiting swarm indecisive but ready. Then they moved at once as a single black body rising above the dead water. When they'd thinned enough to show the lake beyond, he saw a spot of frothing water. A single point a mile out bubbled like dry ice in a dirty pool. From that point he traced low rumbling waves spreading outward. These drove the flies and startled birds—seagulls and cranes—into the air, taking flight in feathered flocks.

He watched the spot and wondered, and when the vapor plume erupted in a fan of steam and algae, his first thought was that it was beautiful and how lucky he was to be there when it happened. He'd need to tell Beth about it when he got home.

The American Clean Air Act was an environmental milestone. Passed in 1963 by a Democratic Congress, it set forth a program within the U.S. Public Health Service to monitor and study air quality across the nation. Information gathered and assessed under the act citing public health concerns led to further environmental regulations and amendments to control pollution. Utah's uniquely pro-business, conservative culture led many of its legislators to fight environmental regulation as the Wasatch Front continually failed National Ambient Air Quality Standards. Citing the unique geography of the valley, they sought to have Utah exempted from the law and it mandates. Critics countered that because of these very factors, the laws and limits should be vigorously adopted and taken further. The debate continued even as studies showed thousands of preventable deaths each year attributable to air pollution, many of them children.

11:10 a.m.

"Yeah it's sick. You even got it there, huh?"

Ezra Anderson talked to his wife on the phone pinched to his shoulder with one ear and listened for the tower over his headphones with the other. He stared down the smoggy runway, but lost sight of the side lights just a few yards away. The little plane's cockpit was cramped and hot, and he was sick of waiting to take off.

"It's like a glacier pouring between the mountains," said his wife. "You can see it from the porch."

"Can't be as bad as it is here."

"No, but I don't remember it ever being this bad down here."

The tower: "Echo three-seven, all commercial aircraft are still grounded at airport number 1. All incoming flights are being diverted to Denver. It is our advice you stay down."

"Tower," he said into his microphone. "I gotta go. Is the runway clear?"

"It's weird," said his wife. "It's like a flowing wall of ugly."

"Yeah, the governor's about to declare a state of emergency. If I don't get up in the next five minutes I'll be stuck here."

"Echo three-seven, do you really want to fly in this crap?"

May 15th

"Tower, I'll be fine once I clear it."

"Negative. There's no way you're going to be able to land in this."

"Check my flight plan. I ain't coming back."

"Provo's no better."

"It's a little better," he said. "But that's just stop and go. We're going to our summer house in Jackson."

"Sorry, echo three-seven. We can't let you fly. The FAA just grounded everything. You missed your chance."

"Honey, I've got to go. Be ready. I'll be there a few minutes."

He hung up the phone and tossed it on the seat beside him. He coughed once into his sleeve and noticed the brown stain it left on his silk shirt. Using the other sleeve, he mopped the hot sweat from his brow and pushed forward the throttle.

"Affirmative tower. Echo three-seven taking off. All clear."

"Negative, Echo three seven. All flights—"

He switched off the radio and pushed the plane into the smog.

The cloud was a tan glow, a glaring mud-colored light that came from all directions. Focusing on the runway lights to his left, Ezra ran the plane parallel to them until his instruments showed he had enough speed to lift. Pulling back on the stick, he was in the air.

He'd spent the last five days working the governor and his people. He represented a list of clients as long as his arm with a combined wealth greater than California's. Their motives were the usual: fear of lawsuits, legal liability, loss of tourist dollars, ideological entrenchment, and profit effecting litigation. He'd done all he could and had already reported to his distant clients—none lived in the valley—how he softened the language and deflected blame to protect their interests. "Acts of God," "climate irregularities," and "unforeseen events" were his contributions to the governor's coming speech. Several of his clients would make a killing selling equipment and services in the short term, others would clean up in the long—there were several hospitals in his stable and a pharmaceutical company that specialized in emphysema treatment.

Watching his radar, he angled the plane upward. The glare was impossible. It reminded him of the time a green laser was aimed at his plane. It had fried his night vision. Now it was day, his glasses were strong aviators, but still his squinting eyes watered. Forgetting the last time, he sneezed into the crook of his arm. Black, brown, and red. Bleeding up there. Not good. He'd be glad to be out of this.

By compass he turned northeast over the Great Salt Lake, looking for clear air before turning south to pick up his family. A thousand feet up and he'd be over the smog like a skater on a pond. Maybe two thousand.

It had been a hard couple of days. The environmental lobby was there in force—local, national, and even some from overseas. The Chinese contingent was particularly alarming, showing how Salt Lake had eclipsed the particulate presence of Beijing at its height. So many people and so much panic just because the weather was bad. All they needed was a little wind and it would be over. The lieutenant governor thought to make their own wind: explode a bomb—a nuclear bomb—over the Great Salt Lake and blow the crap out. To the governor's credit, he didn't entertain that plan for long.

Long term solutions were bandied about and then the alarms finally went off. The governor had to act. All non-essential government activity would be shut down; voluntary driving restrictions would be expanded to essential driving and carpooling only. A shelter was being set up in the basketball arena, and an informational hotline was going live in an hour. Nothing too bad. Early summer recess for schools, some bad PR.

The light shifted from brown to yellow to white, and he was over the lake and could see a horizon, the distant mountains of Nevada ahead of him. He banked the plane over the water and coughed again.

Skirting the edge of the cloud, he pointed his plane south and leveled off.

He saw the plume to his right. The motion of it caught his eye. It was like a long grey white feather waving over an expanse of water

May 15th

rising slowly into the air. It ascended like a slow-motion flowing geyser, falling over itself, growing higher as if the pressure were slowly being increased. Steam roiled around it in boiling clouds. No sound, but it grew bigger by the moment. Ezra wondered if the governor had changed his mind about the nuke as the plume reached his altitude and went higher.

From about five miles away he saw it reach an apex half again higher than his plane. There the pressure failed and the steam or gas or whatever it was, for the color was wrong—grey green, not ivory white as real steam should be—there, at a certain altitude above him in the sky, it spread. Like a liquid upon a glass, it flowed outward into the air. But not evenly. It flowed toward the city, the grey green cloud rushing toward the smog as some unseen pressure drove it into the inversion.

It was because he was watching the plume, the spread of it and the wondering about nuclear bombs, that he failed to see the cloud of insect and birds.

Ezra Anderson managed a short five second mayday call before falling off the radar and crashing into the lake.

> The ancient pluvial Lake Bonneville occupied much of the great basin in present day Utah, Idaho, and Nevada. In area it was about 20,000 square miles with a maximum depth of over a thousand feet, making it larger and deeper than present day Lake Superior. Formed after the last glaciation 32,000 years ago, it receded after 17,000 years and then to the boundaries of the present Great Salt Lake about 12,000 years ago.
>
> The alkali deposits left by the prehistoric lake made human habitation of the area difficult. Early settlers remarked that the natives avoided the area and referred to the lake in particular with a word meaning "poisonous." Modern scholars have since come to translate that word as "malevolent."

11:20 a.m.

Corey watched the plume spread over the heavens like an inverted spilled drink—a thick gas that flowed like liquid picking up speed as it hurried toward the city.

It brought with it a wind that blew the brine flies into his windshield, splattering them in streaks as if he'd been driving though a swarm.

The smell he'd come for was the plume. He watched it move like a gargantuan ghost, a grey green gas that engulfed the sky and fell on his truck.

He felt it in his throat first, then his chest. A reaction. A chemical reaction. He thought of vinegar and baking soda, a Cub Scout science fair in his childhood. Then he thought only of air. His lungs rejected the gas as the unfit poison it was, and he began to suffocate for want of air.

Gasping and grasping, he fell to the floor, dragging his case down beside him. It buckled open and spilled his samples. In the under-dash light of his department issued truck, Cody's last sight was of a fragile, little brine shrimp dancing in a test tube, yet to be named.

Though the released gas was surely deadly—killing by supplanting breathable air with a heavy asphyxiating miasma—it alone could never have wrought the level of carnage experienced on May 15th. Indications show that a complex organic chemical reaction between the lake gas and the compound pollution hovering over the city that summer created a new and never-before imagined alkali toxin. Fueled by the heat locked under the inversion in a greenhouse effect, the reaction spread at approximately thirty miles per hour from the epicenter of the lake into the capital and across the Wasatch Front along the inversion flow. The resulting product—a mutagenic nerve gas—was corrosive, immediately reactive, and a hundred percent lethal at levels a fraction of what the inhabitants were exposed to.

May 15th

Though some outer areas received warnings there was little the population could do to prepare. What could one do when the air itself was coming to kill you?

11:40 a.m.

It wasn't a fire drill. It took Ms. Alsop a minute to recognize it for what it was: an earthquake alarm.

"Everyone get under your desks!" she shouted. "Hands over your head and under your desk."

There was a moment of stillness and then a rushing of moving children.

Ms. Alsop looked over her kids and saw they were all under their desks as they were taught. It was ridiculous. If the roof came down, how would the little desks be any help? It was the same drill as a nuclear attack, she remembered, and that made her afraid because she hadn't felt any tremor. Nor had she been told of any drill today. Would they not tell the teachers? Was this a new kind of drill?

Her eyes itched. She rubbed them. The kids beneath their desks, she moved to crawl under her own but paused to look out the window.

The light was different. The smog different. The air different. It moved and undulated in some unfelt wind. It churned like a soup, grey-yellow-green. She imagined faces and eyes in it, human, demonic, old, and young. Angry and cold. Vengeful and coming. The shapes turned, seethed and spun like obscene cotton candy. Black streaks like infection, red puffs like sores. It slid and slipped and poured through the cracks under the window like a hungry mist.

A scream, short and cut off.

A grunt.

A gurgle and a tumble.

A heavy stillness.

Around her ankles the cloud crept up. Ms. Alsop's legs cramped, hurt and burned, then went numb and cold.

The children, forty-three in this class under their desks—beautiful, smart, eager hopeful children—all stared at her through the churning cloud, their glassy lifeless eyes beseeching her for help, for hope, for explanation.

She gagged and drew breath to scream, but the exhalation never came.

Engulfed in swirling death without and within, her cells were murdered. They collapsed upon themselves in reactive ripples. They swelled, split, and ruptured as if each were drowned and then popped like a bubble. The pain would have been unimaginable had not her nerve cells been among the first to die.

3.5 million people perished within two hours in Utah along the Wasatch Front on May 15th. CDC estimates another 1.3 million died after an unseasonable high pressure ridge developed near Cedar City and dispersed the cloud on May 21st. The weakened cloud fled into neighboring regions, overleaping mountains, spanning deserts, following rivers and natural contours of the Great Basin to where people naturally collect. Recent projections suggest another million long term chronic deaths from near exposure and unknown numbers globally from long-term environmental impact related to the event, localized ecosystem collapses, poisoned rivers, dead livestock and tainted crops being the biggest contributors. In a joint letter, NASA and the United Nations Committee on Science and Research declared May 15th "an acute example of the ongoing Holocene extinction event." The Holocene extinction or "Sixth Extinction" of species on planet Earth is characterized as being mainly due to human activity.

Though the Wasatch Front remains under quarantine, scientists have entered the area to study it. One team reported seeing what appeared to be a dead homeless man sitting under a clogged overpass with a hand-written cardboard sign still on his lap. The sign read only "Consequences."

Johnny Worthen

Johnny Worthen is an award-winning, best-selling author, voyager, and damn fine human being! He is the tie-dye wearing, multi-genre writer of books and stories. Trained in modern literary criticism and cultural studies, when not writing, Johnny is a frequent public speaker, teacher, and blogger. "I write what I like to read," he says. "That guarantees me at least one fan."